高级实用英语系列教材

西方文学选读

Selected Readings of Western Literature

主　编　季　峥

副主编　龙　亚　毕丽君　雷定坤

中国人民大学出版社

·北京·

本书为“入典华裔美国作家作品的中国影响研究（国家社科基金西部项目，批准号：16XWW006）”的研究成果之一

Selected Readings of Western Literature

前言

本教材由希腊神话故事、《圣经》故事、诗歌、散文、戏剧、小说六个大的部分组成。其中，小说部分分为长篇小说与短篇小说。作为西方文学、文化的两大源泉，我们从希腊神话与《圣经》中选取了具有代表性的故事及章节，在让学生了解西方耳熟能详的神话、《圣经》故事的同时，也为他们理解文学作品中常见的相关典故做好准备。其他四个部分入选的皆为西方经典作家的经典作品，同时我们尽量避免国内其他同类教材经常入选的作品，以给学生更多新的选择。每个部分之前都有对该文学体裁的导读，简单介绍了该体裁的发展历史、特点以及学习方法。每篇选文均有注释、作家简介、赏析以及思考题。赏析部分为中文，以方便学生理解。赏析仅仅为学生提供某一个分析文本的视角，主要起抛砖引玉的作用。我们鼓励学生从多角度思考、理解文本。

本教材适合高等学校英语类专业（英语语言文学、翻译、商务英语）本科阶段的学生使用，也可用于大学英语文学文化类拓展课。同时可供非英语专业高年级或非英语专业研究生，以及所有爱好西方文学的学习者使用。本教材的编写源自重庆工商大学英语系为英语专业大一、大二学生开设的“英文名作导读”课程。该课程旨在鼓励学生阅读英文原版名作，帮助学生在大量、优质的英语语言输入中潜移默化地学习英语语言、了解英美文化以及提升文学素养，为高年级的专业学习甚至研究打下基础。该课程由一批经验丰富的教师带领学生一起赏析英文名作。在过去的几年里，选入课堂导读的作品包括:《德伯家的苔丝》《1984》《动物农场》《了不起的盖茨比》《麦田里的守望者》《战地春梦》《喜福会》等。导读课深受学生欢迎，任课教师也由此萌发了将课件、选文编纂成册的念头，以期望更多爱好文学的同学加入到西方经典文学原著的阅读中来，并从中收获阅读带来的惊喜与愉悦。

目录

Part 1 Greek Mythology ········ 001

Zeus ········ 002
Hera ········ 008
Theseus ········ 013
Jason ········ 018

Part 2 The Bible ········ 024

Genesis 1–3 ········ 025
Genesis 4 ········ 029
Genesis 6-9 ········ 030
Genesis 11 ········ 034

Part 3 Poetry ········ 039

Sonnet 29 ········ 040
I Wandered Lonely as a Cloud ········ 042
O Captain! My Captain! ········ 045
There's a Certain Slant of Light ········ 048
The Lake Isle of Innisfree ········ 050
The Road Not Taken ········ 052
Digging ········ 055
Eating Alone ········ 057

Part 4 Prose ········ **060**

The Republic: Book X（Excerpt）········ 061
The Poetics (I–V) ········ 076
Of Travel ········ 082
The Declaration of Independence ········ 084
Nature ········ 088

Part 5 Drama ········ **092**

Romeo and Juliet (Excerpt) ········ 093
Long Day's Journey into Night (Excerpt) ········ 105
No Exit (Excerpt) ········ 117
The Dumb Waiter (Excerpt) ········ 129
Buried Child (Excerpt) ········ 149
Death of a Salesman (Excerpt) ········ 173

Part 6 Fiction ········ **194**

American Fiction ········ 195
Young Goodman Brown (Excerpt) ········ 195
The Purloined Letter（Excerpt）········ 203
The Awakening ········ 211
Martin Eden (Excerpt) ········ 218
British Fiction ········ 225
David Copperfield (Excerpt) ········ 225
Frankenstein (Excerpt) ········ 234
Heart of Darkness (Excerpt) ········ 240
The Mark on the Wall (Excerpt) ········ 245
Short Stories ········ 252
A Sunrise on the Veld ········ 253
The Garden Party (Excerpt) ········ 261
The Heart of a Broken Story ········ 269
Eveline ········ 278

Bibliography ········ **283**

后记 ········ **284**

Part 1
Greek Mythology

Definition of Greek Mythology

Greek mythology is the myths and teachings that belong to the ancient Greeks, about their gods and heroes, the nature of the world, and the origins and significance of their own ritual practices. It was a part of the religion in ancient Greece. Modern scholars refer to and study the myths in an attempt to shed light on the religious and political institutions of ancient Greece and its civilization, and to learn the nature of myth-making itself.

Sources of Greek Mythology

Greek mythology is explicitly embodied in a large collection of narratives, and implicitly in Greek representational arts, such as ancient vase-paintings and votive gifts. Greek myth attempts to explain the origins of the world, and details the lives and adventures of a wide variety of gods, goddesses, heroes, heroines and mythological creatures. These accounts initially were disseminated in an oral-poetic tradition; today the Greek myths are known primarily from ancient Greek literature. The oldest known Greek literary sources, Homer's epic poems *Iliad* and *Odyssey*, focus on the Trojan War and its aftermath. Two poems by Homer's near contemporary Hesiod, the *Theogony* and the *Works and Days*, contain accounts of the genesis of the world, the succession of divine rulers, the succession of human ages, the origin of human woes, and the origin of sacrificial practices.

Myths are also preserved in the Homeric Hymns, in fragments of epic poems of the Epic Cycle, in lyric poems, in the works of the tragedians and comedians of the fifth century BC, in writings of scholars and poets of the Hellenistic Age, and in texts from the time of the Roman Empire by writers such as Plutarch and Pausanias.

Influences of Greek Mythology

Greek mythology has had an extensive influence on the culture, arts, and literature of

Western civilization and remains part of Western heritage and language. Poets and artists from ancient times to the present have derived inspiration from Greek mythology and have discovered contemporary significance and relevance in the themes.

Methods to Study Greek Mythology

The stories of Gods and mortals created by the Greeks thousands of years ago are all around us still today, from terms like "Oedipal complex" and "Pandora's box" to Hollywood movies like *Clash of the Titans*, *Hercules*, and *Troy*. Knowing Greek mythology will make you more culturally literate.

(1) Learn the gods. Greek mythology has a dizzying cast of characters. You don't need to know them all, but learning the major Olympian gods is an important first step in understanding Greek mythology.

(2) Get to know the great heroes of Greek mythology. While the same gods appear in myth after myth, they are rarely the protagonists the leading characters of Greek myths, who are typically human or half-human (quite a few have one divine parent). These heroes are famous for a variety of reasons, from fighting monsters to winning glory on the battlefield to suffering family tragedies.

(3) Study the major myths. While the heroes each have their own stories, there are a number of other myths featuring less prominent protagonists that have become famous, such as the story of Narcissus, who was so vain that he became transfixed upon seeing his reflection in a pond, and stayed staring at it until he died.

Selections of the Greek Mythology

Zeus

Zeus is the child of Cronus and Rhea, the youngest of his siblings to be born. He was respected as an allfather who was chief of the gods and assigned the others to their roles: "Even the gods who are not his natural children address him as Father, and all the gods rise in his presence." "Zeus is king in heaven" is a saying common to all men. Zeus' symbols are the thunderbolt, eagle, bull, and oak. In most traditions, he is married to Hera, by whom he is usually said to have fathered Ares, Hebe, and Hephaestus. At the oracle of Dodona, his consort was said to be Dione, by whom the *Iliad* states that he fathered Aphrodite. Zeus was also infamous for his erotic escapades. These resulted in many godly and heroic offspring, including Athena, Apollo, Artemis, Hermes, Persephone, Perseus, Heracles, Helen of Troy, Minos, and the Muses.

King of All Gods

After the battle with the titans and the giants, and putting out the revolt by Olympian gods and goddesses led by Hera, Zeus became the absolute supreme god of the heavens and the earth. He ordered the heavenly bodies, made laws, enforced oaths, and pronounced oracles. He dominated his kingdom with his two brothers, making himself king of the heavens and the earth, Poseidon king of the sea, and Hades king of the underworld. But he was always the head of the Olympian family, although his authority was sometimes challenged and tested by other deities, especially the goddesses. For instance, Hera was able to thwart now and then, his plans; Aphrodite could bend all the gods to her will, including Zeus, and Demeter forced Zeus to intervene and come to terms with her after her daughter Persephone was abducted by Hades. What's more, Zeus must yield to the fates, although this wasn't always the case.

Zeus was, first of all, the god of weather. He could whistle up a furious storm in the clearest of skies, or calm a gale down to a gentle spring breeze. He gave the world life in the form of rain. In essence, all life was dependent on him for this. Without him, everything that had been created on the earth would perish, and would have to begin anew. Zeus was also the god of the sky and thunder, and often seen as the patron of hospitality and the keeper of oaths. Though often despotic, petty and malicious, Zeus was upheld as the highest authority in preserving order and justice. This is perhaps best exemplified in his punishment of Hera, Poseidon and Apollo[1], and of Lycaon, Tantalus and Atreus[2] to observe the cosmic law and order, he struck the overambitious Asclepius[3], son of Apollo, to death with his thunderbolt; he turned Pandareus to stone for stealing the golden dog from one of his temples on Crete; he killed Salmoneus with a thunderbolt for attempting to equal him by riding around on a bronze chariot and loudly imitating thunder; he condemned the disrespectful nymph named Chelone[4] to eternal silence and together with Hera, he turned the vain king Haemus and queen Rhodope[5] into mountains. He made the decision to marry Aphrodite off to Hephaestus in order to prevent violent conflict between the many gods who lusted after her beauty. He turned Periphas into an eagle after his death, as a reward for being righteous and just. And when Memnon died, he felt pity for his mother, Eos, the dawn goddess, and granted him immortality. A well-known story of Zeus as god of justice and hospitality is related to a marvelous tree in the Phrygian hill country. It is said that sometimes when Zeus grew tired of eating ambrosia, drinking nectar, and even a little weary of hearing Apollo's lyre and watching the Graces dance, he would come down to the earth. He would often disguise himself as a mere mortal and walk around with Hermes. On a voyage to the earth, it was their attempt to see what hospitality was to be met there, for he was the protector of all who sought shelter in a strange land. The two gods, accordingly, took on the appearance of lowly vagabonds. They walked door to door asking each home to admit them and provide food, but none would let them in and the door was often barred to them. However, as they reached the last house, one poorer than all the rest, the door opened and a warm and cheerful voice bade them enter.

As they entered, the old man set a bench near the fire and told them to rest and stretch out their tired limbs. The old woman threw a soft covering over the bench. Her name was Philemon, she told the strangers, and her husband's was Baucis. As the visitors sat at the dining table, they noticed that one leg was propped up by a piece of broken dish for it was shorter than the rest. As they served the food and the diluted wine, the couple realized that the mixing bowl kept full no matter how much had been taken out. As they saw this overcome with terror, they dropped their eyes and prayed silently. Instead of trembling, they told their guests they had a goose and the old man attempted to catch it but failed in doing so. But when he panted, exhausted from the chase, the gods felt that it was time to take some action. "You have been hosts to gods," they said, "and you shall have your reward. This wicked country which despises the poor shall be punished, but not you." They then led the elderly couple out of the hut. The old couple saw in amazement that the countryside that they had known for life had disappeared, and instead a great lake surrounded them. Their lowly hut began to change into a stately pillared temple of whitest marble with a golden roof. The gods granted the two a wish, and the couple huddled and whispered. They had two requests: the first was that they become priest and priestess of this temple, and the second was that they never die alone. The gods agreed and were pleased with their requests. A long time they served in the grand edifice. When they were in extreme old age and exchanged memories of their past life, each suddenly saw the other put forth leaves. Then bark grew around them both. They had time only to cry, "Farewell, dear companion." As the words passed their lips, they became trees, but still they were together. The linden and the oak grew from one trunk.

Zeus and Hera

After establishing his kingdom, Zeus took his youngest sister, Hera, as his wife and queen, but he was by far the most unfaithful of all the gods. Prior to his marriage to Hera, he was said to have married first Metis, and then Themis. His third wife was Mnemosyne, and he was also involved with Leto shortly before his marriage to Hera. As a married god, he was famous for his many extramarital affairs with various goddesses—notably Demeter, Dione and Maia. His marriage with Hera did not stop him from siring countless other children. The immortal children born from these goddesses would eventually join the Olympian pantheon, or become part of the major Olympian gods. Apollo and Artemis, Aphrodite and Hermes are all progeny of his extramarital affairs. Hera was aware of her husband's unfaithfulness, and she did all she could to stop it before it even happened. She was furiously jealous, and vented her wrath on the women Zeus sought after. For a time, a nymph named Echo had the job of distracting Hera from Zeus' affairs by incessantly talking. When Hera discovered the deception, she cast a curse on Echo so that she could only speak or rather, repeat the words of others. Whenever Hera flew into fits of rage, she was unstoppable, even by Zeus. The helpless women would fall prey to her curses and hexes, often ruthlessly tortured as a reminder of what they had done. Zeus feared Hera in her rages, and more often than not, would let her deal her punishment onto the women, and then try to alleviate the harm done. As she was a master in the art of magic, her spells were woven so tightly that even Zeus couldn't unravel them. Thus the couple lived forever in this bizarre marriage loving each other despite the troubles they brought each other. Their marriage left upon people a tableau with Zeus as the harassed, vexed and philandering husband who had countless affairs and was constantly upbraided and intimidated by a self-righteous nagging wife.

Zeus and His Lovers

As the supreme god, Zeus had easy access to both the goddesses and women of the earth and took full advantage of this privilege. Also, his power and charm made him difficult to resist. After defeating his mother Rhea, who foresaw what trouble his lust would cause and tried to prevent him from marriage, Zeus began his long journey of love adventures and of his numerous affairs with mortal women. The most notable are those with Io, Europa, Danae and Leda. Europa was the daughter of king Agenor of Sidon in Asia Minor and the sister of Cadmus. One night, Europa had a dream. In this dream two continents in the forms of two women were arguing over her. Asia, one of the women maintained that since Europa had been born in Asia she belonged to it. The other woman, or continent, which was nameless, said that her birth was not important, and that Zeus would give her to Europe. It was early morning, and disturbed by the dream, Europa did not go back to sleep. She summoned her companions, who were all daughters of nobility and of her age. It was a beautiful day and they went off gathering flowers by the sea. Zeus noticed this charming group, particularly Europa, who was the prettiest of the maidens. Some say that Eros had induced him into action with one of his darts, although Zeus often had enough self-motivation. In any case, Zeus approached the group as a white bull, which was more beautiful than any other, a bull that smelt of flowers and lowed musically, a bull so obviously gentle that all the maidens rushed to stroke and pet it. The bull lay down in front of Europa. She slid on to its back instantly, when the bull charged off, plunging into the sea, and began to swim rapidly from the shore. Europa saw that a procession had joined them: Nereids[6] rode dolphins, Triton blew his horn, and even Poseidon was there. From this she realized that the bull must be a god. She pleaded with him to pity her. Zeus spoke to her and explained his love. He took her to Crete, where he had been raised, and promised that she would bear him many famous sons, including Minos and Rhadamanthus. Thus, Europa had the continent of Europe named after her. And miraculously Hera was somewhat distracted at the time and never punished her.

Zeus also fell in love with Io, the beautiful princess of Argos and seduced her. To keep Hera from noticing, he covered the area with a thick blanket of clouds. However, this backfired, arousing Hera's suspicions. She came down from mount Olympus and began dispersing the clouds. Zeus did some quick thinking and changed Io's form. So as the clouds dispersed, Hera found Zeus standing next to a white heifer. He swore that he had never seen the cow before. It had just sprung right out of the earth. Seeing right through this, Hera complimented the beautiful cow and asked to have it as a present. As turning such a reasonable request down would have given the whole thing away, Zeus agreed. Hera sent the cow away and arranged Argus Panoptes to watch over it. Since Argus had a hundred eyes and could have some of them sleep while others were awake, he made a fine watchman. Desperate, Zeus sent Hermes to fetch Io. Disguised as a shepherd, Hermes had to employ all his skill as a musician and storyteller to gain Argus' confidence and lull him to sleep. Once Argus closed all his eyes, Hermes killed him. As a memorial, Hera took Argus' hundred eyes and set them into the tail of her favorite bird, the peacock. Now that Io was free, Hera sent gadflies to sting the running cow, with the ghost of Argus pursuing her as well. This pushed poor Io near madness. Trying to escape, she wandered all over the world. One day she came across the chained Prometheus at Caucasus. He gave her hope. He predicted that she would have to wander for many years, but would eventually be changed back into human form and would bear a child, whose descendant would be a great hero and set him free. Prometheus' prediction came true. During her wanderings, many geographical locations were named after her, including the Ionian Sea and the Bosphorus (which means "of the cow"). She eventually reached the Nile where Zeus restored her to human form. She bore Epaphus and eleven generations later her descendant Heracles set Prometheus free.

Zeus' Descendants

Zeus had many children by mortals and immortals alike. With Hera, he had four children: Ares, Eris, Eileithyia[7] and Hebe. Another account says that there was a fifth, Hephaestus, although some people say that he was conceived through the will of Hera on her own, with no help from Zeus. Among his other children were Apollo and Artemis, the twin deities born of Leto, a Titaness; Dionysus, the god of wine and ecstasy, was born of the mortal princess Semele; the messenger of the gods, Hermes, was born of the Titaness Maia; Athena, goddess of wisdom, strategy and crafts, was born of Metis, the Titaness of wisdom, whom Zeus swallowed upon finding out that she would be a threat to him; with the Titaness of memory, Mnemosyne, Zeus fathered the nine muses; from the goddess Eurynome, the three Graces were born; Persephone, queen of the underworld, was born of his sister Demeter; Helen, the most beautiful mortal woman to have ever existed, was born of mortal Leda, after Zeus seduced her in the form of a swan; Perseus, the hero who slew the gorgon Medusa, was born of Danae, princess of Argos; Alcmene, queen of Thebes, who slept with both Zeus and her husband Amphitryon on the same night, gave birth to twin sons: the weak and feeble Iphicles, a mortal boy, and the strong and beautiful Heracles, who lived on to become one of the very few mortals ever made immortal through their heroic deeds. There are countless others.

NOTES

1. Zeus punished Poseidon and Apollo by sending them to Laomedon as bond slaves to build the walls of Troy.
2. All of them killed their children and served them as food, and were severely punished in Tartarus.
3. Asclepius restored several dead people to life with his medicine.
4. Chelone was changed into a tortoise for refusing to attend the wedding ceremony of Zeus and Hera. She was condemned to perpetual silence for ridiculing these deities.
5. The couple were so vain that they assumed the name of Zeus and Hera.
6. The Nereids were daughters of Poseidon and Doris and attendants of Poseidon.
7. Eileithyia was seldom mentioned as Zeus and Hera's child. This version may have to do with the fact that as a goddess of childbirth, she was often in the company of Hera.

Appreciation:

中国的英语学习者在接触以希腊神话为代表的西方神话的过程中，不可避免地会把自己对中国古代神话的理解投射到希腊神话中去。然后，一旦有了主观意识的介入，再来学习希腊神话，将会对正确理解希腊神话故事及其意义产生负面影响。因此，为了更好地学习希腊神话，我们不妨先了解东西方神话故事的差别。

中国上古神话有着极为鲜明的尚德精神，这一点在与西方神话特别是希腊神话进行比较时显得更加突出。中国上古神话中的大神均有不食人间烟火、没有凡人情欲的神格特征；神话中充满对远古英雄和帝王献身精神的讴歌与礼赞，以及对神话人物保民佑民的职分要求。“不食人间烟火，没有平凡人的情欲”，这是中国上古神话中的主要大神们神格的重要特征。在中国的很多经史典籍中，中国上古的主要大神们，诸如伏羲、女娲、炎帝、黄帝、颛顼、帝喾、尧、舜、禹等等，都是崇高和圣洁的。他们不苟言笑，从不戏谑人类，更不会嫉妒和残害人类。在个人的私生活上，他们从来都是十分规矩和检点的，十分注重小节、注重品行和德操的修养，并且尊贤重能。几乎每一位神王都没有“红杏出墙”或“乱播爱情种子”的现象。在他们的身上，只有神圣的光环、纯洁的品性和高尚的情操。

古希腊的神话与传说表现出了与中国神话大不相同的文化特色。在古希腊神话中，天神与人类一样，也表现出爱、恨、怒、欲望、嫉妒等凡俗的情感。本书希腊神话选文选择了宙斯和赫拉两位主神的故事，以及忒修斯和伊阿宋两位英雄人物的故事，特别展现了在希腊神话中，无论神还是英雄，他们都有不完美的一面，也即所谓充满了人性的一面。

在关于宙斯的这一选文中，我们将会读到在古希腊神话中，宙斯是世俗的、满身人间烟火味的形象：众神之王狂放不羁，拈花惹草，在神界与人间留下了一大串风流债，更严重的是他任意行事、不讲原则、充满欲望和个人爱好。

Questions:

1. How would you comment on Zeus?

2. Which would you value more, the virtues displayed in Chinese mythology or those in Greek mythology, and why?

Hera

Hera, the youngest sister and the last wife of Zeus, was queen of the Heavens. She was also the goddess of marriage, the patroness of marital fidelity, childbirth and family life. Being the queen of heavens, she reigned with Zeus as the pair-ruler like their predecessors Gaia and Uranus, Rhea and Cronus. However, after the failure of her revolt against Zeus, the pattern of pair-ruler reign was changed to that of single-ruler reign with Zeus as the supreme god, and her status was reduced to a less important one. However, Hera was equal to Zeus in one thing: she could bestow the gift of prophecy on any man or beast and she could metamorphose her rivals into animals or drive them mad. As in the case of Callisto and Lamia[1]; and she turned Galanthis, servant of Alcmene, into a weasel for she foiled Hera by saying that Alcmene had already delivered a baby, thus thwarting Hera's plan to prevent the birth of Heracles. She even granted the best gift that a god could give a mortal—to die in sleep—to two brothers Biton and Cleobis for their devotion to their mother Cydippe, a priestess of Hera. Curses and hexes were also her specialties and she could devastate any being that she hated with a simple phrase, as she cursed Echo to speak or repeat only the words of others; her curse on Leto caused her great suffering and delayed her delivery of Artemis and Apollo; and her hatred for Pelias, who had murdered his step-grandmother, Sidero, in a temple to Hera, prompted her later to manipulate Jason and Pelias and Medea into killing.

Conflicts Between Hera and Zeus

Hera's marriage to Zeus was filled with strife. When Zeus first decided to court Hera, she resisted. No matter what gifts Zeus gave her or what he did for her, she remained completely indifferent. Zeus had then to resort to trickery. One night, he summoned a rainstorm. Taking the form of a cuckoo bird, he flew up to Hera's window and perched there, soaking wet and shivering from the cold. Hera took pity on the bird and brought it in, holding it in her arms against her breast to keep it warm. It was then that Zeus assumed his true form, took advantage of the chance and raped her. Hera thereafter agreed to marry him to cover the shame. Their wedding was such a grand event that every deity was invited to attend. Gifts were showered upon the new queen of the gods. The most cherished gift was given to her by Gaia: a small apple tree that bore fruit of pure gold, and each time an apple was picked another would grow back immediately in its place. All the gods marveled at this gift with greedy eyes, thinking of stealing some of the fruit. Hera saw this, and to safeguard her tree, she took it to the end of the world to the garden of Hesperides[2]. There she also set the great dragon Ladon as well as three apple nymphs to help guard it. Any visitor to the garden would fall prey to the divine charms of the three nymphs, who smelt of the sweetest apple blossoms that would bring a state of euphoria to anyone who breathed it in. The nymphs would then dance with the visitor toward a high cliff until he eventually fell off the cliff.

Zeus and Hera constantly quarreled with each other. Vexed by his infidelities, Hera often humiliated him by her scheming ways. Though he would confide his secrets to her, and sometimes accept her advice, he never fully trusted Hera. She knew that if offended beyond a certain point, Zeus would fly into a rage or even strike her with his thunderbolt. Therefore, she often resorted to ruthless intrigue or spent most of her time plotting revenge on the women that Zeus consorted with.

Once when Zeus was being particularly overbearing to the other gods, Hera convinced them to join a revolt against him. Her role in the revolt was to drug Zeus and she was successful. Then Poseidon, Apollo, Athena and the other deities, except Hestia, bound the sleeping Zeus to a couch with raw-hide thongs knotted into a hundred knots, so that he could not move. After this, they began to discuss who was to be his successor. Overhearing the arguments, Thetis, the Nereid, foresaw a civil war on Olympus, and hurried to get Briareus to help untie the knots. After being released, Zeus sprang from the couch and grabbed his thunderbolt. The gods fell to their knees, begging and pleading for mercy. Zeus punished Poseidon and Apollo by sending them as bondservants to king Laomedon of Troy. Since it was Hera who had led the conspiracy against him, Zeus hung her up from the sky with golden chains. She wept in pain all night, but no one dared to interfere. In the end, Zeus undertook to free her if she swore never more to rebel against him. She had no choice but to agree. Though she never rebelled again, she often intrigued against Zeus' plans, and was sometimes able to outwit him.

Ability of Parthenogenesis

Gaia had the ability to give birth to her offspring without the help of a god. Like her mother Gaia, Hera also had this ability, which showed her superiority to other goddesses.

As Hera watched more and more beautiful children of Zeus' enter the pantheon, she soon became jealous and convinced herself that she could conceive the most beautiful child on her own. Some versions say that Hera was jealous of Zeus giving birth to Athena without her, so she decided to give birth to Hephaestus without him. An alternative version discounts this and says Zeus and Hera were both parents of Hephaestus. Working her magic, she was able to become pregnant and give birth on her own all in one day. However, the baby she gave birth to turned out to be the exact opposite of what she wanted, a pitiful shriveled child that Hera was so disgusted at the ugliness of the baby that she flung him off Mount Olympus, although another account says that because Hephaestus had taken Hera's side against his father Zeus and Zeus threw him off Mount Olympus. He fell for a full day, and landed on a deserted beach shattering his legs. He was later rescued by an ancient ocean goddess, and grew up to become Hephaestus. Later Hephaestus gained revenge against Hera for rejecting him by making her a magical throne, which, when she sat on it, didn't allow her to leave. The other gods begged Hephaestus to return to Olympus and release her, but he refused repeatedly. So Dionysus got him drunk and took him back to Olympus on the back of a mule. Then Hephaestus released Hera after being given Aphrodite as his wife.

A Nagging and Jealous Wife

Though queen of the heavens, Hera still shared the features of most earthly women: vain, jealous and nagging. She entered into competition with Athena and Aphrodite for Eris' apple—the prize of beauty. After the Trojan prince Paris gave the apple to Aphrodite as the fairest of the three goddesses, Hera was very annoyed and became his enemy ever since. Therefore, she favored the Greek army during the Trojan War. She even encouraged Diomedes[3] to attack her own son, Ares, who was fighting on the Trojans' side.

As goddess of marriage, Hera, however, was helpless in safeguarding her own marriage. She was always watching Zeus to ensure that he didn't fall in love or consort with any other female, mortal or immortal, even before it happened. However, most of the time, her efforts ended in failure. She was enraged by Zeus' blatant disregard for the vows of their marriage, but there was nothing she could do to prevent his endless love affairs as his wandering eyes would always spot pretty women. Since she could neither stop this nor harm Zeus, the all-powerful god, she vented all her anger on the innocent female involved, and devoted herself to punishing the lovers of Zeus and ruining the life of their children. Of all the cases of her persecuting the innocent women, the most notable were alluring to death of Semele, Dionysus' mother; torturing Io by sending gadflies to sting her; preventing Leto's delivery of Artemis and Apollo; metamorphosing Callisto into a bear and driving Lamia crazy. And she also resorted to ruthless intrigues to destroy the children born from Zeus' extramarital affairs, as in the matter of Heracles' birth. Even after Heracles reached manhood she would not reconcile with him. She drove him mad and attempted to make almost each one of his twelve labors more difficult than they needed to be. When Heracles fought the Lernaean Hydra, Hera sent a crab to bite his feet in the hope of distracting him. To annoy Heracles after he took the cattle of Geryon, Hera sent a gadfly to bite the cattle in an effort to irritate and scatter them. Hera then sent a flood, which raised the water level of a river to the extent that Heracles could not ford the cattle. He had to pile stones into the river to make the water shallower.

Hera's merciless intrigues in persecuting Zeus' lovers and extramarital children have been well-known and frequently mentioned. Callisto and Lamia are but two examples. As a follower of Artemis, Callisto took a vow to remain a virgin. But Zeus fell in love with her and disguised himself as Apollo in order to lure her. Outraged, the jealous Hera turned Callisto into a bear. An alternative version says that, Callisto, one of Artemis' companions, lost her virginity to Zeus, who disguised himself as Artemis. Enraged, Artemis changed her into a bear. Later, Callisto's son by Zeus, Arcas, almost killed Callisto while hunting, for he didn't know that the bear was his mother. But luckily, Zeus saw this, snatched them away and placed them both in the sky as the constellations Ursa Major and Ursa Minor, the Great Bear and the Little Bear, or the Big Dipper and the Little Dipper. Hera was not pleased with the placement of Callisto and Arcas in the sky, so she asked the marine goddess, Tethys, for help, who cursed the constellations to forever circle the sky and never drop below the horizon, hence explaining why they are circumpolar.

Lamia was a queen of Libya, whom Zeus loved. She bore Zeus several children, who were all killed by Hera for jealousy, except Scylla, and Lamia herself was turned into a monster by Hera. Another version says that Hera killed Lamia's children and the grief turned her into a monster. Lamia was envious of other mothers and took her revenge by eating the children of others. Besides, Lamia was cursed with the inability to close her eyes for sleep: she would always be obsessed by the image of her dead children. Later Zeus bestowed upon her the power to take her eyes out to rest, and then put them back in at will.

NOTES

1. Lamia was turned into a monster, who had the face and breasts of a woman and the body of a serpent.
2. The Hesperides were the daughters of Atlas, the titan who bore the weight of the sky on his shoulders as a punishment for rebelling against the Olympians.
3. Diomedes was the son of Tydeus and the king of Aetolia. He was one of the bravest Greek chieftains in the Trojan War, a loyal supporter of Agamemnon, a favorite of Athena, and the second mightiest hero among the Greeks. He wounded Aeneas and Ares.

Appreciation:

希腊神话中的众神之王后赫拉是一个嫉妒心极强的女人，她憎恨每一个与她丈夫有亲密关系的人，她利用权力和地位惩罚那些女人。赫拉早已熟知丈夫对自己的不忠，她也从不掩饰她的愤怒与嫉妒。她密切注视着丈夫的一举一动，除了常常破坏宙斯偷情，赫拉还会严惩宙斯的情人，甚至是与情敌有关的一切事物也难以忍受，比如情敌为宙斯所生的子女也难逃赫拉的惩戒。赫拉的嫉妒以及为报复宙斯而进行的复仇行为，常常给众神和人类带来巨大的灾难。

Questions:

1. How would you comment on Hera?

2. It is said that Hera punished only the lovers of Zeus without successfully disciplining her own husband. Why did not Hera punish Zeus directly?

Theseus

Theseus was the mythical king and founder-hero of Athens. Theseus battled and overcame foes that were identified with an archaic religious and social order. Theseus was a founding hero for the Athenians in the same way that Heracles was the founding hero for the Dorians. The Athenians regarded Theseus as a great reformer. The myths surrounding Theseus—his journeys, exploits, and family—have provided material for fiction throughout the ages.

Birth and Growth

Theseus was the son of Aegeus, king of Athens, who had, in drunkenness slept with Aethra, a virgin who was hopelessly waiting for Bellerophon[1], with whom she was engaged. Some versions say that he was the son of Poseidon and Aethra, who waded out to Sphairia after sleeping with Aegeus, and lay there with Poseidon. The next day, Aegeus, who had been visiting Troezen, left for home city of Athens. As he left, he left a pair of sandals and a sword under a large rock. Should she bear a male child, he told Aethra, she should bring him up secretly and send him to Athens to claim his birthright as soon as he was old enough to lift the rock and retrieve the items. Aethra gave birth to Theseus, who, when coming of age, lifted the rock and retrieved the sword and sandals, and set off for Athens to look for his father. Before Theseus left home, his maternal grandfather had left a ship for his journey to Athens because there were many bandits that roamed the countryside, but Theseus declined the offer. He decided to travel by land because he wanted to become a great hero at a young age as his famous cousin, Heracles, and he believed that the safety of a ship was not the way to go about this.

So Theseus made the trip by land. On his way, he encountered and defeated many murderous adversaries by adopting the same method that each of them had used to kill his victims. At the narrowest point of the Isthmus, Theseus met Sinis, nicknamed "pine-bender," a man famous for killing people by strapping them to the trunks of two pine trees that were bent to the ground. Sinis would then let the trees stand straight again, thus hurling the victims that were strapped to the trees through the air to their death. Theseus killed Sinis by this method.

On reaching attic Corydallus, he slew Sinis' father Procrustes, who lived beside the road and had two beds in his house, one small and one large. Offering a night's lodging to travelers, he would lay short men on the large bed, and racked them out to fit the large bed; but if they were longer than the small bed he would cut off their legs to suit the bed. Theseus served Procrustes as he had served the others.

At Epidaurus, Theseus ran into a son of Hephaestus named Periphetes, who was armed with a club of iron, which made all travelers stand in terror of his violence. When he saw Theseus approach, he assailed him, but soon fell beneath the blows of the young hero, who took possession of his club and bore it ever afterward as a memorial of his victory.

In similar manner, Theseus got rid of Sciron who kicked travelers off the narrow path on the sea cliffs into the sea, where a huge turtle devoured them; and he wrestled with and killed the wrestler Cercyon of Eleusis.

Having overcome all the perils on the road, Theseus at length reached Athens, where new dangers awaited him. Medea, the sorceress, who had fled from Corinth and Jason, had become wife of Aegeus. Knowing by her magic who the young man was, and fearing the loss of her influence over her husband, if Theseus should be acknowledged as his son, Medea persuaded Aegeus to kill Theseus by having him capture the savage Marathonian bull. After Theseus conquered the beast, she continued to fill the mind of Aegeus with suspicions saying that Theseus was so popular with the people because he had killed the bandits and rid their land of beasts that they might make him the king. She induced the old king to poison the young rival. But when Theseus stepped forward for the poisoned wine, unwillingly revealing the sword of his father, the tragedy was prevented at the last moment. Medea fled once more from her deserved punishment, and Theseus was acknowledged by his father and declared his successor.

Killing of the Minotaur

Theseus' most important feat was the killing of the Minotaur. Years before the arrival of Theseus at Athens, a terrible misfortune had fallen upon the city Minos, the ruler of Crete, lost his only son, Androgeus, who, on a visit to Athens was sent on a dangerous expedition to hunt the Marathonian bull[2], and was killed. To avenge the death of his son, Minos invaded the city and threatened to demolish it unless king Aegeus sent seven maidens and seven youths to Crete every nine years. The Athenian victims were to be sacrificed to the Minotaur and devoured by it.

Before he ascended the throne of Crete, Minos, who was struggling with his brothers for the right to rule, had prayed to Poseidon to send him a snow-white bull as a sign of approval by the gods for his reign and promised to sacrifice the bull. Poseidon then gave the bull to Minos, who, however, liked the bull and kept it for himself. Poseidon was angered, and he made Minos' wife Pasiphae fall madly in love with the bull. Pasiphae had Daedalus, the famous architect, make a wooden cow for her. She climbed into the decoy and fooled the white bull into mating with her. The Minotaur, the offspring of this union, was a big creature with the head of a bull and the body of a man. It was captured and locked in the labyrinth made by Daedalus, from which escape was impossible, and every ninth year Minotaur would devour fourteen children.

When Theseus learned of the Minotaur and the sacrifices, he decided to put an end to this. Despite his old father's plea, he volunteered to go to Crete as one of the victims before departure, he told his father that if he was successful, he would change the sail of the ship that carried the victims from black to white. Upon his arrival at Crete, Theseus met Ariadne, Minos' lovely daughter, who became deeply enamored of him. She promised she would provide the means of escape from the labyrinth if he agreed to marry her. When Theseus gladly accepted the offer, she gave him a ball of thread and told him to fasten it close to the entrance of the labyrinth and follow it all the way back. He made his way through the maze, meanwhile unwinding the thread, until he stumbled upon the sleeping Minotaur. He killed the monster and led the other victims back to the entrance by rolling up the thread into a ball again. Under the cover of darkness, Theseus led the victims aboard and set sail home. He brought Ariadne with him as he had promised. Some days later, after disembarking on the island then named Dia, but now known as Naxos, Theseus left Ariadne asleep on the shore and sailed away. Why he did so remained a mystery. Ariadne was soon to take revenge on him. Whether in grief for her loss or in joy for the sight of Attic coast, from which he had been so long absent, Theseus forgot his promise to hoist the white sail. Aegeus, who was standing watching for his son on the acropolis, saw the black sail, swooned, and deliberately cast himself into the sea, which was thenceforth named the Aegean.

Theseus' Love

Theseus had relations with quite a number of women, but this was also his undoing. His first important love was Ariadne, who helped him kill the Minotaur. He took her with him, but deserted her while she was sleeping on the island of Naxos. Another version says that Ariadne became seasick. As a result of this, she was left on the island while Theseus stayed on the ship to do some necessary work. A terrible storm carried him out to the sea, and when he returned, he found that Ariadne had died. And other people say that Dionysus appeared to him in a dream and threateningly demanded Ariadne for himself. So Theseus left her there to marry the god of wine. Theseus' second love was Antiope, or alternatively, Hippolyta, queen of the Amazons. He had joined Heracles in his ninth labor to fight the Amazons, the women warriors, and brought away their queen, by whom he fathered Hippolytus. After the birth of Hippolytus, the Amazons came to Greece to rescue their queen. They invaded Attica and some say they made it as far as Athens itself but were defeated by Theseus' army. After this, no other enemy invaded Greece as long as Theseus lived.

After the death of Hippolyta, Theseus married Phaedra, daughter of king Minos, and sister of Ariadne. Great misfortunes fell upon them as a result of this. When Hippolytus grew up to be a great hunter and a strong man, he despised people who lived in luxury and people who were silly enough to fall in love. As a result, he praised Artemis and disliked Aphrodite, who punished him by making his stepmother Phaedra fall deeply in love with him. When he rejected Phaedra, she killed herself, leaving a letter to Theseus, in which she said that she had been raped by Hippolytus. In anger, Theseus punished his son by sending him away in exile and asked Poseidon for revenge. When Hippolytus was traveling in his chariot along the coast, a large sea monster suddenly emerged from the water, shocking the horses and knocking the chariot over. Hippolytus was dragged to death. Later Theseus was told the truth by Artemis and he was sorrow-stricken.

Other Adventures and Death

Theseus took part in many adventures. He was one of the most famous monster slayers and defenders of men, comparable even to the great Heracles. He also took part in the Calydonian boar hunt, where he saved the life of Peirithous, king of the Lapithae, who was a man as adventurous as Theseus and later became his best friend. The two had some adventures together. One was at the wedding of Peirithous and Hippodamia. Many centaurs, relatives of the bride, were invited to the reception. They became drunk and seized the women. Theseus came to the defense of the bride, who was being carried off. A battle resulted from this incident between the centaurs and the Lapithae. Theseus helped to finally drive off the entire race of centaurs from where the Lapithae lived. After the death of his first wife, king Peirithous attempted to get another one. He and Theseus, wishing to marry daughters of the almighty Zeus, began their quest by abducting the ten-year-old Helen. Theseus won the bet and got Helen, but he must accompany Peirithous to Hades to recover Persephone for him. Theseus agreed to help his friend because he liked such a dangerous and nearly impossible undertaking. It is said that when Helen's two brothers, Castor and Pollux, arrived where Helen was kept, Peirithous and Theseus could not be found because they had slipped into the underworld, where Hades "welcomed" the two, and instructed them to sit on two chairs known as the Chairs of Forgetfulness. Anyone who sat on these chairs would forget everything and could not move himself from the chair. Peirithous remained on the chair forever, but Theseus was lifted from the chair and brought back to earth by his cousin Heracles, when he traveled to the underworld to fetch Cerberus.

As king of Athens, Theseus also did two noble things to Thebes: accepting the exiled Oedipus at Colonus, and helping Adrastus bury the seven heroes, who had fallen in the battle against Thebes. Although he had lived a life of adventure and was renowned for his bravery and intelligence, Theseus' death was wretched and ignoble indeed. During his absence in the underworld, the Dioscuri, Helen' s twin brothers, assembled an army marched against Athens and demanded the return of the abducted Helen. They ransacked the city and, finally told of Helen's hiding place, got her back. After that they installed Menestheus, son of Peteus, who was banished by Aegeus, as regent of Athens. When Theseus returned from the underworld, he found it impossible to resume his throne and restore order and peace to Athens. With a curse, he sailed for Crete, but a storm blew his ship off course and he found himself landing on the island of Scyrus, where king Lycomedes, a friend of Menestheus, received him. For some unknown reason, he was pushed off a cliff by Lycomedes. Or, as some say, he fell off the cliff by himself. Anyway, he died a similar death as his father.

NOTES

1. Bellerophon was a grandson of Sisyphus, and son of Glaucus and Eurymede. He was one of the seven great destroyers of monsters, slayer of the chimera, and conqueror of the Solymi and the amazons. He tried to fly to heaven on the winged horse Pegasus and perished.
2. After Heracles captured this bull in his seventh labor, he rode it from Crete to Greece, and then turned it loose to roam the countryside. The bull roamed on the plains of marathon and ravaged the neighboring territory. Aegeus, king of Athens, had sent Androgeus, who had won in all the Panathenean games to kill the beast. Later, the beast was killed by Theseus.

Appreciation:

希腊神话中的英雄人物，最后基本都难逃悲剧的命运。这也是与中国神话故事中的英雄不一样的地方。忒修斯是雅典国王，他歼除过很多著名的强盗，杀死过无数怪物，解开米诺斯的迷宫，并战胜了米诺陶诺斯；基本上他的前半生都是高大伟岸正直的形象，但是到了后期，忒修斯似乎逐渐丧失了对神的敬畏，他和希波吕忒结婚，又劫持海伦，还试图劫持冥王哈迪斯的妻子珀耳塞福涅，因此被扣留在冥界，后来虽然被赫拉克勒斯救出，但是等到再回到雅典时，他已失掉了王位和权力，最后客死他乡。

Questions:

1. To you, does Theseus look like a traditional hero?
2. From Theseus' story, what lesson do you learn?

Jason

Jason was an ancient Greek mythological hero, who was the leader of the Argonauts whose quest for the Golden Fleece featured in Greek literature. He was the son of Aeson, the rightful king of Iolcos. He was married to the sorceress Medea. He was also the great-grandson of the messenger god Hermes, through his mother's side. Jason appeared in various literary works in the classical world of Greece and Rome, including the epic poem *Argonautica* and the tragedy *Medea*.

The Trip to Colchis

Jason was the son of the lawful king of Iolcus, but his uncle Pelias had usurped the throne. Pelias lived in constant fear of losing what he had taken so unjustly. He kept Jason's father a prisoner and would certainly have murdered Jason at birth. But Jason's mother deceived Pelias by mourning as if Jason had died. Meanwhile the infant was bundled off to the wilderness cave of Chiron[1]. Chiron tutored Jason in the lore of plants, the hunt and the civilized arts.

When Jason came of age, he set out like a proper hero to claim his rightful throne. But his uncle Pelias had no intention of giving it up, so Pelias offered a deal as to trade the Golden Fleece for the throne. Jason agreed to bring the Golden Fleece, and immediately started to gather volunteers to join him in this expedition. He sought the help of Argus, who, on the advice of Athena, built a fifty-oared ship, the Argo. Athena herself had cut a beam from her father Zeus' oak, gave it a power of speech and prophecy and fitted it into the Argo's prow. With the help of gods, the Argo became the strongest and fastest ship.

Among the 50 heroes who went with Jason to Colchis for the Golden Fleece were, to name a few, Acastus, son of king Pelias; Heracles and Hylas, squire to Heracles; Orpheus, the great Thracian musician; Peleus, Achilles' father; Butes, Aphrodite's lover; Zetes and Calais, sons of Boreas, God of north wind; Pollux and Castor, the twin brothers of Helen; Admetus, prince of Pherae; Tiphys, the helmsman, and even Asclepius came as the ship's physician.

The Argonauts gathered at Pagasae, where they sacrificed to Apollo. The omens were good. On the way to Colchis, they made the first stop at Aphetae to renew their water supplies. Chased by storms, the Argonauts reached the island of Lemnos, where only women lived. Only one man, the king, was left on the island. Although the women had risen up against the men on the island by killing them, they gladly helped the Argonauts with gifts of food and wine after they had promised to treat them as wives. The Argonauts stayed on the island for one or two years, and boarded the ship either on Heracles intervention or attracted by Orpheus' song. Behind them were left numerous descendants.

On Orpheus' advice the Argonauts first sailed from Lemnos to Samothrace. Then, they made their way through the Strait of Hellespont and reached the Propontis. Soon, they approached the land of the Doliones, who were the descendants of Poseidon and were ruled by king Cyzicus. When the Argonauts arrived, Cyzicus had just married Clite. During the wedding banquet, the six-handed giants attacked the Argonauts. They were all killed by Heracles. The next day, the Argonauts continued their journey, but were thrown back by a storm. Thinking that pirates were landing, the Doliones attacked the Argonauts and, in the fierce night battle, Jason killed king Cyzicus. So Jason and his friends stayed to take part in the magnificent funeral activities organized for the dead king. Because of the unfavorable wind, the Argonauts extended their stay in the land of the Doliones for another twelve days.

In order to reach their destination sooner, Heracles initiated a rowing competition. When they reached Mysia, near the mouth of the river Chius, Heracles' oar broke and they had to land to get a new oar, as well as to stock up water supplies. While the dinner was being prepared, Heracles went into a forest to find some wood for his oar, and his squire Hylas went to find water. At Pegae Wellspring, Hylas met a nymph, who, enchanted by his beauty, lured him to the water and drowned him or made him her lover. Pollux heard Hylas' cries and hurried to save him. On his way, he met Heracles who joined him. While they were looking for Hylas in vain, the Argonauts continued the journey.

After some time, the Argo landed in the country of Bebryces in Bithynia, which was ruled by the savage king Amycus, son of Poseidon, a famous boxer, who challenged all travelers to fight him. Those who refused were thrown into the sea, and those who accepted were killed in the match. Amycus approached the Argonauts and refused them any food or water, until one of them fought with him in the ring. Pollux, who was the champion in boxing, accepted the challenge. Although stronger and younger, Amycus was soon defeated by the skill of Pollux. In some versions, Pollux killed Amycus, while in others he just knocked him out and made him promise he would stop harming strangers in future.

On the following day, the Argonauts set sail again and soon they arrived at the land of king Phineus. Apollo gave Phineus the gift of prophecy, but after he revealed their plans to mortals, or rather Zeus unfaithfulness to Hera, Zeus punished him by blinding him and plagued him with a group of harpies, the ugly winged female creatures with hooked beaks and long razor-like claws, who snatched away his food and fouled what was left. Phineus grew thinner and thinner, and began to lose his vision. Phineus promised Jason that he would tell him how to reach Colchis and win the Golden Fleece, if he freed him from the harpies. Calais and Zetes, the winged sons of Boreas, took this task on themselves. The next time when the harpies descended, Calais and Zetes killed them. Some other versions say that they chased the harpies into the air and far across the sea to the Strophades islands, where they spared their lives after the harpies had sworn never to harass Phineus again. At last Phineus instructed Jason how to take the ship between the Symplegades rocks that guarded the entrance to the Bosphorus. He also told Jason what weather and fortune to expect on his way to Colchis, and advised him to trust in Aphrodite once he reached Colchis.

On their way through the Strait of Bosphorus[2], the Argonauts reached the Symplegades rocks, also known as the clashing rocks, between which no ship had ever passed, for the rocks drove together and crushed whatever ship that attempted to pass between them. As Phineus had advised them, they let a dove fly in front of the Argo. The dove managed to get through the channel before the moving rocks closed the passage, losing just a few of tail feathers. When the rocks separated again, the Argonauts rowed through in full speed, with the help of Hera and Athena, and lost only their stern ornament. From then on the rocks remained motionless, as the prophecy said that once a ship passed between them safely, they could move no more.

When the Argonauts sailed along the southern shore, they reached the island of Thynias. From there, they sailed to the land of the Mariandyni, where they were warmly welcomed by king Lycus, who was glad that his bitter enemy Amycus had been killed by the Argonauts. Grateful, he offered them his son Dascylus to guide them on their voyage along the coast. Through the mouth of the river Phasis, the Argonauts, having overcome so many hardships, finally arrived at Colchis, the land of Helius' son, king Aeetes.

Seizure of the Fleece

As soon as he disembarked, Jason presented himself to king Aeetes, told him the reason for his mission to Colchis, and demanded the Golden Fleece. Remembering an old prophecy saying that he would rule as long as he possessed the Golden Fleece, king Aeetes felt scared for his life and crown, and decided to kill Jason. He promised the young man the Golden Fleece, on condition that he should yoke two brazen-footed, fire-breathing bulls, the creations of Hephaestus. After that, he would have to plough the field of Ares and sow it with the dragon's teeth. Jason would have never performed the difficult tasks without the help of Aeetes' daughter Medea, the famous sorceress. Actually, it were Athena and Hera who had approached Aphrodite, who then sent her son Eros to wound Medea's heart with an arrow and made her fall madly in love with

Jason.

After Jason had promised to marry her and take her to Greece, Medea gave him a magic ointment, with which Jason was to cover his body, spear and shield before he attacked the fire bulls. And he managed to yoke the bulls and plough the field. From the sowed dragon's teeth an army of armed men immediately sprouted, but Jason, as Medea had told him, threw a stone among them, and the men started to attack and kill each other. As they were paying no attention to Jason, he slew them easily. At last Jason finished the almost impossible task.

Jason then went to Aeetes and demanded the Golden Fleece again, but Aeetes refused to give it to Jason. Medea took Jason to the precinct of Ares where the Golden Fleece was kept. There, the Golden Fleece were guarded by a huge dragon. Medea put a spell on the dragon, and Jason easily unfastened the fleece from the tree or according to some versions, Jason fought with the dragon and killed it. Then they hurried down to the beach where the other Argonauts were waiting on the ship, ready for escape. Aeetes raised an alarm and ordered to chase them, but Medea killed her half-brother Apsyrtus, cut him into pieces, and then threw his flesh piece by piece into the sea. While the Colchians were searching the sea for the body pieces of Apsyrtus, the Argo escaped.

Returning to Greece and Taking Revenge

The adventures of the Argonauts on their way home were similar to those of Odysseus. They passed the island of the sirens where they would have all died if Orpheus' song wasn't louder than the singing of the sirens. Only Butes responded to the voices of these bird-women and jumped into the sea, but he was rescued by Aphrodite who took him to Lilybaeum in Sicily and made him her lover. Then, the Argonauts passed through the straits of Scylla and Charybdis, and the island of Thrinacia, where the cattle of Helius grazed, and then they arrived at Corcyra in the land of the Phaeacians. After that, the Argonauts hardly set sail again, when a strong storm drove them to the shores of Libya. They had to carry the Argo on their shoulders for twelve days until they reached Lake Tritonis, where the sea god Triton appeared, and showed them the way to the Mediterranean Sea. The Argonauts continued their journey and soon reached Crete. When they tried to disembark, they were attacked by Talos who hurled big stones at the Argo. Talos was a bronze giant created by Hephaestus, whose task was to protect the island from strangers. He was invulnerable except in the lower part of his leg, where there was a vein closed at the top by a bronze nail. Medea swiftly approached Talos and gave him a magic potion that put him into sleep. Then she opened a vein above one of his ankles through which his life-supporting ichor leaked out and Talos died.

When the Argonauts finally arrived at Iolcus, they found no one to greet them. Jason soon learned that Pelias had killed his parents, as well as their newborn son Promachus. When Medea heard the story, she decided to punish Pelias for his crimes. Or, as some say, Jason asked Medea for ways to punish Pelias. She went to the court of Pelias, claiming that the goddess Artemis had sent her to rejuvenate him. She convinced Pelias that there was a way to make the old young again. To prove this, Medea took an old ram and sacrificed it using one of her charms. She turned the old ram, which was in boiling water into a young lamb. So, to make Pelias young again, Medea convinced Pelias' four daughters to cut their father into pieces and boil the pieces in the same way. However, when this was completed, Medea vanished, and thus ended the life of Pelias.

The Tragic End of His Life

After this terrible murder, Jason and Medea lost the trust of the Iolcan people and were sentenced to banishment by the Iolcan court. Therefore, Jason had to give up his throne and, together with Medea, moved to Corinth. There they had two sons. Medea missed her family in Colchis, and yet her love for Jason seemed to be more important. But soon Jason decided to abandon Medea, for he wanted to fulfill his ambitions for power by marrying Glauce, the princess of Corinth. As the king of Corinth feared the powers of Medea, he ordered Medea and her two helpless children out of the country. Desperate, Medea sought revenge and decided to kill Jason's bride and her father. She took a wedding dress and smeared it with deadly drugs. She then placed it into a casket and told her sons to deliver it to the new bride as a gift. The princess received the gift and tried it on at once. No sooner had she put it on than a fire devoured her and her father who came to her rescue, melting their flesh away. They both died rather pathetically. When Medea learned that the deed was done, she turned her mind to one more dreadful task: killing her own sons by Jason. She did so, without feeling sorrow for what she had done. When Jason realized Medea had killed his bride, he was determined to kill Medea. But when he arrived at Medea's house she had already escaped to Athens in her grandfather Helius' chariot drawn by winged dragons. Later she married the old king Aegeus.

After this, Jason cursed her, but not himself, for what had happened. Now bereft of friends and family, Jason sat under the prow of the rotting Argo, the ship of his former glory, and was killed by a fallen beam which hit him on the head.

NOTES

1. Chiron is a wise and noble-hearted centaur, often given charge of the young heroes of

Greek mythology. With his many talents and his gentle nature, he can train the heroes in everything from the deadly arts of hunting and archery to the delicate arts of music and healing.

2. Bosphorus now is one of the world's most strategic waterways, between the Black Sea and the Sea of Marmara; Bosphorus comes from a Tracian word of unknown origin, interpreted in Greek as meaning "Ford of the Cow," from the legend of Io, one of the many lovers of Zeus, who swam across the sea here as a cow chased and continuously disturbed by flies sent by Hera.

Appreciation:

伊阿宋，古希腊神话人物。希腊神话中夺取金羊毛的主要英雄。伊阿宋是埃宋的儿子，克瑞透斯的孙子。叔父珀利阿斯篡夺王位后，令伊阿宋去科尔喀斯觅取金羊毛。伊阿宋得赫拉之助，与赫拉克勒斯、墨勒阿革洛斯等英雄，乘坐"阿尔戈号"，历经艰险到达科尔喀斯，并赢得该国公主美狄亚的爱情和帮助最终取得金羊毛。仅看其夺取金羊毛的故事，伊阿宋绝对是"典型的"英雄人物。但是，我们说过，希腊神话中的英雄，是富有人性的形象，因此在他们身上或多或少都有所谓的"缺点"。伊阿宋在逃去邻国并与美狄亚生子之后，觊觎王权的野心再次燃起，因此不惜在爱情上背叛美狄亚，但最终也因此落得家破人亡的悲惨境遇。

Questions:

1. Betrayal is said to be the key factor to Jason's tragical fate. What is your understanding of loyalty and betrayal?

2. If without the betrayal to Medea, what fate would Jason have? If you were Jason, what would you do at that time?

Part 2
The Bible

Definition of the Bible

The Bible is a collection of sacred texts or scriptures that Jews and Christians consider to be a product of divine inspiration and a record of the relationship between God and humans.

Sources of the Bible

Many different authors contributed to the Bible. What is regarded as canonical text differs depending on traditions and groups; a number of Bible canons have evolved, with overlapping and diverging contents. The Christian *Old Testament* overlaps with the Hebrew Bible and the Greek Septuagint; the Hebrew Bible is known in Judaism as the *Tanakh*. The *New Testament* is a collection of writings by early Christians, believed to be mostly Jewish Disciples of Christ, written in first-century Koine Greek. These early Christian Greek writings consist of narratives, letters, and apocalyptic writings. Among Christian denominations there is some disagreement about the contents of the canon, primarily the Apocrypha, a list of works that are regarded with varying levels of respect.

Influences of the Bible

With estimated total sales of over 5 billion copies, the Bible is widely considered to be the best-selling book of all time. It has estimated annual sales of 100 million copies, and has been a major influence on literature and history, especially in the West, where the Gutenberg Bible was the first book printed using movable type.

Methods to Study the Bible

(1) Book Studies

When you become interested in the Bible you can study it in-depth. The best way to start the Bible study is to find an overview of the Bible to give you a general idea of the outline and

contents of the material. Summaries will tell you who the author was and when the book was written. They will also tell you the general themes covered in the Bible with a quick overview of the stories. From this summary you are ready to study the Bible in detail.

(2) Chapter Studies

To do a proper chapter study you need to understand the chapter in context. Don't pull a chapter out of a book and try to interpret it without the context with which it was intended. A good concordance or topical Bible can help you find other verses related to the chapter you are studying.

(3) Biographical Studies

Studying the life of a person in the Bible can be rewarding and enlightening. Many Bible characters will show up in only one book; but there are some who span multiple books or are referenced many times in the Scriptures.

(4) Topical Studies

Another fun study is to find a topic and follow it through the Bible. This can be based on a single word or teaching. Again, a good study Bible or concordance will help here. There are even topical Bibles that do much of the work for you. Sometimes they are called topical Bibles, but they are also known as reference Bibles.

(5) Keep Notes

Whichever Bible study method you employ, remember to write down what you learn. You will benefit personally from looking over your notes as you pass through certain books and chapters in your future reading time.

Selections of the Bible

The Bible: The Old Testament (Hebrew, ca. 1000 B.C.–300 B.C.)

Genesis[1] 1–3

[The Creation—The Fall]

1. In the beginning God created the heaven and the earth. And the earth was without form, and void; and darkness was upon the face of the deep[2]. And the Spirit of God[3] moved upon the face of the waters.

And God said, Let there be light: and there was light. And God saw the light, that it was good: and God divided the light from the darkness. And God called the light Day, and the darkness he called Night. And the evening and the morning were the first day[4].

And God said, Let there be a firmament in the midst of the waters, and let it divide the waters from the waters. And God made the firmament, and divided the waters which were under the firmament from the waters which were above the firmament: and it was so. And God called the firmament Heaven. And the evening and the morning were the second day.

And God said, Let the waters under the heaven be gathered together unto one place, and let the dry land appear: and it was so. And God called the dry land Earth; and the gathering together of the waters called he Seas: and God saw that it was good. And God said, Let the earth bring forth grass, the herb yielding seed, and the fruit tree yielding fruit after his kind, whose seed is in itself, upon the earth: and it was so. And the earth brought forth grass, and herb yielding seed after his kind, and the tree yielding fruit, whose seed [was] in itself, after his kind: and God saw that it was good. And the evening and the morning were the third day.

And God said, Let there be lights[5] in the firmament of the heaven to divide the day from the night; and let them be for signs, and for seasons, and for days, and years. And let them be for lights in the firmament of the heaven to give light upon the earth: and it was so. And God made two great lights; the greater light to rule the day, and the lesser light to rule the night: he made the stars also. And God set them in the firmament of the heaven to give light upon the earth. And to rule over the day and over the night, and to divide the light from the darkness: and God saw that it was good. And the evening and the morning were the fourth day. And God said, Let the waters bring forth abundantly the moving creature that hath life, and fowl [that] may fly above the earth in the open firmament of heaven. And God created great whales, and every living creature that moveth, which the waters brought forth abundantly, after their kind, and every winged fowl after his kind: and God saw that it was good. And God blessed them, saying, Be fruitful, and multiply, and fill the waters in the seas, and let fowl multiply in the earth. And the evening and the morning were the fifth day.

And God said, Let the earth bring forth the living creature after his kind, cattle, and creeping thing, and beast of the earth after his kind: and it was so. And God made the beast of the earth after his kind, and cattle after their kind, and every thing that creepeth upon the earth after his kind: and God saw that it was good.

And God said, Let us make man[6] in our image, after our likeness: and let them have dominion over the fish of the sea, and over the fowl of the air, and over the cattle, and over all the earth, and over every creeping thing that creepeth upon the earth. So God created man in his own image, in the image of God created he him; male and female created he them. And God blessed them, and God said unto them, Be fruitful, and multiply, and replenish the earth, and subdue it: and have dominion over the fish of the sea, and over the fowl of the air, and over every living thing that moveth upon the earth.

And God said, Behold, I have given you every herb bearing seed, which is upon the face of all the earth, and every tree, in the which is the fruit of a tree yielding seed; to you it shall be for meat. And to every beast of the earth, and to every fowl of the air, and to every thing that creepeth upon the earth, wherein there is life, I have given every green herb for meat[7]: and it was so. And God saw every thing that he had made, and, behold, it was very good. And the evening and the morning were the sixth day.

2. Thus the heavens and the earth were finished, and all the host of them. And on the seventh day God ended his work which he had made; and he rested on the seventh day from all his work which he had made. And God blessed the seventh day, and sanctified it[8]: because that in it he had rested from all his work which God created and made.

These are the generations of the heavens and of the earth when they were created, in the day[9] that the LORD God made the earth and the heavens, And every plant of the field before it was in the earth, and every herb of the field before it grew: for the LORD God had not caused it to rain upon the earth, and there was not a man to till the ground. But there went up a mist[10] from the earth, and watered the whole face of the ground. And the LORD God formed man of the dust of the ground[11], and breathed into his nostrils the breath of life; and man became a living soul.

And the LORD God planted a garden eastward in Eden[12]; and there he put the man whom he had formed. And out of the ground made the LORD God to grow every tree that is pleasant to the sight, and good for food; the tree of life also in the midst of the garden, and the tree of knowledge of good and evil. And a river went out of Eden to water the garden; and from thence it was parted, and became into four heads. The name of the first is Pison: that is it which compasseth the whole land of Havilah, where there is gold; And the gold of that land is good: there is bdellium and the onyx stone. And the name of the second river is Gihon: the same is it that compasseth the whole land of Ethiopia. And the name of the third river is Hiddekel: that is it which goeth toward the east of Assyria. And the fourth river is Euphrates. And the LORD God took the man, and put him into the garden of Eden to dress[13] it and to keep[14] it. And the LORD God commanded the man, saying, Of every tree of the garden thou mayest freely eat: but of the tree of the knowledge of good and evil, thou shalt not eat of it: for in the day that thou eatest thereof thou shalt surely die.

And the LORD God said, It is not good that the man should be alone; I will make him an help meet[15] for him. And out of the ground the LORD God formed every beast of the field, and every fowl of the air; and brought them unto Adam to see what he would call them: and whatsoever Adam called every living creature, that was the name thereof. And Adam gave names to all cattle, and to the fowl of the air, and to every beast of the field; but for Adam there was not found an help meet for him. And the LORD God caused a deep sleep to fall upon Adam and he slept: and he took one of his ribs, and closed up the flesh instead thereof; And the rib, which the LORD God had taken from man, made he a woman, and brought her unto the man. And Adam said, This is now bone of my bones, and flesh of my flesh: she shall be called Woman, because she was taken out of Man. Therefore shall a man leave his father and his mother, and shall cleave unto his wife: and they shall be one flesh. And they were both naked, the man and his wife, and were not ashamed.

3. Now the serpent was more subtil than any beast of the field which the LORD God had made. And he said unto the woman, Yea, hath God said, Ye shall not eat of every tree of the garden? And the woman said unto the serpent, We may eat of the fruit of the trees of the garden: But of the fruit of the tree which is in the midst of the garden, God hath said, Ye shall not eat of it, neither shall ye touch it, lest ye die. And the serpent said unto the woman, Ye shall not surely die: for God doth know that in the day ye eat thereof, then your eyes shall be opened, and ye shall be as gods, knowing good and evil. And when the woman saw that the tree was good for food, and that it was pleasant to the eyes, and a tree to be desired to make one wise, she took of the fruit thereof, and did eat, and gave also unto her husband with her; and he did eat. And the eyes of them both were opened, and they knew that they were naked; and they sewed fig leaves together, and made themselves aprons. And they heard the voice of the LORD God walking in the garden in the cool of the day: and Adam and his wife hid themselves from the presence of the LORD God amongst the trees of the garden. And the LORD God called unto Adam, and said unto him, Where art thou? And he said, I heard thy voice in the garden, and I was afraid, because I was naked; and I hid myself. And he said, Who told thee that thou wast naked? Hast thou eaten of the tree, whereof I commanded thee that thou shouldest not eat? And the man said, The woman whom thou gavest to be with me, she gave me of the tree, and I did eat. And the LORD God said unto the woman, What is this that thou hast done? And the woman said, The serpent beguiled me, and I did eat. And the LORD God said unto the serpent, Because thou hast done this, thou art cursed above all cattle, and above every beast of the field; upon thy belly shalt thou go, and dust shalt thou eat all the days of thy life: And I will put enmity between thee and the woman, and between thy seed and her seed; it shall bruise thy head, and thou shalt bruise his heel. Unto the woman he said, I will greatly multiply thy sorrow and thy conception; in sorrow thou shalt

bring forth children; and thy desire shall be to thy husband, and he shall rule over thee. And unto Adam he said, Because thou hast hearkened unto the voice of thy wife, and hast eaten of the tree, of which I commanded thee, saying, Thou shalt not eat of it: cursed is the ground for thy sake; in sorrow shalt thou eat of it all the days of thy life; Thorns also and thistles shall it bring forth to thee; and thou shalt eat the herb of the field; In the sweat of thy face shalt thou eat bread, till thou return unto the ground; for out of it wast thou taken: for dust thou art, and unto dust shalt thou return. And Adam called his wife's name Eve; because she was the mother of all living. Unto Adam also and to his wife did the LORD God make coats of skins, and clothed them.

And the LORD God said, Behold, the man is become as one of us, to know good and evil: and now, lest he put forth his hand, and take also of the tree of life, and eat, and live for ever: therefore the LORD God sent him forth from the garden of Eden, to till the ground from whence he was taken. So he drove out the man; and he placed at the east of the garden of Eden Cherubims, and a flaming sword which turned every way, to keep the way of the tree of life.

Genesis 4

[The First Murder]

4. And Adam knew Eve his wife; and she conceived[16], and bare Cain, and said, I have gotten a man from the LORD. And she again bare his brother Abel. And Abel was a keeper of sheep, but Cain was a tiller of the ground. And in process of time it came to pass, that Cain brought of the fruit of the ground an offering unto the LORD. And Abel, he also brought of the firstlings of his flock and of the fat thereof. And the LORD had respect unto Abel and to his offering: but unto Cain and to his offering he had not respect. And Cain was very wroth, and his countenance fell. And the LORD said unto Cain, Why art thou wroth? and why is thy countenance fallen? If thou doest well, shalt thou not be accepted? and if thou doest not well, sin lieth at the door. And unto thee shall be his desire, and thou shalt rule over him. And Cain talked with Abel his brother: and it came to pass, when they were in the field, that Cain rose up against Abel his brother, and slew him.

And the LORD said unto Cain, Where is Abel thy brother? And he said, I know not: am I my brother's keeper? And he said, What hast thou done? the voice of thy brother's blood crieth unto me from the ground. And now art thou cursed from the earth, which hath opened her mouth to receive thy brother's blood from thy hand; when thou tillest the ground, it shall not henceforth yield unto thee her strength; a fugitive and a vagabond shalt thou be in the earth. And Cain said unto the LORD, My punishment is greater than I can bear. Behold, thou hast driven me out this day from the face of the earth; and from thy face shall I be hid; and I shall be a fugitive and a vagabond in the earth; and it shall come to pass, that every one that findeth me shall slay me. And the LORD said unto him, Therefore whosoever slayeth Cain, vengeance shall be taken on him sevenfold. And the LORD set a mark upon Cain, lest any finding him should kill him. And Cain went out from the presence of the LORD, and dwelt in the land of Nod[17], on the east of Eden. And Cain knew his wife; and she conceived, and bare Enoch: and he builded a city, and called the name of the city, after the name of his son, Enoch. And unto Enoch was born Irad: and Irad begat Mehujael: and Mehujael begat Methusael: and Methusael begat Lamech. And Lamech took unto him two wives: the name of the one was Adah, and the name of the other Zillah. And Adah bare Jabal: he was the father of such as dwell in tents, and of such as have cattle. And his brother's name was Jubal: he was the father of all such as handle the harp and organ. And Zillah, she also bare Tubal-cain, an instructor of every artificer in brass and iron: and the sister of Tubal-cain was Naamah. And Lamech said unto his wives, Adah and Zillah, Hear my voice; ye wives of Lamech, hearken unto my speech: for I have slain a man to my wounding, and a young man to my hurt. If Cain shall be avenged sevenfold, truly Lamech seventy and sevenfold. And Adam knew his wife again; and she bare a son, and called his name Seth: For God, said she, hath appointed me another seed instead of Abel, whom Cain slew. And to Seth, to him also there was born a son; and he called his name Enos: then began men to call upon the name of the LORD.

Genesis 6–9

[The Flood]

6. …… And GOD saw that the wickedness of man was great in the earth, and that every imagination of the thoughts of his heart was only evil continually. And it repented the LORD that he had made man on the earth, and it grieved him at his heart. And the LORD said, I will destroy man whom I have created from the face of the earth; both man, and beast, and the creeping thing, and the fowls of the air; for it repenteth me that I have made them. But Noah found grace in the eyes of the LORD.

These are the generations of Noah: Noah was a just man and perfect in his generations, and Noah walked with God. And Noah begat three sons, Shem, Ham, and Japheth.

The earth also was corrupt before God, and the earth was filled with violence. And God looked upon the earth, and, behold, it was corrupt; for all flesh had corrupted his way upon the earth. And God said unto Noah, The end of all flesh is come before me; for the earth is filled with violence through them; and, behold, I will destroy them with the earth. Make thee an ark of gopher wood; rooms shalt thou make in the ark, and shalt pitch it within and without with pitch. And this is the fashion which thou shalt make it of: The length of the ark shall be three hundred cubits[18], the breadth of it fifty cubits, and the height of it thirty cubits. A window shalt thou make to the ark, and in a cubit shalt thou finish it above; and the door of the ark shalt thou set in the side thereof; with lower, second, and third stories shalt thou make it. And, behold, I, even I, do bring a flood of waters upon the earth, to destroy all flesh, wherein is the breath of life, from under heaven; and every thing that is in the earth shall die. But with thee will I establish my covenant; and thou shalt come into the ark, thou, and thy sons, and thy wife, and thy sons' wives with thee. And of every living thing of all flesh, two of every sort shalt thou bring into the ark, to keep them alive with thee; they shall be male and female. Of fowls after their kind, and of cattle after their kind, of every creeping thing of the earth after his kind, two of every sort shall come unto thee, to keep them alive. And take thou unto thee of all food that is eaten, and thou shalt gather it to thee; and it shall be for food for thee, and for them. Thus did Noah; according to all that God commanded him, so did he.

7. …… And Noah was six hundred years old when the flood of waters was upon the earth. And Noah went in, and his sons, and his wife, and his sons' wives with him, into the ark, because of the waters of the flood. Of clean beasts, and of beasts that are not clean, and of fowls, and of every thing that creepeth upon the earth, there went in two and two unto Noah into the ark, the male and the female, as God had commanded Noah. And it came to pass after seven days, that the waters of the flood were upon the earth. In the six hundredth year of Noah's life, in the second month, the seventeenth day of the month, the same day were all the fountains of the great deep broken up, and the windows of heaven were opened. And the rain was upon the earth forty days and forty nights. In the selfsame day entered Noah, and Shem, and Ham, and Japheth, the sons of Noah, and Noah's wife, and the three wives of his sons with them, into the ark; they, and every beast after his kind, and all the cattle after their kind, and every creeping thing that creepeth upon the earth after his kind, and every fowl after his kind, every bird of every sort. And they went in unto Noah into the ark, two and two of all flesh, wherein is the breath of life. And they that went in, went in male and female of all flesh, as God had commanded him: and the LORD shut him in. And the flood was forty days upon the earth; and the waters increased, and bare up the ark, and it was lift up above the earth. And the waters prevailed, and were increased greatly upon the

earth; and the ark went upon the face of the waters. And the waters prevailed exceedingly upon the earth; and all the high hills, that were under the whole heaven, were covered. Fifteen cubits upward did the waters prevail; and the mountains were covered. And all flesh died that moved upon the earth, both of fowl, and of cattle, and of beast, and of every creeping thing that creepeth upon the earth, and every man: All in whose nostrils was the breath of life, of all that was in the dry land, died. And every living substance was destroyed which was upon the face of the ground, both man, and cattle, and the creeping things, and the fowl of the heaven; and they were destroyed from the earth: and Noah only remained alive, and they that were with him in the ark. And the waters prevailed upon the earth an hundred and fifty days.

8. And God remembered Noah, and every living thing, and all the cattle that was with him in the ark: and God made a wind to pass over the earth, and the waters assuaged; The fountains also of the deep and the windows of heaven were stopped, and the rain from heaven was restrained; And the waters returned from off the earth continually: and after the end of the hundred and fifty days the waters were abated. And the ark rested in the seventh month, on the seventeenth day of the month, upon the mountains of Ararat. And the waters decreased continually until the tenth month: in the tenth month, on the first day of the month, were the tops of the mountains seen.

And it came to pass at the end of forty days, that Noah opened the window of the ark which he had made: and he sent forth a raven, which went forth to and fro, until the waters were dried up from off the earth. Also he sent forth a dove from him, to see if the waters were abated from off the face of the ground; but the dove found no rest for the sole of her foot, and she returned unto him into the ark, for the waters were on the face of the whole earth: then he put forth his hand, and took her, and pulled her in unto him into the ark. And he stayed yet other seven days; and again he sent forth the dove out of the ark; and the dove came in to him in the evening; and, lo, in her mouth was an olive leaf pluckt off: so Noah knew that the waters were abated from off the earth. And he stayed yet other seven days; and sent forth the dove; which returned not again unto him any more.

And it came to pass in the six hundredth and first year, in the first month, the first day of the month, the waters were dried up from off the earth: and Noah removed the covering of the ark, and looked, and, behold, the face of the ground was dry. And in the second month, on the seven and twentieth day of the month, was the earth dried.

And God spake unto Noah, saying, Go forth of the ark, thou, and thy wife, and thy sons, and thy sons' wives with thee. Bring forth with thee every living thing that is with thee, of all flesh, both of fowl, and of cattle, and of every creeping thing that creepeth upon the earth; that they may breed abundantly in the earth, and be fruitful, and multiply upon the earth. And Noah went forth, and his sons, and his wife, and his sons' wives with him: Every beast, every creeping thing, and every fowl, and whatsoever creepeth upon the earth, after their kinds, went forth out of the ark. And Noah builded an altar unto the LORD; and took of every clean beast, and of every clean fowl, and offered burnt offerings on the altar. And the LORD smelled a sweet savour; and the LORD said in his heart, I will not again curse the ground any more for man's sake; for the imagination of man's heart is evil from his youth; neither will I again smite any more every thing living, as I have done. While the earth remaineth, seedtime and harvest, and cold and heat, and summer and winter, and day and night shall not cease.

9. And God blessed Noah and his sons, and said unto them, Be fruitful, and multiply, and replenish the earth. And the fear of you and the dread of you shall be upon every beast of the earth, and upon every fowl of the air, upon all that moveth upon the earth, and upon all the fishes of the sea; into your hand are they delivered. Every moving thing that liveth shall be meat for you; even as the green herb have I given you all things. But flesh with the life thereof, which is the blood thereof, shall ye not eat. And surely your blood of your lives will I require; at the hand of every beast will I require it, and at the hand of man; at the hand of every man's brother will I require the life of man. Whoso sheddeth man's blood, by man shall his blood be shed: for in the image of God made he man. And you, be ye fruitful, and multiply; bring forth abundantly in the earth, and multiply therein.

And God spake unto Noah, and to his sons with him, saying, And I, behold, I establish my covenant with you, and with your seed after you; And with every living creature that is with you, of the fowl, of the cattle, and of every beast of the earth with you; from all that go out of the ark, to every beast of the earth. And I will establish my covenant with you; neither shall all flesh be cut off any more by the waters of a flood; neither shall there any more be a flood to destroy the earth. And God said, This is the token of the covenant which I make between me and you and every living creature that is with you, for perpetual generations: I do set my bow in the cloud, and it shall be for a token of a covenant between me and the earth. And it shall come to pass, when I bring a cloud over the earth, that the bow shall be seen in the cloud: And I will remember my covenant, which is between me and you and every living creature of all flesh; and the waters shall no more become a flood to destroy all flesh. And the bow shall be in the cloud; and I will look upon it, that I may remember the everlasting covenant between God and every living creature of all flesh that is upon the earth. And God said unto Noah, This is the token of the covenant, which I have established between me and all flesh that is upon the earth. And the sons of Noah, that went forth of the ark, were Shem, and Ham, and Japheth: and Ham is the father of Canaan. These are the three sons of Noah: and of them was the whole earth overspread. And Noah began to be an husbandman, and he planted a vineyard: And he drank of the wine, and was drunken; and he was uncovered within his tent. And Ham, the father of Canaan, saw the nakedness of his father, and told his two brethren without. And Shem and Japheth took a garment, and laid it upon both their shoulders, and went backward, and covered the nakedness of their father; and their faces were backward, and they saw not their father's nakedness. And Noah awoke from his wine, and knew what his younger son had done unto him. And he said, Cursed be Canaan; a servant of servants shall he be unto his brethren. And he said, Blessed be the LORD God of Shem; and Canaan shall be his servant. God shall enlarge Japheth, and he shall dwell in the tents of Shem; and Canaan shall be his servant. And Noah lived after the flood three hundred and fifty years. And all the days of Noah were nine hundred and fifty years: and he died.

Genesis 11

[The Origin of Languages]

11. And the whole earth was of one language, and of one speech. And it came to pass, as they journeyed from the east, that they found a plain in the land of Shinar; and they dwelt there. And they said one to another, Go to, let us make brick, and burn them throughly. And they had brick for stone, and slime had they for morter. And they said, Go to, let us build us a city and a tower, whose top may reach unto heaven; and let us make us a name, lest we be scattered abroad upon the face of the whole earth. And the LORD came down to see the city and the tower, which the children of men builded. And the LORD said, Behold, the people is one, and they have all one language; and this they begin to do: and now nothing will be restrained from them, which they have imagined to do. Go to, let us go down, and there confound their language, that they may not understand one another's speech. So the LORD scattered them abroad from thence upon the face of all the earth: and they left off to build the city. Therefore is the name of it called Babel; because the LORD did there confound the language of all the earth: and from thence did the LORD scatter them abroad upon the face of all the earth.

NOTES

1. Genesis, late Old English, via Latin from Greek, means "generation, creation, nativity,

horoscope," from the base of gignesthai "be born or produced." The name was given to the first book of the *Old Testament* in the Greek translation (*The Septuagint*), hence in the Latin translation (*The Vulgate*). Genesis is the first book of the biblical scriptures of both Judaism and Christianity—describing the creation of the Earth and of mankind. Longinus, points out in his "On the Sublime" (Section 9, Chapter 9), the first chapters in Genesis illustrate the great glory of God, that is an example of sublime.

2. the deep: the Ocean.
3. the Spirit of God: gas and wind.
4. And the evening and the morning were the first day: Hebrew counts their day from the evening, from 6 p.m. to 6 a.m. is one day.
5. Let there be lights: here refers to the sun, the moon and the stars, etc., illuminant body.
6. Let us make man: (1) the plural of Majesty; (2) the plural of Deliberation.
   Man, mankind generally.
7. meat: food.
8. And God blessed the seventh day, and sanctified it: The seventh day becomes the sabbath day which the Hebrew people are commanded to remember and keep holy in the fourth of the Ten Commandments (Exodus 20).
9. in the day: The 24 hours that constitutes what we consider a day, was not established until the 14th century (first proposed by Greek Mathematician Hipparchus), quite some time after the Bible was written. Therefore, we cannot be certain about the length of the intervals between the chronological order of the events described in the Genesis account.
10. mist: "Mist" could be translated as "flow." This indicated that water came up from beneath the ground as springs and spread over the whole earth in an uninterrupted cycle of water.
11. And the LORD God formed man of the dust of the ground: Hence the name Adam, from the Hebrew "adamah," meaning "ground" or "earth."
12. Note that Eden is not the name of the garden, but that the garden is located in the land of Eden. The term "eastward" means that Eden itself is to the east, this is presumed to be east of Canaan – the focal point of the rest of the Bible and the home of the writers and readers of Genesis.
13. "dress" is more closely translated as "tend", since the meaning of "dress" has changed since 1611, where it originally meant "to set in order" but gradually became more decorative. It is from the Hebrew abad, meaning "to work or serve." It can be also defined as "to till or cultivate."

14. keep (Hebrew "shamar"): means "to exercise great care over," "to guard," or "to preserve."
15. meet: The word "meet" is one of those words that has archaic meanings. The link shows that it can be used to mean "suitable," "tight," or "proper." Any of those words would be an acceptable substitute in this sentence. It should be noted in light of this etymology, "help meet" should not be interpreted as an early form of "a help mate," but rather as something closer to "a suitable help," or, more loosely, "a helpful partner."
16. And Adam knew Eve his wife; and she conceived: This is where the phrase "know her/him in the Biblical sense" as a euphemism for sexual intercourse comes from.
17. Nod: "Nod" does not have a specific identified region. The Hebrew word "Nod" is related to the term meaning "wanderer"; therefore to dwell in the land of Nod is usually taken to mean that one takes up a wandering life.
18. cubits: The cubit is an ancient unit based on the forearm length from the middle finger tip to the elbow bottom.

About the Author:

The Bible or The Holy Scriptures is composed of two parts: *The Old Testament* and *The New Testament*. *The Old Testament* is mainly written in Hebrew, while *The New Testament* is in Greek, which is called Judeo-Greek or Hellenistic-Greek. The Christian Old Testament overlaps with the Hebrew Bible and the Greek Septuagint. "Septuagint" in Greek means "seventy," for the Bible is translated by 72 Jewish scholars, according to the tale. The oldest extant copy of a complete Bible is an early 4th-century parchment book preserved in the Vatican Library, and it is known as the *Codex Vaticanus*. The oldest copy of the *Tanakh* in Hebrew and Aramaic dates from the 10th century CE. The oldest copy of a complete Latin (Vulgate) Bible is the *Codex Amiatinus*, dating from the 8th century, which is widely used by Catholic Church.

The King James Version (KJV, or the Authorized Version) of the Bible, which is the version found here, was composed around the time of Shakespeare, by a group of learned scholars headed by Bishop Lancelot Andrewes (1555–1626). It predates the discovery of the Dead Sea Scrolls. The KJV is now in the public domain. It was the KJV that was vastly important in shaping Anglo-American culture and literature, language and politics. It was this edition that was shipped out to colonies, used to educate generations, and shaped the way we speak today.

Appreciation:

《圣经》是英美社会文化的基石，对英美文学产生了深远而巨大的影响。《圣经》简洁、明晰的叙事风格影响了海明威，“罪”与“救赎”的观念影响了乔叟、莎士比亚、约翰·班扬、惠特曼、霍桑、福克纳……而其中的母题、意象、人物原型、结构原型也深深影响了英美文学名著。了解《圣经》能帮助读者看到文学名著幕后的本质，听出作品的弦外之音，读出作品的言外之意，从而更深刻地领悟文学作品的深奥底蕴。

《创世记》第 1 章讲述了天地或宇宙之开辟，以及创世的后果，理智、秩序和善良。开篇的诗行，匀称、反复但又不失变化。古罗马哲学家卢克莱修（Lucretius）在其作品《论宇宙的本质》（*On the Nature of the Universe*）中，约翰·弥尔顿（John Milton）在《失乐园》（*Paradise Lost*）中，柯勒律治（S. T. Coleridge）在《文学传记》（*Biographia Literaria*）中，雪莱（P. S. Shelley）在《诗辩》（*Defense of Poetry*）中，玛丽·雪莱（Mary B. Shelley）在《弗兰克斯坦》（*Frankenstein*）中，阿道司·赫胥黎（Aldous Huxley）在《美丽新世界》中，都引用了《圣经》并讨论了永恒、人性、女性的作用、神的本质等文学和哲学主题。

在第 2、3 章中，讨论了诱惑和罪的主题。在第 4 章中，讲述了人类的第一次谋杀，堕落的开始。在西方文学作品中，该隐的罪恶作为母题出现，“该隐的标记”出现在一些神话和神秘故事中，鬼怪都是该隐的后裔。在《贝奥武夫》中，戈兰德尔（Grendel）和他的妈妈就是来自该隐一族。在现代安妮·赖斯（Anne Rice）的恐怖小说，吸血鬼系列中，吸血鬼们也是该隐的后代。约翰·斯坦贝克在他的作品《伊甸园之东》中指出，只有了解该隐和亚伯的故事，才能更好地理解作品。而且，斯坦贝克认为该隐和亚伯的故事以及夏娃从伊甸园的堕落是全人类症结的基础。他还认为，如果没有这两个故事，心理医生也就失业了。《伊甸园之东》的叙述者在书中第四部分讲到，“人类被自己困在信仰中，在思想中，在饥饿和野心中，在贪婪和残忍中，以及善意和慷慨中——在善与恶的网中”。

罪与罪的后果促使上帝展开救赎。第 6 至 9 章，描述关于罪与救赎。大洪水和诺亚方舟是《圣经》中有名的故事。这个故事在现代流行文化中也多次被刻画和重现。电影《2012》中世界末日能够拯救人类的方舟也脱胎于《圣经》故事。

《创世记》第 11 章，是西方文明的基础文本之一，在艺术、诗歌和小说中都有重现。

对这个故事，有着不同的阐释：有的说文本从历史、权威的角度解释了语言的多样性，有的说，故事进一步表现了人类的傲慢、罪恶和道德沦丧。而巴别塔成为了反叛上帝、亵渎神灵的象征。

《圣经》和古希腊罗马神话是西方文学文化的两大源泉。文学评论家诺恩罗普·弗莱说道：“学习英语文学的学生如果不了解《圣经》，那么对于他所学的东西就会七窍通了六窍——还有一窍不通。”为了准确无误、完整无缺地解读西方文学作品，就必须了解《圣经》。

Questions:

1. Why should students know the Holy Bible?

2. How do you understand the thought presented in the Bible?

3. Who were Adam and Eve? What does Eden symbolize?

4. Find out the influence of the story of Cain in western literature and culture.

5. Why do we say the Bible has shaped Western culture more decisively than anything else ever written?

Part 3
Poetry

Definition of Poetry

Poetry is a comprehensive term which can be taken to cover any kind of metrical composition.

Major Types of Poetry

Epic: A long narrative poem that is about a serious subject, told in a formal and elevated style, centering on a heroic or quasi-divine individual on whose actions depends the fate of a tribe, a nation or the human race.

Lyric: A short poem in which a single speaker expresses a state of mind or a process of perception, thought and feeling. Most lyric speakers usually muse in solitude.

Ballad: A poem originally sung that tells a story in rhyme, usually transmitted orally.

Elegy: A poem that is on the lamentation and mourning for the dead; it is also a poem about the subjects of change and loss in the elegiac form, such as the complaints about love.

Pastoral: A deliberately conventional poem expressing a poet's, especially an urban poet's longing and nostalgic image of the idealized peace and simplicity of rural life in contrast with the corruption in the city.

Forms of Poetry

Forms of poetry range from the variable, the fixed, the visual, the hybrid and the "formless." The Variable forms of poetry include Ode, Epigram, Epitaph, Dramatic monologue and Blank Verse; the Fixed forms contain Sonnet, Haiku, Limerick, Villanelle and Fixed French forms; the Visual forms include Concrete (or pattern) poems and Acrostics; the Hybrid forms include Verse drama and Verse novel; and the "Formless" forms contain Free verse and Prose poetry.

Rhyme

Rhyme refers to the repetition of identical or similar sounds of the last stressed vowel and of all the speech sounds following that vowel, usually at the end of poetic lines, that is, End Rhyme, but sometimes, the Internal Rhyme happens. Rhyme is usually thought of as the defining feature that distinguishes poetry from prose. Its appeal to the ear keeps us engaged as we listen for matching sounds and the way it brings words together unexpectedly can be surprising and even revolutionary, such as the revolution by means of rhyme in John Milton's *Paradise Lost*. While the rhyme seems to be an aesthetic question, it is of some political significance sometimes.

Rhyme Scheme

It refers to the ordered pattern of end-rhymes across a poem. To identify a rhyme scheme, take a poem and give a letter, in alphabetical order, to each different sound you hear at the end of each. Thus, label the sound of the first end of line with "a" and then label any subsequent repeats of that sound also with "a". Give the next different sound of the end of line a "b", together with subsequent occurrences of that sound, and so on. In the case of the Sonnet, rhyme schemes can be associated with particular traditions, for example, the quatrains of a Petrarchan sonnet have "a-b-b-a" rhyme schemes, while the quatrains of a Shakespearean one have "a-b-a-b" rhyme schemes.

Stanza

Stanza refers to a group of poetic lines, defined by its arrangement of metre and rhyme. It includes one-line stanzas, two-line stanzas (couplets), three-line stanzas (tercets), four-line stanzas (quatrains), longer-length stanzas which may vary from five-line stanzas (quintains), six-line stanzas (sestains), seven-line stanzas (septets), to eight-line stanzas (octets) etc.

Sonnet[1] 29

When, in disgrace[2] with Fortune and men's eyes,
I all alone beweep[3] my outcast state,
And trouble deaf heaven with my bootless[4] cries,
And look upon myself and curse my fate,
Wishing me like to one more rich in hope,
Featured like him, like him with friends possessed,
Desiring this man's art and that man's scope[5],
With what I most enjoy contented least;
Yet in these thoughts myself almost despising,

Haply I think on thee, and then my state
(Like to the lark at break of day arising
From sullen[6] earth) sings hymns at heaven's gate;
For thy sweet love remembered such wealth brings
That then I scorn to change my state with kings.

NOTES

1. 十四行诗源于意大利，以但丁（Dante）和彼特拉克（Petrarch）为代表，其一般由前八行诗歌（Octave）和后六行诗（Sestet）组成，前八行一般是语气比较强烈的问题陈述，后六行一般是对前部分问题的解决。其韵脚常常是 abba abba cde cde。十四行诗传入英国经过怀亚特（Thomas Wyatt）、斯宾塞（Edmund Spenser）等人对韵律的改进，莎士比亚在其改进的基础上调整修改了十四行诗的韵脚，一般由三个四行诗（Quatrains）加一个对句（Couplet）组成，一般称为莎士比亚式十四行诗。其韵脚一般有两种：abab cdcd efef gg; abba cddc effe gg。文中所选莎士比亚的这首十四行诗采用的是前种韵脚，即 abab cdcd efef gg。
2. disgrace: 耻辱，丢脸，不光彩，丢脸的人（或事）
3. beweep：悲伤，哀叹
4. bootless: 无用的，无益的
5. scope: 眼界，见识
6. sullen: 阴沉的，阴暗的

About the Author:

William Shakespeare was born in a small town Stratford-upon-Avon in April (probably April 23, regarding that a new born baby is usually christened three days after he was born, and Shakespeare's christening date is April 26), 1564. There are no documented records about his youth but some legends which are hard to tell whether real or not. The first documented fact is his marriage in 1582 when he was 18 years old to Anne Hathaway, eight years senior to him. They had twins Hamnet and Judith in 1585. By 1592, Shakespeare was already in London as an actor and a well-known playwright, who wrote comedies and history plays. Between 1601 to 1607, Shakespeare wrote famous tragedies from *Othello, King Lear, Macbeth, Anthony and Cleopatra,* to *Corilanus.* Very few plots of Shakespeare's plays are original, and mostly based on the stories in history and classic works, such as novels, poems and plays, etc. Though he was chiefly celebrated in the centuries after his death as a playwright, his early poetry ranging from sonnets to lyrics deserve close attention. Shakespeare's sonnets are quite original both in form and subject. His most frequently used rhyme scheme in the sonnets is abab cdcd efef gg, known as *Shakespearean sonnet*, different from long stand Petrarchan sonnet with rhyme scheme abba abba cde cde. When it comes to the subject, Shakespeare's sonnets are mainly about the praise of love and tribute to a beautiful young man instead of a lady, and when they do speak about a lady, his choice is special too. He chose a sexually promiscuous mistress with dark complexion instead of a usual chaste and aloof blonde. Shakespeare went back to his hometown in his later years and passed away there on April 23, 1616 after a happy meal with his friend. Ben Jonson spoke of William Shakespeare in *To the Memory of My Beloved, The Author, Mr. William Shakespeare, and What He Hath Left Us*:

Triumph, my Britain; thou hast one to show
To whom all scenes of Europe homage owe.
He was not of an age, but for all time!

Appreciation:

莎士比亚的十四行诗或是献给一个黑美人，或是献给一个俊秀青年，多是情诗。这首诗中尤是如此。诗歌的前八行，叙述者怨天尤人似地抱怨哭泣自己的悲惨命运，希望自己如别人一样充满希望，或是拥有满座高朋，更或是希望自己有别人的技艺与见识。然而这首十四行诗的后六行笔锋一转，叙述者意识到自己拥有的比什么都珍贵，珍贵到即使君王拿王国换他也不屑。那是什么呢？是“你甜美的爱”。这是这首十四行诗的最后两行，即莎士比亚式十四行诗中的对句所强调的内容。前后两部分中叙述者内心状态的对比与反差更突出了其爱人的爱在他生命中的珍贵意义。

Questions:

1. What's the similarity between "summer's day" and the speaker's beloved?
2. What made the miserable speaker realize his own wealth?

I Wandered Lonely as a Cloud[1]

I wandered lonely as a Cloud
That floats on high o'er Vales and Hills,
When all at once I saw a crowd
A host of [2]dancing Daffodils;
Along the Lake, beneath the tress,

Ten thousand dancing in the breeze.

The waves beside them danced, but they
Outdid the sparkling waves in glee:—
A Poet could not but be gay
In such a laughing company:
I gazed—and gazed—but little thought
What wealth the shew to me had brought:

For oft when on my couch I lie
In vacant[3] or in pensive[4] mood,
They flash upon that inward eye
Which is the bliss of solitude,
And then my heart with pleasure fills,
And dances with the Daffodils.

NOTES

1. 这首诗在国内常以《咏水仙》为题，但华兹华斯在世时所出版的所有的诗集中，皆是用第一句《我孤独地漫游，像一朵云》为题。这首诗初次发表于华兹华斯出版于1807年的诗集《两卷本诗集》（*Poems, in Two Volumes*）的第二卷中。上文所节选的三节诗的版本与国内其他选集中所节选的四节诗有所不同，这三节诗是华兹华斯最初发表的版本。1815年出版《诗集》（*Poems*）时，华兹华斯加入了另外一个诗节，成了后人广为流传的版本。国内的诗歌选集中，几乎没有涉及华兹华斯这一最初的版本，所以此处特别选择它，以供读者与另外一个版本进行对比赏读。
2. a host of: 许多
3. vacant: 茫然若失的
4. pensive: 沉思的，深思的

About the Author:

William Wordsworth, a great English Romantic poet, was born on April 7th, 1770 in Cockermouth in the Lake District. After education in Hawkshead Grammar School and St. John College, Cambridge, he lived an unsettled life in France, London, Southern part of England before he finally settled down in the Lake District. During his unsettled years, he got to know several radical thinkers, such as William Godwin, John Thelwall and Joseph Fawcett, etc. and responded to their thoughts and causes in his play, prose and poems at that time and later in his life. During his stay in southern England, he made acquaintance of Samuel Taylor Coleridge and got soon very intimate with each other. The intimate relationship with Samuel Taylor Coleridge inspired both his genius and Coleridge's, which led to their collaborated works *Lyrical Ballads* in 1798. Anonymously published in the first edition, soon the second edition was published in 1800 with Wordsworth's own name on. The collection established his fame as a poet. In 1799, he came back to the Lake District, where he first lived in Townend, Grasmere in a two-storey cottage, now famous as Dove Cottage, for nine years, then moved to Allan Bank, a town centre house and finally settled in Rydal Mount in the village Rydal near Grasmere until the end of his life. He married his childhood friend Mary Hutchinson in 1802, and they had five children, two of whom died young. In order to support his family and have time to write poetry, he started working as a Stamp Distributor in 1813 until very late in his life. He became Poet Laureate to the young Queen Victoria in 1843, the honour which he finally accepted after having declined several times only on the condition that he did not need to compose poetry for the court. Seven years later, he died on April 23rd, 1850 when the church bell tolled 12 at noon. Wordsworth's wife Mary published his autobiographical poem which she named it *The Prelude* the same year after he died.

Appreciation:

这首诗的第一诗节中的意象以诗人的孤独无依（lonely as a cloud）与水仙花的花团锦簇（a host of, ten thousand）和安然快乐（along the lake, beneath the trees, dancing）形成鲜明对比，给读者的阅读体验带来一种张力。第二诗节中，诗人由远及近，来到水仙花近旁，对比了湖水与水仙花的欢愉，当然，还是水仙花更胜一筹。更重要的是，孤独的诗人，因为水仙花而有了陪伴，不再觉得孤独，而且“怎能不心旷神怡”（could not but be gay）（杨德豫译）。水仙花的舞动与快乐给孤独的诗人以陪伴与欢愉，然而还不仅如此，在第三节中，诗人描述了日后独处感到多思与迷茫之时，曾经让他快乐的水仙花又在他心中舞动。而这是当时的诗人所没有料到的。这首诗中诗人展示了孤独的双面性，孤独有沉郁、迷茫之时，孤独亦是一种福祉。在第一节中，诗人的孤独让他感觉如孤独无依的云；在第三节中，孤独中的他也曾感到迷茫多思。然而，也是孤独让他更加体会水仙花及其所代表的大自然传递的欢乐，是孤独，让他感觉到回忆的慰藉。为了对应这种观察与沉思的节奏，华兹华斯在此诗中选用了英国诗歌中常用的六行诗节（sesta rima, 即一个四行诗 quatrain 加对句 couplet, 韵脚 abab cc）。每个六行诗节中的前四行似乎创造了一个音景（soundscape），最后的对句似是音景的回声。

与此诗相关的有趣典故有二。第一，这首诗并非诗人“强烈情感的自然流露”的即兴之作，而是诗人在两年后的沉思中回忆，并且参考多萝茜的日志所作。华兹华斯并非如诗中所言，独自漫步，而是与妹妹一起经过湖区的第二大湖埃尔茨湖畔（Ullswater）时，被风中舞动的水仙吸引。多萝茜当天（1802 年 4 月 15 日）的日志中是这样描述水仙的：

> *在树枝下，在湖边*，我们看到一长片水仙花……我从没见过如此漂亮的水仙。它们长在生满苔藓的岩石中间。有些水仙花慵懒地倚在石头上休息，石头宛如它们的枕头。其他的来回*舞动，摇摆*（tossed, and reeled and danced），而且看上去好像它们在与风一起欢笑。它们看上去如此*欢乐*（*gay*）。风儿掠过湖水吹在它们身上。它们看上去如此*欢乐*（gay），*一直在跳舞*（ever glancing），*永远在变化*（ever changing）……

诗中有这样的诗句："蓦然举目，我望见一丛／金黄的水仙，缤纷茂密；／在湖水之滨，树荫之下，／正随风摇曳，舞姿潇洒……／湖面的涟漪也迎风起舞，／水仙的欢悦却胜似涟漪；有了这样愉快的伴侣，／诗人怎能不心旷神怡（gay）！"（杨德豫 译）这个典故有助于读者了解华兹华斯"强烈情感的自然流露"与"深思了很久"这两种截然不同的诗学理念。

第二，此诗中，第三节中的两句"they flash upon that inward eye/which is the bliss of solitude"是华兹华斯认为全诗最好的两句，但并非出自诗人之手，而是出自他的妻子玛丽·华兹华斯之手。

Questions:

1. How do you understand the role of "solitude" in inspiring the poem?
2. What is the part that Nature plays in the poet's mind according to the poem?

O Captain! My Captain!

O Captain! My Captain! Our fearful trip is done,
The ship has weather'd[1] every rack, the prize we sought is won,
The port is near, the bells I hear, the people all exulting[2],
While follow eyes the steady keel[3], the vessel grim and daring;
But O heart! heart! heart!
O the bleeding drops of red!
Where on the deck my Captain lies,

Fallen cold and dead.

O Captain! My Captain! Rise up and hear the bells;
Rise up—for you the flag is flung[4]—for you the bugle[5] trills[6],
For you bouquets and ribbon'd wreaths—for you the shores a-crowding[7],
For you they call, the swaying mass, their eager faces turning;
Here Captain! Dear father!
This arm beneath your head!
It is some dream that on the deck,
You've fallen cold and dead.

My Captain does not answer, his lips are pale and still,
My father does not feel my arm, he has no pulse nor will,
The ship is anchor'd safe and sound, its voyage closed and done,
From fearful trip the victor ship comes in with object won;
Exult, o shore, and ring, O bells!
But I, with mournful tread[8],
Walk the deck my Captain lies,
Fallen cold and dead.

NOTES

1. weather'd: 经受住
2. exulting: 狂喜，欢跃
3. keel: (船的)龙骨
4. flung: 扬起
5. bugle: 号角
6. trills: 响起
7. a-crowding: 挤满了人群
8. tread: 脚步

About the Author:

Walt Whitman was born in May, 1819 in West Hills, Long Island, New York. Whitman did not get too much education at school. He left school very early at eleven and became an office boy in a law firm. After that, he worked for a doctor briefly. He was employed in the printing industry since then, and at the same time he started writing poetry. By his mid-teens, he contributed to the famous newspaper, *The Mirror*. He left the printing industry due to two big fires in 1835 and then began to be a teacher for five years. From 1840 through the end of 1854 when he decided to concentrate on poetry writing, he worked for different papers, including the *New World*, *Aurora*,

Star, etc. and he never stopped writing and publishing works. His novel *Franklin Evans* was published during that period. In 1855, he published the *Leaves of Grass*, and the image of him on this book's frontispiece rejected the conventional suit and tie style, instead, it was a bearded Whitman with a workingman's hat on. He defied the tradition both with the unconventional image and his experimental poems in the collection. The outbreak of the Civil War drew his attention to the wounded soldiers. During the war, he once worked as a hospital attendant in the war field. At the same time, he worked on his series of war poems, and published the collection *Drum-Taps* in 1865. Lincoln's assassination drove him to reissue this collection with a sequel including "O Captain! My Captain!" and "When Lilacs Last in the Dooryard Bloom'd," which he dedicated to their assassinated president. Whitman revolutionized American poetry, and wrote in response to what Emerson advocated in "The Poet" (1842) an American Bard is supposed to express. The bold style in the *Leaves of Grass* led to his being fired by the department where he worked. He then worked as a clerk in the attorney general's office, but lost the job due to his stroke and the ill health. He was acknowledged as a great poet across Europe and America in his last twenty years. His later years were spent on poetry writing, editing and lecturing on some political figures or thinkers. He stayed in Camden, a cottage he bought, since 1884 until the end of his life. There, he was visited by several leading literary figures at that time, such as Oscar Wilde and Longfellow. In 1891, he edited his own prose and poetry collection. He died in Camden on March 26, 1892.

Appreciation:

1865 年 4 月，在南北内战中做出重要贡献的林肯总统遇刺，惠特曼深受震动，于 1865 年 11 月发表了这首挽诗。这是惠特曼最著名的诗作之一，同时，也因为诗人饱含着感情，所以也是他最伤感的一首。

这首诗中，倒下的船长便是林肯总统，他的"可怕的旅途"到达了终点。这首诗中长短句的交错对应诗人起伏激动的情绪。同时，在这首诗中，大海的意象贯穿始终。在第二诗节中，画面集中在总统的灵柩。海岸边挤满的人群、花束、带丝带的花环都将人们的悲伤表达得淋漓尽致。在诗的第三节，诗人又回归传统的诗歌语言与海的意象。第二、三诗节中提到的"父"(father) 对应民众对林肯的昵称"亚伯拉罕老爹"(Father Abraham)，情感饱满、真挚，反映了全国人民的无言悲痛。然而，诗人惠特曼后来对这首诗的公众性与直接性表达了遗憾，再兼之这首诗创作得匆忙，他甚至遗憾地说希望自己从来没有创作过这首诗作。然而，无论如何，这首诗成为惠特曼最受欢迎的作品之一。

Questions:

1. Why did the poet name Lincoln as Captain in the poem?
2. What did the ship in the poem symbolize?

There's a Certain Slant of Light

There's a certain[1] Slant[2] of light,
Winter Afternoons—
That oppresses, like the Heft[3]
Of Cathedral Tunes—

Heavenly Hurt, it gives us—
We can find no scar,
But internal difference—
Where the Meanings, are—

None my teach it—Any—
'Tis the Seal Despair—
An imperial[4] affliction
Sent us of the Air—

When it comes, the Landscape listens—
Shadows—hold their breath—
When it goes, 'tis like the Distance
On the look of Death

NOTES

1. certain: 特定的；确定的。在此处，此词可以有这两种含义。
2. Slant: 斜线；倾斜的
3. Heft: 重量
4. imperial: 庄严的

About the Author:

Emily Dickinson was born on December 10, 1830, in Amherst, Massachusetts. She spent most of her life in the spacious Dickinson family house in Amherst called the Homestead. She attended Amherst Academy from 1840 to 1846 for education, and then went to board in a female seminary which was ten miles from her hometown. However, Dickinson quit in less than a year due to her homesickness. After back home, she embarked on lifelong reading as well as poetry writing. She wrote about various subjects, including religion, science, nature, books, music, national and local events in her time. To all those readers who viewed her as a recluse who stayed at home most of her life, it's surprising to find that she wrote several poems about the Civil War and expressed her concerns in her letters. Apart from the variety of the subjects, Dickinson was very experimental in the poetry forms. For example, she used dashes and syntactical fragments which are very typical of her poetry to convey her pursuit of the truth. Various subjects and experimental forms contributed in establishing Dickinson as one of the greatest American poets. She wrote nearly eighteen hundred poems throughout her life, very few of which were published in her life-time, however. Only around a dozen of them were known to the public. Suffering from health problems in her later years, Dickinson died on May 15, 1886. Most of her poems and letters were published posthumously.

Appreciation:

狄金森主要在这首诗中描写了大自然带给人的绝望等负面影响。在第一诗节中，诗人首先以冬日午后倾斜的阳光引入，这种阳光独特而又确定。诗人将它比作教堂音乐，这种比喻突出了午后这一缕阳光的有形与无形的重量。第一诗节中的 oppresses 表明了无形的重量所指的是叙述者心中的重压。第二节、第三节与第四节中所用的词汇，如，Hurt、difference、Despair、affliction、Shadows、Distance 与 Death 都传递了同样的沉重，反映了大自然对人的负面影响，诗人在第二诗节的第一行 Heavenly 中所采用的扬抑抑格（dactyl，即一个长重音节由两个短音节相随）也对应叙述者在这种重压下的沉闷。第一诗节中所强调的冬日午后，让读者联想到与此相关的贫瘠，这种贫瘠亦是与诗人在最后一诗节所提到的 Shadow、Death 相关。这种负面力量给人的伤害不会留下有形的伤疤，只会给人带来内心的冲击，困惑人对意义的思忖。这束斜光所代表的自然的神秘无人能将其启示阐释，那是一种绝望，一种创伤。倾听的风景与毫无生息的阴影也在分享我们对这束斜光的忧虑。然而，最让人恐惧的不是它的降临，而是它的离去，这种离去在诗中暗示我们望向逝去亲人最后一眼的别离。

Questions:

1. How do you understand the slash used by the poet in the poem?
2. What does "it" refer to in the first line of the third stanza "None may teach it—Any—"?

The Lake Isle of Innisfree[1]

I will arise and go now, and go to Innisfree,
And a small cabin build there, of clay and wattles[2] made:
Nine bean-rows will I have there, a hive for the honey-bee,
And live alone in the bee-loud glade[3].

And I shall have some peace there, for peace comes dropping slow,
Drooping from the veils of the morning to where the cricket sings;
There midnight's all a glimmer[4], and noon a purple glow,
And evening full of the linnet's[5] wings.

I will arise and go now, for always night and day
I hear lake water lapping[6] with low sounds by the shore;
While I stand on the roadway, or on the pavements[7] grey,
I hear it in the deep heart's core.

NOTES

1. Innisfree: 因尼斯弗里，又名石南岛，是爱尔兰西部斯莱戈(Sligo)附近吉尔湖(Lough Gill) 上的小岛。
2. wattles: 枝条编成的篱笆
3. glade: 林中空地
4. glimmer: 微光，闪光
5. linnet: 红雀
6. lapping: 此处指湖水轻轻地拍击
7. pavements: 人行道

About the Author:

William Butler Yeats was born in 1865 in Dublin. The Yeats family stayed in London from 1874 to 1900 when they went back to Dublin. He was interested in arts and went to art school after high school, but he soon gave up the art after several attempts and started to concentrate on poetry. Dublin, London and Sligo which is his mother's hometown, witnessed Yeats' childhood and young manhood, and these three places inspired his poetic development in various ways. In Dublin, he founded the National Literary Society, there he came to see the positive and powerful influence of his poetry on the development of Irish culture. In London, he met the important poets of the day, with whose influence he founded his early language style which are dreamy and ethereal. From Sligo, he gained a knowledge of country life and of relevant folklores, which made up his poetry subjects. In 1889, Yeats met Irish nationalist Maud Gonne who was a beautiful actress, with whom he was desperately and despairingly in love for many years when Gonne persistently refused to marry him. She became the subject of his love poems, such as "When You Are Old." He was influenced greatly by American poet Ezra Pound from 1913 to 1916 when they stayed together in Sussex, England. Inspired by Pound, Yeats decided to develop a less mannered and much clearer style which is different from his early times. In the poems of the 1920s and 1930s, he wrote visionary poems, such as "The Second Coming" and "Leda and the Swan," etc. The poems in his last several years, such as "Under Ben Bulben" and "Man and the Echo," etc. were written with controlled emotions, but embodied a startling wilderness. Yeats was awarded the Nobel Prize for Literature in 1923 for "his always inspired poetry, which in a highly artistic form gives expression to the spirit of a whole nation." Yeats died in 1939 and left a huge body of poems, which constituted an enduring influence on poets of more than English-language around the world.

Appreciation:

这首诗创作于1890年，叶芝曾经在自传中提到他自己自从在斯莱戈的十几岁时便梦想着在因尼斯弗里岛上模仿梭罗在瓦尔登湖的隐居经历。叶芝回忆自己走在伦敦舰队街（Fleet Street）上非常想家的时候，突然听到了水流的声音，于是想起了因尼斯弗里岛，他的回忆便成就了这首著名的抒情诗。

在这首诗中叙述者“我”在诗的开始便下定决心“现在”要起身去因尼斯弗里这个湖心岛，他想象了自己在那里用篱笆和泥巴建座小屋。而且他还要种豆子、养蜜蜂，要在蜂鸣中独自住在那里。叙述者就这样在第一诗节中搭建了自己的房子，安置好植物（豆子）与动物（蜜蜂）所代表的大自然的陪伴。在第二诗节中，叙述者继续畅想自己安居在那里之后的生活状态，白天充满安静祥和，夜晚充满了光。第二诗节中呈现的是一个没有尘世喧嚣打扰的安静自然的世界。在第三诗节中，叙述者从想象中回到现实，继续下定决心要前往湖心岛，去日日夜夜倾听那里湖水拍打岸边的声音。这种决心似是现实中灰色的水泥路也无法阻挡。

叙述者直抒胸臆的叙述充满激情又非常自然，诗的韵律也对应着这种节奏。第二诗节中，诗人从这首诗中多用的抑扬格（iambic, 一个两个音节的音步，第一个是非重读音节，第二个是重读音节）会忽然转换成抑抑扬格（anapaest，一个音步，由两个非重读音加一个重读音组成）以对应叙述者的情绪，比如，from the **veils** of the **morning**，诗歌的节奏感与音乐性在这种转变中得到凸显。另一点需要注意的是，虽然诗人在这首诗中描述了一个超越现实非常理想的世界，但他却使用了极其日常普通的词汇，比如，cabin、lake water 等。这种对比一方面让读者联想到最擅长此书写方式的华兹华斯，另一方面也给读者一种扑面而来的清新感。这或许也是此诗成为叶芝最受欢迎的诗歌之一的缘由。

Questions:

1. Could you think of any other poems with similar theme of Nature and City?
2. Did the speaker finally manage to go to the Innisfree? How could you tell?

The Road Not Taken

Two roads diverged[1] in a yellow wood,
And sorry I could not travel both
And be one traveler, long I stood
And looked down one as far as I could
To where it bent in the undergrowth[2];

Then took the other, as just as fair,
And having perhaps the better claim[3],
Because it was grassy and wanted[4] wear[5];
Though as for that, the passing there
Had worn them really about the same,

And both that morning equally lay

In leaves no step had trodden[6] black.
Oh, I kept the first for another day!
Yet knowing how way leads on to way,
I doubted if I should ever come back.

I shall be telling this with a sigh
Somewhere ages and ages hence:
Two roads diverged in a wood, and I—
I took the one less traveled by,
And that has made all the difference.

NOTES

1. diverged: 分歧，分岔
2. undergrowth: 矮树丛，灌木丛
3. claim: 断言，主张
4. wanted: 缺少
5. wear: 磨损，与 wanted 连用表示“人迹罕至”的意思
6. trodden: 踩，踏

About the Author:

Robert Frost was born in 1874 in California, U.S. and stayed there until eleven. His family moved to New England, which he identified as his hometown. He went to Dartmouth College but dropped out soon. He then went to Harvard from 1897 to 1899, but left there because of ill health. In 1912, he moved to England with his family, and published his first poetry collection *A Boy's Will* (1913) which won Ezra Pound's favorable review, and thus with the help of Pound, his second poetry collection *North of Boston* (1914) was published, which won him a great success. The success affected his determination to be back to America. Then with his family, he returned to his motherland as a successful poet. In the following decades, Frost turned out to be one of the most celebrated poets in America. He was awarded Pulitzer Prizes four times in his life and was nominated for the Nobel Prize for Literature more than thirty times. Frost was invited to read his poem "The Gift Outright" at John F. Kennedy's presidential inauguration in 1961. In the last twenty years of his life, he spent more time as a lecturer at Amherst, at Dartmouth, at Harvard, etc. and more activities were involved, such as reading his poetry and giving talks about poetry, including his own poetry. He died in 1963, and one quote from his poetry became his epitaph: "I had a lover's quarrel with the World."

Appreciation:

这首诗是罗伯特·弗罗斯特在英国得到盛名决定回到美国前的心态的一种反映。弗罗斯特在美国开始写诗时并没有得到多少认可，所以他决定与全家人移居英国，不料，在英国一举成名。而这时的他，反而决定回到自己的祖国美国。这是一个大胆的决定，但也反映出作者内心的犹豫。就如诗歌中所言，他对自己的选择的理由解释是那条路很少有人走，但他内心也知道，虽然希望自己哪天能再走一遍那条他没有选择的路，在选择的当下，已经什么都不一样了。然而事实证明，弗罗斯特的选择非常成功，他回到美国后，虽然人生经历了种种折磨与苦难，但在诗歌方面光芒大绽，成为美国最伟大的诗人之一。这首诗也成为弗罗斯特最著名、被引用最多的作品。

第一诗节中，叙述者站在树林前，面对两条路，遗憾自己一人不能走两路，但他久久伫立，极目远望其中一条路，直到其消失在灌木丛林（undergrowth）中，在第一诗节最后一个词中，诗人采用了扬抑抑格（dactyl），以给读者一种庄严的体验。扬抑抑格的采用多为产生一种庄严的效果，又或是要预示什么不好的事情发生。在这首诗中，它的效果表现为，叙述者并没有选择他极目远望至灌木丛的这条路，而是选择了另外一条。叙述者为自己的选择所做的解释稍显牵强，因为他首先解释选择的理由是这条路走的人少，但他随即又承认，他极目远望的那条路也差不多情况。那么，在这种情况下，第三诗节中的遗憾才自然而然。因为叙述者非常清楚，每一个选择以及这种选择带来的变化都是不可逆转的，所以他其实怀疑自己是否真能在某一天回来再走那条没有选择的路。于是，第四诗节也就是最后一个诗节中，叙述者的叹息是这种遗憾的自然反映，他想象自己在将来的某一天叹息自己在过去面对两条路时的选择以及这种选择所带来的无法重来的改变。这种改变是好是坏？到底有多大？叙述者把这些全部留给了读者来思索。诗中的路与叙述者能给读者无限的想象，可能是面对留在英国还是回美国的诗人，可能是面对人生抉择的我们自己，也可能是在十字路口的俄狄浦斯，或是进入地狱前经过昏暗的树林的但丁。他们所具有的这种现实、神话与宗教等的维度也是这首诗的生命力所在。

Questions:

1. Do you think whether the speaker was convinced of his own reason to choose the road less trodden?

2. Have you ever had a similar dilemma of choice?

Digging

Between my finger and my thumb
The squat[1] pen rests; snug[2] as a gun.

Under my window, a clean rasping[3] sound
When the spade[4] sinks into gravelly[5] ground:
My father, digging. I look down

Till his straining[6] rump[7] among the flowerbeds
Bends low, comes up twenty years away
Stooping[8] in rhythm through potato drills[9]
Where he was digging.

The coarse boot nestled[10] on the lug[11], the shaft[12]
Against the inside knee was levered[13] firmly.
He rooted out tall tops, buried the bright edge deep
To scatter new potatoes that we picked
Loving their cool hardness in our hands.

By God, the old man could handle a spade.
Just like his old man.

My grandfather cut more turf[14] in a day
Than any other man on Toner's bog[15].
Once I carried him milk in a bottle
Corked[16] sloppily with paper. He straightened up
To drink it, then fell to right away
Nicking[17] and slicing[18] neatly, heaving[19] sods
Over his shoulder, going down and down
For the good turf. Digging.

The cold smell of potato mould[20], the squelch[21] and slap[22]

Of soggy[23] peat[24], the curt [25]cuts of an edge
Through living roots awaken in my head.
But I've no spade to follow men like them.

Between my finger and my thumb
The squat pen rests.
I'll dig with it.

NOTES

1. squat: 矮胖的，粗矮的，此处指粗短的、粗壮的
2. snug: 舒适，自在
3. rasping: 刺耳的摩擦声
4. spade: 铁铲，铁锹
5. gravelly: 铺有碎石的，由碎石构成的
6. straining: 用尽全力的
7. rump: 臀部
8. stooping: 弯腰，弯曲
9. drills: 播种种子的犁沟
10. nestled: 紧贴着
11. lug: 手柄
12. shaft: 柄，轴
13. levered: 撬动
14. turf: 厚泥炭
15. bog: 沼泽地
16. corked: 用软木塞塞住，此处指用纸塞住
17. nicking: 割断
18. slicing: 切下
19. heaving: 举起，扔去
20. mould: 霉菌
21. squelch: 吧唧声
22. slap: 拍击声
23. soggy: 潮湿的
24. peat: 泥炭
25. curt: 草率的，简短的

About the Author:

Seamus Heaney was born in 1939 in County Derry, Northern Ireland. He was born the year when a great Irish poet W.B. Yeats died. He was educated at St. Columb's College first, and then to Queen's university in Belfast. He held a professorship at Harvard University for many years, and was once Oxford Professor of Poetry too. He published several poems collections, such as *Death of a Naturalist* (1966), *Selected Poems 1965–1975*(1980), *Government of the Tongue* (1988), *Opened Ground: Poems 1966–1996* (1998), etc. Apart from poetry, he wrote drama and critical essays. Memory is an important theme both in his poems and other forms of works, among which, the poem "Digging" is the most representative one. He was awarded the Nobel Prize for Literature in 1995 "for works of lyrical beauty and ethical depth, which exalt everyday miracles and the living past," and he donated the prize money to the Wordsworth Trust for the founding of Jerwood Centre in Grasmere to pay respect to the great romantic poet William Wordsworth, whom he admired and was influenced by. He had been suffering from a stroke for several years in his later life and died in 2013.

Appreciation:

希尼望向窗外，感觉到了他与父辈的距离。他没有祖父、父亲都有的铁锹去深挖土豆地，为他们的生计劳作。虽然他没有铁锹来传承父辈的传统，但他有一支笔，一支"粗壮"的笔，他可以借此来挖掘并推广爱尔兰的文化传统。希尼的笔如他手中的枪，有其破坏性的一面，表现在他与自己观望反思的传统的割裂；这支笔也有其创造性的一面，那是希尼所示范的，要重新换一种方式给这片"沼泽地"带来生机，从而避免爱尔兰文化的石化。希尼的笔触不仅这么有力，凸显他作为一个诗人与爱尔兰公民的责任与抱负，而且充满温情，他对祖父、父亲挖土豆的辛劳画面的摹写让人感动潸然。

Questions:

1. How did the speaker's digging differ from his father's and ancestor's digging?
2. What is the most important message that the poet wanted to convey through the poem?

Eating Alone

I've pulled the last of the year's young onions.
The garden is bare now. The ground is cold,
brown and old. What is left of the day flames[1]
in the maples[2] at the corner of my
eye. I turn, a cardinal[3] vanishes.
By the cellar[4] door, I wash the onions,
then drink from the icy metal spigot[5].

Once, years back, I walked beside my father

among the windfall pears. I can't recall
our words. We may have strolled in silence. But
I still see him bend that way—left hand braced[6]
on knee, creaky[7]—to lift and hold to my
eye a rotten pear. In it, a hornet[8]
spun crazily, glazed[9] in slow, glistening juice.

It was my father I saw this morning
waving to me from the trees. I almost
called to him, until I came close enough
to see the shovel[10], leaning where I had
left it, in the flickering[11], deep green shade.

White rice steaming, almost done. Sweet green peas
fried in onions. Shrimp braised[12] in sesame
oil and garlic. And my own loneliness,
What more could I, a young man, want.

NOTES

1. flames: 发光，燃烧
2. maples: 枫树
3. cardinal: 大红色，深红色
4. cellar: 地下室
5. spigot: 室外水龙头
6. braced: 支撑，撑着
7. creaky: 嘎吱作响
8. hornet: 大黄蜂，马蜂
9. glazed: 变得光滑
10. shovel: 铲子，铁锹
11. flickering: 闪烁的，摇曳的，忽隐忽现的
12. braised: 炖熟

About the Author:

LI-YOUNG LEE was born in 1957 in Jakarta, Indonesia. He moved to America with his family in 1959. His father was a Presbyterian minister in a small town in western Pennsylvania. Lee studied at the University of Arizona, and the State University of New York College at Brockport. He attended the University of Pittsburgh too, where he developed his love for writing. His love of writing developed with his father's passionate reading to him. His poems have been influenced by classic Chinese poets, such as Li Bai, Du Fu, etc. as well as American poets, such as Walt Whitman and James Wright, etc. Most of his poems expressed his longing to remember and understand his father's life and come to terms with his own different life. The poem collections, such as *City in Which I Love You* (1990), *Book of My Nights* (2001), and *Behind My Eyes* (2008), illustrate his sense of the past, where his father played a very important part. Memory, and smell, sound, touch in memory permeated through his poems. He has won many awards, among which the most representative ones are the American Book Award in 1995 and William Carlos Williams Award in 2002.

Appreciation:

这首诗是诗人对已故父亲的追忆。诗人在第一诗节看到的萧瑟、感受到的寒冷与他看到那一抹亮红的消逝，反映出他失去父亲后内心的寒凉与孤独。然而，在第二诗节中，诗人追忆与父亲沉默同行于果林中的画面却明亮温暖。父亲弯腰的动作、父亲将熟透而被风吹落的梨子及困在其中的马蜂举在他面前的画面，反映着回忆中儿子与父亲同在的温馨。然而同时，“被风吹落的梨子”也预示了死亡与终结。盘旋在其中的马蜂在梨子内部所展示的生与死的对比，也暗示了回忆中的儿子与已故父亲生死两隔的悲伤事实。在第三诗节中，诗人以超现实的笔触表达了儿子对父亲的深深思念。他将树荫下的铁铲看成了父亲。诗人的这种恍惚与误认传递出一种悲伤。然而，这也同时说明，父亲与儿子曾经父子情深，曾经共度很多时光。花园、闪烁不定的树荫都曾见证。因此，该诗的最后一节，诗人回到现实中，厨房中快要做好的饭，在某种程度上代表了诗人对父亲离去这一事实的接受。虽然孤独，但他拥有夏天一样温暖的回忆。所以最后一句诗，诗人虽然是在提一个问题，但并没加问号。是的，作为一个年轻人，虽然失去了父亲，虽然感到非常孤单，但他拥有满满的与父亲在一起的或是与父亲有关的回忆。他还需要什么呢？他什么都不需要，故诗人用句号完成了这个问题。

Questions:

1. Why do you think that the poet did not capitalize the first letter of the first word in each line?
2. What changed the speaker's melancholy and sad mood in the poem?

Part 4
Prose

Definition of Prose

Prose is a form of language which applies ordinary grammatical structure and natural flow of speech rather than rhythmic structure (as in traditional poetry). The common unit of prose is purely grammatical, such as a sentence or a paragraph. While there are critical debates on the construction of prose, its simplicity and loosely defined structure has led to its adoption for the majority of spoken dialogue, factual discourse as well as topical and fictional writing.

The Origins of Prose

The word "prose" didn't appear in English until the 14th century. It is derived from the Old French *prose*. Isaac Newton in *The Chronology of Ancient Kingdoms* wrote "The Greek Antiquities are full of Poetical Fictions, because the Greeks wrote nothing in Prose. Then, Pherecydes, Scyrius and Cadmus Milesius introduced the writing in Prose." In the west, prose first formally appeared in *Proverbs* and *Ecclesiastes* in the Bible. Literally, prose is the record of one's reflection and contemplation on wit, fortune, marriage and personal relationship, etc. It's the product of the speculative thinking through the ages.

Structure of Prose

Prose lacks the more formal metrical structure of verse that can be found in traditional poetry. Prose comprises full grammatical sentences, which then constitute paragraphs while overlooking aesthetic appeal. Some works of prose contain traces of metrical structure or versification and a conscious blend of the two literature formats known as prose poetry. Different from verse which is considered to be more systematic or formulaic, prose is the most reflective of ordinary (often conversational) speech. In this sense, as Samuel Taylor Coleridge put it, "the definition of prose is that prose is the words in their best order."

Types of Prose

Many types of prose exist, which include nonfictional prose, heroic prose, prose poem, polyphonic prose, alliterative prose, prose fiction, and village prose in Russian literature.

How to Effectively Read a Prose

a. Pay attention to the background information of each prose;
b. Try to appreciate the writing style of the prose;
c. Pay attention to the fascinating words and expressions applied in the prose;
d. Pay attention to the structure and organization of the prose;
e. Pay attention to the messages and emotions delivered by the writers;
f. Pay attention to the philosophical ideas expressed by the writers;
g. Use associations with the writers' vivid descriptions;
h. Learn to read between the lines and infer from the writing.

The Republic: Book X (Excerpt)

OF THE many excellences which I perceive in the order of our State, there is none which upon reflection pleases me better than the rule about poetry.

To what do you refer?

To the rejection of imitative poetry, which certainly ought not to be received; as I see far more clearly now that the parts of the soul have been distinguished.

What do you mean?

Speaking in confidence, for I should not like to have my words repeated to the tragedians and the rest of the imitative tribe—but I do not mind saying to you, that all poetical imitations are ruinous to the understanding of the hearers, and that the knowledge of their true nature is the only antidote to them.

Explain the purport of your remark.

Well, I will tell you, although I have always from my earliest youth had an awe and love of Homer, which even now makes the words falter on my lips, for he is the great captain and teacher of the whole of that charming tragic company; but a man is not to be reverenced more than the truth, and therefore I will speak out.

Very good, he said.

Listen to me then, or rather, answer me.

Put your question.

Can you tell me what imitation is? for I really do not know.

A likely thing, then, that I should know.

Why not? for the duller eye may often see a thing sooner than the keener.

Very true, he said; but in your presence, even if I had any faint notion, I could not muster courage to utter it. Will you enquire yourself?

Well then, shall we begin the enquiry in our usual manner: Whenever a number of individuals have a common name, we assume them to have also a corresponding idea or form. Do you understand me?

I do.

Let us take any common instance; there are beds and tables in the world—plenty of them, are there not?

Yes.

But there are only two ideas or forms of them—one the idea of a bed, the other of a table.

True.

And the maker of either of them makes a bed or he makes a table for our use, in accordance with the idea—that is our way of speaking in this and similar instances—but no artificer makes the ideas themselves: how could he?

Impossible.

And there is another artist,—I should like to know what you would say of him.

Who is he?

One who is the maker of all the works of all other workmen.

What an extraordinary man!

Wait a little, and there will be more reason for your saying so. For this is he who is able to make not only vessels of every kind, but plants and animals, himself and all other things—the earth and heaven, and the things which are in heaven or under the earth; he makes the gods also.

He must be a wizard and no mistake.

Oh! you are incredulous, are you? Do you mean that there is no such maker or creator, or that in one sense there might be a maker of all these things but in another not? Do you see that there is a way in which you could make them all yourself?

What way?

An easy way enough; or rather, there are many ways in which the feat might be quickly and easily accomplished, none quicker than that of turning a mirror round and round—you would soon enough make the sun and the heavens, and the earth and yourself, and other animals and plants, and all the, other things of which we were just now speaking, in the mirror.

Yes, he said; but they would be appearances only.

Very good, I said, you are coming to the point now. And the painter too is, as I conceive, just such another—a creator of appearances, is he not?

Of course.

But then I suppose you will say that what he creates is untrue. And yet there is a sense in which the painter also creates a bed?

Yes, he said, but not a real bed.

And what of the maker of the bed? Were you not saying that he too makes, not the idea which, according to our view, is the essence of the bed, but only a particular bed?

Yes, I did.

Then if he does not make that which exists he cannot make true existence, but only some semblance of existence; and if any one were to say that the work of the maker of the bed, or of any other workman, has real existence, he could hardly be supposed to be speaking the truth.

At any rate, he replied, philosophers would say that he was not speaking the truth.

No wonder, then, that his work too is an indistinct expression of truth.

No wonder.

Suppose now that by the light of the examples just offered we enquire who this imitator is?

If you please.

Well then, here are three beds: one existing in nature[1], which is made by God, as I think that we may say—for no one else can be the maker?

No.

There is another which is the work of the carpenter?

Yes.

And the work of the painter is a third?

Yes.

Beds, then, are of three kinds, and there are three artists who superintend them: God, the maker of the bed, and the painter?

Yes, there are three of them.

God, whether from choice or from necessity, made one bed in nature and one only; two or more such ideal beds neither ever have been nor ever will be made by God.

Why is that?

Because even if He had made but two, a third would still appear behind them which both of them would have for their idea, and that would be the ideal bed and the two others.

Very true, he said.

God knew this, and He desired to be the real maker of a real bed, not a particular maker of a particular bed, and therefore He created a bed which is essentially and by nature one only.

So we believe.

Shall we, then, speak of Him as the natural author or maker of the bed?

Yes, he replied; inasmuch as by the natural process of creation He is the author of this and of all other things.

And what shall we say of the carpenter—is not he also the maker of the bed?

Yes.

But would you call the painter a creator and maker?

Certainly not.

Yet if he is not the maker, what is he in relation to the bed?

I think, he said, that we may fairly designate him as the imitator of that which the others make.

Good, I said; then you call him who is third in the descent from nature an imitator?

Certainly, he said.

And the tragic poet is an imitator, and therefore, like all other imitators, he is thrice removed from the king [2] and from the truth?

That appears to be so.

Then about the imitator we are agreed. And what about the painter?—I would like to know whether he may be thought to imitate that which originally exists in nature, or only the creations of artists?

The latter.

As they are or as they appear? You have still to determine this.

What do you mean?

I mean, that you may look at a bed from different points of view, obliquely or directly or from any other point of view, and the bed will appear different, but there is no difference in reality. And the same of all things.

Yes, he said, the difference is only apparent.

Now let me ask you another question: Which is the art of painting designed to be—an imitation of things as they are, or as they appear—of appearance or of reality?

Of appearance.

Then the imitator, I said, is a long way off the truth, and can do all things because he lightly touches on a small part of them, and that part an image. For example: A painter will paint a cobbler, carpenter, or any other artist, though he knows nothing of their arts; and, if he is a good artist, he may deceive children or simple persons, when he shows them his picture of a carpenter from a distance, and they will fancy that they are looking at a real carpenter.

Certainly.

And whenever any one informs us that he has found a man knows all the arts, and all things else that anybody knows, and every single thing with a higher degree of accuracy than any other man—whoever tells us this, I think that we can only imagine to be a simple creature who is likely to have been deceived by some wizard or actor whom he met, and whom he thought all-knowing, because he himself was unable to analyze the nature of knowledge and ignorance and imitation.

Most true.

And so, when we hear persons saying that the tragedians, and Homer, who is at their head, know all the arts and all things human, virtue as well as vice, and divine things too, for that the good poet cannot compose well unless he knows his subject, and that he who has not this knowledge can never be a poet, we ought to consider whether here also there may not be a similar illusion. Perhaps they may have come across imitators and been deceived by them; they may not have remembered when they saw their works that these were but imitations thrice removed from the truth, and could easily be made without any knowledge of the truth, because they are appearances only and not realities? Or, after all, they may be in the right, and poets do really know the things about which they seem to the many to speak so well?

The question, he said, should by all means be considered.

Now do you suppose that if a person were able to make the original as well as the image, he would seriously devote himself to the image-making branch? Would he allow imitation to be the ruling principle of his life, as if he had nothing higher in him?

I should say not.

The real artist, who knew what he was imitating, would be interested in realities and not in imitations; and would desire to leave as memorials of himself works many and fair; and, instead of being the author of encomiums, he would prefer to be the theme of them.

Yes, he said, that would be to him a source of much greater honour and profit.

Then, I said, we must put a question to Homer; not about medicine, or any of the arts to which his poems only incidentally refer: we are not going to ask him, or any other poet, whether he has cured patients like Asclepius, or left behind him a school of medicine such as the Asclepiads were, or whether he only talks about medicine and other arts at second hand; but we have a right to know respecting military tactics, politics, education, which are the chiefest and noblest subjects of his poems, and we may fairly ask him about them. "Friend Homer," then we say to him, "if you are only in the second remove from truth in what you say of virtue, and not in the third—not an image maker or imitator—and if you are able to discern what pursuits make men better or worse in private or public life, tell us what State was ever better governed by your help? The good order of Lacedaemon is due to Lycurgus, and many other cities great and small have been similarly benefited by others; but who says that you have been a good legislator to them and have done them any good? Italy and Sicily boast of Charondas, and there is Solon who is renowned among us; but what city has anything to say about you?" Is there any city which he might name?

I think not, said Glaucon; not even the Homerids themselves pretend that he was a legislator.

Well, but is there any war on record which was carried on successfully by him, or aided by his counsels, when he was alive?

There is not.

Or is there any invention of his, applicable to the arts or to human life, such as Thales the Milesian or Anacharsis the Scythian[3], and other ingenious men have conceived, which is attributed to him?

There is absolutely nothing of the kind.

But, if Homer never did any public service, was he privately a guide or teacher of any? Had he in his lifetime friends who loved to associate with him, and who handed down to posterity an Homeric way of life, such as was established by Pythagoras who was so greatly beloved for his wisdom, and whose followers are to this day quite celebrated for the order which was named after him?

Nothing of the kind is recorded of him. For surely, Socrates, Creophylus, the companion of Homer, that child of flesh, whose name always makes us laugh, might be more justly ridiculed for his stupidity, if, as is said, Homer was greatly neglected by him and others in his own day when he was alive?

Yes, I replied, that is the tradition. But can you imagine, Glaucon, that if Homer had really been able to educate and improve mankind—if he had possessed knowledge and not been a mere imitator—can you imagine, I say, that he would not have had many followers, and been honoured and loved by them? Protagoras of Abdera, and Prodicus of Ceos, and a host of others, have only to whisper to their contemporaries: "You will never be able to manage either your own house or your own State until you appoint us to be your ministers of education"—and this ingenious device of theirs has such an effect in making them love them that their companions all but carry them about on their shoulders. And is it conceivable that the contemporaries of Homer, or again of Hesiod, would have allowed either of them to go about as rhapsodists, if they had really been able to make mankind virtuous? Would they not have been as unwilling to part with them as with gold, and have compelled them to stay at home with them? Or, if the master would not stay, then the disciples would have followed him about everywhere, until they had got education enough?

Yes, Socrates, that, I think, is quite true.

Then must we not infer that all these poetical individuals, beginning with Homer, are only imitators; they copy images of virtue and the like, but the truth they never reach? The poet is like a painter who, as we have already observed, will make a likeness of a cobbler though he understands nothing of cobbling; and his picture is good enough for those who know no more than he does, and judge only by colours and figures.

Quite so.

In like manner the poet with his words and phrases may be said to lay on the colours of the several arts, himself understanding their nature only enough to imitate them; and other people, who are as ignorant as he is, and judge only from his words, imagine that if he speaks of cobbling, or of military tactics, or of anything else, in metre and harmony and rhythm, he speaks very well—such is the sweet influence which melody and rhythm by nature have. And I think that you must have observed again and again what a poor appearance the tales of poets make when stripped of the colours which music puts upon them, and recited in simple prose.

Yes, he said.

They are like faces which were never really beautiful, but only blooming; and now the bloom of youth has passed away from them?

Exactly.

Here is another point: The imitator or maker of the image knows nothing of true existence; he knows appearances only. Am I not right?

Yes.

Then let us have a clear understanding, and not be satisfied with half an explanation.

Proceed.

Of the painter we say that he will paint reins, and he will paint a bit?

Yes.

And the worker in leather and brass will make them?

Certainly.

But does the painter know the right form of the bit and reins? Nay, hardly even the workers in brass and leather who make them; only the horseman who knows how to use them—he knows their right form.

Most true.

And may we not say the same of all things?

What?

That there are three arts which are concerned with all things: one which uses, another which makes, a third which imitates them?

Yes.

And the excellence or beauty or truth of every structure, animate or inanimate, and of every action of man, is relative to the use for which nature or the artist has intended them.

True.

Then the user of them must have the greatest experience of them, and he must indicate to the maker the good or bad qualities which develop themselves in use; for example, the flute-player will tell the flute-maker which of his flutes is satisfactory to the performer; he will tell him how he ought to make them, and the other will attend to his instructions?

Of course.

The one knows and therefore speaks with authority about the goodness and badness of flutes, while the other, confiding in him, will do what he is told by him?

True.

The instrument is the same, but about the excellence or badness of it the maker will only attain to a correct belief; and this he will gain from him who knows, by talking to him and being compelled to hear what he has to say, whereas the user will have knowledge?

True.

But will the imitator have either? Will he know from use whether or not his drawing is correct or beautiful? Or will he have right opinion from being compelled to associate with another who knows and gives him instructions about what he should draw?

Neither.

Then he will no more have true opinion than he will have knowledge about the goodness or badness of his imitations?

I suppose not.

The imitative artist will be in a brilliant state of intelligence about his own creations?

Nay, very much the reverse.

And still he will go on imitating without knowing what makes a thing good or bad, and may be expected therefore to imitate only that which appears to be good to the ignorant multitude?

Just so.

Thus far then we are pretty well agreed that the imitator has no knowledge worth mentioning of what he imitates. Imitation is only a kind of play or sport, and the tragic poets, whether they write in iambic or in Heroic verse, are imitators in the highest degree?

Very true.

And now tell me, I conjure you, has not imitation been shown by us to be concerned with that which is thrice removed from the truth?

Certainly.

And what is the faculty in man to which imitation is addressed?

What do you mean?

I will explain: The body which is large when seen near, appears small when seen at a distance?

True.

And the same object appears straight when looked at out of the water, and crooked when in the water; and the concave becomes convex, owing to the illusion about colours to which the sight is liable. Thus every sort of confusion is revealed within us; and this is that weakness of the human mind on which the art of conjuring and of deceiving by light and shadow and other ingenious devices imposes, having an effect upon us like magic.

True.

And the arts of measuring and numbering and weighing come to the rescue of the human understanding—there is the beauty of them—and the apparent greater or less, or more or heavier, no longer have the mastery over us, but give way before calculation and measure and weight?

Most true.

And this, surely, must be the work of the calculating and rational principle in the soul.

To be sure.

And when this principle measures and certifies that some things are equal, or that some are greater or less than others, there occurs an apparent contradiction?

True.

But were we not saying that such a contradiction is the same faculty cannot have contrary opinions at the same time about the same thing?

Very true.

Then that part of the soul which has an opinion contrary to measure is not the same with that which has an opinion in accordance with measure?

True.

And the better part of the soul is likely to be that which trusts to measure and calculation?

Certainly.

And that which is opposed to them is one of the inferior principles of the soul?

No doubt.

This was the conclusion at which I was seeking to arrive when I said that painting or drawing, and imitation in general, when doing their own proper work, are far removed from truth, and the companions and friends and associates of a principle within us which is equally removed from reason, and that they have no true or healthy aim.

Exactly.

The imitative art is an inferior who marries an inferior, and has inferior offspring.

Very true.

And is this confined to the sight only, or does it extend to the hearing also, relating in fact to what we term poetry?[4]

Probably the same would be true of poetry.

Do not rely, I said, on a probability derived from the analogy of painting; but let us examine further and see whether the faculty with which poetical imitation is concerned is good or bad.

By all means.

We may state the question thus:—Imitation imitates the actions of men, whether voluntary or involuntary, on which, as they imagine, a good or bad result has ensued, and they rejoice or sorrow accordingly. Is there anything more?

No, there is nothing else.

But in all this variety of circumstances is the man at unity with himself—or rather, as in the instance of sight there was confusion and opposition in his opinions about the same things, so here also is there not strife and inconsistency in his life? Though I need hardly raise the question again, for I remember that all this has been already admitted; and the soul has been acknowledged by us to be full of these and ten thousand similar oppositions occurring at the same moment?

And we were right, he said.

Yes, I said, thus far we were right; but there was an omission which must now be supplied.

What was the omission?

Were we not saying that a good man, who has the misfortune to lose his son or anything else which is most dear to him, will bear the loss with more equanimity than another?

Yes.

But will he have no sorrow, or shall we say that although he cannot help sorrowing, he will moderate his sorrow?

The latter, he said, is the truer statement.

Tell me: will he be more likely to struggle and hold out against his sorrow when he is seen by his equals, or when he is alone?

It will make a great difference whether he is seen or not.

When he is by himself he will not mind saying or doing many things which he would be ashamed of any one hearing or seeing him do?

True.

There is a principle of law and reason in him which bids him resist, as well as a feeling of his misfortune which is forcing him to indulge his sorrow?

True.

But when a man is drawn in two opposite directions, to and from the same object, this, as we affirm, necessarily implies two distinct principles in him?

Certainly.

One of them is ready to follow the guidance of the law?

How do you mean?

The law would say that to be patient under suffering is best, and that we should not give way to impatience, as there is no knowing whether such things are good or evil; and nothing is gained by impatience; also, because no human thing is of serious importance, and grief stands in the way of that which at the moment is most required.

What is most required? he asked.

That we should take counsel about what has happened, and when the dice have been thrown order our affairs in the way which reason deems best; not, like children who have had a fall, keeping hold of the part struck and wasting time in setting up a howl, but always accustoming the soul forthwith to apply a remedy, raising up that which is sickly and fallen, banishing the cry of sorrow by the healing art.

Yes, he said, that is the true way of meeting the attacks of fortune.

Yes, I said; and the higher principle is ready to follow this suggestion of reason?

Clearly.

And the other principle, which inclines us to recollection of our troubles and to lamentation, and can never have enough of them, we may call irrational, useless, and cowardly?

Indeed, we may.

And does not the latter—I mean the rebellious principle—furnish a great variety of materials for imitation? Whereas the wise and calm temperament, being always nearly equable, is not easy to imitate or to appreciate when imitated, especially at a public festival when a promiscuous crowd is assembled in a theatre. For the feeling represented is one to which they are strangers.

Certainly.

Then the imitative poet who aims at being popular is not by nature made, nor is his art intended, to please or to affect the principle in the soul; but he will prefer the passionate and fitful temper, which is easily imitated?

Clearly.

And now we may fairly take him and place him by the side of the painter, for he is like him in two ways: first, inasmuch as his creations have an inferior degree of truth—in this, I say, he is like him; and he is also like him in being concerned with an inferior part of the soul; and therefore we shall be right in refusing to admit him into a well-ordered State, because he awakens and nourishes and strengthens the feelings and impairs the reason. As in a city when the evil are permitted to have authority and the good are put out of the way, so in the soul of man, as we maintain, the imitative poet implants an evil constitution, for he indulges the irrational nature which has no discernment of greater and less, but thinks the same thing at one time great and at another small—he is a manufacturer of images and is very far removed from the truth.

Exactly.

But we have not yet brought forward the heaviest count in our accusation:—the power which poetry has of harming even the good (and there are very few who are not harmed), is surely an awful thing?

Yes, certainly, if the effect is what you say.

Hear and judge: The best of us, as I conceive, when we listen to a passage of Homer, or one of the tragedians, in which he represents some pitiful hero who is drawling out his sorrows in a long oration, or weeping, and smiting his breast—the best of us, you know, delight in giving way to sympathy, and are in raptures at the excellence of the poet who stirs our feelings most.

Yes, of course I know.

But when any sorrow of our own happens to us, then you may observe that we pride ourselves on the opposite quality—we would fain be quiet and patient; this is the manly part, and the other which delighted us in the recitation is now deemed to be the part of a woman.

Very true, he said.

Now can we be right in praising and admiring another who is doing that which any one of us would abominate and be ashamed of in his own person?

No, he said, that is certainly not reasonable.

Nay, I said, quite reasonable from one point of view.

What point of view?

If you consider, I said, that when in misfortune we feel a natural hunger and desire to relieve our sorrow by weeping and lamentation, and that this feeling which is kept under control in our own calamities is satisfied and delighted by the poets;—the better nature in each of us, not having been sufficiently trained by reason or habit, allows the sympathetic element to break loose because the sorrow is another's; and the spectator fancies that there can be no disgrace to himself in praising and pitying any one who comes telling him what a good man he is, and making a fuss about his troubles; he thinks that the pleasure is a gain, and why should he be supercilious and lose this and the poem too? Few persons ever reflect, as I should imagine, that from the evil of other men something of evil is communicated to themselves. And so the feeling of sorrow which has gathered strength at the sight of the misfortunes of others is with difficulty repressed in our own.

How very true!

And does not the same hold also of the ridiculous? There are jests which you would be ashamed to make yourself, and yet on the comic stage, or indeed in private, when you hear them, you are greatly amused by them, and are not at all disgusted at their unseemliness;—the case of pity is repeated;—there is a principle in human nature which is disposed to raise a laugh, and this which you once restrained by reason, because you were afraid of being thought a buffoon, is now let out again; and having stimulated the risible faculty at the theatre, you are betrayed unconsciously to yourself into playing the comic poet at home.

Quite true, he said.

And the same may be said of lust and anger and all the other affections, of desire and pain and pleasure, which are held to be inseparable from every action—in all of them poetry feeds and waters the passions instead of drying them up; she lets them rule, although they ought to be controlled, if mankind are ever to increase in happiness and virtue.

I cannot deny it.

Therefore, Glaucon, I said, whenever you meet with any of the eulogists of Homer declaring that he has been the educator of Hellas, and that he is profitable for education and for the ordering of human things, and that you should take him up again and again and get to know him and regulate your whole life according to him, we may love and honour those who say these things—they are excellent people, as far as their lights extend; and we are ready to acknowledge that Homer is the greatest of poets and first of tragedy writers; but we must remain firm in our conviction that hymns to the gods and praises of famous men are the only poetry which ought to be admitted into our State. For if you go beyond this and allow the honeyed muse to enter, either in epic or lyric verse, not law and the reason of mankind, which by common consent have ever been deemed best, but pleasure and pain will be the rulers in our State.

That is most true, he said.

And now since we have reverted to the subject of poetry, let this our defence serve to show the reasonableness of our former judgment in sending away out of our State an art having the tendencies which we have described; for reason constrained us. But that she[5] may impute to us any harshness or want of politeness, let us tell her that there is an ancient quarrel between philosophy and poetry; of which there are many proofs, such as the saying of "the yelping hound howling at her lord," or of one "mighty in the vain talk of fools," and "the mob of sages circumventing Zeus," and the "subtle thinkers who are beggars after all"; and there are innumerable other signs of ancient enmity between them. Notwithstanding this, let us assure our sweet friend and the sister arts of imitation that if she will only prove her title to exist in a well-ordered State we shall be delighted to receive her—we are very conscious of her charms; but we may not on that account betray the truth. I dare say, Glaucon, that you are as much charmed by her as I am, especially when she appears in Homer?

Yes, indeed, I am greatly charmed.

Shall I propose, then, that she be allowed to return from exile, but upon this condition only—that she make a defence of herself in lyrical or some other metre?

Certainly.

And we may further grant to those of her defenders who are lovers of poetry and yet not poets the permission to speak in prose on her behalf: let them show not only that she is pleasant but also useful to States and to human life, and we will listen in a kindly spirit; for if this can be proved we shall surely be the gainers—I mean, if there is a use in poetry as well as a delight?

Certainly, he said, we shall be the gainers.

If her defence fails, then, my dear friend, like other persons who are enamoured of something, but put a restraint upon themselves when they think their desires are opposed to their interests, so too must we after the manner of lovers give her up, though not without a struggle. We too are inspired by that love of poetry which the education of noble States has implanted in us,[6] and therefore we would have her appear at her best and truest; but so long as she is unable to make good her defence, this argument of ours shall be a charm to us, which we will repeat to ourselves while we listen to her strains; that we may not fall away into the childish love of her which captivates the many. At all events we are well aware that poetry being such as we have described is not to be regarded seriously as attaining to the truth; and he who listens to her, fearing for the safety of the city which is within him, should be on his guard against her seductions and make our words his law.

Yes, he said, I quite agree with you.

Yes, I said, my dear Glaucon, for great is the issue at stake, greater than appears, whether a man is to be good or bad. And what will any one be profited if under the influence of honor or money or power, aye, or under the excitement of poetry, he neglect justice and virtue?

Yes, he said; I have been convinced by the argument, as I believe that any one else would have been.

NOTES

1. 本质的“床”，床的理念
2. 真理的，最高的
3.《名哲言行家》中提到的几位能工巧匠。其中 Anacharsis 据说是锚和陶轮的发明者。
4. 古代诗歌只有两种，悲剧和喜剧，都是用唱的形式，观众要用耳朵听。
5. 这里“she”指的是诗歌。
6. 这句话是反语，事实上诗歌没有那么美妙，我们的制度也没有那么美好。

About the Author:

As a philosopher in Classical Greece, Plato (about 427 BC–347 BC) appears to have been the founder of Western political philosophy, with his *Republic*, and *Laws*, providing some of the earliest extant treatments of political questions from a philosophical perspective. Widely considered as the most influential figure in the field of philosophy, Plato has made impact on the world for over 2,400 years. Along with his teacher, Socrates, and his most famous student, Aristotle, Plato has laid the very foundations of Western philosophy and science. Alfred North Whitehead once noted: “The safest general characterization of the European philosophical tradition is that it consists of a series of footnotes to Plato.” He is not only a foundational figure for Western science, philosophy, and mathematics, but also one of the founders of Western religion and spirituality. In addition, Plato is the innovator of the written dialogue and dialectic forms in philosophy. Plato used to be described as “...one of the most dazzling writers in the Western literary tradition and one of the most penetrating, wide-ranging, and influential authors in the history of philosophy.”

Appreciation:

《理想国》一书是柏拉图的一篇重要对话录，对话录里柏拉图以苏格拉底之口通过与其他人对话的方式设计了一个真、善、美相统一的政体，即可以达到公正的理想国。柏拉图的理想国是人类历史上最早的乌托邦。在他的理想国里统治者必须是哲学家，他认为现存的政治都是坏的，人类的真正出路在于哲学家掌握政权，也只有真正的哲学家才能拯救当时城邦所处的危机。这种信念构成了柏拉图成熟的政治哲学体系的核心。在他的眼里“哲学家”有着特殊的内涵。他认为哲学家是最高尚、最有学识的人，而这种贤人统治下的贤人政体就是最好的政体。所以，只有以哲学家为国王的国家才是最理想的国家。这个国家就是存在于天上的模范国家。

在节选的《理想国》第十章卷中，柏拉图借苏格拉底之口，与其表弟格劳孔展开一番对话。他基于个人的假设，主张把诗人从理想国中驱逐出去。首先，因为他认为“天下文章一大抄”，诗人和作家们无非是你抄袭我，我剽窃你，没什么创作的新意；其次，他认为诗人在写诗的时候，完全不受自己控制地陷入一种癫狂状态，失去理性；最后，诗人们的种种行为只会引领着人们越来越偏离真理的轨道。

Questions:

1. Why does Plato criticize the poetry in the passage?
2. According to Plato, how can a good poet describe things well?
3. What does the writer think of the imitative art?

The Poetics (I–V)

I

I propose to treat of Poetry in itself and of its various kinds, noting the essential quality of each, to inquire into the structure of the plot as requisite to a good poem; into the number and nature of the parts of which a poem is composed; and similarly into whatever else falls within the same inquiry. Following, then, the order of nature, let us begin with the principles which come first.

Epic poetry and Tragedy, Comedy also and Dithyrambic[1] poetry, and the music of the flute and of the lyre in most of their forms, are all in their general conception modes of imitation. They differ, however, from one another in three respects—the medium, the objects, the manner or mode of imitation, being in each case distinct.

For as there are persons who, by conscious art or mere habit, imitate and represent various objects through the medium of color and form[2], or again by the voice; so in the arts above mentioned, taken as a whole, the imitation is produced by rhythm, language, or "harmony," either singly or combined.

Thus in the music of the flute and of the lyre, "harmony" and rhythm alone are employed; also in other arts, such as that of the shepherd's pipe, which are essentially similar to these. In dancing, rhythm alone is used without "harmony"; for even dancing imitates character, emotion, and action, by rhythmical movement.

There is another art which imitates by means of language alone, and that either in prose or verse—which verse, again, may either combine different meters or consist of but one kind—but this has hitherto been without a name. For there is no common term we could apply to the mimes of Sophron and Xenarchus and the Socratic dialogues on the one hand; and, on the other, to poetic imitations in iambic, elegiac, or any similar meter. People do, indeed, add the word "maker" or "poet" to the name of the meter, and speak of elegiac poets, or epic (that is, hexameter) poets, as if it were not the imitation that makes the poet, but the verse that entitles them all to the name. Even when a treatise on medicine or natural science is brought out in verse, the name of poet is by custom given to the author; and yet Homer and Empedocles have nothing in common but the meter, so that it would be right to call the one poet, the other physicist rather than poet. On the same principle, even if a writer in his poetic imitation were to combine all meters, as Chaeremon did in his Centaur, which is a medley composed of meters of all kinds, we should bring him too under the general term poet. So much then for these distinctions.

There are, again, some arts which employ all the means above mentioned—namely, rhythm, tune, and meter. Such are Dithyrambic and Nomic poetry, and also Tragedy and Comedy; but between them originally the difference is, that in the first two cases these means are all employed in combination, in the latter, now one means is employed, now another.

Such, then, are the differences of the arts with respect to the medium of imitation.

II

Since the objects of imitation are men in action, and these men must be either of a higher or a lower type (for moral character mainly answers to these divisions, goodness and badness being the distinguishing marks of moral differences), it follows that we must represent men either as better than in real life, or as worse, or as they are. It is the same in painting. Polygnotus depicted men as nobler than they are, Pauson as less noble, Dionysius drew them true to life.

Now it is evident that each of the modes of imitation above mentioned will exhibit these differences, and become a distinct kind in imitating objects that are thus distinct. Such diversities may be found even in dancing, flute-playing, and lyre-playing. So again in language, whether prose or verse unaccompanied by music. Homer, for example, makes men better than they are; Cleophon as they are; Hegemon the Thasian, the inventor of parodies, and Nicochares, the author of the Deiliad, worse than they are. The same thing holds good of Dithyrambs and Nomes; here too one may portray different types, as Timotheus and Philoxenus differed in representing their Cyclopes. The same distinction marks off Tragedy from Comedy; for Comedy aims at representing men as worse, Tragedy as better than in actual life.

III

There is still a third difference—the manner in which each of these objects may be imitated. For the medium being the same, and the objects the same, the poet may imitate by narration—in which case he can either take another personality as Homer does, or speak in his own person, unchanged—or he may present all his characters as living and moving before us.

These, then, as we said at the beginning, are the three differences which distinguish artistic imitation—the medium, the objects, and the manner. So that from one point of view, Sophocles is an imitator of the same kind as Homer—for both imitate higher types of character; from another point of view, of the same kind as Aristophanes—for both imitate persons acting and doing. Hence, some say, the name of "drama" is given to such poems, as representing action. For the same reason the Dorians claim the invention both of Tragedy and Comedy. The claim to Comedy is put forward by the Megarians—not only by those of Greece proper, who allege that it originated under their democracy, but also by the Megarians of Sicily, for the poet Epicharmus, who is much earlier than Chionides and Magnes, belonged to that country. Tragedy too is claimed by certain Dorians of the Peloponnese. In each case they appeal to the evidence of language. The outlying villages, they say, are by them called komai[3], by the Athenians demoi[4]: and they assume that comedians were so named not from komazein, "to revel," but because they wandered from village to village (kata komas), being excluded contemptuously from the city. They add also that the Dorian word for "doing" is dran[5], and the Athenian, prattein[6].

This may suffice as to the number and nature of the various modes of imitation.

IV

Poetry in general seems to have sprung from two causes, each of them lying deep in our nature. First, the instinct of imitation is implanted in man from childhood, one difference between him and other animals being that he is the most imitative of living creatures, and through imitation learns his earliest lessons; and no less universal is the pleasure felt in things imitated. We have evidence of this in the facts of experience. Objects which in themselves we view with pain, we delight to contemplate when reproduced with minute fidelity: such as the forms of the most ignoble animals and of dead bodies. The cause of this again is, that to learn gives the liveliest pleasure, not only to philosophers but to men in general; whose capacity, however, of learning is more limited. Thus the reason why men enjoy seeing a likeness is, that in contemplating it they find themselves learning or inferring, and saying perhaps, "Ah, that is he." For if you happen not to have seen the original, the pleasure will be due not to the imitation as such, but to the execution, the coloring, or some such other cause.

Imitation, then, is one instinct of our nature. Next, there is the instinct for "harmony" and rhythm, meters being manifestly sections of rhythm. Persons, therefore, starting with this natural gift developed by degrees their special aptitudes, till their rude improvisations gave birth to Poetry.

Poetry now diverged in two directions, according to the individual character of the writers. The graver spirits imitated noble actions, and the actions of good men. The more trivial sort imitated the actions of meaner persons, at first composing satires, as the former did hymns to the gods and the praises of famous men. A poem of the satirical kind cannot indeed be put down to any author earlier than Homer; though many such writers probably there were. But from Homer onward, instances can be cited—his own Margites, for example, and other similar compositions. The appropriate meter was also here introduced; hence the measure is still called the iambic or lampooning measure, being that in which people lampooned one another. Thus the older poets were distinguished as writers of heroic or of lampooning[7] verse.

As, in the serious style, Homer is pre-eminent among poets, for he alone combined dramatic form with excellence of imitation so he too first laid down the main lines of comedy, by dramatizing the ludicrous instead of writing personal satire. His Margites bears the same relation to comedy that the *Iliad* and *Odyssey* do to tragedy. But when Tragedy and Comedy came to light, the two classes of poets still followed their natural bent: the lampooners became writers of Comedy, and the Epic poets were succeeded by Tragedians, since the drama was a larger and higher form of art.

Whether Tragedy has as yet perfected its proper types or not; and whether it is to be judged in itself, or in relation also to the audience—this raises another question. Be that as it may, Tragedy—as also Comedy—was at first mere improvisation. The one originated with the authors of the Dithyramb, the other with those of the phallic songs, which are still in use in many of our cities. Tragedy advanced by slow degrees; each new element that showed itself was in turn developed. Having passed through many changes, it found its natural form, and there it stopped.

Aeschylus first introduced a second actor; he diminished the importance of the Chorus, and assigned the leading part to the dialogue. Sophocles raised the number of actors to three, and added scene-painting. Moreover, it was not till late that the short plot was discarded for one of greater compass, and the grotesque diction of the earlier satyric form for the stately manner of Tragedy. The iambic measure then replaced the trochaic tetrameter, which was originally employed when the poetry was of the satyric order, and had greater with dancing. Once dialogue had come in, Nature herself discovered the appropriate measure. For the iambic is, of all measures, the most colloquial we see it in the fact that conversational speech runs into iambic lines more frequently than into any other kind of verse; rarely into hexameters, and only when we drop the colloquial intonation. The additions to the number of "episodes" or acts, and the other accessories of which tradition tells, must be taken as already described; for to discuss them in detail would, doubtless, be a large undertaking.

V

Comedy is, as we have said, an imitation of characters of a lower type—not, however, in the full sense of the word bad, the ludicrous being merely a subdivision of the ugly. It consists in some defect or ugliness which is not painful or destructive. To take an obvious example, the comic mask is ugly and distorted, but does not imply pain.

The successive changes through which Tragedy passed, and the authors of these changes, are well known, whereas Comedy has had no history, because it was not at first treated seriously. It was late before the Archon granted a comic chorus to a poet; the performers were till then voluntary. Comedy had already taken definite shape when comic poets, distinctively so called, are heard of. Who furnished it with masks, or prologues, or increased the number of actors—these and other similar details remain unknown. As for the plot, it came originally from Sicily; but of Athenian writers Crates was the first who abandoning the "iambic" or lampooning form, generalized his themes and plots.

Epic poetry agrees with Tragedy in so far as it is an imitation in verse of characters of a higher type. They differ in that Epic poetry admits but one kind of meter and is narrative in form. They differ, again, in their length: for Tragedy endeavors, as far as possible, to confine itself to a single revolution of the sun, or but slightly to exceed this limit, whereas the Epic action has no limits of time. This, then, is a second point of difference; though at first the same freedom was admitted in Tragedy as in Epic poetry.

Of their constituent parts some are common to both, some peculiar to Tragedy: whoever, therefore knows what is good or bad Tragedy, knows also about Epic poetry. All the elements of an Epic poem are found in Tragedy, but the elements of a Tragedy are not all found in the Epic poem.

NOTES

1. 歌颂酒神的诗歌
2. 指一些绘画和雕像
3. 村庄
4. 城镇和村庄
5. 相当于英语中的 to do
6. 相当于英语中的 to do
7. 强烈讽刺的

About the Author:

Aristotle (about 384 BC–322 BC) is an ancient Greek philosopher and scientist. When he was 17 or 18 years old, he joined Plato's Academy in Athens and remained there until the age of 37(347 BC). His writings touch upon many subjects, including physics, biology, zoology, metaphysics, logic, ethics, aesthetics, poetry, theater, music, rhetoric, linguistics, politics and government. For the first time, he helps develop the comprehensive system of western philosophy. *The Poetics* is the earliest work of dramatic theory which focuses on literary theory in the west. In the book, Aristotle accounts for the definition of "poetry." According to him, poetry includes drama, comedy, tragedy, satyr play, lyric poetry and epic poetry as well.

Appreciation:

《诗学》是古希腊著名美学家亚里士多德所著，原名为《论诗》，据说是亚里士多德的讲义。有佚失，现存 26 章，主要讨论悲剧和史诗。有人认为失传的第二卷可能是讨论喜剧的。对现存 26 章的内容，有六分说、五分说、三分说三个分法。《诗学》里亚里士多德表达了对艺术及悲剧的观点，认为艺术的本质是摹仿；而悲剧是对于一个严肃、完整、有一定长度的行动的摹仿。《诗学》对国人也有较深的影响。本文节选的是《诗学》的第一部分，包括第一章至第五章。主要分析了各种艺术所摹仿的对象、摹仿所采用的媒介和方式，由于对象不同（好人或坏人）、媒介不同（颜色、声音、节奏、语言或音调）、方式不同（叙述或表演），也就形成艺术之间的差异以及各种艺术由此而形成的差别，进而指出了诗的起源。除此之外，亚里士多德在本文中还追溯了悲剧与喜剧的历史发展进程。

Questions:

1. In what ways is one art different from another?
2. What does Aristotle think of the origin of the poetry?
3. What are the elements of comedy and tragedy?

Of Travel

Travel, in the younger sort, is a part of education, in the elder, a part of experience. He that travelleth[1] into a country, before he hath some entrance into the language, goeth[2] to school, and not to travel. That young men travel under some tutor, or grave servant, I allow well; so that he be such a one that hath the language, and hath been in the country before; whereby he may be able to tell them what things are worthy to be seen, in the country where they go; what acquaintances they are to seek; what exercises, or discipline, the place yieldeth[3]. For else, young men shall go hooded, and look abroad little. It is a strange thing, that in sea voyages, where there is nothing to be seen, but sky and sea, men should make diaries; but in land-travel, wherein so much is to be observed, for the most part they omit it; as if chance were fitter to be registered, than observation. Let diaries, therefore, be brought in use. The things to be seen and observed are: the courts of princes, especially when they give audience to ambassadors; the courts of justice, while they sit and hear causes; and so of consistories ecclesiastic; the churches and monasteries, with the monuments which are therein extant; the walls and fortifications of cities, and towns, and so the heavens and harbors; antiquities and ruins; libraries; colleges, disputations, and lectures, where any are; shipping and navies; houses and gardens of state and pleasure, near great cities; armories; arsenals; magazines; exchanges; burses; warehouses; exercises of horsemanship, fencing, training of soldiers, and the like; comedies, such whereunto the better sort of persons do resort; treasuries of jewels and robes; cabinets and rarities; and, to conclude, whatsoever is memorable, in the places where they go. After all which, the tutors, or servants, ought to make diligent inquiry. As for triumphs, masks, feasts, weddings, funerals, capital executions, and such shows, men need not to be put in mind of them; yet are they not to be neglected. If you will have a young man to put his travel into a little room, and in short time to gather much, this you must do. First, as was said, he must have some entrance into the language before he goeth[4]. Then he must have such a servant, or tutor, as knoweth[5] the country, as was likewise said. Let him carry with him also, some card or book, describing the country where he travelleth; which will be a good key to his inquiry. Let him keep also a diary. Let him not stay long, in one city or town; more or less as the place deserveth, but not long; nay, when he stayeth[6] in one city or town, let him change his lodging from one end and part of the town, to another; which is a great adamant of acquaintance. Let him sequester himself, from the company of his countrymen, and diet in such places, where there is good company of the nation where he travelleth. Let him, upon his removes from one place to another, procure recommendation to some person of quality, residing in the place whither he removeth[7]; that he may use his favor, in those things he desireth[8] to see or know. Thus he may abridge his travel, with much profit. As for the acquaintance, which is to be sought in travel; that which is most of all profitable, is acquaintance with the secretaries and employed men of ambassadors: for so in travelling in one country, he shall suck the experience of many. Let him also see, and visit, eminent persons in all kinds, which are of great name abroad; that he may be able to tell, how the life agreeth[9] with the fame. For quarrels, they are with care and discretion to be avoided. They are commonly for mistresses, healths, place, and words. And let a man beware, how he keepeth[10] company with choleric and quarrelsome persons; for they will engage him into their own quarrels. When a traveller returneth[11] home, let him not leave the countries, where he hath[12] travelled, altogether behind him; but maintain a correspondence by letters, with those of his acquaintance. which are of most worth. And let his travel appear rather in his discourse, than his apparel or gesture; and in his discourse, let him be rather advised in his answers, than forward to tell stories; and let it appear that he doth[13] not change his country manners, for those of foreign parts; but only prick in some flowers, of that he hath learned abroad, into the customs of his own country.

NOTES

1—11. -eth=-s 或者 -es, 为一般现在时动词的变化形式。

12. hath=has

13. doth=does

About the Author:

As an English philosopher, statesman, scientist, jurist, orator, and author, Francis Bacon (1561–1626) also serves both as Attorney General and as Lord Chancellor of England. After his death, he remained extremely influential through his works, especially as philosophical advocate and practitioner of the scientific method during the scientific revolution. Having been called "the father of empiricism," he argued for the possibility of scientific knowledge based upon inductive reasoning and careful observation of events in nature. Most importantly, he noted that this could be achieved by means of a skeptical and methodical approach. While his *Baconian Method* has not exerted a long lasting influence, the general idea of the importance and possibility of a skeptical methodology makes Bacon "the father of scientific method," which marks a new turn in the rhetorical and theoretical framework for science and is still central in debates about science and methodology today.

Appreciation:

培根是文艺复兴时期的哲学家和文学家，在《论旅行》中他结合了文艺复兴时期典型的时代特色论述了旅行的意义并表达了自己对于旅行的见解。培根说，对于年轻人来说，“旅行”是一种学习知识的过程和方式；而对于成年人，旅行则是丰富人生经验的最佳途径。从“旅行”一词说起。人们常用“旅行”一词而不是“旅游”，“行”与“游”差异明显。“行”是行走，而“游”是游玩；“行”目的是增长见识，而“游”是为了达到休闲娱乐的目的。关于旅行应观看和观察的事情，培根的建议是君主的宫殿、正在审理案件的法庭、教堂和修道院、城市的墙垣和堡垒等等。这与当今的旅行观念大有不同，培根着重的是文化的气息与沉淀，让旅行者沉浸其中，领略带有岁月痕迹的珍贵遗产。在旅行时，如果条件允许，还可以去拜访一下当地有名望的贤达人士。旅行归来，切记保持与朋友们的联系。另外，在言谈中不能骄傲自满地讲述旅行中的见闻，而应审慎回答。炫耀所见所闻并不是旅行的初衷，旅行的意义在于将一路的所见所闻所感融入我们自身的修养与谈吐之中。旅行，是为了寻找更好的自己。

Questions:

1. What does the author think of the significance or the benefits of traveling?
2. What are your own opinions about traveling?

The Declaration of Independence

When in the Course of human events, it becomes necessary for one people to dissolve the political bands which have connected them with another, and to assume among the powers of the earth, the separate and equal station to which the Laws of Nature and of Nature's God entitle them, a decent respect to the opinions of mankind requires that they should declare the causes which impel them to the separation.

We hold these truths to be self-evident, that all men are created equal, that they are endowed by their Creator with certain unalienable Rights, that among these are Life, Liberty and the pursuit of Happiness. —That to secure these rights, Governments are instituted among Men, deriving their just powers from the consent of the governed, —That whenever any Form of Government becomes destructive of these ends, it is the Right of the People to alter or to abolish it, and to institute new Government, laying its foundation on such principles and organizing its powers in such form, as to them shall seem most likely to affect their Safety and Happiness. Prudence, indeed, will dictate that Governments long established should not be changed for light and transient causes; and accordingly all experience hath shown, that mankind are more disposed to suffer, while evils are sufferable, than to right themselves by abolishing the forms to which they are accustomed. But when a long train of abuses and usurpations, pursuing invariably the same Object evinces a design to reduce them under absolute Despotism, it is their right, it is their duty, to throw off such Government, and to provide new Guards for their future security. Such has been the patient sufferance of these Colonies; and such is now the necessity which constrains them to alter their former Systems of Government. The history of the present King of Great Britain[1] is a history of repeated injuries and usurpations, all having in direct object the establishment of an absolute Tyranny over these States. To prove this, let Facts be submitted to a candid world.

He has refused his Assent to Laws, the most wholesome and necessary for the public good.

He has forbidden his Governors to pass Laws of immediate and pressing importance, unless suspended in their operation till his Assent should be obtained; and when so suspended, he has utterly neglected to attend to them.

He has refused to pass other Laws for the accommodation of large districts of people, unless those people would relinquish the right of Representation in the Legislature, a right inestimable to them and formidable to tyrants only. He has called together legislative bodies at places unusual, uncomfortable, and distant from the depository of their public Records, for the sole purpose of fatiguing them into compliance with his measures.

He has dissolved Representative Houses repeatedly, for opposing with manly firmness his invasions on the rights of the people.

He has refused for a long time, after such dissolutions, to cause others to be elected; whereby the Legislative powers, incapable of Annihilation, have returned to the People at large for their exercise; the State remaining in the mean time exposed to all the dangers of invasion from without, and convulsions within.

He has endeavored to prevent the population of these States; for that purpose obstructing the Laws for Naturalization of Foreigners; refusing to pass others to encourage their migrations hither, and raising the conditions of new Appropriations of Lands.

He has obstructed the Administration of Justice, by refusing his Assent to Laws for establishing Judiciary powers.

He has made Judges dependent on his Will alone, for the tenure of their offices, and the amount and payment of their salaries.

He has erected a multitude of New Offices, and sent hither swarms of Officers to harass our people, and eat out their substance.

He has kept among us, in times of peace, Standing Armies without the Consent of our legislatures. He has affected to render the Military independent of and superior to the Civil power.

He has combined with others[2] to subject us to a jurisdiction foreign to our constitution, and unacknowledged by our laws; giving his Assent to their Acts of pretended Legislation:

For Quartering large bodies of armed troops among us:

For protecting them, by a mock Trial, from punishment for any Murders which they should commit on the Inhabitants of these States:

For cutting off our Trade with all parts of the world: For imposing Taxes on us without our Consent:

For depriving us in many cases, of the benefits of Trial by Jury:

For transporting us beyond Seas to be tried for pretended offences:

For abolishing the free System of English Laws in a neighbouring Province[3], establishing therein an Arbitrary government, and enlarging its Boundaries so as to render it at once an example and fit instrument for introducing the same absolute rule into these Colonies:

For taking away our Charters, abolishing our most valuable Laws, and altering fundamentally the Forms of our Governments:

For suspending our own Legislatures, and declaring themselves invested with power to legislate for us in all cases whatsoever.

He has abdicated Government here, by declaring us out of his Protection and waging War against us.

He has plundered our seas, ravaged our Coasts, burnt our towns, and destroyed the lives of our people.

He is at this time transporting large Armies of foreign Mercenaries[4] to complete the works of death, desolation and tyranny, already begun with circumstances of Cruelty & perfidy scarcely paralleled in the most barbarous ages, and totally unworthy of the Head of a civilized nation.

He has constrained our fellow Citizens taken Captive on the high Seas to bear Arms against their Country, to become the executioners of their friends and Brethren, or to fall themselves by their Hands.

He has excited domestic insurrections amongst us, and has endeavored to bring on the inhabitants of our frontiers, the merciless Indian Savages, whose known rule of warfare, is an undistinguished destruction of all ages, sexes and conditions.

In every stage of these Oppressions We have Petitioned for Redress in the most humble terms: Our repeated Petitions have been answered only by repeated injury. A Prince whose character is thus marked by every act which may define a Tyrant, is unfit to be the ruler of a free people.

Nor have We been wanting in attentions to our British brethren. We have warned them from time to time of attempts by their legislature to extend an unwarrantable jurisdiction over us. We have reminded them of the circumstances of our emigration and settlement here. We have appealed to their native justice and magnanimity, and we have conjured them by the ties of our common kindred to disavow these usurpations, which, would inevitably interrupt our connections and correspondence. They too have been deaf to the voice of justice and of consanguinity. We must, therefore, acquiesce in the necessity, which denounces[5] our Separation, and hold them, as we hold the rest of mankind, Enemies in War, in Peace Friends.

We, therefore, the Representatives of the United States of America, in General Congress, Assembled, appealing to the Supreme Judge of the world for the rectitude of our intentions, do, in the Name, and by Authority of the good People of these Colonies, solemnly publish and declare, That these United Colonies are, and of Right ought to be Free and Independent States; that they are Absolved from all Allegiance to the British Crown, and that all political connection between them and the State of Great Britain, is and ought to be totally dissolved; and that as Free and Independent States, they have full Power to levy War, conclude Peace, contract Alliances, establish Commerce, and to do all other Acts and Things which Independent States may of right do.

And for the support of this Declaration, with a firm reliance on the protection of divine Providence, we mutually pledge to each other our Lives, our Fortunes and our sacred Honor.

NOTES

1. 指 George III：乔治三世，英国国王（1760—1820），当政期间由于采取高压殖民政策，激起北美人民反抗英国殖民统治的斗争
2. 指 the British Parliament: 英国议会
3. 指 the Province of Quebec

4. 指 German soldiers：受雇于英国殖民军队的德国士兵
5. 宣称，=proclaim

About the Author:

Thomas Jefferson is the author of *The Declaration of Independence,* third president of the United States. He used to be the founder of the University of Virginia—voiced the aspirations of a new America as no other individual of his era. As a public official, historian, philosopher, and plantation owner, he served his country for over five decades.

Appreciation:

《独立宣言》包括三个部分：第一部分阐明政治哲学 —— 民主与自由的哲学，包括人人平等、天赋人权等等，以及政府的组成和社会契约等内容。并且，对于英国政府的行为，从哲学的角度给予了抨击。这主要得益于启蒙思想的传播。第二部分列举共 29 款不平等事例，来证明乔治三世和整个英国政府对于北美殖民地的迫害。在第三部分中，《独立宣言》郑重立誓，宣布美国的独立。宣誓的誓词，以基督教和契约理论作为依据，体现了北美殖民地人民已经在语言、宗教信仰、社会思想的基础上达到了统一，崭新的美利坚民族已经宣告诞生！ 尽管《独立宣言》满篇都是关于自由的宣言，但同时也传递出一个更为重要的信息，即：当滥用权力、巧取豪夺的现象大量出现的时候，就表明政府企图把人民置于专制暴政之下。人民有权利、有义务抛弃这样的政府，为他们以后的安全提供新的守卫。

Questions:

1. What are the main ideas of the Declaration? How do you think these ideas affect human beings in the world?

2. The Declaration is considered as a turning point in American people's lives. What contributions has it made in the U.S.A? And how does it influence the life of the Americans?

Nature

To go into solitude, a man needs to retire as much from his chamber as from society. I am not solitary whilst I read and write, though nobody is with me. But if a man would be alone, let him look at the stars. The rays that come from those heavenly worlds, will separate between him and what he touches. One might think the atmosphere was made transparent with this design, to give man, in the heavenly bodies, the perpetual presence of the sublime. Seen in the streets of cities, how great they are! If the stars should appear one night in a thousand years, how would men believe and adore; and preserve for many generations the remembrance of the city of God[1] which had been shown! But every night come out these envoys of beauty, and light the universe with their admonishing smile.

The stars awaken a certain reverence, because though always present, they are inaccessible; but all natural objects make a kindred impression[2], when the mind is open to their influence. Nature never wears a mean appearance. Neither does the wisest man extort her secret, and lose his curiosity by finding out all her perfection. Nature never became a toy to a wise spirit. The flowers, the animals, the mountains, reflected the wisdom of his best hour, as much as they had delighted the simplicity of his childhood.

When we speak of nature in this manner, we have a distinct but most poetical sense in the mind. We mean the integrity of impression made by manifold natural objects. It is this which distinguishes the stick of timber of the wood-cutter, from the tree of the poet. The charming landscape which I saw this morning, is indubitably made up of some twenty or thirty farms. Miller owns this field, Locke that, and Manning the woodland beyond. But none of them owns the landscape. There is a property in the horizon which no man has but he whose eye can integrate all the parts, that is, the poet. This is the best part of these men's farms, yet to this their warranty-deeds[3] give no title.

To speak truly, few adult persons can see nature. Most persons do not see the sun. At least they have a very superficial seeing. The sun illuminates only the eye of the man, but shines into the eye and the heart of the child. The lover of nature is he whose inward and outward senses are still truly adjusted to each other; who has retained the spirit of infancy even into the era of manhood. His intercourse with heaven and earth, becomes part of his daily food. In the presence of nature, a wild delight runs through the man, in spite of real sorrows. Nature says,—he is my creature, and maugre[4] all his impertinent griefs, he shall be glad with me. Not the sun or the summer alone, but every hour and season yields its tribute of delight; for every hour and change corresponds to and authorizes a different state of the mind, from breathless noon to grimmest midnight. Nature is a setting that fits equally well a comic or a mourning piece. In good health, the air is a cordial[5] of incredible virtue. Crossing a bare common, in snow puddles, at twilight, under a clouded sky, without having in my thoughts any occurrence of special good fortune, I have enjoyed a perfect exhilaration. I am glad to the brink of fear. In the woods too, a man casts off his years, as the snake his slough, and at what period soever of life, is always a child. In the woods, is perpetual youth. Within these plantations of God, a decorum and sanctity[6] reign, a perennial festival is dressed, and the guest sees not how he should tire of them in a thousand years. In the woods, we return to reason and faith. There I feel that nothing can befall me in life, —no disgrace, no calamity, (leaving me my eyes,) which nature cannot repair. Standing on the bare ground, —my head bathed by the blithe air, and uplifted into infinite space, —all mean egotism vanishes. I become a transparent eye-ball; I am nothing; I see all; the currents of the Universal Being circulate through me; I am part or particle of God. The name of the nearest friend sounds then foreign and accidental: to be brothers, to be acquaintances, —master or servant, is then a trifle and a disturbance. I am the lover of uncontained and immortal beauty. In the wilderness, I find something more dear and connate than in streets or villages. In the tranquil landscape, and especially in the distant line of the horizon, man beholds somewhat as beautiful as his own nature.

The greatest delight which the fields and woods minister, is the suggestion of an occult relation between man and the vegetable. I am not alone and unacknowledged. They nod to me, and I to them. The waving of the boughs in the storm, is new to me and old. It takes me by surprise, and yet is not unknown. Its effect is like that of a higher thought or a better emotion coming over me, when I deemed I was thinking justly or doing right.

Yet it is certain that the power to produce this delight, does not reside in nature, but in man, or in a harmony of both. It is necessary to use these pleasures with great temperance. For, nature is not always tricked in holiday attire, but the same scene which yesterday breathed perfume and glittered as for the frolic of the nymphs[7], is overspread with melancholy today. Nature always wears the colors of the spirit. To a man laboring under calamity, the heat of his own fire hath sadness in it. Then, there is a kind of contempt of the landscape felt by him who has just lost by death a dear friend. The sky is less grand as it shuts down over less worth in the population.

NOTES

1. 天国
2. 互相关联的、同源的印象
3. 地产契约
4. （古语）虽然，尽管
5. 爽心的饮料
6. 恰到好处而又神圣
7. 仙女的嬉闹

About the Author:

Ralph Waldo Emerson is an American essayist, lecturer, and poet. He is also the major representative of the transcendentalist movement of the mid-19th century. Seen as a champion of individualism and a prescient critic of the countervailing pressures of society, he disseminated his thoughts through dozens of published essays and more than 1,500 public lectures across the country. In Emerson's writings, he has written on a number of subjects, developing certain ideas such as individuality, freedom, the ability for human kind to realize almost anything, and the relationship between the soul and the surrounding world. Apart from that, Emerson takes a more pantheist or pandeist approach by rejecting views of God as separate from the world.

Appreciation:

正如爱默生在《论自然》中第一章里写到的那样，"人不仅要远离社会，还需远离书房，方可进入孤独的境界"。远离人，远离社会，直面自然，比如星空，它能让你体验孤独。

《论自然》第一章从自然、物质、美、语言、知识、理念、精神和未来等八个方面阐述了大自然的丰富意蕴和作者自身的独特见解。在爱默生看来，自然都是人的精神化身，欢乐的自然呈现着欢乐，而忧伤的自然则呈现着哀愁。他主张修身养性，认为只有在孤身独处时，人的各种内在天赋才能得到充分发展。同时爱默生又提到"自然，即外界各种事物给予的完整的印象"，表明作者视整个世界为一个有机整体的浪漫主义自然观。他主张人应当回到原始的物质状态中去单纯地观察世界。接下来又是一段精彩的话："我站在空地上，头沐浴在和煦的空气里，仰望着无垠的太空，小我的一切都消失了，我变成了一只透明的眼球；本身不复存在；我洞察一切；上帝的精气神在我周身循环；我变成了上帝的一部分。"这一段描述实际上也体现了作者的超验主义观念。

Questions:

1. Try to find the philosophical ideas implied in the chapter.
2. What is the necessary quality to be a poet according to the author?
3. "Nature always wears the color of the spirit." Do you agree? Why or why not?

Part 5
Drama

Definition of Drama

Drama is a genre of literature, in which the words are mainly dialogue. People talking is the basic dramatic action. Wordless activity may interrupt the talk, but it is the context of dialogue that gives significance to such activity.

Elements of Drama

"Drama" comes from a Greek word "dran," meaning "thing done," "action," or "deed." Aristotle, first and still the single most important theorist of drama, called drama "imitated human action." Professor J. M. Manly saw three necessary elements in drama: (1) a story (2) told in action (3) by actors who impersonate the characters of the story. Aristotle in his *Poetics*, listed the six elements of drama in order of importance: plot, character, thought, diction, music, and spectacle.

The Origins of Drama

There are three independent origins of drama. Drama began with pagan religious rites in Greece. It evolved from certain religious ceremonies. It is generally believed that Greek tragedy developed from certain Dionysian rites dealing with life and death, while Greek comedy arose from the Dionysian rites which dealt with the theme of fertility. And medieval drama came out of rites commemorating the birth and the resurrection of Christ.

Drama as Performance

Unlike poetry and fiction, drama is theater. What the dramatist writes is a performable script. Theatre is always more than mere language. Language alone can be read, but true theatre can become manifested only in performance. So a performance of drama is much more than just an art of words. The thoughtful efforts of perhaps a hundred people—actors, director, producer, stage designer, costumer, makeup artist, and technicians, ect.—have to go into a production. Another difference between fiction and drama is that dramatic effects are stage effects. Plays appeal directly to the auditory and visionary senses. Characters exist directly before audiences in their own immediate field of experience.

How to Effectively Read Drama

(1) Try to envisage the set clearly.

(2) Pay attention to the introduction of characters.

(3) Pay attention to the stage directions.

(4) Pay attention to whatever sound effects are specified in the play.

(5) Pay attention to the eloquent silences, including pauses within speeches or between speeches.

(6) Pay attention to the revealing remark or gesture of the characters.

A Selection of Plays:

Romeo and Juliet (Excerpt)

Script of Act II Scene II. Capulet's orchard.

Enter ROMEO ROMEO

He jests at scars that never felt a wound.

JULIET appears above at a window.

But, soft! what light through yonder window breaks?
It is the east, and Juliet is the sun.
Arise, fair sun, and kill the envious moon,
Who is already sick and pale with grief,
That thou her maid art far more fair than she:
Be not her maid, since she is envious;
Her vestal livery is but sick and green

And none but fools do wear it; cast it off.
It is my lady, O, it is my love!
O, that she knew she were!
She speaks yet she says nothing: what of that?
Her eye discourses; I will answer it.
I am too bold, 'tis not to me she speaks:
Two of the fairest stars in all the heaven,
Having some business, do entreat her eyes
To twinkle in their spheres till they return.
What if her eyes were there, they in her head?
The brightness of her cheek would shame those stars,
As daylight doth a lamp; her eyes in heaven
Would through the airy region stream so bright
That birds would sing and think it were not night.
See, how she leans her cheek upon her hand!
O, that I were a glove upon that hand,
That I might touch that cheek!

JULIET

Ay me!

ROMEO

She speaks:
O, speak again, bright angel! for thou art
As glorious to this night, being o'er my head
As is a winged messenger of heaven
Unto the white-upturned wondering eyes
Of mortals that fall back to gaze on him
When he bestrides the lazy-pacing clouds
And sails upon the bosom of the air.

JULIET

O Romeo, Romeo! wherefore art thou Romeo?
Deny thy father and refuse thy name;

Or, if thou wilt not, be but sworn my love,
And I'll no longer be a Capulet.

ROMEO

[Aside] Shall I hear more, or shall I speak at this?

JULIET

'Tis but thy name that is my enemy;
Thou art thyself, though not a Montague.
What's Montague? it is nor hand, nor foot,
Nor arm, nor face, nor any other part
Belonging to a man. O, be some other name!
What's in a name? that which we call a rose
By any other name would smell as sweet;
So Romeo would, were he not Romeo call'd,
Retain that dear perfection which he owes
Without that title. Romeo, doff thy name,
And for that name which is no part of thee
Take all myself.

ROMEO

I take thee at thy word:
Call me but love, and I'll be new baptized;
Henceforth I never will be Romeo.

JULIET

What man art thou that thus bescreen'd in night
So stumblest on my counsel?

ROMEO

By a name
I know not how to tell thee who I am:
My name, dear saint, is hateful to myself,
Because it is an enemy to thee;

Had I it written, I would tear the word.

JULIET

My ears have not yet drunk a hundred words
Of that tongue's utterance, yet I know the sound:
Art thou not Romeo and a Montague?

ROMEO

Neither, fair saint, if either thee dislike.

JULIET

How camest thou hither, tell me, and wherefore?
The orchard walls are high and hard to climb,
And the place death, considering who thou art,
If any of my kinsmen find thee here.

ROMEO

With love's light wings did I o'er-perch these walls;
For stony limits cannot hold love out,
And what love can do that dares love attempt;
Therefore thy kinsmen are no let to me.

JULIET

If they do see thee, they will murder thee.

ROMEO

Alack, there lies more peril in thine eye
Than twenty of their swords: look thou but sweet,
And I am proof against their enmity.

JULIET

I would not for the world they saw thee here.

ROMEO

I have night's cloak to hide me from their sight;
And but thou love me, let them find me here:
My life were better ended by their hate,
Than death prorogued, wanting of thy love.

JULIET

By whose direction found'st thou out this place?

ROMEO

By love, who first did prompt me to inquire;
He lent me counsel and I lent him eyes.
I am no pilot; yet, wert thou as far
As that vast shore wash'd with the farthest sea,
I would adventure for such merchandise.

JULIET

Thou know'st the mask of night is on my face,
Else would a maiden blush bepaint my cheek
For that which thou hast heard me speak to-night
Fain would I dwell on form, fain, fain deny
What I have spoke: but farewell compliment!
Dost thou love me? I know thou wilt say "Ay,"
And I will take thy word: yet if thou swear'st,
Thou mayst prove false; at lovers' perjuries
Then say, Jove laughs. O gentle Romeo,
If thou dost love, pronounce it faithfully:
Or if thou think'st I am too quickly won,
I'll frown and be perverse an say thee nay,
So thou wilt woo; but else, not for the world.
In truth, fair Montague, I am too fond,
And therefore thou mayst think my 'havior light:
But trust me, gentleman, I'll prove more true
Than those that have more cunning to be strange.

I should have been more strange, I must confess,
But that thou overheard'st, ere I was ware,
My true love's passion: therefore pardon me,
And not impute this yielding to light love,
Which the dark night hath so discovered.

ROMEO

Lady, by yonder blessed moon I swear
That tips with silver all these fruit-tree tops—

JULIET

O, swear not by the moon, the inconstant moon,
That monthly changes in her circled orb,
Lest that thy love prove likewise variable.

ROMEO

What shall I swear by?

JULIET

Do not swear at all;
Or, if thou wilt, swear by thy gracious self,
Which is the god of my idolatry,
And I'll believe thee.

ROMEO

If my heart's dear love—

JULIET

Well, do not swear: although I joy in thee,
I have no joy of this contract to-night:
It is too rash, too unadvised, too sudden;
Too like the lightning, which doth cease to be
Ere one can say "It lightens." Sweet, good night!
This bud of love, by summer's ripening breath,

May prove a beauteous flower when next we meet.
Good night, good night! as sweet repose and rest
Come to thy heart as that within my breast!

ROMEO

O, wilt thou leave me so unsatisfied?

JULIET

What satisfaction canst thou have to-night?

ROMEO

The exchange of thy love's faithful vow for mine.

JULIET

I gave thee mine before thou didst request it:
And yet I would it were to give again.

ROMEO

Wouldst thou withdraw it? for what purpose, love?

JULIET

But to be frank, and give it thee again.
And yet I wish but for the thing I have:
My bounty is as boundless as the sea,
My love as deep; the more I give to thee,
The more I have, for both are infinite.

Nurse calls within

I hear some noise within; dear love, adieu!
Anon, good nurse! Sweet Montague, be true.
Stay but a little, I will come again.

Exit, above

ROMEO

O blessed, blessed night! I am afeard.
Being in night, all this is but a dream,
Too flattering-sweet to be substantial.

Re-enter JULIET, above

JULIET

Three words, dear Romeo, and good night indeed.
If that thy bent of love be honourable,
Thy purpose marriage, send me word to-morrow,
By one that I'll procure to come to thee,
Where and what time thou wilt perform the rite;
And all my fortunes at thy foot I'll lay
And follow thee my lord throughout the world.

Nurse

[Within] Madam!

JULIET

I come, anon.—But if thou mean'st not well,
I do beseech thee—

Nurse

[Within] Madam!

JULIET

By and by, I come:—
To cease thy suit, and leave me to my grief:
To-morrow will I send.

ROMEO

So thrive my soul—

JULIET

A thousand times good night!

Exit, above

ROMEO

A thousand times the worse, to want thy light.
Love goes toward love, as schoolboys from
their books,
But love from love, toward school with heavy looks.

Retiring

Re-enter JULIET, above

JULIET

Hist! Romeo, hist! O, for a falconer's voice,
To lure this tassel-gentle back again!
Bondage is hoarse, and may not speak aloud;
Else would I tear the cave where Echo lies,
And make her airy tongue more hoarse than mine,
With repetition of my Romeo's name.

ROMEO

It is my soul that calls upon my name:
How silver-sweet sound lovers' tongues by night,
Like softest music to attending ears!

JULIET

Romeo!

ROMEO

My dear?

JULIET

At what o'clock to-morrow
Shall I send to thee?

ROMEO

At the hour of nine.

JULIET

I will not fail: 'tis twenty years till then.
I have forgot why I did call thee back.

ROMEO

Let me stand here till thou remember it.

JULIET

I shall forget, to have thee still stand there,
Remembering how I love thy company.

ROMEO

And I'll still stay, to have thee still forget,
Forgetting any other home but this.

JULIET

'Tis almost morning; I would have thee gone:
And yet no further than a wanton's bird;
Who lets it hop a little from her hand,
Like a poor prisoner in his twisted gyves,
And with a silk thread plucks it back again,
So loving-jealous of his liberty.

ROMEO

I would I were thy bird.

JULIET

Sweet, so would I:
Yet I should kill thee with much cherishing.
Good night, good night! parting is such
sweet sorrow,
That I shall say good night till it be morrow.

Exit above

ROMEO

Sleep dwell upon thine eyes, peace in thy breast!
Would I were sleep and peace, so sweet to rest!
Hence will I to my ghostly father's cell,
His help to crave, and my dear hap to tell.

Exit

About the Playwright:

William Shakespeare is the most important English playwright and poet with the greatest works in the history of English literature.

Shakespeare was assumed to be born on April 23, 1564. In 1582, 18-year-old Shakespeare got married to Anne Hathaway, twenty-six years old at the time. In 1586, Shakespeare left Stratford for London to make his fortune, where there already was an established community of playwrights. By 1595, Shakespeare was sufficiently successful to be named as one of senior members of the Lord Chamberlain's men, an acting company that performed frequently before court. This was no small honor; this prominent theatre company later became the royal company called the King's Men, making Shakespeare an official playwright to the King of England. Shakespeare's fortunes were also improving as his fame. In 1597 he purchased the second largest house in Stratford which he called New Place and began buying up land around Stratford. One year later, Shakespeare became a ten percent owner of the famous Globe Theatre in London, where so many of his plays would later be performed. By 1611, Shakespeare retired, returning to Stratford and in 1616 Shakespeare died, famously bequeathing his second-best bed to his wife, often seen as a sign that his marriage may be far from happiness.

Shakespeare's works are often divided into four periods with the starting of what is referred to as an experimental period, approximately from 1591 and to 1593, with the works of *Titus Andronicus, Love's Labour's Lost, The Two Gentlemen of Verona, The Comedy of Errors* and *The Taming of the Shrew.* The second period ending around 1601, marks the establishment of Shakespeare with the tragedy *Romeo and Juliet*, the comedies, *The Merchant of Venice, A Midsummer-Night's Dream, Much Ado about Nothing, The Merry Wives of Windsor* and the history plays, *Henry IV, Parts I and II, Henry V, Richard II, King John* and *Julius Caesar*. The third period ending around 1610 marks perhaps the apex of Shakespeare's work with the tragedies, *Hamlet, Othello, Macbeth, King Lear* but also comedies such as *Twelfth Night, All's Well that Ends Well* and the epic history play, *Antony and Cleopatra.* The final period ends around 1611 with the plays, *Cymbeline, Henry VIII* and romances such as *The Tempest* and *The Winter's Tale.*

Appreciation:

《罗密欧与朱丽叶》，英文原名为 *The Most Excellent and Lamentable Tragedy of Romeo and Juliet*，简写为 *Romeo and Juliet*，是英国剧作家莎士比亚著名的剧目。但罗密欧与朱丽叶这个悲剧故事并非莎士比亚原创，据传是改编自阿瑟·布卢克（Arthur Broke）1562 年的小说《罗密欧与朱丽叶的悲剧历史》（*The Tragical History of Romeus and Juliet*），当然也有说是改编自意大利文艺复兴时期小说家马泰奥·班戴洛（1480?—1561）创作的一部小说。

《罗密欧与朱丽叶》讲述的是在意大利的小城维洛那的两大家族——蒙太古和凯普莱特家族间的宿仇背景下所产生的一段凄美的爱情故事。蒙太古家的儿子罗密欧与凯普莱特家的女儿朱丽叶在一次宴会中一见钟情，共沐爱河。罗密欧请求劳伦斯神父为他们举行秘密婚礼，好心的神父很乐意成全他们，并希望他们的结合可以使两家冰释前嫌，重修旧好。然而悲剧却发生了：罗密欧的好朋友茂丘西奥因为帮罗密欧出头而被朱丽叶的表哥提伯尔特一剑刺死。迫于正义的呼唤，也为了替朋友报仇，罗密欧不得不拔剑杀死了提伯尔特。朱丽叶焦急万分，请求劳伦斯长老帮助，长老急中生智，一面让朱丽叶在婚前的夜晚服下他的假药，一面派人送信给罗密欧，让他适时赶来带走朱丽叶。朱丽叶依计行事，可是送信的人却没有如期找到罗密欧。罗密欧听到朱丽叶的死讯，悲痛欲绝，匆匆回到维洛那城，来到朱丽叶的墓地，以死殉情。当朱丽叶从假死中醒过来后，发现罗密欧已经死去后，她不顾外面喧嚣的人声，也不顾长老的劝告，立即决定同罗密欧死在一起，于是她果敢地拿起匕首，刺进了自己的心脏。罗密欧与朱丽叶的爱情虽然毁灭了，却因此赢得了两家人的悔悟，换来了两家人的世代和平。

《罗密欧与朱丽叶》最为突出的写作特色为大量的抒情意象形式，这是莎士比亚其他悲剧中所没有的。戏剧中的男女主人公完全沉浸在对爱情的热忱、向往之中。特别是第二幕第二场凯普莱特家花园中，抒情意象尤为突出。男女主人公借助对月的抒怀，表现了他们炙热的情感交流和惜别时的难舍难分，弹奏的是一曲情意缠绵的爱情颂歌。

Questions:

1. What is the theme of *Romeo and Juliet*?
2. What is your reflections on this play?

Long Day's Journey into Night (Excerpt)

Act IV

....

JAMIE [*in a cruel, sneering tone with hatred in it*] Where's the hophead? Gone to sleep?

Edmund jerks as if he'd been struck. There is a tense silence. Edmund's face looks stricken and sick. Then in a burst of rage he springs from his chair.

EDMUND. You dirty bastard!

He punches his brother in the face, a blow that glances off the cheekbone. For a second Jamie reacts pugnaciously and half rises from his chair to do battle, but suddenly he seems to sober up to a shocked realization of what he has said and he sinks back limply.

JAMIE [*miserably*] Thanks, Kid. I certainly had that coming. Don't know what made me—booze talking—You know me, Kid.

EDMUND [*his anger ebbing*] I know you'd never say that unless—But God, Jamie, no matter how drunk you are, it's no excuse! [*He pauses—miserably*] I'm sorry I hit you. You and I never scrap—that bad. [*He sinks back on his chair.*]

JAMIE [*huskily*] It's all right. Glad you did. My dirty tongue. Like to cut it out. [*He hides his face in his hands—dully.*] I suppose it's because I feel so damned sunk. Because this time Mama had me fooled. I really believed she had it licked. She thinks I always believe the worst, but this time I believed the best. [*His voice flutters.*] I suppose I can't forgive her—yet. It meant so much. I'd begun to hope, if she'd beaten the game, I could, too. [*He begins to sob, and the horrible part of his weeping is that it appears sober, not the maudlin tears of drunkenness.*]

EDMUND [*blinking back tears himself*] God, don't I know how you feel! Stop it, Jamie!

JAMIE [*trying to control his sobs*] I've known about Mama so much longer than you. Never forget the first time I got wise. Caught her in the act with a hypo. Christ, I'd never dreamed before that any women but whores took dope! [*He pauses.*] And then this stuff of you getting consumption. It's got me licked. We've been more than brothers. You're the only pal I've ever had. I love your guts. I'd do anything for you.

EDMUND [*reaches out and pats his arm*] I know that, Jamie.

JAMIE [*his crying over—drops his hands from his face—with a strange bitterness*] Yet I'll bet you've heard Mama and old Gaspard spill so much bunk about my hoping for the worst, you suspect right now I'm thinking to myself that Papa is old and can't last much longer, and if you were to die, Mama and I would get all he's got, and so I'm probably hoping—

EDMUND [*indignantly*] Shut up, you damned fool! What the hell put that in your nut? [*He stares at his brother accusingly.*] Yes, that's what I'd like to know. What put that in your mind?

JAMIE [*confusedly—appearing drunk again*] Don't be a dumbbell! What I said! Always suspected of hoping for the worst. I've got so I can't help—[*Then drunkenly resentful*] What are you trying to do, accuse me? Don't play the wise guy with me! I've learned more of life than you'll ever know! Just because you've read a lot of highbrow junk, don't think you can fool me! You're only an overgrown kid! Mama's baby and Papa's pet! The family White Hope! You've been getting a swelled head lately. About nothing! About a few poems in a hick town newspaper! Hell, I used to write better stuff for the Lit magazine in college! You better wake up! You're setting no rivers on fire! You let hick town boobs flatter you with bunk about your future—[*Abruptly his tone changes to disgusted contrition. Edmund has looked away from him, trying to ignore this tirade.*] Hell, Kid, forget it. That goes for Sweeny. You know I don't mean it. No one hopes more than I do you'll knock'em all dead. No one is prouder you've started to make good. [*Drunkenly assertive*] Why shouldn't I be proud? Hell, it's purely selfish. You reflect credit on me. I've had more to do with bringing you up than anyone. I wised you up about women, so you'd never be a fall guy, or make any mistakes you didn't want to make! And who steered you on to reading poetry first? Swinburne, for example? I did! And because I once wanted to write, I planted it in your mind that someday you'd write! Hell, you're more than my brother. I made you! You're my Frankenstein!

He has risen to a note of drunken arrogance. Edmund is grinning with amusement now.

EDMUND. All right, I'm your Frankenstein. So let's have a drink. [*He laughs.*] You crazy nut!

JAMIE [*thickly*] I'll have a drink. Not you. Got to take care of you. [*He reaches out with a foolish grin of doting affection and grabs his brother's hand.*] Don't be scared of this sanatorium business. Hell, you can beat that standing on your head. Six months and you'll be in the pink. Probably haven't got consumption at all. Doctors lot of fakers. Told me years ago to cut out booze or I'd soon be dead—and here I am. They're all con men[1]. Anything to grab your dough. I'll bet this state farm stuff is political graft game. Doctors get a cut for every patient they send.

EDMUND [*disgustedly amused*] You're the limit! At the Last Judgment, you'll be around telling everyone it's in the bag.

JAMIE. And I'll be right. Slip a piece of change to the Judge and be saved, but if you're broke you can go to hell! [*He grins at this blasphemy and Edmund has to laugh. Jamie goes on.*] "Therefore put money in thy purse." That's the only dope[*Mockingly*]. The secret of my success! Look what it's got me! [*He lets Edmund's hand go to pour a big drink, and gulps it down. He stares at his brother with bleary affection—takes his hand again and begins to talk thickly but with a strange, convincing sincerity.*] Listen, Kid, you'll be going away. May not get another chance to talk. Or might not be drunk enough to tell you truth. So got to tell you now. Something I ought to have told you long ago—for your own good. [*He pauses—struggling with himself. Edmund stares, impressed and uneasy. Jamie blurts out.*] Not drunken bull, but "in vino veritas"[2] stuff. You better take it seriously. Want to warn you—against me. Mama and Papa are right. I've been rotten bad influence. And worst of it is, I did it on purpose.

EDMUND [*uneasily*] Shut up! I don't want to hear—

JAMIE. Nix, Kid! You listen! Did it on purpose to make a bum of you. Or part of me did. A big part. That part that's been dead so long. That hates life. My putting you wise so you'd learn from my mistakes. Believed that myself at times, but it's a fake. Made my mistakes look good. Made getting drunk romantic. Made whores fascinating vampires instead of poor, stupid, diseased slobs they really are. Made fun of work as sucker's game. Never wanted you succeed and make me look even worse by comparison. Wanted you to fail. Always jealous of you. Mama's baby, Papa's pet! [*He stares at Edmund with increasing enmity.*] And it was your being born that started Mama on dope. I know that's not your fault, but all the same, God damn you, I can't help hating your guts—!

EDMUND [*almost frightenedly*] Jamie! Cut it out! You're crazy!

JAMIE. But don't get wrong idea, Kid. I love you more than I hate you. My saying what I'm telling you now proves it. I run the risk you'll hate me—and you're all I've got left. But I didn't mean to tell you that last stuff—go that far back. Don't know what made me. What I wanted to say is, I'd like to see you become the greatest success in the world. But you'd better be on your guard. Because I'll do my damnedest to make you fail. Can't help it. I hate myself. Got to take revenge. On everyone else. Especially you. Oscar Wilde's "Reading Gaol" has the dope twisted. The man was dead and so he had to kill the thing he loved.[3] That's what it ought to be. The dead part of me hopes you won't get well. Maybe he's even glad the game has got Mama again! He wants company, he doesn't want to be the only corpse around the house! [*He gives a hard, tortured laugh.*]

EDMUND. Jesus, Jamie! You really have gone crazy!

JAMIE. Think it over and you'll see I'm right. Think it over when you're away from me in the sanatorium. Make up your mind you've got to tie a can to me—get me out of your life—think of me as dead—tell people, "I had a brother, but he's dead." And when you come back, look out for me. I'll be waiting to welcome you with that "my old pal" stuff, and give you the glad hand, and at the first good chance I get stab you in the back.

EDMUND. Shut up! I'll be God-damned if I'll listen to you any more—

JAMIE [*as if he hadn't heard*] Only don't forget me. Remember I warned you—for your sake. Give me credit. Greater love hath no man than this, that he saveth his brother from himself.[4] [*Very drunkenly, his head bobbing*] That's all. Feel better now. Gone to confession. Know you absolve me, don't you, Kid? You understand. You're a damned fine kid. Ought to be. I made you. So go and get well. Don't die on me. You're all I've got left. God bless you, Kid. [*His eyes close. He mumbles.*] That last drink—the old K. O.

He falls into a drunken doze, not completely asleep. Edmund buries his face in his hands miserably. Tyrone comes in quietly through the screen door from the porch, his dressing gown wet with fog, the collar turned up around his throat. His face is stern and disgusted but at the same time pitying. Edmund does not notice his entrance.

TYRONE [*in a low voice*] Thank God he's asleep. [*Edmund looks up with a start.*] I thought he'd never stop talking. [*He turns down the collar of his dressing gown.*] We'd better let him stay where he is and sleep it off. [*Edmund remains silent. Tyrone regards him—then goes on.*] I heard the last part of his talk. It's what I've warned you. I hope you'll heed the warning, now it comes from his own mouth. [*Edmund gives no sign of having heard. Tyrone adds pityingly*] But don't take it too much to heart, lad. He loves to exaggerate the worst of himself when he's drunk. He's devoted to you. It's the one good thing left in him. [*He looks down on Jamie with a bitter sadness.*] A sweet spectacle for me! My first-born, who I hoped would bear my name in honor and dignity, who showed such brilliant promise!

EDMUND [*miserably*] Keep quiet, can't you, Papa?

TYRONE [*pours a drink*] A waste! A wreck, a drunken hulk, done with and finished!

He drinks. Jamie has become restless, sensing his father's presence, struggling up from his stupor. Now he gets his eyes open to blink up at Tyrone. The latter moves back a step defensively, his face growing hard.

JAMIE [*suddenly points a finger at him and recites with dramatic emphasis*]

"Clarence is come, false, fleeting, perjured Clarence,
That stabbed me in the field by Tewksbury.

Seize on him, Furies, take him into torment."[5]

[*Then resentfully*] What the hell are you staring at? [*He recites sardonically from Rossetti.*]

"Look in my face. My name is Might-Have-Been;

I am also called No More, Too Late, Farewell."[6]

TYRONE. I'm well aware of that, and God knows I don't want to look at it.

EDMUND. Papa! Quit it!

JAMIE [*derisively*] Got a great idea for you, Papa. Put on revival of "The Bells"[7] this season. Great part in it you can play without make-up. Old Gaspard, the miser!

Tyrone turns away, trying to control his temper.

EDMUND. Shut up, Jamie!

JAMIE [*jeeringly*] I claim Edwin Booth[8] never saw the day when he could give as good a performance as a trained seal. Seals are intelligent and honest. They don't put up any bluffs about the Art of Acting. They admit they're just hams earning their daily fish.

TYRONE [*stung, turns on him in a rage*] You loafer!

EDMUND. Papa! Do you want to start a row that will bring Mama down? Jamie, go back to sleep! You've shot off your mouth too much already.

Tyrone turns away.

JAMIE [*thickly*] All right, Kid. Not looking for argument. Too damned sleepy.

He closes his eyes, his head nodding. Tyrone comes to the table and sits down, turning his chair so he won't look at Jamie. At once he becomes sleepy, too.

TYRONE [*heavily*] I wish to God she'd go to bed so that I could, too. [*Drowsily*] I'm dog tired. I can't stay up all night like I used to. Getting old—old and finished. [*With a bone-cracking yawn*] Can't keep my eyes open. I think I'll catch a few winks. Why don't you do the same, Edmund? It'll pass the time until she—

His voice trails off. His eyes close, his chin sags, and he begins to breathe heavily through his mouth. Edmund sits tensely. He hears something and jerks nervously forward in his chair, staring through the front parlor into the hall. He jumps up with a hunted, distracted expression. It seems for a second he is going to hide in the back parlor. Then he sits down again and waits, his eyes averted, his hands gripping the arms of his chair. Suddenly all five bulbs of the chandelier in the front parlor are turned on from a wall switch, and a moment later someone starts playing the piano in there—the opening of one of Chopin's simpler waltzes, done with a forgetful, stiff-fingered groping, as if an awkward schoolgirl were practicing it for the first time, Tyrone starts to wide-awakeness and sober dread, and Jamie's head jerks back and his eyes open. For a moment they listen frozenly. The playing stops as abruptly as it began, and Mary appears in the doorway.

She wears a sky-blue dressing gown over her nightdress, dainty slippers with pompons on her bare feet. Her face is paler than ever. Her eyes look enormous. They glisten like polished black jewels. The uncanny thing is that her face now appears so youthful. Experience seems ironed out of it. It is a marble mask of girlish innocence, the mouth caught in a shy smile. Her white hair is braided in two pigtails which hang over her breast. Over one arm, carried neglectfully, trailing on the floor, as if she had forgotten she held it, is an old-fashioned white satin wedding gown, trimmed with duchesse lace. She hesitates in the doorway, glancing round the room, her forehead puckered puzzledly, like someone who has come to a room to get something but has become absent-minded on the way and forgotten what it was. They stare at her. She seems aware of them merely as she is aware of other objects in the room, the furniture, the windows, familiar things she accepts automatically as naturally belonging there but which she is too preoccupied to notice.

JAMIE [*breaks the cracking silence—bitterly, self-defensively sardonic*] The Mad Scene. Enter Ophelia![9]—

His father and brother both turn on him fiercely. Edmund is quicker. He slaps Jamie across the mouth with the back of his hand.

TYRONE [*his voice trembling with suppressed fury*] Good boy, Edmund. The dirty blackguard! His own mother!

JAMIE [*mumbles guiltily, without resentment*] All right, Kid. Had it coming. But I told you how much I'd hoped—[*He puts his hands over his face and begins to sob.*]

TYRONE. I'll kick you out in the gutter tomorrow, so help me God. [*But Jamie's sobbing breaks his anger, and he turns and shakes his shoulder, pleading*] Jamie, for the love of God, stop it!

Then Mary speaks, and they freeze into silence again, staring at her. She has paid no attention whatever to the incident. It is simply a part of the familiar atmosphere of the room, a background which does not touch her preoccupation; and she speaks aloud to herself, not to them.

MARY. I play so badly now. I'm all out of practice. Sister Theresa will give me a dreadful scolding. She'll tell me it isn't fair to my father when he spends so much money for extra lessons. She's quite right, it isn't fair, when he's so good and generous, and so proud of me. I'll practice every day from now on. But something horrible has happened to my hands. The fingers have gotten so stiff—[*She lifts her hands to examine them with a frightened puzzlement.*] The knuckles are all swollen. They're so ugly. I'll have to go to the Infirmary and show Sister Martha. [*With a sweet smile of affectionate trust*] She's old and a little cranky, but I love her just the same, and she has things in her medicine chest that'll cure anything. She'll give me something to rub on my hands, and tell me to pray to the Blessed Virgin, and they'll be well again in no time. [*She forgets her hands and comes into the room, the wedding gown trailing on the floor. She glances around vaguely, her forehead puckered again.*] Let me see. What did I come here to find? It's terrible, how absent-minded I've become. I'm always dreaming and forgetting.

TYRONE [*in a stifled voice*]What's that she's carrying, Edmund?

EDMUND [*dully*] Her wedding gown, I suppose.

TYRONE. Christ! [*He gets to his feet and stands directly in her path—in anguish.*] Mary! Isn't it bad enough—? [*Controlling himself—gently persuasive*] Here, let me take it, dear. You'll only step on it and tear it and get it dirty dragging it on the floor. Then you'd be sorry afterwards.

She lets him take it, regarding him from somewhere far away within herself, without recognition, without either affection or animosity.

MARY [*with the shy politeness of a well-bred young girl toward an elderly gentleman who relieves her of a bundle*] Thank you. You are very kind. [*She regards the wedding gown with a puzzled interest.*] It's a wedding gown. It's very lovely, isn't it? [*A shadow crosses her face and she looks vaguely uneasy.*] I remember now. I found it in the attic hidden in a trunk. But I don't know what I wanted it for. I'm going to be a nun—that is, if I can only find—[*She looks around the room, her forehead puckered again.*] What is it I'm looking for? I know it's something I lost. [*She moves back from Tyrone, aware of him now only as some obstacle in her path.*]

TYRONE [*in hopeless appeal*] Mary!

But it cannot penetrate her preoccupation. She doesn't seem to hear him. He gives up helplessly, shrinking into himself, even his defensive drunkenness taken from him, leaving him sick and sober. He sinks back on his chair, holding the wedding gown in his arms with an unconscious clumsy, protective gentleness.

JAMIE [*drops his hand from his face, his eyes on the table top. He has suddenly sobered up, too—dully*] It's no good, Papa. [*He recites from Swinburne's "A Leave-taking" and does it well, simply but with a bitter sadness.*]

"Let us rise up and part; she will not know.
Let us go seaward as the great winds go,
Full of blown sand and foam; what help is here?
There is no help, for all these things are so,
And all the world is bitter as a tear.
And how these things are, though ye strove to show,
She would not know."

MARY [*looking around her*] Something I miss terribly. It can't be altogether lost. [*She starts to move around in back of Jamie's chair.*]

JAMIE [*turns to look up into her face—and cannot help appealing pleadingly in his turn*] Mama! [*She does not seem to hear. He looks away hopelessly.*] Hell! What's the use? It's no good. [*He recites from "A Leave-taking" again with increased bitterness.*]

"Let us go hence, my songs; she will not hear.
Let us go hence together without fear;
Keep silence now, for singing-time is over,
And over all old things and all things dear.
She loves not you nor me as all we love her.
Yea, though we sang as angels in her ear,
She would not hear."

MARY [*looking around her*] Something I need terribly. I remember when I had it I was never lonely nor afraid. I can't have lost it forever, I would die if I thought that. Because then there would be no hope. [*She moves like a sleepwalker, around the back of Jamie's chair, then forward toward left front, passing behind Edmund.*]

EDMUND [*turns impulsively and grabs her arm. As he pleads he has the quality of a bewilderedly hurt little boy*] Mama! It isn't a summer cold! I've got consumption!

MARY [*for a second he seems to have broken through to her. She trembles and her expression becomes terrified. She calls distractedly, as if giving a command to herself*] No! [*And instantly she is far away again. She murmurs gently but impersonally.*] You must not try to touch me. You must not try to hold me. It isn't right, when I am hoping to be a nun.

He lets his hand drop from her arm. She moves left to the front end of the sofa beneath the windows and sits down, facing front, her hands folded in her lap, in a demure schoolgirlish pose.

JAMIE [*gives Edmund a strange look of mingled pity and jealous gloating*] You damned fool. It's no good. [*He recites again from the Swinburne poem.*]

"Let us go hence, go hence; she will not see.
Sing all once more together; surely she,
She too, remembering days and words that were,
Will turn a little toward us, sighing; but we,
We are hence, we are gone, as though we had not been there.
Nay, and though all men seeing had pity on me,
She would not see."

TYRONE [*trying to shake off his hopeless stupor*] Oh, we're fools to pay any attention. It's the damned poison. But I've never known her to drown herself in it as deep as this. [*Gruffly*] Pass me that bottle, Jamie. And stop reciting that damned morbid poetry. I won't have it in my house!

Jamie pushes the bottle toward him. He pours a drink without disarranging the wedding gown he holds carefully over his other arm and on his lap, and shoves the bottle back. Jamie pours his and passes the bottle to Edmund, who, in turn, pours one. Tyrone lifts his glass and his sons follow suit mechanically, but before they can drink Mary speaks and they slowly lower their drinks to the table, forgetting them.

MARY [*staring dreamily before her. Her face looks extraordinarily youthful and innocent. The shyly eager, trusting smile is on her lips as she talks aloud to herself*] I had a talk with Mother Elizabeth. She is so sweet and good. A saint on earth. I love her dearly. It may be sinful of me but I love her better than my own mother. Because she always understands, even before you say a word. Her kind blue eyes look right into your heart. You can't keep any secrets from her. You couldn't deceive her, even if you were mean enough to want to. [*She gives a little rebellious toss of her head—with girlish pique.*] All the same, I don't think she was so understanding this time. I told her I wanted to be a nun. I explained how sure I was of my vocation, that I had prayed to the Blessed Virgin to make me sure, and to find me worthy. I told Mother I had had a true vision when I was praying in the shrine of Our Lady of Lourdes[10], on the little island in the lake. I said I knew, as surely as I knew I was kneeling there, that the Blessed Virgin had smiled and blessed me with her consent. But Mother Elizabeth told me I must be more sure than that, even, that I must prove it wasn't simply my imagination. She said, if I was so sure, then I wouldn't mind putting myself to a test by going home after I graduated, and living as other girls lived, going out to parties and dances and enjoying myself; and then if after a year or two I still felt sure, I could come back to see her and we would talk it over again. [*She tosses her head—indignantly.*] I never dreamed Holy Mother would give me such advice! I was really shocked. I said, of course, I would do anything she suggested, but I knew it was simply a waste of time. After I left her, I felt all mixed up, so I went to the shrine and prayed to the Blessed Virgin and found peace again because I knew she heard my prayer and would always love me and see no harm ever came to me so long as I never lost my faith in her. [*She pauses and a look of growing uneasiness comes over her face. She passes a hand over her forehead as if brushing cobwebs from her brain—vaguely.*] That was in the winter of senior year. Then in the spring something happened to me. Yes, I remember. I fell in love with James Tyrone and was so happy for a time.

She stares before her in a sad dream. Tyrone stirs in his chair. Edmund and Jamie remain motionless.

CURTAIN

NOTES

1. con man: a person who deceives other people by making them believe something false or making them give money away
2. in vino veritas: (Latin) there is truth in wine
3. Oscar Wilde's long poem "Reading Gaol" was written after his two years of imprisonment (1895–1897) for having a homosexual lover. What Jamie mentions are from its most famous stanza:
   Yet each man kills the thing he loves,
   By each let this be heard.
   Some do it with a bitter look,
   Some with a flattering word.
   The coward does it with a kiss,
   The brave man with a sword!
4. "Greater love hath no man than this...": a variant of *John* 15:13.
5. The lines are from Act One, Scene Four of William Shakespeare's *Richard III*. In that scene, the imprisoned Duke of Clarence describes a nightmare he has had in which a ghostly figure cries out these words at the sight of him.
6. The lines are from Dante Gabriel Rossetti's "A Superscription." They express the feeling of hollowness and failure in life and death.
7. *The Bells* is a play in three acts translated by Leopold Davis Lewis from the 1867 play *Le Juif Polonais* (*The Polish Jew*) by Erckmann-Chatrian.
8. Edwin Thomas Booth (1833–1893) was a most famous American actor of Shakespearean plays, who toured throughout America and the major capitals of Europe. Previously in Act Four, Tyrone tells Edmund that as a young actor, after a performance of Shakespeare's *Othello* in which he played Othello to Edwin Booth's Iago, Booth said that Tyrone was playing Othello better than he ever had himself, and that he was so touched by Booth's words that he asked the theatre manager to write them down.
9. This alludes to Act Four, Scene Four of William Shakespeare's *Hamlet*. In that scene, Gertrude hears that Ophelia has lost her sanity.
10. "Our Lady of Lourdes" refers to an image of the Blessed Virgin Mary specifically associated with the numerous appearances of her apparitions in the vicinity of Lourdes, France.

About the Playwright:

Eugene Gladstone O'Neill (October 16, 1888 – November 27, 1953) was an American playwright and Nobel laureate in Literature. The drama *Long Day's Journey into Night* is regarded as one of the finest American plays in the 20th century.

It was O'Neill's plays that first included speeches in American vernacular and involved characters on the fringes of society. These characters strive to maintain their hopes and aspirations, but ultimately slide into disillusionment and despair. Almost all his works involve some degree of tragedy and personal pessimism.

Eugene O'Neill wrote *Long Day's Journey into Night* for his wife on the occasion of their 12th wedding anniversary in 1940. The playwright wanted to create a play that would lay forth his own background in a forgiving nature, which is why he strove not to bias the play against any one character. The drama is very similar to O'Neill's family situation as a young man, but more importantly, it has become a universal play representing the problems of a family that cannot live in the present, mired in the dark recesses of a bitter, troubled past. Because of its deeply personal nature, O'Neill requested that the play be published posthumously, which meant that the play was not revealed to the world until O'Neill's death in 1956.

To be sure, O'Neill has always been seen as one of the greatest American playwrights. He was the only American dramatist to be awarded the Nobel Prize. He won the Pulitzer Prize for four times. Besides *Long Day's Journey into Night*, his other best known plays are *The Iceman Cometh*, *Mourning Becomes Electra, Ah Wilderness!, Strange Interlude,* and *The Hairy Ape.* O'Neill was a huge Broadway success during his own adult life.

Appreciation:

《长夜漫漫路迢迢》是诺贝尔文学奖得主美国剧作家尤金·奥尼尔的同名自传剧，亦是一部关于剧作家青春岁月的家庭伦理剧。1939 年暮夏，尤金·奥尼尔决心将自己家中不可告人之事以戏剧的形式无保留地公之于世。为什么呢？“他向我解释，他不能不写这部关于他青春岁月和他的家庭的戏。这些往事如同幽灵一样纠缠着他，逼他非写不可；仿佛在他心灵深处跟他在作祟，不尽心倾吐，他永远无法安宁……”奥尼尔第三任妻子卡洛泰日后回忆说。1940 年 9 月剧本脱稿后，奥尼尔却踌躇起来，不知这样做到底对不对？于是他把稿子交给兰登书屋封存，说好要等他死后 25 年再发表。1953 年，饱受身心折磨的奥尼尔在悲惨中过世。三年之后，卡洛泰决意解封，并把首演机会交给斯德哥尔摩的瑞典皇家剧院。首演结束，这一部长达四个钟头的舞台剧震撼了包括瑞典国王和王后的所有观众。报纸评论认为奥尼尔的成就已超越现代的易卜生和史特林堡，他被称为美国的“莎士比亚”。

《长夜漫漫路迢迢》讲述的是提罗恩一家的悲剧故事。提罗恩是一位十分出色的演员，但在现实生活中却是一位不折不扣的悭吝之徒。他儿时随父母从爱尔兰移民至美国，但父亲随后抛妻弃子，使得他的童年生活十分艰难，从而造就了人格缺失的提罗恩。成年之后，作为生活的不幸者，提罗恩又给自己的家庭带来了更多的不幸。

他的妻子曾经是一位美貌无双，弹得一手好钢琴的多才女子，但在婚后不得不长期跟随丈夫奔波在各个演出城市，独自一人饱尝颠沛流离之苦。尤其是第二个孩子出生后不幸遇难，提罗恩夫人的精神开始焦虑。随着埃德蒙德的出生，她身体每况愈下，亟待调理休养。但丈夫提罗恩却为了省钱，随便找了一个价格便宜的医生诊治，结果庸医竟然开出了用毒品止痛的方子，从此提罗恩夫人被迫成为“瘾君子”，长期备受煎熬，开始漫长而无望的戒毒之旅。

第一幕。提罗恩一家在早餐后，两个孩子在饭桌上继续说着玩笑话，而书房里提罗恩夫人显得容光焕发，然而变形的双手直指过去不堪的折磨。老提罗恩十分高兴妻子所表现出明显的戒毒后的健康状态。一切似乎都很美好。然而小儿子埃德蒙德生病了，且很有可能是和提罗恩夫人的父亲一样的痨病。妈妈显得有些焦虑不安，希望儿子没事。然而一切都朝着不可预知的方向发展着……

在第二幕和第三幕中，提罗恩夫人因为无法忍受过去和现在的种种，重新开始注射毒品，埃德蒙德最终被确诊为痨病，而年迈的提罗恩仍旧不管不顾地只知道买地皮，并计划着要把得了会死的病的儿子送往救济院。一系列的无望，最终在第四幕达到高潮。在酒精的作用下，提罗恩对夫人说出久抑心中的厌烦，最终在儿子的指责下他终于妥协愿意送他去好一点的疗养院。

全剧最终是提罗恩夫人的一句话结尾：那是在我毕业的那年冬天，然后，在春天的时候我遇到一件事情，是的，我想起来了……我爱上了詹姆斯·提罗恩。那时，我多么幸福啊……

该剧创作最为突出的特点为象征手法的广泛运用。例如，剧作家用雾霭的变化贯穿全剧，颇具深意。早晨，晴空万里，前天晚上的雾散了，剧中人物的心境此时也是明朗的，家庭还算和谐，夫妻逗趣，兄弟聊天，亲人间其乐融融；中午，空气渐渐变得潮湿，开始起雾，悲剧渐起，妈妈忍受不住内心焦灼的煎熬而复吸毒品；黄昏时分，雾气弥漫，妈妈内心崩溃，从而自暴自弃，同时丈夫和两个儿子也躲到外面喝酒；午夜，剧情到了高潮，矛盾也到了顶峰，妈妈彻底癫狂，而此时雾浓如铁。

Questions:

1. Discuss O'Neill's use of broken dreams in the play. What do they mean to the characters, and what do they symbolize? How are the dynamics between characters affected by broken

dreams?

2. How does the title of the play "*Long Day's Journey into Night*" impress you? What associations would you make with the title?

No Exit (Excerpt)

Wait a minute, there's a snag somewherc; something disagreeable. Why, now, should it be disagreeable?...Ah, I see; it's life without a break. (Jean Paul Sartre—Huis Clos)

…

GARCIN: What do you want of me?

ESTELLE: You can help ME, anyhow.

GARCIN: If you want help, apply to her.

ESTELLE: I implore you, Garcin—you gave me your promise, didn't you? Help me quick. I don't want to be left alone. Olga's taken him to a cabaret.

INEZ: Taken whom?

ESTELLE: Peter...Oh, now they're dancing together.

INEZ: Who's Peter?

ESTELLE: Such a silly boy. He called me his glancing stream—just fancy! He was terribly in love with me... She's persuaded him to come out with her tonight.

INEZ: Do you love him?

ESTELLE: They're sitting down now. She's puffing like a grampus. What a fool the girl is to insist on dancing! But I dare say she does it to reduce...No, of course I don't love him. He's only eighteen, and I'm not a baby-snatcher.

INEZ: Then why bother about them? What difference does it make?

ESTELLE: He belonged to me.

INEZ: Nothing on earth belongs to you any more.

ESTELLE: I tell you he was mine. All mine.

INEZ: Yes, he was yours—once. But now—try to make him hear, try to touch him. Olga can touch him, talk to him as much as she likes. That's so, isn't it? She can squeeze his hands, rub herself against him—

ESTELLE: Yes, look! She's pressing her great fat chest against him, puffing and blowing his face. But, my poor little lamb, can't you see how ridiculous she is? Why don't you laugh at her? Oh, once I'd have only had to glance at them and she'd have slunk away. Is there really nothing, nothing left of me?

INEZ: Nothing whatever. Nothing of you's left on earth—not even a shadow. All you own is here. Would you like that paper-knife? Or that ornament on the mantelpiece? That blue sofa's yours. And I, my dear, am yours forever.

ESTELLE: You mine! That's good! Well, which of you two would dare to call me his glancing stream, his crystal girl? You know too much about me, you know I'm rotten through and through... Peter, dear, think of me, fix your thoughts on me, and save me. All the time you're thinking "my glancing stream, his crystal girl," I'm only half here. I'm only half wicked, and half of me is down there with you, clean and bright and crystal-clear as running water...Oh, just look at her face, all scarlet, like a tomato. No, it's absurd, we've laughed at her together, you and I, often and often... What's that tune?—I always loved it. Yes, the "St. Louis Blues"....All right, dance away, dance away. Garcin, I wish you could see her, you'd die of laughing. Only—she'll never know I SEE her. Yes, I see you, Olga, with your hair all anyhow, and you do look like a dope, my dear. Oh, now you're treading on his toes. It's a scream! Hurry up! Quicker! Quicker! He's dragging her along, bundling her round and round—it's too ghastly! He always said I was so light, he loved to dance with me. I tell you, Olga, I can see you. No, she doesn't care, she's dancing through my gaze. What's that? What's that you said? "Our poor dear Estelle"? Oh, don't be such a humbug! You didn't even shed a tear at the funeral...And she has the nerve to talk to him about her poor dear friend Estelle! How dare she discuss me with Peter? Now then, keep time. She never could dance and talk at once. Oh, what's that? No, no. Don't tell him. Please, please don't tell him. You can keep him, do what you like with him, but please don't tell him about—that! All right. You can have him now. Isn't it FOUL, Garcin? She's told him everything, about Roger, my trip to Switzerland, the baby. "Poor Estelle wasn't exactly—" "No, I wasn't exactly—True enough." He's looking grave, shaking his head, but he doesn't seem so much surprised, not what one would expect. Keep him then—I won't haggle with you over his long eyelashes, his pretty girlish face. They're yours for the asking. His glancing stream, his crystal. Well, the crystal's shattered into bits. "Poor Estelle!" Dance, dance, dance. On with it. But do keep time. One, two. One, two. How I'd love to go down to earth for just a moment, and dance with him again. The music's growing fainter. They've turned down the lights, as they do for a tango. Why are they playing so softly? Louder, please. I can't hear. It's so far away, so far away. I—I can't hear a sound. All over. It's the end. The earth has left me. Don't turn from me—please.

Take me in your arms.

INEZ: Now then, Garcin!

GARCIN: It's to her you should say that.

ESTELLE: Don't turn away. You're a man, aren't you, and surely I'm not a fright as all that! Everyone says I've lovely hair and after all, a man killed himself on my account. You have to look at something, and there's nothing here to see except the sofas and that awful ornament and the table. Surely I'm better to look at that a lot of stupid furniture. Listen! I've dropped out of their heart like a little sparrow fallen from its nest. So gather me up, dear, fold me to your heart—and you'll see how nice I can be.

GARCIN: I tell you it's to that lady you should speak.

ESTELLE: To her? But she doesn't count, she's a woman.

INEZ: Oh, I don't count? Is that what you think? But, my poor little fallen nestling, you've been sheltering in my heart for ages, though you didn't realize it. Don't be afraid; I'll keep looking at you for ever and ever, without a flutter of my eyelids, and you'll live in my gaze like a mote in a sunbeam.

ESTELLE: A sunbeam indeed! Don't talk such rubbish! You've tried that trick already, and you should know it doesn't work.

INEZ: Estelle! My glancing stream! My crystal!

ESTELLE: YOUR crystal? It's grotesque. Do you think you can fool me with that sort of talk? Everyone know by now what I did to my baby. The crystal's shattered, but I don't care. I'm just a hollow dummy, all that's left of me is the outside—but it's not for you.

INEZ: Come to me, Estelle. You shall be whatever you like: a glancing stream, a muddy stream. And deep down in my eyes you'll see yourself just as you want to be.

ESTELLE: Oh, leave me in peace. You haven't any eyes. Oh, damn it, isn't there anything I can do to get rid of you? I've an idea. (Spits in Garcin's face.) There!

INEZ: Garcin, you shall pay for this.

GARCIN: So it's a man you need?

ESTELLE: Not any man. You.

GARCIN: No humbug now. Any man would do your business. As I happen to be here, you want me. Right! Mind, I'm not your sort at all, really; I'm not a young nincompoop and I don't dance the tango.

ESTELLE: I'll take you as you are. And perhaps I shall change you.

GARCIN: I doubt it. I shan't pay much attention; I've other things to think about.

ESTELLE: What things?

GARCIN: They wouldn't interest you.

ESTELLE: I'll sit on your sofa and wait for you to take some notice of me. I promise not to bother you at all.

INEZ: That's right, fawn on him, like the silly bitch you are. Grovel and cringe! And he hasn't even good looks to commend him!

ESTELLE: Don't listen to her. She has no eyes, no ears. She's—nothing.

GARCIN: I'll give you what I can. It doesn't amount to much. I shan't love you; I know you too well.

ESTELLE: Do you want me, anyhow?

GARCIN: Yes.

ESTELLE: I ask no more.

GARCIN: In that case—

INEZ: Estelle! Garcin! You must be going crazy. You're not alone. I'm here too.

GARCIN: Of course—but what does it matter?

INEZ: Under my eyes? You couldn't—couldn't do it.

ESTELLE: Why not? I often undressed with my maid looking on.

INEZ: Let her alone. Don't paw her with your dirty man's hands.

GARCIN: Take care. I'm no gentleman, and I'd have no compunction about striking a woman.

INEZ: But you promised me; you promised. I'm only asking you to keep your word.

GARCIN: Why should I, considering you were the first to break our agreement?

INEZ: Very well, have it your own way. I'm the weaker party, one against two. But don't forget I'm here, and watching. I shan't take my eyes off you, Garcin; when you're kissing her, you'll feel them boring into you. Yes, have it your own way, make love and get it over. We're in hell; my turn will come.

GARCIN: Now then. Your lips. Give me your lips.

ESTELLE: Really! Didn't I tell you not to pay attention to her?

GARCIN: You've got it wrong. It's Gomez; he's back in the press-room. They've shut the windows; it must be winter down there. Six months since I—Well, I warned you I'd be absent-minded sometimes, didn't I? They're shivering, they've kept their coats on. Funny they should feel the cold like that, when I'm feeling so hot. Ah, this time he's talking about me.

ESTELLE: Is it going to last long? You might at least tell me what he's saying.

GARCIN: Nothing. Nothing worth repeating. He's a swine, that's all. A god-damned bloody swine. Let's come back to—to ourselves. Are you going to love me?

ESTELLE: I wonder now!

GARCIN: Will you trust me?

ESTELLE: What a quaint thing to ask! Considering you'll be under my eyes all the time, and I don't think I've much to fear from Inez, so far as you're concerned.

GARCIN: Obviously. I was thinking of another kind of trust. Talk away, talk away, you swine. I'm not there to defend myself. Estelle, you MUST give me your trust.

ESTELLE: Oh, what a nuisance you are! I'm giving you my mouth, my arms, my whole body—and everything could be so simple...My trust! I haven't any to give, I'm afraid, and you're making me terribly embarrassed. You must have something pretty ghastly on your conscience to make such a fuss about my trusting you.

GARCIN: They shot me.

ESTELLE: I know. Because you refused to fight. Well, why shouldn't you?

GARCIN: I—I didn't exactly refuse. I must say he talks well, he makes out a good case against me, but he never says what I should have done instead. Should I have gone to the general and said: "General, I decline to fight"? A mug's game; they'd have promptly locked me up. But I wanted to show my colors, my true colors, do you understand? I wasn't going to be silenced. So I—I took the train.... They caught me at the frontier.

ESTELLE: Where were you trying to go?

GARCIN: To Mexico. I meant to launch a pacifist newspaper down there. Well, why don't you speak?

ESTELLE: What could I say? You acted quite rightly, as you didn't want to fight. But, darling, how on earth can I guess what you want me to answer?

INEZ: Can't you guess? Well, I can. He wants you to tell him that he bolted like a lion. For "bolt" he did, and that's what biting him.

GARCIN: "Bolted," "went away,"—we won't quarrel over words.

ESTELLE: But you had to run away. If you'd stayed they'd have sent you to jail, wouldn't they?

GARCIN: Of course. Well, Estelle, am I a coward?

ESTELLE: How can I say? Don't be so unreasonable, darling. I can't put myself in your skin. You must decide that for yourself.

GARCIN: I can't decide.

ESTELLE: Anyway, you must remember. You must have had reasons for acting as you did.

GARCIN: I had.

ESTELLE: Well?

GARCIN: But were they the real reasons?

ESTELLE: You've a twisted mind, that's your trouble. Plaguing yourself over such trifles!

GARCIN: I'd thought it all out, and I wanted to make a stand. But was that my real motive?

INEZ: Exactly. That's the question. Was that your real motive? No doubt you argued it out with yourself, you weighed the pros and cons, you found good reasons for what you did. But fear and hatred and all the dirty little instincts one keeps dark—they're motives too. So carry on, Mr. Garcin, and try to be honest with yourself—for once.

GARCIN: Do I really need you to tell me that? Day and night I paced my cell, from the window to the door, from the door to the window. I pried into my heart, I sleuthed myself like a detective. By the end of it I felt as if I'd given my whole life to introspection. But always I harked back to the one thing certain—that I had acted as I did, I'd taken that train to the frontier. But why? Why? Finally I thought: My death will settle it. If I face death courageously, I'll prove I am no coward.

INEZ: And how did you face death?

GARCIN: Miserably. Rottenly. Oh, it was only a physical lapse—that might happen to anyone; I'm not ashamed of it. Only everything's been left in suspense forever. Come here, Estelle. Look at me. I want to feel someone looking at me while they're talking about me on earth... I like green eyes.

INEZ: Green eyes! Just hark to him! And you, Estelle, do you like cowards?

ESTELLE: If you knew how little I care! Coward or hero, it's all one—provided he kisses well.

GARCIN: There they are, slumped in their chairs, sucking at their cigars. Bored they look. Half-asleep. They're thinking: "Garcin's a coward." But only vaguely, dreamily. One's got to think of something. "That chap Garcin was a coward." That's what they've decided, those dear friends of mine. In six months' time they'll be saying: "Cowardly as that skunk Garcin." You're lucky, you two; no one on earth is giving you another thought. But I—I'm long in dying.

INEZ: What about your wife, Garcin?

GARCIN: Oh, didn't I tell you? She's dead.

INEZ: Dead?

GARCIN: Yes, she died just now. About two months ago.

INEZ: Of grief?

GARCIN: What else should she die of? So all is for the best, you see; the war's over, my wife's dead, and I've carved out my place in history.

ESTELLE: My poor darling! Look at me. Please look. Touch me. Touch me. There! Keep your hand there. No, don't move. Why trouble what those men are thinking? They'll die off one by one. Forget them. There's only me, now.

GARCIN: But THEY won't forget me, not they! They'll die, but others will come after them to carry on the legend. I've left my fate in their hands.

ESTELLE: You think too much, that's your trouble.

GARCIN: What else is there to do now? I was a man of action once... Oh, if only I could be with them again, for just one day—I'd fling their lie in their teeth. But I'm locked out; they're passing judgment on my life without troubling about me, and they're right, because I'm dead. Dead and done with. A back number.

ESTELLE: Garcin.

GARCIN: Still there? Now listen! I want you to do me a service. No, don't shrink away. I know it must seem strange to you, having someone asking you for help; you're not used to that. But if you'll make the effort, if you'll only WILL it hard enough, I dare say we can really love each other. Look at it this way. A thousand of them are proclaiming I'm a coward; but what do numbers matter? If there's someone, just one person, to say quite positively I did not run away, that I'm not the sort who runs away, that I'm brave and decent and the rest of it—well, that one person's faith would save me. Will you have that faith in me? Then I shall love you and cherish you for ever. Estelle—will you?

ESTELLE: Oh, you dear silly man, do you think I could love a coward?

GARCIN: But just now you said—

ESTELLE: I was only teasing you. I like men, my dear, who're real men, with tough skin and strong hands. You haven't a coward's chin, or a coward's mouth, or a coward's voice, or a coward's hair. And it's for your mouth, your hair, your voice, I love.

GARCIN: Do you mean this? REALLY mean it?

ESTELLE: Shall I swear it?

GARCIN: Then I snap my fingers at them all, those below and those in here. Estelle, we shall climb out of hell. (Inez laughs.) What's that?

INEZ: But she doesn't mean a word of what she says. How can you be such a simpleton? "Estelle, am I a coward?" As if she cared a damn either way.

ESTELLE: Inez, how dare you? Don't listen to her. If you want me to have faith in you, you must begin by trusting me.

INEZ: That's right! That's right! Trust away! She wants a man—that far you can trust her—she wants a man's arm round her waist, a man's smell, a man's eyes glowing with desire. And that's all she wants. She'd assure you you were God Almighty if she thought it would give you pleasure.

GARCIN: Estelle, is it true? Answer me. Is it true?

ESTELLE: What do you expect me to say? Don't you realize how maddening it is to have to answer questions one can't make head or tail of? You do make things difficult...Anyhow, I'd love you just the same, even if you were a coward. Isn't that enough?

GARCIN: You disgust me, both of you.

ESTELLE: What are you up to?

GARCIN: I'm going.

INEZ: You won't get far. The door is locked.

GARCIN: I'll MAKE them open it.

ESTELLE: Please! Please!

INEZ: Don't worry, my pet. The bell doesn't work.

GARCIN: I tell you they shall open. I can't endure it any longer, I'm through with you both. Go away.(to Estelle) You're even fouler than she. I won't let myself get bogged in your eyes. You're soft and slimy. Ugh! Like an octopus. Like a quagmire.

ESTELLE: I beg you, oh, I beg you not to leave me. I'll promise not to speak again, I won't trouble you in any way—but don't go. I daren't be left alone with Inez, now she's shown her claws.

GARCIN: Look after yourself. I never asked you to come here.

ESTELLE: Oh, how mean you are! Yes, it's quite true you're a coward.

INEZ: Well, my little sparrow fallen from the nest, I hope you're satisfied now. You spat in my face—playing up to him, of course—and we had a tiff on his account. But he's going, and a good riddance it will be. We two women will have the place to ourselves.

ESTELLE: You won't gain anything. If that door opens, I'm going too.

INEZ: Where?

ESTELLE: I don't care where. As far from you as I can.

GARCIN: Open the door! Open, blast you! I'll endure anything, your red-hot tongs and molten lead, your racks and prongs and garrotes—all your fiendish gadgets, everything that burns and flays and tears—I'll put up with any torture you impose. Anything, anything would be better than this agony of mind, this creeping pain that gnaws and fumbles and caresses one and never hurts quite enough. Now will you open? (THE DOOR FLIES OPEN: a long silence.)

INEZ: Well, Garcin? You're free to go.

GARCIN: Now I wonder why that door opened.

INEZ: What are you waiting for? Hurry up and go.

GARCIN: I shall not go.

INEZ: And you, Estelle? So what? Which shall it be? Which of the three of us will leave? The barrier's down, why are we waiting? But what a situation! It's a scream! We're inseparables!

ESTELLE: Inseparables? Garcin, come and lend a hand. Quickly. We'll push her out and slam the door on her. That'll teach her a lesson.

INEZ: (Struggling with Inez) Estelle, I beg you, let me stay. I won't go, I won't go! Not into the passage.

GARCIN: Let go of her.

ESTELLE: You're crazy. She hates you.

GARCIN: It's because of her I'm staying here.

INEZ: Because of me? All right, shut the door. It's ten times hotter here since it opened. Because of me, you said?

GARCIN: Yes. YOU, anyhow, know what it means to be a coward.

INEZ: Yes, I know.

GARCIN: And you know what wickedness is, and shame, and fear. There were days when you peered into yourself, into the secret places of your heart, and what you saw there made you faint with horror. And then, next day, you didn't know what to make of it, you couldn't interpret the horror you had glimpsed the day before. Yes, you know what evil costs. And when you say I'm a coward, you know from experience what that means. Is that so?

INEZ: Yes.

GARCIN: So it's you whom I have to convince; you are of my kind. Did you suppose I meant to go? No, I couldn't leave you here, gloating over my defeat, with all those thoughts about me running in your head.

INEZ: Do you really wish to convince me?

GARCIN: That's the one and only thing I wish for now. I can't hear them any longer, you know. Probably that means they're through with me. For good and all. The curtain's down, nothing of me is left on earth—not even the name of coward. So, Inez, we're alone. Only you two remain to give a thought to me. She—she doesn't count. It's you who matter; you who hate me. If you'll have faith in me, I'm saved.

INEZ: It won't be easy. Have a look at me. I'm a hard-headed woman.

GARCIN: I'll give you all the time that's needed.

INEZ: Yes, we've lots of time in hand. ALL time.

GARCIN: Listen! Each man has an aim in life, a leading motive; that's so, isn't it? Well, I didn't give a damn for wealth, or for love. I aimed at being a real man. A tough, as they say. I staked everything on the same horse... Can one possibly be a coward when one's deliberately courted danger at every turn? And can judge a life by a single action?

INEZ: Why not? For thirty years you dreamt you were a hero, and condoned a thousand petty lapses—because a hero, of course, can do no wrong. An easy method, obviously. Then a day came when you were up against it, the red light of real danger—and you took the train to Mexico.

GARCIN: I "dreamt," you say. It was no dream. When I chose the hardest path, I made my choice deliberately. A man is what he wills himself to be.

INEZ: Prove it. Prove it was no dream. It's what one does, and nothing else, that shows the stuff one's made of.

GARCIN: I died too soon. I wasn't allowed time to—to do my deeds.

INEZ: One always dies too soon—or too late. And yet one's whole life is complete at that moment, with a line drawn neatly under it, ready for the summing up. You are—your life, and nothing else.

GARCIN: What a poisonous woman you are! With an answer for everything.

INEZ: Now then! Don't lose heart. It shouldn't be so hard, convincing me. Pull yourself together, man, rake up some arguments. Ah, wasn't I right when I said you were vulnerable? Now you're going to pay the price, and what a price! You're a coward, Garcin, because I wish it! I wish it—do you hear?—I wish it. And yet, just look at me, see how weak I am, a mere breath on the air, a gaze observing you, a formless thought that thinks you. Ah, they're open now, those big hands, those coarse, man's hands! But what do you hope to do? You can't throttle thoughts with hands. So you've no choice, you must convince me, and you're at my mercy.

ESTELLE: Garcin!

GARCIN: What?

ESTELLE: Revenge yourself.

GARCIN: How?

ESTELLE: Kiss me, darling—then you'll hear her squeal.

GARCIN: That's true, Inez. I'm at your mercy, but you're at mine as well.

INEZ: Oh, you coward, you weakling, running to women to console you!

ESTELLE: That's right, Inez. Squeal away.

INEZ: What a lovely pair you make! If you could see his big paw splayed out on your back, rucking up your skin and creasing the silk. Be careful, though! He's perspiring, his hand will leave a blue stain on your dress.

ESTELLE: Squeal away, Inez, squeal away!...Hug me tight, darling; tighter still—that'll finish her off, and a good thing too!

INEZ: Yes, Garcin, she's right. Carry on with it, press her to you till you feel your bodies melting into each other; a lump of warm, throbbing flesh... Loe's a grand solace, isn't it, my friend? Deep and dark as sleep. But I'll see you don't sleep.

ESTELLE: Don't listen to her. Press your lips to my mouth. Oh, I'm yours, yours, yours.

INEZ: Well, what are you waiting for? Do as you're told. What a lovely scene: coward Garcin holding baby-killer Estelle in his manly arms! Make your stakes, everyone. Will coward Garcin kiss the lady, or won't he dare? What's the betting? I'm watching you, everybody's watching, I'm a crowd all by myself. Do you hear the crowd? Do you hear them muttering, Garcin? "Coward! Coward!"—that's what they're saying...It's no use trying to escape, I'll never let you go. What do you hope to get from her silly lips? Forgetfulness? But I shan't forget you, not I! "It's I you must convince." So come to me. I'm waiting. Come along, now...Look how obedient he is, like a well-trained dog who comes when his mistress calls. You can't hold him, and you never will.

GARCIN: Will night never come?

INEZ: Never.

GARCIN: You will always see me?

INEZ: Always.

GARCIN: This bronze. Yes, now's the moment; I'm looking at this thing on the mantelpiece, and I understand that I'm in hell. I tell you, everything's been throughout beforehand. They knew I'd stand at the fireplace stroking this thing of bronze, with all those eyes intent on me. Devouring me. What? Only two of you? I thought there were more; many more. So this is hell. I'd never have believed it. You remember all we were told about the torture-chambers, the fire and brimstone, the "burning marl." Old wives' tales! There's no need for red-hot pokers. HELL IS—OTHER PEOPLE!

ESTELLE: My darling! Please—

GARCIN: No, let me be. She is between us. I cannot love you when she's watching.

ESTELLE: Right! In that case, I'll stop her watching. (She picks up the PAPER knife and stabs Inez several times.)

INEZ: But, you crazy creature, what do you think you're doing? You know quite well I'm dead.

ESTELLE: Dead?

INEZ: Dead! Dead! Dead! Knives, poison, ropes—useless. It has happened already, do you understand? Once and for all. So here we are, forever.

ESTELLE: Forever. My God, how funny! Forever.

GARCIN: For ever, and ever, and ever.

(A long silence.)

GARCIN: Well, well, let's get on with it...

About the Playwright:

Jean-Paul Charles Aymard Sartre (June 21, 1905 –April 15, 1980) was a French philosopher, playwright, novelist, political activist, biographer, and literary critic. He was one of the key figures in the philosophy of existentialism and phenomenology, and one of the leading figures in 20th-century French philosophy and Marxism.

Sartre was also noted for his open relationship with prominent feminist and fellow existentialist philosopher and writer Simone de Beauvoir. Together, Sartre and de Beauvoir challenged the cultural and social assumptions and expectations of their upbringings, which they considered bourgeois, in both lifestyle and thought.

The conflict between oppressive, spiritually destructive conformity and an "authentic" way of "being" became the dominant theme of Sartre's early work, a theme embodied in his principal philosophical work *Being and Nothingness* (1943). Sartre's introduction to his philosophy is his work *Existentialism and Humanism* (1946), originally presented as a lecture.

He was awarded the 1964 Nobel Prize in Literature but refused it, saying that he always declined official honours and that "a writer should not allow himself to be turned into an institution."

Appreciation:

《密室》是法国哲学家、戏剧家萨特于1944年创作的剧本。《密室》剧情发生的地点是一间地狱里的房间，剧中有三个鬼魂：被处决的逃兵叛徒加尔散，勾引并折磨弟弟的妻子以致被弟妻开煤气谋杀了的变态女同性恋者伊内斯，溺死了私生子的艾丝黛尔。三个鬼魂生活在同一间密室里，相互交往，但这种交往是一种互相的折磨和纠缠。只要有两个鬼魂在一起表示亲近，第三个就会过来破坏。这是一种绝妙的平衡关系，就如伊内斯所说："我们当中的每一个人都是另外两个人的刽子手。"在相互折磨至巅峰的时候，本来纳闷为什么地狱里没有刑具的加尔散明白了，"无需赤热的烤架，地狱就是他人！"

1946年萨特在一篇以英文发表的文章中指出该剧的创作特点："我们的剧作是激烈而短促的，仅围绕一个事件展开，只有很少的几名演员。故事常被压缩在很短的时间内，有时仅几个小时。因为它遵循一种稍加更新变换的'三一律'。（剧中）只有一个布景，几次上下场以及剧中人满怀激情为捍卫个人的权利而进行的激烈辩论。"此外，该剧所使用的语言是通俗易懂的，使观众更易于理解萨特深奥的哲学观点，产生强烈共鸣，这使该剧获得巨大成功，成为萨特戏剧的代表作。本剧是他所创作的戏剧作品中最受欢迎、上演次数最多的剧目。

Questions:

1. Examine the masculine-feminine dynamic in the play. What does Sartre seem to be saying about the battle of the sexes? Is it even important that Inez and Estelle are women, and Garcin a man? Is Sartre's argument gender-based or gender-neutral?

2. Analyze the play's title. Be sure to consider the original French: *Huis Clos*.

The Dumb Waiter (Excerpt)

Scene: *A basement room. Two beds, flat against the back wall. A serving hatch*[1]*, closed, between the beds. A door to the kitchen and lavatory, left. A door to a passage, right.*

…

BEN. Are you feeling all right?

GUS. Sure.

BEN. Go and make the tea.

GUS. Yes, sure.

GUS *exits, left,* BEN *looks after him. He then takes his revolver from under the pillow and checks it for ammunition.* GUS *re-enters.*

The gas has gone out.

BEN. Well, what about it?

GUS. There's a meter.

BEN. I haven't got any money.

GUS. Nor have I.

BEN. You'll have to wait.

GUS. What for?

BEN. For Wilson.

GUS. He might not come. He might just send a message. He doesn't always come.

BEN. Well, you'll have to do without it, won't you?

GUS. Blimey[2].

BEN. You'll have a cup of tea afterwards. What's the matter with you?

GUS. I like to have one before.

BEN *holds the revolver up to the light and polishes it.*

BEN. You'd better get ready anyway.

GUS. Well, I don't know, that's a bit much, you know, for my money.

He picks up a packet of tea from the bed and throws it into the bag.

I hope he's got a shilling, anyway, if he comes. He's entitled to have. After all, it's his place, he could have seen there was enough gas for a cup of tea.

BEN. What do you mean, it's his place?

GUS. Well, isn't it?

BEN. He's probably only rented it. It doesn't have to be his place.

GUS. I know it's his place. I bet the whole house is. He's not even laying on any gas now either.

GUS *sits on his bed.*

It's his place all right. Look at all the other places. You go to this address, there's a key there, there's a teapot, there's never a soul in sight—(*He pauses.*) Eh, nobody ever hears a thing, have you ever thought of that? We never get any complaints, do we, too much noise or anything like that? You never see a soul, do you?—except the bloke who comes. You ever noticed that? I wonder if the walls are sound-proof. (*He touches the wall above his bed.*) Can't tell. All you do is wait, eh? Half the time he doesn't even bother to put in an appearance, Wilson.

BEN. Why should he? He's a busy man.

GUS (*thoughtfully*). I find him hard to talk to, Wilson. Do you know that, Ben?

BEN. Scrub round it[3], will you?

Pause.

GUS. There are a number of things I want to ask him. But I can never get round to it, when I see him.

Pause.

I've been thinking about the last one.

BEN. What last one?

GUS. That girl.

BEN *grabs the paper, which he reads.*

(*Rising, looking down at* BEN). How many times have you read that paper?

BEN *slams the paper down and rises.*

BEN (*angrily*). What do you mean?

GUS. I was just wondering how many times you'd—

BEN. What are you doing, criticizing me?

GUS. No, I was just—

BEN. You'll get a swipe[4] round your earhole if you don't watch your step.

GUS. Now look here, Ben—

BEN. I'm not looking anywhere! (*He addresses the room.*) How many times have I—! A bloody liberty[5]!

GUS. I didn't mean that.

BEN. You just get on with it, mate. Get on with it, that's all.

BEN *gets back on the bed.*

GUS. I was just thinking about that girl, that's all.

GUS *sits on his bed.*

She wasn't much to look at, I know, but still. It was a mess though, wasn't it? What a mess. Honest, I can't remember a mess like that one. They don't seem to hold together like men, women. A looser texture, like. Didn't she spread, eh? She didn't half spread. Kaw! But I've been meaning to ask you.

BEN *sits up and clenches*[6] *his eyes.*

Who clears up after we've gone? I'm curious about that. Who does the clearing up? Maybe they don't clear up. Maybe they just leave them there, eh? What do you think? How many jobs have we done? Blimey, I can't count them. What if they never clear anything up after we've gone.

BEN (*pityingly*). You mutt. Do you think we're the only branch of this organization? Have a bit of common[7]. They got departments for everything.

GUS. What cleaners and all?

BEN. You birk[8]!

GUS. No, it was that girl made me start to think—

There is a loud clatter and racket in the bulge of wall between the beds, of something descending. They grab their revolvers, jump up and face the wall. The noise comes to a stop. Silence. They look at each other. BEN *gestures sharply towards the wall.* GUS *approaches the wall slowly. He bangs it with his revolver. It is hollow.* BEN *moves to the head of his bed, his revolver cocked.* GUS *puts his revolver on his bed and pats along the bottom of the centre panel. He finds a rim. He lifts the panel. Disclosed is a serving-hatch, a "dumb waiter." A wide box is held by pulleys.* GUS *peers into the box. He brings out a piece of paper.*

BEN. What is it?

GUS. You have a look at it.

BEN. Read it.

GUS (*reading*). Two braised[9] steak and chips. Two sago[10] puddings. Two teas without sugar.

BEN. Let me see that. (*He takes the paper.*)

GUS (*to himself*). Two teas without sugar.

BEN. Mmnn.

GUS. What do you think of that?

BEN. Well—

The box goes up. BEN *levels his revolver.*

GUS. Give us a chance! They're in a hurry, aren't they?

BEN *re-reads the note.* GUS *looks over his shoulder.*

That's a bit—that's a bit funny, isn't it?

BEN (*quickly*). No. It's not funny. It probably used to be a café here, that's all. Upstairs. These places change hands very quickly.

GUS. A café?

BEN. Yes.

GUS. What, you mean this was the kitchen, down here?

BEN. Yes, they change hands overnight, these places. Go into liquidation. The people who run it, you know, they don't find it a going concern[11], they move out.

GUS. You mean the people who ran this place didn't find it a going concern and moved out?

BEN. Sure.

GUS. WELL, WHO'S GOT IT NOW?

Silence.

BEN. What do you mean, who's got it now?

GUS. Who's got it now? If they moved out, who moved in?

BEN. Well, that all depends—

The box descends with a clatter and bang. BEN *levels his revolver.* GUS *goes to the box and brings out a piece of paper.*

GUS (*reading*). Soup of the day. Liver and onions. Jam tart[12].

A pause. GUS *looks at* BEN. BEN *takes the note and reads it. He walks slowly to the hatch.* GUS *follows.* BEN *looks into the hatch but not up it.* GUS *puts his hand on* BEN*'S shoulder.* BEN *throws it off.* GUS *puts his finger to his mouth. He leans on the hatch and swiftly looks up it.* BEN *flings him away in alarm.* BEN *looks at the note. He throws his revolver on the bed and* *speaks with decision.*

BEN. We'd better send something up.

GUS. Eh?

BEN. We'd better send something up.

GUS. Oh! Yes. Yes. Maybe you're right.

They are both relieved at the decision.

BEN (*purposefully*). Quick! What have you got in that bag?

GUS. Not much.

GUS *goes to the hatch and shouts up it.*

Wait a minute!

BEN. Don't do that!

GUS *examines the contents of the bag and brings them out, one by one.*

GUS. Biscuits. A bar of chocolate. Half a pint of milk.

BEN. That all?

GUS. Packet of tea.

BEN. Good.

GUS. We can't send the tea. That's all the tea we've got.

BEN. Well, there's no gas. You can't do anything with it, can you?

GUS. Maybe they can send us down a bob[13].

BEN. What else is there?

GUS (*reaching into bag*). One Eccles cake[14].

BEN. One Eccles cake?

GUS. Yes.

BEN. You never told me you had an Eccles cake.

GUS. Didn't I?

BEN. Why only one? Didn't you bring one for me?

GUS. I didn't think you'd be keen.

BEN. Well, you can't send up one Eccles cake, anyway.

GUS. Why not?

BEN. Fetch one of those plates.

GUS. All right.

GUS *goes towards the door, left, and stops.*

Do you mean I can keep the Eccles cake then?

BEN. Keep it?

GUS. Well, they don't know we've got it, do they?

BEN. That's not the point.

GUS. Can't I keep it?

BEN. No, you can't. Get the plate.

GUS *exits, left.* BEN *looks in the bag. He brings out a packet of crisps*[15]. *Enter* GUS *with a plate.*

(*Accusingly, holding up the crisps*). Where did these come from?

GUS. What?

BEN. Where did these crisps come from?

GUS. Where did you find them?

BEN (*hitting him on the shoulder*). You're playing a dirty game, my lad!

GUS. I only eat those with beer!

BEN. Well, where were you going to get the beer?

GUS. I was saving them till I did.

BEN. I'll remember this. Put everything on the plate.

They pile everything on to the plate. The box goes up without the plate.

Wait a minute!

They stand.

GUS. It's gone up.

BEN. It's all your stupid fault, playing about!

GUS. What do we do now?

BEN. We'll have to wait till it comes down.

BEN *puts the plate on the bed, puts on his shoulder holster*[16], *and starts to put on his tie.*

You'd better get ready.

GUS *goes to his bed, puts on his tie, and starts to fix his holster.*

GUS. Hey, Ben.

BEN. What?

GUS. What's going on here?

Pause.

BEN. What do you mean?

GUS. How can this be a café?

BEN. It used to be a café.

GUS. Have you seen the gas stove?

BEN. What about it?

GUS. It's only got three rings.

BEN. So what?

GUS. Well, you couldn't cook much on three rings, not for a busy place like this.

BEN (*irritably*). That's why the service is slow!

BEN *puts on his waistcoat.*

GUS. Yes, but what happens when we're not here? What do they do then? All these menus coming down and nothing going up. It might have been going on like this for years.

BEN *brushes his jacket.*

What happens when we go?

BEN *puts on his jacket.*

They can't do much business.

The box descends. They turn about. GUS *goes to the hatch and brings out a note.*

GUS (*reading*). Macaroni Pastitsio. Ormitha Macarounada.[17]

BEN. What was that?

GUS. Macaroni Pastitsio. Ormitha Macarounada.

BEN. Greek dishes.

GUS. No.

BEN. That's right.

GUS. That's pretty high class.

BEN. Quick before it goes up.

GUS *puts the plate in the box.*

GUS (*calling up the hatch*). Three McVitie and Price! One Lyons Red Label! One Smith's Crisps! One Eccles cake! One Fruit and Nut[18]!

BEN. Cadbury's[19].

GUS (*up the hatch*). Cadbury's!

BEN (*handing the milk*). One bottle of milk.

GUS (*up the hatch*). One bottle of milk! Half a pint! (*He looks at the label.*) Express Dairy! (*He puts the bottle in the box.*)

The box goes up.

Just did it.

BEN. You shouldn't shout like that.

GUS. Why not?

BEN. It isn't done.

BEN *goes to his bed.*

Well, that should be all right, anyway, for the time being.

GUS. You think so, eh?

BEN. Get dressed, will you? It'll be any minute now.

GUS *puts on his waistcoat.* BEN *lies down and looks up at the ceiling.*

GUS. This is some place. No tea and no biscuits.

BEN. Eating makes you lazy, mate. You're getting lazy, you know that? You don't want to get slack[20] on your job.

GUS. Who me?

BEN. Slack, mate, slack.

GUS. Who me? Slack?

BEN. Have you checked your gun? You haven't even checked your gun. It looks disgraceful, anyway. Why don't you ever polish it?

GUS *rubs his revolver on the sheet.* BEN *takes out a pocket mirror and straightens his tie.*

GUS. I wonder where the cook is. They must have had a few, to cope with that. Maybe they had a few more gas stoves. Eh! Maybe there's another kitchen along the passage.

BEN. Of course there is! Do you know what it takes to make an Ormitha Macarounada?

GUS. No, what?

BEN. An Ormitha—! Buck your ideas up[21], will you?

GUS. Takes a few cooks, eh?

GUS *puts his revolver in its holster.*

The sooner we're out of this place the better.

He puts on his jacket.

Why doesn't he get in touch? I feel like I've been here years. (*He takes his revolver out of its holster to check the ammunition.*) We've never let him down though, have we? We've never let him down. I was thinking only the other day, Ben. We're reliable, aren't we?

He puts his revolver back in its holster.

Still, I'll be glad when it's over tonight.

He brushes his jacket.

I hope the bloke's not going to get excited tonight, or anything. I'm feeling a bit off[22]. I've got a splitting headache.

Silence.

The box descends. BEN *jumps up.*

Gus *collects the note.*

(*Reading.*) One Bamboo Shoots, Water Chestnuts and Chicken. One Char Siu and

Beansprouts.[23]

BEN. Beansprouts?

GUS. Yes.

BEN. Blimey.

GUS. I wouldn't know where to begin.

He looks back at the box. The packet of tea is inside it. He picks it up.

They've sent back the tea.

BEN (*anxious*). What'd they do that for?

GUS. Maybe it isn't tea-time.

The box goes up. Silence.

BEN (*throwing the tea on the bed, and speaking urgently*). Look here. We'd better tell them.

GUS. Tell them what?

BEN. That we can't do it, we haven't got it.

GUS. All right then.

BEN. Lend us your pencil. We'll write a note.

GUS, *turning for a pencil, suddenly discovers the speaking-tube*[24]*, which hangs on the right wall of the hatch facing his bed.*

GUS. What's this?

BEN. What?

GUS. This.

BEN (*examining it*). This? It's a speaking-tube.

GUS. How long has that been there?

BEN. Just the job. We should have used it before, instead of shouting up there.

GUS. Funny I never noticed it before.

BEN. Well, come on.

GUS. What do you do?

BEN. See that? That's a whistle.

GUS. What, this?

BEN. Yes, take it out. Pull it out.

GUS *does so.*

That's it.

GUS. What do we do now?

BEN. Blow into it.

GUS. Blow?

BEN. It whistles up there if you blow. Then they know you want to speak. Blow.

GUS *blows. Silence.*

GUS (*tube at mouth*). I can't hear a thing.

BEN. Now you speak! Speak into it!

GUS *looks at* BEN, *then speaks into the tube.*

GUS. The larder's[25] bare!

BEN. Give me that!

He grabs the tube and puts it to his mouth.

(*Speaking with great deference.*) Good evening. I'm sorry to—bother you, but we just thought we'd better let you know that we haven't got anything left. We sent up all we had. There's no more food down here.

He brings the tube slowly to his ear.

What?

To mouth.

What?

To ear. He listens. To mouth.

No, all we had we sent up.

To ear. He listens. To mouth.

Oh, I'm very sorry to hear that.

To ear. He listens. To GUS.

The Eccles cake was stale.

He listens. To GUS.

The chocolate was melted.

He listens. To GUS.

The milk was sour.

GUS. What about the crisps?

BEN (*listening*). The biscuits were mouldy.

He glares at GUS. *Tube to mouth.*

Well, we're very sorry about that.

Tube to ear.

What?

To mouth.

What?

To ear.

Yes. Yes.

To mouth.

Yes certainly. Certainly. Right away.

To ear. The voice has ceased. He hangs up the tube.

(*Excitedly*). Did you hear that?

GUS. What?

BEN. You know what he said? Light the kettle! Not put on the kettle! Not light the gas! But light the kettle!

GUS. How can we light the kettle?

BEN. What do you mean?

GUS. There's no gas.

BEN (*clapping hand to head*). Now what do we do?

GUS. What did he want us to light the kettle for?

BEN. For tea. He wanted a cup of tea.

GUS. He wanted a cup of tea! What about me? I've been wanting a cup of tea all night!

BEN (*despairingly*). What do we do now?

GUS. What are we supposed to drink?

BEN *sits on his bed, staring.*

What about us?

BEN *sits.*

I'm thirsty too. I'm starving. And he wants a cup of tea. That beats the band[26], that does.

BEN *lets his head sink on to his chest.*

I could do with a bit of sustenance[27] myself. What about you? You look as if you could do with something too.

GUS *sits on his bed.*

We send him up all we've got and he's not satisfied. No, honest, it's enough to make the cat laugh. Why did you send him up all that stuff? (*Thoughtfully.*) Why did I send it up?

Pause.

Who knows what he's got upstairs? He's probably got a salad bowl. They must have something up there. They won't get much from down here. You notice they didn't ask for any salads? They've probably got a salad bowl up there. Cold meat, radishes, cucumbers. Watercress. Roll mops.[28]

Pause.

Hardboiled eggs.

Pause.

The lot. They've probably got a crate of beer too. Probably eating my crisps with a pint of beer now. Didn't have anything to say about those crisps, did he? They do all right, don't worry about that. You don't think they're just going to sit there and wait for stuff to come up from down here, do you? That'll get them nowhere.

Pause.

They do all right.

Pause.

And he wants a cup of tea.

Pause.

That's past a joke, in my opinion.

He looks over at BEN, *rises, and goes to him.*

What's the matter with you? You don't look too bright. I feel like an Alka-Seltzer[29] myself.

BEN *sits up.*

BEN (*in a low voice*). Time's getting on.

GUS. I know. I don't like doing a job on an empty stomach.

BEN (*wearily*). Be quiet a minute. Let me give you your instructions.

GUS . What for? We always do it the same way, don't we?

BEN. Let me give you your instructions.

GUS *sighs and sits next to* BEN *on the bed. The instructions are stated and repeated automatically.*

When we get the call, you go over and stand behind the door.

GUS. Stand behind the door.

BEN. If there's a knock on the door you don't answer it.

GUS. If there's a knock on the door I don't answer it.

BEN. But there won't be a knock on the door.

GUS. So I won't answer it.

BEN. When the bloke comes in—

GUS. When the bloke comes in—

BEN. Shut the door behind him.

GUS. Shut the door behind him.

BEN. Without divulging[30] your presence.

GUS. Without divulging my presence.

BEN. He'll see me and come towards me.

GUS. He'll see you and come towards you.

BEN. He won't see you.

GUS (*absently*). Eh?

BEN. He won't see you.

GUS. He won't see me.

BEN. But he'll see me.

GUS. He'll see you.

BEN. He won't know you're there.

GUS. He won't know you're there.

BEN. He won't know *you're* there.

GUS. He won't know I'm there.

BEN. I take out my gun.

GUS. You take out your gun.

BEN. He stops in his tracks.

GUS. He stops in his tracks.

BEN. If he turns round—

GUS. If he turns round—

BEN. You're there.

GUS. I'm here.

BEN *frowns and presses his forehead.*

You've missed something out.

BEN. I know. What?

GUS. I haven't taken my gun out, according to you.

BEN. You take your gun out—

GUS. After I've closed the door.

BEN. After you've closed the door.

GUS. You've never missed that out before, you know that?

BEN. When he sees you behind him—

GUS. Me behind him—

BEN. And me in front of him—

GUS. And you in front of him—

BEN. He'll feel uncertain—

GUS. Uneasy.

BEN. He won't know what to do.

GUS. So what will he do?

BEN. He'll look at me and he'll look at you.

GUS. We won't say a word.

BEN. We'll look at him.

GUS. He won't say a word.

BEN. He'll look at us.

GUS. And we'll look at him.

BEN. Nobody says a word.

Pause.

GUS. What do we do if it's a girl?

BEN. We do the same.

GUS. Exactly the same?

BEN. Exactly.

Pause.

GUS. We don't do anything different?

BEN. We do exactly the same.

GUS. Oh.

GUS *rises, and shivers.*

Excuse me.

He exits through the door on the left. BEN *remains sitting on the bed, still.*

The lavatory chain is pulled once off left, but the lavatory does not flush.

Silence.

GUS *re-enters and stops inside the door, deep in thought. He looks at* BEN, *then walks slowly across to his own bed. He is troubled. He stands, thinking. He turns and looks at* BEN. *He moves a few paces towards him.*

(*Slowly in a low, tense voice.*) Why did he send us matches if he knew there was no gas?

Silence.

BEN *stares in front of him.* GUS *crosses to the left side of* BEN, *to the foot of his bed, to get to his other ear.*

BEN. Why did he send us matches if he knew there was no gas?

BEN *looks up.*

Why did he do that?

BEN. Who?

GUS. Who sent us those matches?

BEN. What are you talking about?

GUS *stares down at him.*

GUS (*thickly*). Who is it upstairs?

BEN (*nervously*). What's one thing to do with another?

GUS. Who is it, though?

BEN. What's one thing to do with another?

BEN *fumbles for his paper on the bed.*

GUS. I asked you a question.

BEN. Enough!

GUS (*with growing agitation*). I asked you before. Who moved in? I asked you. You said the people who had it before moved out. Well, who moved in?

BEN (*hunched*). Shut up.

GUS. I told you, didn't I?

BEN (*standing*). Shut up!

GUS (*feverishly*). I told you before who owned this place, didn't I? I told you.

BEN *hits him viciously on the shoulder.*

I told you who ran this place, didn't I?

BEN *hits him viciously on the shoulder.*

(*Violently.*) Well, what's he playing all these games for? That's what I want to know. What's he doing it for?

BEN. What games?

GUS (*passionately, advancing*). What's he doing it for? We've been through our tests, haven't we? We got right through our tests, years ago, didn't we? We took them together, don't you remember, didn't we? We've proved ourselves before now, haven't we? We've always done our job. What's he doing all this for? What's the idea? What's he playing these games for?

The box in the shaft comes down behind them. The noise is this time accompanied by a shrill whistle, as it falls. GUS *rushes to the hatch and seizes the note.*

(*Reading.*) Scampi[31]!

He crumples the note, picks up the tube, takes out the whistle, blows and speaks.

WE'VE GOT NOTHING LEFT! NOTHING! DO YOU UNDERSTAND?

BEN *seizes the tube and flings* GUS *away. He follows* GUS *and slaps him hard, back-handed, across the chest.*

BEN. Stop it! You maniac!

GUS. But you heard!

BEN (*savagely*). That's enough! I'm warning you!

Silence.

BEN *hangs the tube. He goes to his bed and lies down. He picks up his paper and reads.*

Silence.

The box goes up.

They turn quickly, their eyes meet. BEN *turns to his paper.*

Slowly GUS *goes back to his bed, and sits.*

Silence.

The hatch falls back into place.

They turn quickly, their eyes meet.

BEN *turns back to his paper.*

Silence.

BEN *throws his paper down.*

BEN. Kaw!

He picks up the paper and looks at it.

Listen to this!

Pause.

What about that, eh?

Pause.

Kaw!

Pause.

Have you ever heard such a thing?

GUS (*dully*). Go on!

BEN. It's true.

GUS. Get away.

BEN. It's down here in black and white.

GUS (*very low*). Is that a fact?

BEN. Can you imagine it?

GUS. It's unbelievable.

BEN. It's enough to make you want to puke, isn't it?

GUS (*almost inaudible*). Incredible.

BEN *shakes his head. He puts the paper down and rises. He fixes the revolver in his holster.*

GUS *stands up. He goes towards the door on the left.*

BEN. Where are you going?

GUS. I'm going to have a glass of water.

He exits. BEN *brushes dust off his clothes and shoes. The whistle in the speaking-tube blows. He goes to it, takes the whistle out and puts the tube to his ear. He listens. He puts it to his mouth.*

BEN. Yes.

To ear. He listens. To mouth.

Straight away. Right.

To ear. He listens. To mouth.

Sure we're ready.

To ear. He listens. To mouth.

Understood. Repeat. He has arrived and will be coming in straight away. The normal method to be employed. Understood.

To ear. He listens. To mouth.

Sure we're ready.

To ear. He listens. To mouth.

Right.

He hangs the tube up.

Gus!

He takes out a comb and combs his hair, adjusts his jacket to diminish the bulge of the revolver. The lavatory flushes off left. BEN *goes quickly to the door, left.*

Gus!

The door right opens sharply. BEN *turns, his revolver leveled at the door.*

GUS *stumbles in.*

He is stripped of his jacket, waistcoat, tie, holster and revolver.

He stops, body stooping, his arms at his sides.

He raises his head and looks at BEN.

A long silence.

They stare at each other.

Curtain

NOTES

1. hatch：升降机通道口
2. blimey：旧式英国英语中的语气词，表示惊讶。
3. scrub round：（口语）取消原先的行动计划。

4. swipe：从侧面猛击，重击。
5. liberty：越轨；言行或举止上的冒犯。
6. clench：紧闭或紧握，通常显示坚定的决心或愤怒。
7. common：common sense，常识。
8. birk：傻瓜，笨蛋。这是一种略带亲昵意味的侮辱性称呼。
9. braised：焖熟的，用文火炖熟的。
10. sago：西米，从西谷椰树提取出的一种粉状淀粉类食物。
11. a going concern：有利可图的生意。
12. jam tart：果酱馅的小烘饼。
13. bob：a shilling，一先令。
14. Eccles：一种葡萄干馅饼，原产于英国兰开夏郡的埃克尔斯镇。
15. crisp：potato chip，薯条。
16. holster：用来装手枪的皮套。
17. Macaroni Pastitsio：焗烤通心面，一种希腊风味的食物。Ormitha Macarounada 也是一种希腊食物。
18. McVitie and Price：饼干品牌。Lyons Red Label：袋泡茶品牌。Smith：薯片品牌。Fruit and Nut：一种水果果仁巧克力。
19. Cadbury's：吉佰利，巧克力品牌。
20. slack：松懈的，懒散的。
21. buck one's ideas up：start thinking in a more positive way，振作起来，打起精神。
22. off：状态不佳。
23. water chestnut：菱角或荸荠。char siu：叉烧。beansprout：豆芽。
24. speaking-tube：speaking trumpet，房间与房间之间的通话管。
25. larder：食品贮藏库。
26. to beat the band：（俚）猛烈地，出众地。That beats the band：这可真叫绝了。
27. sustenance：维持生命或健康的物质；食物。
28. radish：小萝卜。cucumber：黄瓜。watercress：豆瓣菜。roll mop：或 rollmop，香料醋渍鲱鱼卷。
29. Alka-Seltzer：德国非处方药品牌，这里指该品牌的药片。
30. divulge：泄露、暴露。
31. scampi：蒜味大虾。

About the Playwright:

Harold Pinter was a British actor, director, poet and screenwriter, but he is best known for his 29 plays, which made him the foremost English playwright of the late-twentieth-century theater and the laureate of the Nobel Prize in Literature of 2005.

Pinter was born in 1930 in a working-class neighborhood of London's East End. He was the only child of a Portuguese Jewish family that Anglicized their name (Da Pinta) for fear of prejudices against Jews. The bombings of London and the Holocaust in Europe during World War II left a permanent impact on Pinter. The theme of loneliness and loss recurs in his plays, especially early works such as *The Room* (1957), *The Birthday Party* (1958), *The Caretaker* (1960) and *The Homecoming* (1965). In these "comedies of menace," Pinter dramatizes a mysterious outside force threatening isolated characters in seemingly comical everyday situations. Since these plays reject consistent characterization and plot, critics usually label them as theatre of the absurd. Pinter himself, too, cited Samuel Beckett as the influence on his early works.

In the late sixties, Pinter turned away from "comedy of menace" to "memory play." He wrote *Landscape* (1969), *Silence* (1969), *Old Times* (1971), *No Man's Land* (1975), *Betrayal* (1978), *Family Voices* (1981), *A Kind of Alaska* (1982), among others, to probe into the elusive human memory. In *Old Times* and *No Man's Land*, in particular, the characters' attempt to verify the past becomes problematic. They each choose to believe their own version of memory, and use it as a means of overcoming their opponents in a dark, if humorously depicted, struggle for control. Variations on this memory theme also occur in some of Pinter's late plays, such as *Moonlight* (1993) and *Ashes to Ashes* (1996), but intertwined with a new concern.

In those plays written in the 1980s and after, starting with *One for the Road* (1984) and *Mountain Language* (1988), Pinter shows an increasingly overt determination to address social issues. Accompanied by his devotion to political activism in public life, his late plays openly indict oppression, war and abuse of human rights. This inclination has also encouraged critics to read his early plays in a new light. Like the Angry Young Men dramas featuring social realism, Pinter's early plays have their roots in the social conditions of post-war Britain. His early drama always carries a political overtone, even though overshadowed by his ambiguous style and his perception of existential absurdity.

Stylistically, too, Pinter draws upon both realism and absurdism. Already showing a gift for acting in his primary school years, Pinter enrolled in the Royal Academy of Dramatic Art (RADA) in 1948 to pursue a career as actor. He dropped out after two terms, but the training at RADA acquainted him with the theories of Stanislavski, the guru of realist acting, whose emphasis on subtext inspired Pinter's plays. The bleakness of Beckett's language, reflecting his characters' failure to communicate, provided another source of inspiration for Pinter's playwriting. Inheriting both traditions, Pinter has forged a style of his own. His dialogue follows the casual, colloquial, everyday speech patterns, but it is also sparse and elliptical, full of non sequiturs, long pauses and silences.

Pinter used to suffer critical flogging for being "obscure." Now the critics have coined the term "Pinteresque" to recognize his innovative art. The one-act play *The Dumb Waiter*, written in 1957, carries the distinct signature of early Pinter both in theme and in style.

Appreciation:

哈罗德·品特 1930 年出生在伦敦一个犹太裁缝家庭，在反犹主义思潮的影响下，走上戏剧之路。品特的作品新颖精炼，形式多样，有独幕和多幕舞台剧，也有电视剧和广播剧。主要作品有：《房屋》（1957）、《送菜升降机》（1957）、《生日晚会》（1958）、《看管人》（1960，作为最佳剧本赢得晚会标准戏剧奖和纽约报纸同业公会的专栏奖）、《侏儒》（1961）、《搜集证据》（1962）、《茶会》（1965）、《回家》（1965，1967 年获百老汇剧评家奖）、《昔日》（1971）和《虚无乡》（1975）等。

除了撰写舞台剧剧本，品特还为广播剧、电影和电视剧撰写过剧本，同时也兼任导演并客串演员，先后获得过两次奥斯卡奖提名和七次英国电影学院奖提名。品特的语言技巧、冷峻的解剖风格影响了整整一代英国戏剧家，在 2005 年，他荣获诺贝尔文学奖，因为"他改变了 20 世纪戏剧舞台的面貌"。

独幕剧《送菜升降机》发表于 1957 年，是品特早期的优秀剧作之一，也是颇具荒诞色彩的"威胁喜剧"。剧本一开始便交代了场景："一个地下室房间。两张床，紧靠着后墙。一个送菜的升降口，封闭着，位于两床之间。左边，一扇门通厨房和厕所。右边，一扇门通过道。"这个地下室里有两个人物：班和格斯。从他们后来的对话中，读者（观众）得知他们两个是受雇于一个神秘公司的杀手。他们在这里听候指示。

他们俩无事可做，班用报纸上的无聊消息作话题来打发时间，格斯不停地问一些不着边际的问题，可班的回答却常常答非所问。突然，一架送菜升降机开动起来，一张菜单被送了下来。两人把能找到的东西都让升降机送了上去。但升降机不断地下来，要求更多的东西、更复杂的食品。后来，他们发现升降机旁有一个通话管，班与格斯与上面的权力者建立了联系。当格斯到左门去倒水时，班从通话管接到指令，要他杀死下一个进入房间的人。这时，左边的厕所传来冲水声。班快步走向左边的门。"右边的门一下子开了。班转身，用枪向门的方向瞄准。格斯踉跄而入。他的上装、背心、领带、枪套和手枪都被剥光了。他停住脚步，弯腰曲背，两只胳膊耷拉在身体两侧。他抬起头来望着班。长时间沉默。他们彼此瞪着眼。——幕落。"

这个独幕剧具有鲜明的"品特风格"，表现出明显的威胁性、荒诞性和喜剧性。但该剧绝非闹剧。剧目的关键定位是"威胁喜剧"。所谓威胁喜剧，是指品特所创作的喜剧强调一种普遍存在的威胁。时至今日，日趋激烈的社会竞争使人们倍感“压力山大”，为此，人们普遍感到安全感缺失，感情生活孤寂……上述令人无所适从的各种环境成为“威胁喜剧”的外部架构。而剧中两个杀手的性格迥异，他们之间答非所问的对话中富含喜剧元素；而人物间所表现的“静默”隐喻使得该剧的喜剧效果得以最大化的彰显。

Questions:

1. Comment on Pinter's use of repetitions and silences in this play. Do they help to convey the themes? Give examples.

2. Do you find the dialogue between Ben and Gus funny? If you do, explain what elements make it funny to you. Does the comedy weaken or strengthen the subject matter of this play?

Buried Child (Excerpt)

Scene: same set. Morning. Bright sun. No sound of rain. Everything has been cleared up again. No sign of carrots. No pail. No stool. Vince's saxophone case and overcoat are still at the foot of the staircase. Bradley is asleep on the sofa under Dodge's blanket, his head toward stage left. Bradley's wooden leg is leaning against the sofa right by his head. The shoe is left on. The harness hangs down. Dodge is sitting on the floor, propped up against the TV set facing stage left, wearing his baseball cap. Shelly's rabbit fur coat covers his chest and shoulders. He stares toward stage left. He seems weaker and more disoriented. The lights rise slowly to the sound of birds. The two men remain for a while in silence. Bradley sleeps very soundly. Dodge hardly moves. Shelly appears from stage left with a big smile, slowly crossing toward Dodge balancing a steaming cup of broth in a saucer. Dodge just stares at her as she gets close to him.

SHELLY

(As she crosses – SAUCER/CUP FOLEY.*)* A nice hot cup of broth. This is going to make all the difference in the world, Grandpa. You don't mind me calling you Grandpa do you? I mean I know you minded when Vince called you that but you don't even know him.

DODGE

I'm nobody's Grandpa. He skipped town with my money you know. I'm gonna hold you as collateral.

SHELLY

He'll be back. Don't worry. He always comes back.

DODGE

The faithful type.

SHELLY

No. Determined. *(She kneels down next to Dodge and* PUTS THE CUP AND SAUCER IN HIS LAP.*)*

DODGE

It's morning already! When did it get to be morning? Not only didn't I get my bottle but he's got my two bucks. I'm surrounded by thieves. What am I doing on the floor?

SHELLY

Try to drink this, okay? Don't spill it.

DODGE

What is it?

SHELLY

Beef bouillon. It'll warm you up.

DODGE

Bouillon! I don't want any goddamn bouillon! Get that stuff away from me!

SHELLY

I just got through making it.

DODGE

I don't care if you just spent all week making it! I ain't drinking it!

SHELLY

Well, what am I supposed to do with it? I'm trying to help you out. Besides, it's good for you.

DODGE

Get it away from me! *(Shelly stands up with cup and saucer.)* What do you know what's good for me anyway?

(She looks at Dodge then turns away from him, crosses to the staircase, sits on bottom step and drinks the bouillon.)

SHELLY

Fine. I'll drink it.

DODGE

(Staring at her.) You know what'd be good for me?

SHELLY

What?

DODGE

A little backrub. A little contact.

SHELLY

Oh no. I've had enough contact for a while. Thanks anyway. *(She keeps sipping the bouillon, stays sitting. Pause as Dodge stares at her.)*

DODGE

Why not? You got nothing better to do. That fella's not gonna be back here. You're not expecting him to show up again are you?

SHELLY

Sure. He'll show up. He left his horn here.

DODGE

His horn? *(Laughs)* You're his horn?

SHELLY

Very funny. His saxophone.

DODGE

He's run off with my money! That's what he did. He's not coming back here.

SHELLY

He'll be back. This is where he's from. He knows that. He's convinced. And so am I.

DODGE

You're a funny chicken, you know that?

SHELLY

Funny?

DODGE

Full of hope. Faith. Faith and hope. You're all alike you hopers. If it's not God then it's a man. If it's not a man then it's a woman. If it's not a woman then it's politics or bee pollen or the future of some kind. Some kind of future.

SHELLY

Bee pollen?

DODGE

Yeah, bee pollen. *(Pause.)*

SHELLY

(Looking toward porch.) I'm glad it stopped raining. *(Dodge looks toward porch then back to Shelly.)*

DODGE

That's what I mean. See, you're glad it stopped raining. Now you think everything's gonna be different. Just 'cause the sun comes out.

SHELLY

It's already different. Last night I was scared.

DODGE

Scared a what?

SHELLY

Just scared.

DODGE

Yeah, well we've all got an instinct for disaster. We can smell it coming.

SHELLY

It was your son, Bradley. He scared me.

DODGE

Bradley? *(Looks at Bradley.)* He's a push-over. 'Specially now. All ya gotta do is take his wooden leg and throw it out the back door. Helpless. Totally helpless. *(Shelly turns and stares at Bradley's wooden leg then looks at Dodge. She sips bouillon.)*

SHELLY

You'd do that?

DODGE

Me? I've hardly got the strength to breathe.

SHELLY

But you'd actually do it if you could?

DODGE

Don't be so easily shocked, girlie. There's nothing a man can't do. You dream it up and he can do it. Anything. It boggles the imagination.

SHELLY

You've tried I guess.

DODGE

Don't sit there sippin' your bouillon and judging me! This is my house!

SHELLY

I forgot.

DODGE

You forgot? Whose house did you think it was?

SHELLY

Mine. *(Dodge just stares at her. Long pause. She sips from cup.)* I know it's not mine but I had that feeling.

DODGE

What feeling?

SHELLY

The feeling that nobody lives here but me. I mean everybody's gone. You're here, but it doesn't seem like you're supposed to be. *(Pointing to Bradley.)* Bradley doesn't seem like he's supposed to be here either. I don't know what it is. It's the house or something. Something familiar. Like I know my way around here. Did you ever get that feeling? *(Dodge stares at her in silence. Pause.)*

DODGE

No. No, I never did. I get lost in the hallway sometimes. *(Shelly gets up. Moves around space holding cup.)*

SHELLY

Last night I went to sleep up there in that room.

DODGE

What room?

SHELLY

That room up there with all the pictures. All the crosses on the wall.

DODGE

Halie's room?

SHELLY

Yeah. Whoever "Halie" is.

DODGE

She's my wife.

SHELLY

So you remember her?

DODGE

Whadya mean! 'Course I remember her. She's only been gone a day—half a day. However long it's been.

SHELLY

Do you remember her when her hair was bright red? Standing in front of an apple tree?

DODGE

What is that, the third degree or something! Who're you to be askin' me personal questions about my wife!

SHELLY

You never look at those pictures up there?

DODGE

What pictures!

SHELLY

Your whole life's up there hanging on the wall. Somebody who looks just like you. Somebody who looks just like you used to look.

DODGE

That isn't me! That never was me! This is me. Right here. This is it. The whole shootin' match, sittin' right here in front of you. That other stuff was a sham.

SHELLY

So the past never happened as far as you're concerned?

DODGE

The past? Jesus Christ. The past is passed. What do you know about the past?

SHELLY

Not much. I know there was a farm. *(Pause.)*

DODGE

A farm?

SHELLY

There's a picture of a farm. A big farm. A bull. Wheat. Corn.

DODGE

Corn?

SHELLY

All the kids are standing out in the corn. They're all waving these big straw hats. One of them doesn't have a hat.

DODGE

Which one was that?

SHELLY

There's a baby. A baby in a woman's arms. The same woman with the red hair. She looks lost standing out there. Like she doesn't know how she got there.

DODGE

She knows! I told her a hundred times it wasn't gonna be the city! I gave her plenty a warning.

SHELLY

She's looking down at the baby like it was somebody else's. Like it didn't even belong to her.

DODGE

That's about enough outta you! You got some funny ideas, sister. Some damn funny ideas. You think just because people propagate they have to love their offspring? You never seen a bitch eat her puppies? Where are you from anyway?

SHELLY

LA. We already went through that.

DODGE

That's right, LA I remember.

SHELLY

Stupid country.

DODGE

That's right! No wonder. Dumber than dirt. *(Pause.)*

SHELLY

What's happened to this family anyway?

DODGE

You're in no position to ask! What do you care? You some kinda social worker?

SHELLY

I'm Vince's friend.

DODGE

Vince's friend! That's rich. That's real rich. "Vince!" "Mr. Vince!" "Mr. Thief!" Is more like it! His name doesn't mean a hoot in hell to me. Not a tinkle in the well. You know how many kids I've spawned? Not to mention grandkids and great-grandkids and great-great-grandkids after them?

SHELLY

And you don't remember any of them?

DODGE

What's to remember? Halie's the one with the family album. She's the one you should talk to. She'll set you straight on the heritage if that's what you're interested in. She's traced it all the way back to the grave.

SHELLY

What do you mean?

DODGE

What do you think I mean? How far back can you go? A long line of corpses! There's not a living soul behind me. Not a one. Who gives a damn about bones in the ground?

SHELLY

What was Tilden trying to tell me last night? *(Dodge stops short. Stares at Shelly. Shakes his head. He looks off L. Dodge's tone changes drastically.)*

DODGE

Tilden? *(Turns to Shelly, calmly.)* Where is Tilden?

SHELLY

What was he trying to say about the baby? *(Pause. Dodge turns toward L.)*

DODGE

What's happened to Tilden? Why isn't Tilden here?

SHELLY

Bradley chased him out.

DODGE

(Looking at Bradley asleep.) Bradley? Why is he on my sofa? *(Turns back to Shelly.)* Have I been here all night? On the floor?

SHELLY

He wouldn't leave. I hid outside until he fell asleep.

DODGE

Outside? Is Tilden outside? He shouldn't be out there in the rain. He'll get himself into trouble. He doesn't know his way around here anymore. Not like he used to. He went out West and got himself into trouble. Deep trouble. We don't want any of that around here.

SHELLY

What did he do? *(Pause.)*

DODGE

(Quietly stares at Shelly.) Tilden? He got mixed up. That's what he did. We can't afford to leave him alone. Not now. *(Sound of Halie laughing comes from off L. Shelly stands, looking in direction of voice, holding cup and saucer, doesn't know whether to stay or run. Motioning to Shelly.)* Sit down! Sit back down! *(Shelly sits. Sound of Halie's laughter again. To Shelly in a heavy whisper, pulling coat up around him.)* Don't leave me alone now! Promise me? Don't go off and leave me alone. I need somebody here with me. Tilden's gone now and I need someone. Don't leave me! Promise!

SHELLY

(Sitting.) I won't. *(Halie appears outside the screen porch door U.L. with Father Dewis. She is wearing a bright yellow dress, no hat, white gloves and her arms are full of yellow roses. Father Dewis is dressed in traditional black suit, white clerical collar and shirt. He is a very*

distinguished gray-haired man in his sixties. They are both slightly drunk and feeling giddy. As they ENTER THE PORCH THROUGH THE SCREEN DOOR, *Dodge pulls the rabbit fur coat over his head and hides. Shelly stands again. Dodge drops the coat and whispers intently to Shelly. Neither Halie nor Father Dewis are aware of the people inside the house.)*

…

SHELLY

I know you've got a secret. You've all got a secret. It's so secret, in fact, you're all convinced it never happened. *(Halie moves to Dewis.)*

HALIE

Oh my God, Father! Who is this person?

DODGE

(Laughing to himself.) She thinks she's going to get it out of us. She thinks she's going to uncover the truth of the matter. Like a detective or something.

BRADLEY

I'm not telling her anything! Nothing's wrong here! Nothing's ever been wrong! Everything's the way it's supposed to be! Nothing ever happened that's bad. Everything is all right here! We're all good people! We've always been good people. Right from the very start.

DODGE

She thinks she's gonna suddenly bring everything out into the open after all these years.

DEWIS

(To Shelly.) Can't you see that these people want to be left in peace? Don't you have any mercy? They haven't done anything to you.

DODGE

She wants to get to the bottom of it. *(To Shelly)* That's it, isn't it? You'd like to get right down to bedrock? Look the beast right dead in the eye. You want me to tell ya? You want me to tell ya what happened? I'll tell ya. I might as well. I wouldn't mind hearing it hit the air after all these years of silence.

BRADLEY

No! Don't listen to him. He doesn't remember anything!

DODGE

I remember the whole thing from start to finish. I remember the day he was born. *(Pause.)*

HALIE

Dodge, if you tell this thing—if you tell this, you'll be dead to me. You'll be just as good as dead.

DODGE

That won't be such a big change, Halie. See this girl, this little girl here, she wants to know. She wants to know something more. And I got this feeling that it doesn't make a bit a difference. I'd sooner tell it to a stranger than anybody else. I'd sooner tell it to the four winds.

BRADLEY

(To Dodge.) We made a pact! We made a pact between us! You can't break that now!

DODGE

I don't remember any pact. *(Silence.)* See, we were a well-established family once. Well-established. All the boys were grown. The farm was producing enough milk to fill Lake Michigan twice over. Me and Halie here were pointed toward what looked like the middle part of our life. Everything was settled with us. All we had to do was ride it out. Then Halie got pregnant again. Out the middle a nowhere, she got pregnant. We weren't planning on havin' any more boys. We had enough boys already. In fact, we hadn't been sleepin' in the same bed for about six years.

HALIE

(Moving toward stairs.) I'm not listening to this! I don't have to listen to this!

DODGE

(Stops Halie.) Where are you going! Upstairs! You'll just be listenin' to it upstairs. You go

outside, you'll be listenin' to it outside. Might as well stay here and listen to it. *(Halie stays by stairs. Pause.)* Halie had this kid see. This baby boy. She had it. I let her have it on her own. All the other boys I had had the best doctors, the best nurses, everything. This one I let her have by herself. This one hurt real bad. Almost killed her, but she had it anyway. It lived, see. It lived. It wanted to grow up in this family. It wanted to be just like us. It wanted to be part of us. It wanted to pretend that I was its father. She wanted me to believe in it. Even when everyone around us knew. Everyone. All our boys knew. Tilden knew.

HALIE

You shut up! Bradley, make him stop!

BRADLEY

I can't.

DODGE

Tilden was the one who knew. Better than any of us. He'd walk for miles with the kid in his arms. Halie let him take it. All night sometimes. He'd walk all night out there in the pasture with it. Talkin' to it. Singin' to it. Used to hear him singing to it. He'd make up stories. He'd tell that kid all kinds a stories. Even when he knew it couldn't understand him. We couldn't let a thing like that continue. We couldn't allow that to grow up right in the middle of our lives. It made everything we'd accomplished look like it was nothin'. Everything was canceled out by this one mistake. This one weakness.

SHELLY

So you…

DODGE

I killed it. I drowned it. Just like the runt of a litter. Just drowned it. There was no struggle. No noise. Life just left it. *(Halie moves toward Bradley.)*

HALIE

(To Bradley.) Ansel would've stopped him! Ansel wouldn've stopped him from telling these lies! He was a hero! A man! A whole man! What's happened to the men in this family! Where are the men! *(***SUDDENLY VINCE COMES CRASHING THROUGH THE SCREEN PORCH DOOR U.L., TEARING IT**

OFF ITS HINGES. *Everyone but Dodge and Bradley back away from the porch and stare at Vince, who has landed on his stomach on the porch in a drunken stupor. He is singing loudly to himself and hauls himself slowly to his feet. He has a paper shopping bag full of empty booze bottles.* HE TAKES THEM OUT ONE AT A TIME AS HE SINGS AND SMASHES THEM AT THE OPPOSITE END OF THE PORCH, *behind the solid interior door, R. Shelly moves slowly toward R., holding wooden leg and watching Vince.)*

VINCE

(Singing loudly as he hurls bottles.) "From the halls of Montezuma to the shores of Tripoli. We will fight our country's battles in the air on land and sea." *(*HE PUNCTUATES THE WORDS "MONTEZUMA," "TRIPOLI," "BATTLES," AND "SEA" WITH A SMASHED BOTTLE EACH. *He stops throwing for a second, stares toward R. of the porch, shades his eyes with his hand as though looking across to a battlefield, then cups his hands around his mouth and yells across the space of the porch to an imaginary army. The others watch in terror and expectation. To imagined army.)* Have you had enough over there! 'Cause there's a lot more here where that came from! *(*JOSTLING THE PAPER BAG FULL OF BOTTLES.*)* A helluva lot more! We got enough over here to blow ya from here to Kingdom come! *(He takes another bottle, makes high whistling sound of a bomb and throws it toward R. porch.* SOUND OF BOTTLE SMASHING AGAINST WALL.

HE KEEPS YELLING AND HEAVING BOTTLES ONE AFTER ANOTHER. *Vince stops for a while, breathing heavily from exhaustion. Long silence as the others watch him. Shelly approaches tentatively in Vince's direction, still holding Bradley's wooden leg.)*

SHELLY

(After a silence.) Vince? *(Vince turns toward her. Peers through screen.)*
What are you doing out on the porch?

VINCE

Who? What? Vince who? Who's that in there? Is someone in there? I can't see you through the screen. *(Vince pushes his face against the screen from the porch and stares in at everyone.)*

DODGE

Where's my goddamn bottle!

VINCE

(Looking in at Dodge.) What? Who is that? Who's speaking. Whose voice is that?

DODGE

It's me! Your grandfather! Don't play stupid with me! Where's my two bucks!

VINCE

Grandfather? Grandfather? You mean the father of my father? The son of my great-grandfather? That one? When did this start?

DODGE

Where's my bottle! *(Halie moves away from Dewis, U., peers out at Vince, trying to recognize him.)*

HALIE

Vincent? Is that you, Vincent? *(Shelly stares at Halie then looks out at Vince.)*

VINCE

(From porch.) Vincent who? What is this! Who are you people?

SHELLY

(To Halie.) Hey, wait a minute. Wait a minute!

HALIE

(Moving closer to porch screen.) We thought you were a murderer or something. Barging in through the door like that.

VINCE

A murderer? No, no, no! How could I be a murderer when I don't exist? A murderer is a living breathing person who takes the life and breath away from another living breathing person. That's a murderer. You've got me mixed up with someone else.

BRADLEY

(Sitting up on sofa.) You get off our front porch you creep! What're you doing out there breaking bottles? Who are these foreigners anyway! Where did they all come from?

HALIE

(Moving toward porch.) Vincent, what's got into you! Why are you acting like this?

VINCE

Who's that? Who's that speaking?

SHELLY

(Approaching Halie.) You mean you know who he is?

HALIE

Of course I know who he is! That's more than I can say for you missie.

DODGE

Where's my goddamn bottle? *(Halie turns back toward Dewis and crosses to him. Vince sings.)*

VINCE

"From the halls of Montezuma to the shores of Tripoli. We will fight our country's battles in the air on land and sea..."

HALIE

(To Dewis.) Father, why are you just standing around here when everything's falling apart? Can't you rectify this situation? *(Dodge laughs, coughs.)*

DEWIS

I'm just a guest here, Halie. I don't know what my position is exactly. This is outside my parish anyway. I'm in the quiet part of town.

SHELLY

Vince! Knock it off will ya! I want to get out of here! This is enough.

VINCE

(To Shelly.) Have they got you prisoner in there, dear? *(Vince starts to sing again, throwing more bottles as things continue.)*

SHELLY

I'm coming out there, Vince! I'm coming out there and I want us to get in the car and drive away from here. Anywhere. Just away from here. Far, far away. *(Shelly moves to R. door and opens it.)*

VINCE

We'd never make it. We'd drive and we'd drive and we'd drive and we'd never make it. We'd think we were getting farther and farther away. That's what we'd think.

SHELLY

I'm coming out there now, Vince.

VINCE

Don't come out. Don't you dare come out here. It's off limits. Taboo territory. But I'm coming in. Right through this goddamn screen. *(Vince pulls out a big folding hunting knife and pulls open the blade. He jabs the blade into the screen and starts cutting a hole big enough to climb through. Bradley cowers in a corner of the sofa as Vince rips open the screen. Dewis takes Halie by the arm and pulls her toward staircase.)*

DEWIS

Halie, maybe we should go upstairs until this blows over. I'm completely at a loss.

HALIE

I don't understand it. I just don't understand it. He was the sweetest little boy! There was no indication. *(Dewis drops the roses beside the wooden leg at the foot of the staircase then escorts Halie quickly up the stairs. Halie keeps looking back at Vince as they climb the stairs.)* There wasn't a mean bone in his body. Everybody loved Vincent. Everyone. He was the perfect baby. So pink and perfect.

DEWIS

He'll be all right after a while. He's just had a few too many that's all.

HALIE

He used to sing in his sleep. He'd sing. In the middle of the night. The sweetest voice. Like an angel. *(She stops for a moment.)* I used to lie awake listening to it. I used to lie awake thinking it was all right if I died. Because Vincent was an angel. A guardian angel. He'd watch over us. He'd watch over all of us. He would see to it that no harm would come. *(Dewis takes her all the way up the stairs. They disappear above. Vince is now climbing through the porch screen onto the sofa. Bradley crashes off the sofa, holding tight to his blanket, keeping it wrapped around him. Shelly is outside on the porch. Vince holds the knife in his teeth once he gets the hole wide enough to climb through. Bradley starts crawling slowly toward his wooden leg, reaching out for it.)*

BRADLEY

My leg! Gotta get to my leg!

*(*VINCE *and* BRADLEY *ad lib about the leg as the scene continues.)*

DODGE

(To Vince.) Go ahead! Take over the house! Take over the whole goddamn house! You can have it! It's yours! It's been a pain in the neck ever since the very first mortgage. I'm gonna die any second now. Any second. You won't even notice. So I'll settle my affairs once and for all. *(As Dodge proclaims his last will and testament, Vince climbs into the room, knife in mouth and strides slowly around the space, inspecting his inheritance. He casually notices Bradley as he crawls toward his leg. Vince moves to the leg and keeps pushing it with his foot so that it's out of Bradley's reach then goes on with his inspection. He picks up the roses and carries them around smelling them. Shelly can be seen outside on the porch, moving slowly C. and staring in at Vince. Vince ignores her.)* The house goes to my grandson, Vincent. That's fair and square. All the furnishings, accoutrements, and paraphernalia therein. Everything tacked to the walls or otherwise resting under this roof. My tools—namely my band saw, my skill saw, my drill press, my chain saw, my lathe, my electric sander all go to my eldest son, Tilden. That is, if he ever shows up again. My Benny Goodman records, my harnesses, my bits, my halters, my brace, my rough rasp, my forge, my welding equipment, my shoeing nails, my levels and bevels, my milking stool—no, not my milking stool—my hammers and chisels and all related materials are to be pushed into a gigantic heap and set ablaze in the very center of my fields. When the blaze is at its highest, preferably on a cold, windless night, my body is to be pitched into the middle of it and burned 'til nothing remains but ash. *(Pause. Vince takes the knife out of his mouth and smells the roses. He's facing toward audience and doesn't turn around to Shelly. He folds up knife and*

pockets it.)

SHELLY

(From porch.) I'm leaving, Vince. Whether you come or not, I'm leaving. I can't stay here.

VINCE

(Smelling roses.) You'll never make it. You'll see.

SHELLY

(Moving toward hole in screen.) You're not coming? *(Vince stays D., turns and looks at her.)*

VINCE

I just inherited a house. I've finally been recognized. Didn't you hear?

SHELLY

(Through hole, from porch.) You want to stay here?

VINCE

(As he pushes Bradley's leg out of reach.) I've gotta carry on the line. It's in the blood. I've gotta see to it that things keep rolling. *(Bradley looks up at him from floor, keeps pulling himself toward his leg. Vince keeps moving it.)*

SHELLY

What happened to you, Vince? You just disappeared. *(Pause. Vince delivers the following speech front.)*

VINCE

I was gonna run last night. I was gonna run and keep right on running. Clear to the Iowa border. I drove all night with the windows open. The old man's two bucks flapping right on the seat beside me. It never stopped raining the whole time. Never stopped once. I could see myself in the windshield. My face. My eyes. I studied my face. Studied everything about it as though I was looking at another man. As though I could see his whole race behind him. Like a mummy's face. I saw him dead and alive at the same time. In the same breath. In the windshield I watched him breathe as though he was frozen in time and every breath marked him. Marked him forever without him knowing. And then his face changed. His face became his father's face. Same bones. Same eyes. Same nose. Same breath. And his father's face changes to his gradfather's face. And it went on like that. Changing. Clear on back to faces I'd never seen before but still recognized. Still recognized the bones underneath. Same eyes. Same mouth. Same breath. I followed my family clear into Iowa. Every last one. Straight into the corn belt and further. Straight back as far as they'd take me. Then it all dissolved. Everything dissolved. Just like that. And that two bucks kept right on flapping on the seat beside me.

(Shelly stares at him for a while.)

SHELLY

Bye Vince. I can't hang around for this. I'm not even related. *(She exits L. off the porch. Vince watches her go. Bradley tries to make a lunge for his wooden leg. Vince quickly picks it up and dangles it over Bradley's head like a carrot. Bradley keeps making desperate grabs at the leg.* [ACTORS AD LIB.] *Dewis comes down the staircase and stops halfway, staring at Vince and Bradley. Vince looks up at Dewis and smiles. He keeps moving backwards with the leg toward U.L. as Bradley crawls after him.)*

VINCE

(To Dewis as he continues torturing Bradley.) Oh, excuse me, Father. Just getting rid of some of the vermin in the house. This is my house now, ya know? All mine. Everything. Except for the power tools and stuff. I'm gonna get all new equipment anyway. New plows, new tractor, everything. All brand-new. Start right off on the ground floor.

VINCE

(Teasing Bradley closer to the U.L. corner of the stage.) Come on, Bradley. You can get it. You want your leg? **(HE THROWS BRADLEY'S WOODEN LEG FAR OFFSTAGE L.)** Crawl for it.

(Bradley follows his leg offstage, pulling himself along on the ground, whimpering. As Bradley exits, Vince pulls the blanket off him and throws it over his own shoulder. He crosses toward Dewis with the blanket and smells the roses. Dewis comes to the bottom of the stairs.)

DEWIS

You'd better go up and see your grandmother. I think you should. It would be the Christian thing.

VINCE

(Looking upstairs, back to Dewis.) My grandmother? There's nobody else in this house. Except for you. And you're leaving aren't you? *(Dewis crosses toward R. door. He turns back to Vince.)*

DEWIS

She's going to need someone. I can't help her. I don't know what to do. I don't know what my position is here. I'm quite out of my depths. I'll be the first to admit it. I thought, by now, the Lord would have given me some sign, some guidepost, but I haven't seen it. No sign at all. Just— *(Vince just stares at him. Dewis goes out the door, crosses porch and exits L. Vince listens to him leaving. He smells roses, looks up the staircase then smells roses again. He turns and looks U. at Dodge. He crosses up to him and bends over, looking at Dodge's open eyes. Dodge is dead. His death should have come completely unnoticed.)*

VINCE

Grandpa? Grandpa? When did you die?

(After a while, Halie is heard coming from above the staircase. The lights start to dim imperceptibly as Halie speaks. Vince keeps staring at the ceiling.)

HALIE'S VOICE

Dodge? Is that you Dodge? Tilden was right about the corn you know. I've never seen such corn. Have you taken a look at it lately? Dazzling. Tall as a man already. This early in the year. Carrots too. Potatoes. Peas. It's like a paradise out there, Dodge. You oughta take a look. A miracle. I've never seen it like this. Maybe the rain did something. Maybe it was the rain. *(As Halie keeps talking offstage, Tilden appears from L., dripping with mud from the knees down. His arms and hands are covered with mud. In his hands he carries the corpse of a small child at chest level, staring down at it. The corpse mainly consists of bones wrapped in muddy, rotten cloth.)*

VINCE

Dad? You're all muddy … where you been?

TILDEN

Out back.

VINCE

What you got in your hands?

TILDEN

A baby … A tiny little baby.

(As Halie continues, Tilden slowly makes his way up the stairs. His eyes never leave the corpse of the child. The lights keep fading.)

HALIE

Good hard rain. Takes everything straight down deep to the roots. The rest takes care of itself. You can't force a thing to grow. You can't interfere with it. It's all hidden. Unseen. You just gotta wait 'til it pops up out of the ground. Tiny little shoot. Tiny little white shoot. All hairy and fragile. Strong though. Strong enough to crack the earth even. It's a miracle, Dodge. I've never seen a crop like this in my whole life. Maybe it's the sun. Maybe that's it. Maybe it's the sun. *(Tilden disappears above. Silence. Lights go to black.)*

MUSIC CUE: Solo dobro or steel guitar.

END

About the Playwright:

Samuel Shepard Rogers III (November, 1943—July, 2017), known professionally as Sam Shepard, is an American playwright, actor, author, screenwriter, and director, whose body of work spans over half a century. He is the author of forty-four plays as well as several books of short stories, essays, and memoirs. Shepard received the Pulitzer Prize for Drama in 1979 for his play *Buried Child*. He was nominated for an Academy Award for Best Supporting Actor for his portrayal of pilot Chuck Yeager in *The Right Stuff* (1983). Shepard received the PEN/Laura Pels International Foundation for Theater Award as a master American dramatist in 2009. New York described him as "the greatest American playwright of his generation."

Shepard's plays are chiefly known for their bleak, poetic, often surrealist elements, black humor and rootless characters living on the outskirts of American society. His style has evolved over the years, from the absurdism of his early Off-Off-Broadway work to the realism of *Buried Child* and *Curse of the Starving Class* (both 1978) and *True West* (1980), which are considered to be his masterpieces as "Family Tragedy Trilogy."

Appreciation:

萨姆·谢泼德被视为当代美国最富有影响的剧作家，他的作品在世界范围内倍受称赞。美国戏剧史家比格斯毕指出：萨姆·谢泼德是20世纪七八十年代美国剧坛上“最重要、最有力的声音”，是一代新人中“最为优秀的剧作家”。他伟大的戏剧创作成就使之成为现代美国戏剧之父尤金·奥尼尔的新一代接班人，与现代美国社会问题剧作家埃尔默·赖斯，现代美国现实主义戏剧作家阿瑟·密勒，现代美国理性戏剧作家田纳西·威廉斯以及第二次世界大战后成长起来的著名剧作家爱德华·阿尔比等优秀的剧作家齐名。

作为一位高产剧作家，萨姆·谢泼德共创作了40余部剧作，并10次获奥比奖。他擅长探讨人的下意识，挖掘人的被压抑的精神世界。他对诸如乱伦、暴力及寻根等题材极感兴趣。失败的家庭关系是他的创作主题之一。其代表作为家庭悲剧三部曲：《饥饿阶级的诅咒》、《被埋葬的孩子》和《真正的西部》。

《被埋葬的孩子》描述以剧作家的故乡——美国中西部的伊利诺伊州的一个农场为背景，以“被隐藏的丑闻”为主题的家庭悲剧。这部剧表面看来情节松散，但立意深刻。它不仅为剧作家赢得1979年的普利策奖，更奠定了他在美国戏剧史上的重要地位。该剧以一位似乎已忘记自己成长经历的青年文斯带着女朋友谢丽回老家去寻根为主线展开。然而，寻根之旅使他大失所望，因为他想象中的能给他“火鸡晚餐和苹果馅饼”的温馨的家庭变成了一个与世隔绝、自我封闭的冷漠家庭：垂死的祖父根本不认识他，老头子所感兴趣的只是整日坐在楼下电视机旁偷偷地喝酒；形容枯槁一身黑衣的祖母自顾自住在楼上为失去的孩子伤心不已；不知为何痴傻癫狂的父亲也把他视为路人。一家人虽然生活在一起，却彼此冷漠，相互折磨。文斯对这种冷漠的环境倍感失落，寻根的梦想好像已经幻灭。而旁观者谢丽却带着对这个家庭的厌恶、恐惧以及好奇的心情揭开了被隐藏了几十年的秘密。原来，屋外埋着一个死去的孩子。它是祖母和父亲乱伦的产物，后被祖父溺死埋在屋外。

剧作家给这个葬子赋予了深刻的含义：它使全家人自我封闭，达成共识，空前团结，因为它是全家人共同竭力保守的秘密；同时，它又使全家人相互埋怨，彼此仇视，分崩离析，因为它是全家人相互伤害的武器；它是全家人痛苦的根源；它是全家人罪孽的象征。

Questions:

1. In *Buried Child* of what importance is Bradly's artificial leg and Dodge's baseball cap and the blanket?

2. What are the symbols, allegories and motifs manifested in this play?

Death of a Salesman (Excerpt)

ACT ONE

A melody is heard played upon a flute. It is small and fine, telling of grass and trees and the horizon. The curtain rises.

Before us is the SALESMAN'S *house. We are aware of towering, angular shapes*[1] *behind it, surrounding it on all sides. Only the blue light of the sky falls upon the house and forestage; the surrounding area shows an angry glow of orange. As more light appears, we see a solid vault of apartment houses around the small, fragile-seeming home. An air of the dream clings to the place, a dream rising out of reality. The kitchen at centre seems actual enough, for there is a kitchen table with three chairs and a refrigerator. But no other fixtures are seen. At the back of the kitchen there is a draped entrance, which leads to the living-room. To the right of the kitchen, on a level raised two feet, is a bedroom furnished only with a brass bedstead and a straight chair. On a shelf over the bed a silver athletic trophy stands. A window opens on to the apartment house at the side.*

Behind the kitchen, on a level raised six and a half feet, is the boys' bedroom, at present barely visible. Two beds are dimly seen, and at the back of the room a dormer window. (This bedroom is above the unseen living-room.) At the left a stairway curves up to it from the kitchen.

The entire setting is wholly or, in some places, partially transparent. The roof-line of the house is one-dimensional[2]*, under and over it we see the apartment buildings. Before the house lies an apron, curving beyond the forestage into the orchestra*[3]*. This forward area serves as the back yard as well as the locale of all Willy's imaginings and of his city scenes. Whenever the action is in the present the actors observe the imaginary wall-lines, entering the house only through its door at the left. But in the scenes of the past these boundaries are broken, and characters enter or leave a room by stepping "through" a wall on to the forestage.*

[*From the right,* WILLY LOMAN, *the Salesman, enters, carrying two large sample cases*[4]*. The flute plays on. He hears but is not aware of it. He is past sixty years of age, dressed quietly. Even as he crosses the stage to the doorway of the house, his exhaustion is apparent. He unlocks the door, comes into the kitchen, and thankfully lets his burden down, feeling the soreness of his palms. A word-sigh escapes his lips—it might be* "Oh, boy, oh, boy." *He closes the door, then carries his cases out into the living-room, through the draped kitchen doorway.* LINDA, *his wife, has stirred in her bed at the right. She gets out and puts on a robe, listening. Most often jovial,* *she has developed an iron repression of her exceptions to* WILLY'S *behaviour*[5]*—she more than loves him, she admires him, as though his mercurial nature, his temper, his massive dreams and little cruelties, served her only as sharp reminders of the turbulent longings within him, longings which she shares but lacks the temperament to utter and follow to their end.*]

Linda [*hearing* WILLY *outside the bedroom, calls with some trepidation*]: Willy!

Willy: It's all right. I came back.

Linda: Why? What happened? [*Slight pause.*] Did something happen, Willy?

Willy: No, nothing happened.

Linda: You didn't smash the car, did you?

Willy [*With casual irritation*]: I said nothing happened. Didn't you hear me?

Linda: Don't you feel well?

Willy: I'm tired to the death. [*The flute has faded away. He sits on the bed beside her, a little numb.*] I couldn't make it. I just couldn't make it, Linda.

Linda: [*very carefully. delicately*]: Where were you all day? You look terrible.

Willy: I got as far as a little above Yonkers. I stopped for a cup of coffee. Maybe it was the coffee.

Linda: What?

Willy [*after a pause*]: I suddenly couldn't drive any more. The car kept going off on to the shoulder[6], y'know?

Linda [*helpfully*]: Oh. Maybe it was the steering again. I don't think Angelo knows the Studebaker.

Willy: No, it's me, it's me. Suddenly I realize I'm goin' sixty miles an hour and I don't remember the last five minutes. I'm—I can't seem to—keep my mind to it.

Linda: Maybe it's your glasses. You never went for your new glasses.

Willy: No, I see everything. I came back ten miles an hour. It took me nearly four hours from Yonkers.

Linda [*resigned*]: Well, you'll just have to take a rest, Willy, you can't continue this way.

Willy: I just got back from Florida[7].

Linda: But you didn't rest your mind. Your mind is overactive, and the mind is what counts, dear.

Willy: I'll start out in the morning. Maybe I'll feel better in the morning. [*She is taking off his shoes.*] These goddam arch supports[8] are killing me.

Linda: Take an aspirin. Should I get you an aspirin? It'll soothe you.

Willy [*with wonder*]: I was driving along, you understand? And I was fine. I was even observing the scenery. You can imagine, me looking at scenery, on the road every week of my life. But it's so beautiful up there, Linda, the trees are so thick, and the sun is warm. I opened the windshield and just let the warm air bathe over me. And then all of a sudden I'm going' off the road! I'm tellin' ya, I absolutely forgot I was driving. If I'd've gone the other way over the white line I might've killed somebody. So I went on again—and five minutes later I'm dreamin' again, and I nearly—[*He presses two fingers against his eyes.*] I have such thoughts, I have such strange thoughts.

Linda: Willy, dear. Talk to them again. There's no reason why you can't work in New York.

Willy: They don't need me in New York. I'm the New England man. I'm vital in New England.

Linda: But you're sixty years old. They can't expect you to keep travelling every week.

Willy: I'll have to send a wire to Portland. I'm supposed to see Brown and Morrison tomorrow morning at ten o'clock to show the line[9]. Goddammit[10], I could sell them! [*He starts putting on his jacket.*]

Linda [*taking the jacket from him*]: Why don't you go down to the place tomorrow and tell Howard you've simply got to work in New York? You're too accommodating, dear.

Willy: If old man Wagner was alive I'da been in charge of New York now! That man was a prince, he was a masterful man. But that boy of his, that Howard, he don't appreciate. When I went north the first time, the Wagner Company didn't know where New England was!

Linda: Why don't you tell those things to Howard, dear?

Willy [*encouraged*]: I will, I definitely will. Is there any cheese?

Linda: I'll make you a sandwich.

Willy: No, go to sleep. I'll take some milk. I'll be up right away. The boys in?

Linda: They're sleeping. Happy took Biff on a date tonight.

Willy [*interested*]: That so?

Linda: It was so nice to see them shaving together, one behind the other, in the bathroom. And going out together. You notice? The whole house smells of shaving lotion.

Willy: Figure it out. Work a lifetime to pay off a house. You finally own it, and there's nobody to live in it.

Linda: Well, dear, life is a casting off. It's always that way.

Willy: No, no, some people—some people accomplish something. Did Biff say anything after I went this morning?

Linda: You shouldn't have criticized him, Willy, especially after he just got off the train.

You mustn't lose your temper with him.

Willy: When the hell did I lose my temper? I simply asked him if he was making any money. Is that a criticism?

Linda: But, dear, how could he make any money?

Willy [*worried and angered*]: There's such an undercurrent in him. He became a moody man. Did he apologize when I left this morning?

Linda: He was crestfallen, Willy. You know how he admires you. I think if he finds himself, then you'll both be happier and not fight any more.

Willy: How can he find himself on a farm? Is that a life? A farmhand? In the beginning, when he was young, I thought, well, a young man, it's good for him to tramp around, take a lot of different jobs. But it's more than ten years now and he has yet to make thirty-five dollars a week!

Linda: He's finding himself, Willy.

Willy: Not finding yourself at the age of thirty-four is a disgrace!

Linda: Shh!

Willy: The trouble is he's lazy, goddammit!

Linda: Willy, please!

Willy: Biff is a lazy bum!

Linda: They're sleeping. Get something to eat. Go on down.

Willy: Why did he come home? I would like to know what brought him home.

Linda: I don't know. I think he's still lost, Willy. I think he's very lost.

Willy: Biff Loman is lost. In the greatest country in the world a young man with such—personal attractiveness, gets lost. And such a hard worker. There's one thing about Biff—he's not lazy.

Linda: Never.

Willy [*with pity and resolve*]: I'll see him in the morning; I'll have a nice talk with him. I'll get him a job selling. He could be big in no time. My God! Remember how they used to follow him around in high school? When he smiled at one of them their faces lit up. When he walked down the street... [*He loses himself in reminiscences.*]

Linda [*trying to bring him out of it*]: Willy, dear, I got a new kind of American-type cheese today. It's whipped.

Willy: Why do you get American when I like Swiss?

Linda: I just thought you'd like a change—

Willy: I don't want a change! I want Swiss cheese. Why am I always being contradicted?

Linda: [*with a covering laugh*]: I thought it would be a surprise.

Willy: Why don't you open a window in here, for God's sake?

Linda [*with infinite patience*]: They're all open, dear.

Willy: The way they boxed us in here. Bricks and windows, windows and bricks.

Linda: We should've bought the land next door.

Willy: The street is lined with cars. There's not a breath of fresh air in the neighbourhood. The grass don't grow any more, you can't raise a carrot in the backyard. They should've had a law against apartment houses. Remember those two beautiful elm trees out there? When I and Biff hung the swing between them?

Linda: Yeah, like being a million miles from the city.

Willy: They should've arrested the builder for cutting those down. They massacred the neighbourhood. [*Lost*] More and more I think of those days, Linda. This time of year it was lilac and wistaria. And then the peonies would come out, and the daffodils. What a fragrance in this room!

Linda: Well, after all, people had to move somewhere.

Willy: No, there's more people now.

Linda: I don't think there's more people, I think—

Willy: There's more people! That's what's ruining this country! Population is getting out of control. The competition is maddening! Smell the stink from that apartment house! And another one on the other side... How can they whip cheese?

[*On* WILLY'S *last line,* BIFF *and* HAPPY *raise themselves up in their beds, listening.*]

Linda: Go down, try it. And be quiet.

Willy [*turning to* LINDA, *guiltily*]: You're not worried about me, are you, sweetheart?

Biff: What's the matter?

Happy: Listen!

Linda: You've got too much on the ball to worry about.

Willy: You're my foundation and my support, Linda.

Linda: Just try to relax, dear. You make mountains out of molehills.

Willy: I won't fight with him any more. If he wants to go back to Texas, let him go.

Linda: He'll find his way.

Willy: Sure. Certain men just don't get started till later in life. Like Thomas Edison, I think. Or B. F. Goodrich. One of them was deaf. [*He starts for the bedroom doorway.*] I'll put my money on Biff.

Linda: And Willy—if it's warm Sunday we'll drive in the country. And we'll open the windshield, and take lunch.

Willy: No, the windshields don't open on the new cars.

Linda: But you opened it today.

Willy: Me? I didn't. [*He stops.*] Now isn't that peculiar! Isn't that a remarkable—[*He breaks off in amazement and fright as the flute is heard distantly.*]

Linda: What, darling?

Willy: That is the most remarkable thing.

Linda: What, dear?

Willy: I was thinking of the Chevvy. [*Slight pause.*] *Nineteen twenty-eight... when I had that red Chevvy*—[*Breaks off.*] That funny? I coulda sworn I was driving that Chevvy today.

Linda: Well, that's nothing. Something must've reminded you.

Willy: Remarkable. Ts. Remember those days? The way Biff used to simonize that car? The dealer refused to believe there was eighty thousand miles on it. [*He shakes his head.*] Heh! [*To* LINDA] Close your eyes, I'll be right up. [*He walks out of the bedroom.*]

Happy [*to* BIFF]: Jesus, maybe he smashed up the car again!

Linda [*calling after* WILLY]: Be careful on the stairs, dear! The cheese is on the middle shelf! [*She turns, goes over to the bed, takes his jacket, and goes out of the bedroom.*]

[*Light has risen on the boys' room. Unseen,* WILLY *is heard talking to himself, "Eighty thousand miles," and a little laugh.* BIFF *gets out of bed, comes downstage a bit, and stands attentively.* BIFF *is two years older than his brother* HAPPY, *well built, but in these days bears a worn air and seems less self-assured. He has succeeded less, and his dreams are stronger and less acceptable than* HAPPY'S. HAPPY *is tall, powerfully made. Sexuality is like a visible colour on him, or a scent that many women have discovered. He, like his brother, is lost, but in a different way, for he has never allowed himself to turn his face toward defeat and is thus more confused and hard-skinned, although seemingly more content.*]

Happy [*getting out of bed*]: He's going to get his licence taken away if he keeps that up. I'm getting nervous about him, y'know, Biff?

Biff: His eyes are going.

Happy: No, I've driven with him. He sees all right. He just doesn't keep his mind on it. I drove into the city with him last week. He stops at a green light and then it turns red and he goes. [*He laughs.*]

Biff: Maybe he's colour-blind.

Happy: Pop? Why, he's got the finest eye for colour in the business. You know that.

Biff [*sitting down on his bed*]: I'm going to sleep.

Happy: You're not still sour on Dad, are you, Biff?

Biff: He's all right, I guess.

Willy [*underneath them, in the living-room*]: Yes, sir, eighty thousand miles—eighty-two thousand!

Biff: You smoking?

Happy [*holding out a pack of cigarettes*]: Want one?

Biff [*taking a cigarette*]: I can never sleep when I smell it.

Willy: What a simonizing job, heh!

Happy [*with deep sentiment*]: Funny, Biff, y'know? Us sleeping in here again? The old beds. [*He pats his bed affectionately.*] All the talk that went across those two beds, huh? Our whole lives.

Biff: Yeah. Lotta dreams and plans.

Happy [*with a deep and masculine laugh*]: About five hundred women would like to know what was said in this room.

[*They share a soft laugh.*]

Biff: Remember that big Betsy something—what the hell was her name—over on Bushwick Avenue?

Happy [*combing his hair*]: With the collie dog!

Biff: That's the one. I got you in there, remember?

Happy: Yeah, that was my first time—I think. Boy, there was a pig! [*They laugh, almost crudely.*] You taught me everything I know about women. Don't forget that.

Biff: I bet you forgot how bashful you used to be. Especially with girls.

Happy: Oh, I still am, Biff.

Biff: Oh, go on.

Happy: I just control it, that's all. I think I got less bashful and you got more so. What happened, Biff? Where's the old humour, the old confidence? [*He shakes* BIFF's *knee.* BIFF *gets up and moves restlessly about the room.*] What's the matter?

Biff: Why does Dad mock me all the time?

Happy: He's not mocking you, he—

Biff: Everything I say there's a twist of mockery on his face. I can't get near him.

Happy: He just wants you to make good, that's all. I wanted to talk to you about Dad for a long time, Biff. Something's—happening to him. He—talks to himself.

Biff: I noticed that this morning. But he always mumbled.

Happy: But not so noticeable. It got so embarrassing I sent him to Florida. And you know something? Most of the time he's talking to you.

Biff: What's he say about me?

Happy: I can't make it out.

Biff: What's he say about me?

Happy: I think the fact that you're not settled, that you're still kind of up in the air...

Biff: There's one or two other things depressing him, Happy.

Happy: What do you mean?

Biff: Never mind. Just don't lay it all to me.

Happy: But I think if you got started—I mean—is there any future for you out there?

Biff: I tell ya, Hap, I don't know what the future is. I don't know—what I'm supposed to want.

Happy: What do you mean?

Biff: Well, I spent six or seven years after high school trying to work myself up. Shipping clerk, salesman, business of one kind or another. And it's a measly manner of existence. To get on that subway on the hot mornings in summer. To devote your whole life to keeping stock, or making phone calls, or selling or buying. To suffer fifty weeks of the year for the sake of a two-week vacation, when all you really desire is to be outdoors, with your shirt off. And always to have to get ahead of the next fella. And still—that's how you build a future.

Happy: Well, you really enjoy it on a farm? Are you content out there?

Biff [*with rising agitation*]: Hap, I've had twenty or thirty different kinds of job since I left home before the war, and it always turns out the same. I just realized it lately. In Nebraska when I herded cattle, and the Dakotas, and Arizona, and now in Texas. It's why I came home now, I guess, because I realized it. This farm I work on, it's spring there now, see? And they've got about fifteen new colts. There's nothing more inspiring or—beautiful than the sight of a mare and a new colt. And it's cool there now, see? Texas is cool now, and it's spring. And whenever spring comes to where I am, I suddenly get the feeling, my God, I'm not gettin' anywhere. What the hell am I doing, playing around with horses, twenty-eight dollars a week! I'm thirty-four years old, I oughta be makin' my future. That's when I come running home. And now, I get here, and I don't know what to do with myself. [*After a pause*] I've always made a point of not wasting my life, and everytime I come back here I know that all I've done is to waste my life.

Happy: You're a poet, you know that, Biff? You're a—you're an idealist!

Biff: No, I'm mixed up very bad. Maybe I oughta get married. Maybe I oughta get stuck into something. Maybe that's my trouble. I'm like a boy. I'm not married, I'm not in business, I just—I'm like a boy. Are you content, Hap? You're a success, aren't you? Are you content?

Happy: Hell, no!

Biff: Why? You're making money, aren't you?

Happy [*moving about with energy, expressiveness*]: All I can do now is wait for the merchandise manager to die. And suppose I get to be merchandise manager? He's a good friend of mine, and he just built a terrific estate on Long Island. And he lived there about two months and sold it, and now he's building another one. He can't enjoy it once it's finished. And I know that's just what I would do. I don't know what the hell I'm workin' for. Sometimes I sit in my apartment—all alone. And I think of the rent I'm paying. And it's crazy. But then, it's what I always wanted. My own apartment, a car, and plenty of women. And still, goddammit, I'm lonely.

Biff [*with enthusiasm*]: Listen, why don't you come out West with me?

Happy: You and I, heh?

Biff: Sure, maybe we could buy a ranch. Raise cattle, use our muscles. Men built like we are should be working out in the open.

Happy [*avidly*]: The Loman Brothers, heh?

Biff [*with vast affection*]: Sure, we'd be known all over the counties!

Happy [*enthralled*]: That's what I dream about, Biff. Sometimes I want to just rip my clothes off in the middle of the store and outbox that goddam merchandise manager. I mean I can outbox, outrun, and outlift anybody in that store, and I have to take orders from those common, petty sons-of-bitches till I can't stand it any more.

Biff: I'm tellin' you, kid, if you were with me I'd be happy out there.

Happy [*enthused*]: See, Biff, everybody around me is so false that I'm constantly lowering my ideals...

Biff: Baby, together we'd stand up for one another, we'd have someone to trust.

Happy: If I were around you—

Biff: Hap, the trouble is we weren't brought up to grub for money. I don't know how to do it.

Happy: Neither can I!

Biff: Then let's go!

Happy: The only thing is—what can you make out there?

Biff: But look at your friend. Builds an estate and then hasn't the peace of mind to live in it.

Happy: Yeah, but when he walks into the store the waves part in front of him. That's fifty-two thousand dollars a year coming through the revolving door, and I got more in my pinky finger than he's got in his head.

Biff: Yeah, but you just said—

Happy: I gotta show some of those pompous, self-important executives over there that Hap Loman can make the grade! I want to walk into the store the way he walks in. Then I'll go with you, Biff. We'll be together yet, I swear. But take those two we had tonight. Now weren't they gorgeous creatures?

Biff: Yeah, yeah, most gorgeous I've had in years.

Happy: I get that any time I want, Biff. Whenever I feel disgusted. The only trouble is, it gets like bowling or something. I just keep knockin' them over and it doesn't mean anything. You still run around a lot?

Biff: Naa. I'd like to find a girl—steady, somebody with substance.

Happy: That's what I long for.

Biff: Go on! You'd never come home.

Happy: I would! Somebody with character, with resistance! Like Mom, y'know? You're gonna call me a bastard when I tell you this. That girl Charlotte I was with tonight is engaged to be married in five weeks. [*He tries on his new hat.*]

Biff: No kiddin'!

Happy: Sure, the guy's in line for the vice-presidency of the store. I don't know what gets into me, maybe I just have an over-developed sense of competition or something, but I went and ruined her, and furthermore I can't get rid of her. And he's the third executive I've done that to. Isn't that a crummy characteristic? And to top it all, I go to their weddings! [*Indignantly, but laughing*] Like I'm not supposed to take bribes. Manufacturers offer me a hundred-dollar bill now and then to throw an order their way. You know how honest I am, but it's like this girl, see. I hate myself for it. Because I don't want the girl, and still, I take it and—I love it!

Biff: Let's go to sleep.

Happy: I guess we didn't settle anything, heh?

Biff: I just got one idea that I think I'm going to try.

Happy: What's that?

Biff: Remember Bill Oliver?

Happy: Sure, Oliver is very big now. You want to work for him again?

Biff: No, but when I quit he said something to me. He put his arm on my shoulder, and he said, "Biff, if you ever need anything, come to me."

Happy: I remember that. That sounds good.

Biff: I think I'll go to see him. If I could get ten thousand or even seven or eight thousand dollars I could buy a beautiful ranch.

Happy: I bet he'd back you. 'Cause he thought highly of you, Biff. I mean, they all do. You're well liked, Biff. That's why I say to come back here, and we both have the apartment. And I'm tellin' you, Biff, any babe you want...

Biff: No, with a ranch I could do the work I like and still be something. I just wonder though. I wonder if Oliver still thinks I stole that carton of basketballs.

Happy: Oh, he probably forgot that long ago, It's almost ten years. You're too sensitive. Anyway, he didn't really fire you.

Biff: Well, I think he was going to. I think that's why I quit. I was never sure whether he knew or not. I know he thought the world of me, though. I was the only one he'd let lock up the place.

Willy [*below*]: You gonna wash the engine, Biff?

Happy: Shh!

[BIFF *looks at* HAPPY, *who is gazing down, listening* WILLY *is mumbling in the parlour.*]

Happy: You hear that?

[*They listen.* WILLY *laughs warmly.*]

Biff [*growing angry*]: Doesn't he know Mom can hear that?

Willy: Don't get your sweater dirty, Biff!

[*A look of pain crosses* BIFF'S *face.*]

Happy: Isn't that terrible? Don't leave again, will you? You'll find a job here. You gotta stick around. I don't know what to do about him, it's getting embarrassing.

Willy: What a simonizing job!

Biff: Mom's hearing that!

Willy: No kiddin', Biff, you got a date? Wonderful!

Happy: Go on to sleep. But talk to him in the morning, will you?

Biff [*reluctantly getting into bed*]: With her in the house. Brother!

Happy [*getting into bed*]: I wish you'd have a good talk with him.

[*The light on their room begins to lade.*]

Biff [*to himself in bed*]: That selfish, stupid...

Happy: Sh ... Sleep, Biff.

[*Their light is out. Well before they have finished speaking,* WILLY's *form is dimly seen below in the darkened kitchen. He opens the refrigerator, searches in there, and takes out a bottle of milk. The apartment houses are fading out, and the entire house and surroundings become covered with leaves. Music insinuates itself as the leaves appear.*]

Willy: Just wanna be careful with those girls, Biff, that's all. Don't make any promises. No promises of any kind. Because a girl, y' know, they always believe what you tell 'em, and you're very young, Biff, you're too young to be talking seriously to girls.

[*Light rises on the kitchen.* WILLY, *talking, shuts the refrigerator door and comes downstage to the kitchen table. He pours milk into a glass. He is totally immersed in himself, smiling faintly.*]

Willy: Too young entirely, Biff. You want to watch your schooling first. Then when you're all set, there'll be plenty of girls for a boy like you. [*He smiles broadly at a kitchen chair.*] That so? The girls pay for you? [*He laughs.*] Boy, you must really be makin' a hit.

[WILLY *is gradually addressing—physically—a point offstage, speaking through the wall of the kitchen, and his voice has been rising in volume to that of a normal conversation.*]

Willy: I been wondering why you polish the car so careful. Ha! Don't leave the hubcaps, boys. Get the chamois to the hubcaps. Happy, use newspaper on the windows, it's the easiest thing. Show him how to do it, Biff! You see, Happy? Pad it up, use it like a pad. That's it, that's it, good work. You're doin' all right, Hap. [*He pauses, then nods in approbation for a few seconds, then looks upward.*] Biff, first thing we gotta do when we get time is clip that big branch over the house. Afraid it's gonna fall in a storm and hit the roof. Tell you what. We get a rope and sling her around, and then we climb up there with a couple of saws and take her down. Soon as you finish the car, boys, I wanna see ya. I got a surprise for you, boys.

Biff [*offstage*]: Whatta ya got, Dad?

Willy: No, you finish first. Never leave a job till you're finished—remember that. [*Looking toward the "big trees"*] Biff, up in Albany I saw a beautiful hammock. I think I'll buy it next trip, and we'll hang it right between those two elms. Wouldn't that be something? Just swingin' there under those branches. Boy, that would be...

[YOUNG BIFF *and* YOUNG HAPPY *appear from the direction* WILLY *was addressing.* HAPPY *carries rags and a pail of water.* BIFF, *wearing a sweater with a block "S", carries a football.*]

Biff [*pointing in the direction of the car offstage*]: How's that, Pop, professional?

Willy: Terrific. Terrific job, boys. Good work, Biff.

Happy: Where's the surprise, Pop?

Willy: In the back seat of the car.

Happy: Boy! [*He runs off.*]

Biff: What is it, Dad? Tell me, what'd you buy?

Willy [*laughing, cuffs him*]: Never mind, something I want you to have.

Biff [*turns and starts off*]: What is it, Hap?

Happy [*offstage*]: It's a punching bag!

Biff: Oh, Pop!

Willy: It's got Gene Tunney's signature on it!

[HAPRY *runs onstage with a punching bag.*]

Biff: Gee, how'd you know we wanted a punching bag?

Willy: Well, it's the finest thing for the timing.

Happy [*lies down on his back and pedals with his feet*]: I'm losing weight, you notice, Pop?

Willy [to HAPPY]: Jumping rope is good too.

Biff: Did you see the new football I got?

Willy [*examining the ball*]: Where'd you get a new ball?

Biff: The coach told me to practise my passing.

Willy: That so? And he gave you the ball, heh?

Biff: Well, I borrowed it from the locker room. [*He laughs confidentially.*]

Willy [*laughing with him at the theft*]: I want you to return that.

Happy: I told you he wouldn't like it!

Biff [*angrily*]: Well, I'm bringing it back!

Willy [*stopping the incipient argument, to* HAPPY]: Sure, he's gotta practise with a regulation ball, doesn't he? [*To* BIFF] Coach'll probably congratulate you on your initiative!

Biff: Oh, he keeps congratulating my initiative all the time, Pop.

Willy: That's because he likes you. If somebody else took that ball there'd be an uproar. So what's the report, boys, what's the report?

Biff: Where'd you go this time, Dad? Gee, we were lonesome for you.

Willy [*pleased, puts an arm around each boy and they come down to the apron*]: Lonesome, heh?

Biff: Missed you every minute.

Willy: Don't say? Tell you a secret, boys. Don't breathe it to a soul. Someday I'll have my own business, and I'll never have to leave home any more.

Happy: Like Uncle Charley, heh?

Willy: Bigger than Uncle Chanley! Because Charley is not—liked. He's liked, but he's not—well liked.

Biff: Where'd you go this time, Dad?

Willy: Well, I got on the road, and I went north to Providence. Met the Mayor.

Biff: The Mayor of Providence!

Willy: He was sitting in the hotel lobby.

Biff: What'd he say?

Willy: He said, "Morning!" And I said, "You got a fine city here, Mayor." And then he had coffee with me. And then I went to Waterbury. Waterbury is a fine city. Big clock city, the famous

Waterbury clock. Sold a nice bill there. And then Boston—Boston is the cradle of the Revolution. A fine city. And a couple of other towns in Mass., and on to Portland and Bangor and straight home!

Biff: Gee, I'd love to go with you sometime, Dad.

Willy: Soon as summer comes.

Happy: Promise?

Willy: You and Hap and I, and I'll show you all the towns. America is full of beautiful towns and fine, upstanding people. And they know me, boys, they know me up and down New England. The finest people. And when I bring you fellas up, there'll be open sesame for all of us, 'cause one thing, boys: I have friends. I can park my car in any street in New England, and the cops protect it like their own. This summer, heh?

Biff and Happy [*together*]: Yeah! You bet!

Willy: We'll take our bathing-suits.

Happy: We'll carry your bags, Pap!

Willy: Oh, won't that be something! Me comin' into the Boston stores with you boys carryin' my bags. What a sensation!

[BIFF *is prancing around, practising passing the ball.*]

Willy: You nervous, Biff, about the game?

Biff: Not if you're gonna be there.

Willy: What do they say about you in school, now that they made you captain?

Happy: There's a crowd of girls behind him every time the classes change.

Biff [*taking* WILLY's *hand*]: This Saturday, Pop, this Saturday—just for you, I'm going to break through for a touchdown.

Happy: You're supposed to pass.

Biff: I'm takin' one play for Pop. You watch me, Pop, and when I take off my helmet, that means I'm breakin' out. Then watch me crash through that line!

Willy [*kisses* BIFF]: Oh, wait'll I tell this in Boston!

[*BERNARD enters in knickers. He is younger than BIFF, earnest and loyal, a worried boy.*]

Bernard: Biff, where are you? You're supposed to study with me today.

Willy: Hey, looka Bernard. What're you lookin' so anaemic about, Bernard?

Bernard: He's gotta study, Uncle Willy. He's got Regents next week.

Happy [*tauntingly, spinning* BERNARD *around*]: Let's box, Bernard!

Bernard: Biff! [*He gets away from* HAPPY.] Listen, Biff, I heard Mr Birnbaum say that if you don't start studyin' math he's gonna flunk you, and you won't graduate. I heard him!

Willy: You better study with him, Biff. Go ahead now.

Bernard: I heard him!

Biff: Oh, Pop, you didn't see my sneakers! [*He holds up a foot for* WILLY *to look at.*]

Willy: Hey, that's a beautiful job of printing!

Bernard [*wiping his glasses*]: Just because he printed University of Virginia on his sneakers doesn't mean they've got to graduate him, Uncle Willy!

Willy [*angrily*]: What're you talking about? With scholarships to three universities they're gonna flunk him?

Bernard: But I heard Mr Birnbaum say—

Willy: Don't be a pest, Bernard! [*To his boys*] What an anaemic!

Bernard: Okay, I'm waiting for you in my house, Biff.

[BERNARD *goes off. The* LOMANS *laugh.*]

Willy: Bernard is not well liked, is he?

Biff: He's liked, but he's not well liked.

Happy: That's right, Pop.

Willy: That's just what I mean, Bernard can get the best marks in school, y'understand, but when he gets out in the business world, y'understand, you are going to be five times ahead of him. That's why I thank Almighty God you're both built like Adonises. Because the man who makes an appearance in the business world, the man who creates personal interest, is the man who gets ahead. Be liked and you will never want. You take me, for instance. I never have to wait in line to see a buyer. "Willy Loman is here!" That's all they have to know, and I go right through.

Biff: Did you knock them dead, Pop?

Willy: Knocked 'em cold in Providence, slaughtered 'em in Boston.

Happy [*on his back, pedalling again*]: I'm losing weight, you notice, Pop?

[LINDA *enters, as of old, a ribbon in her hair, carrying a basket of washing.*]

Linda [*with youthful energy*]: Hello, dear!

Willy: Sweetheart!

Linda: How'd the Chevvy run?

Willy: Chevrolet, Linda, is the greatest car ever built. [*To the boys*] Since when do you let your mother carry wash up the stairs?

Biff: Grab hold there, boy!

Happy: Where to, Mom?

Linda: Hang them up on the line. And you better go down to your friends, Biff. The cellar is full of boys. They don't know what to do with themselves.

Biff: Ah, when Pop comes home they can wait!

Willy [*laughs appreciatively*]: You better go down and tell them what to do, Biff.

Biff: I think I'll have them sweep out the furnace room.

Willy: Good work, Biff.

Biff [*goes through wall-line of kitchen to doorway at back and calls down*]: Fellas! Everybody sweep out the furnace room! I'll be right down!

***Voices*:** All right! Okay, Biff.

Biff: George and Sam and Frank, come out back! We're hangin' up the wash! Come on, Hap, on the double! [*He and* HAPPY *carry out the basket.*]

Linda: The way they obey him!

Willy: Well, that's training, the training. I'm tellin' you, I was sellin' thousands and thousands, but I had to come home.

Linda: Oh, the whole block'll be at that game. Did you sell anything?

Willy: I did five hundred gross in Providence and seven hundred gross in Boston.

Linda: No! Wait a minute, I've got a pencil. [*She pulls pencil and paper out of her apron pocket.*] That makes your commission... Two hundred, my God! Two hundred and twelve dollars!

Willy: Well, I didn't figure it yet, but….

Linda : How much did you do?

Willy: Well, I—I did—about a hundred and eighty gross in Providence. Well, no—it came to—roughly two hundred gross on the whole trip.

Linda [*without hesitation*]: Two hundred gross. That's ... [*She figures.*]

Willy: The trouble was that three of the stores were halfclosed for inventory in Boston. Otherwise I woulda broke records.

Linda : Well, it makes seventy dollars and some pennies. That's very good.

Willy: What do we owe?

Linda : Well, on the first there's sixteen dollars on the refrigerator—

Willy: Why sixteen?

Linda : Well, the fan belt broke, so it was a dollar eighty.

Willy: But it's brand new.

Linda : Well, the man said that's the way it is. Till they work themselves in, y'know.

[*They move through the wall-line into the kitchen.*]

Willy: I hope we didn't get stuck on that machine.

Linda : They got the biggest ads of any of them!

Willy: I know, it's a fine machine. What else?

Linda : Well, there's nine-sixty for the washing-machine. And for the vacuum cleaner there's three and a half due on the fifteenth. Then the roof, you got twenty-one dollars remaining.

Willy: It don't leak, does It?

Linda : No, they did a wonderful job. Then you owe Frank for the carburettor.

Willy: I'm not going to pay that man! That goddam Chevrolet, they ought to prohibit the manufacture of that car!

Linda : Well, you owe him three and a half. And odds and ends, comes to around a hundred and twenty dollars by the fifteenth.

Willy: A hundred and twenty dollars! My God, if business don't pick up I don't know what I'm gonna do!

Linda : Well, next week you'll do better.

Willy: Oh, I'll knock 'em dead next week. I'll go to Hartford. I'm very well liked in Hartford. You know, the trouble is, Linda, people don't seem to take to me.

[*They move on to the forestage.*]

Linda : Oh, don't be foolish.

Willy: I know it when I walk in. They seem to laugh at me.

Linda : Why? Why would they laugh at you? Don't talk that way, Willy.

[WILLY *moves to the edge of the stage.* LINDA *goes into the kitchen and starts to darn stockings.*]

Willy: I don't know the reason for it, but they just pass me by. I'm not noticed.

Linda : But you're doing wonderful, dear. You're making seventy to a hundred dollars a week.

Willy: But I gotta be at it ten, twelve hours a day. Other men—I don't know—they do it easier. I don't know why—I can't stop myself—I talk too much. A man oughta come in with a few words. One thing about Charley. He's a man of few words, and they respect him.

Linda : You don't talk too much, you're just lively.

Willy [*smiling*]: Well, I figure, what the hell, life is short, a couple of jokes. [*To himself*] I joke too much! [*The smile goes.*]

Linda: Why? You're—

Willy: I'm fat. I'm very—foolish to look at, Linda. I didn't tell you, but Christmas-time I happened to be calling on F. H. Stewarts, and a salesman I know, as I was going in to see the buyer I heard him say something about—walrus. And I—I cracked him right across the face. I won't take that. I simply will not take that. But they do laugh at me. I know that.

Linda: Darling...

Willy: I gotta overcome it. I know I gotta overcome it. I'm not dressing to advantage, maybe.

Linda: Willy, darling, you're the handsomest man in the world—

Willy: Oh, no, Linda.

Linda: To me you are. [*Slight pause.*] The handsomest.

[*From the darkness is heard the laughter of a woman.* WILLY *doesn't turn to it, but it continues through* LINDA'S *lines.*]

Linda: And the boys, Willy. Few men are idolized by their children the way you are.

[*Music is heard as behind a scrim, to the left of the house, the* WOMAN, *dimly seen, is dressing.*]

Willy [*with great feeling*]: You're the best there is, Linda, you're a pal, you know that? On the road—on the road I want to grab you sometimes and just kiss the life outa you.

[*The laughter is loud now, and he moves into a brightening area at the left, where the* WOMAN *has come from behind the scrim and is standing, putting on her hat, looking into a "mirror", and laughing.*]

Willy: 'Cause I get so lonely—especially when business is bad and there's nobody to talk to. I get the feeling that I'll never sell anything again, that I won't make a living for you, or a business, a business for the boys. [*He talks through the* WOMAN'S *subsiding laughter; the* WOMAN *primps at the "mirror".*] There's so much I want to make for—

The Woman: Me? You didn't make me, Willy. I picked you.

Willy [*pleased*]: You picked me?

The Woman [*who is quite proper-looking, Willy's age*]: I did. I've been sitting at that desk watching all the salesmen go by, day in, day out. But you've got such a sense of humour, and we do have such a good time together, don't we?

Willy: Sure, sure. [*He takes her in his arms.*] Why do you have to go now?

The Woman: It's two o'clock...

Willy: No, come on in! [*He pulls her.*]

The Woman: ... my sisters'll be scandalized. When'll you be back?

Willy: Oh, two weeks about. Will you come up again?

The Woman: Sure thing. You do make me laugh. It's good for me. [*She squeezes his arm, kisses him.*] And I think you're a wonderful man.

Willy: You picked me, heh?

The Woman: Sure. Because you're so sweet. And such a kidder.

Willy: Well, I'll see you next time I'm in Boston.

The Woman: I'll put you right through to the buyers.

Willy [*slapping her bottom*]: Right. Well, bottoms up!

The Woman [*slaps him gently and laughs*]: You just kill me, Willy. [*He suddenly grabs her and kisses her roughly.*] You kill me. And thanks for the stockings. I love a lot of stockings. Well, good night.

Willy: Good night. And keep your pores open!

The Woman: Oh, Willy!

…

CURTAIN

NOTES

1. towering, angular shapes: 高耸、呈尖角的轮廓，指周围的公寓大楼
2. the roof-line of the house is one-dimensional: 屋顶的轮廓呈线条状（不用实景屋顶）
3. before the house lies ... into the orchestra: 屋前的台口在前台成弧形，伸进乐池中
4. sample case: 装样品的箱子
5. most often jovial, she has ... to Willy's behavior: 她极大部分时间都笑嘻嘻的，以坚定的意志抑制自己对威利任何行为的不同看法，完全成了她的习惯
6. the shoulder: 公路两边不铺柏油的路肩
7. I just got back from Florida: Willy 显然刚从 Florida 休假回来。Florida: 佛罗里达州是美国著名的旅游、度假胜地。
8. arch supports: 鞋楦
9. show the line: 让他们看货。line:（美语）a stock of goods of a particular type, 某类各种规格商品的存货（样品）
10. Goddammit 即 God damn it

About the Author:

Arthur Miller was born on October 17, 1915 in Manhattan, a middle-class Jewish family who studied journalism and won a scriptwriting award in Michigan. In 1947, he created *All My Son*, which made him famous. Two years later, Miller wrote the *Death of a Salesman* and won three awards, including the Pulitzer Prize, which at the same time earned him an international reputation. Many critics described *Death of a Salesman* as a great American tragedy. Miller earned his outstanding position as a dramatist who understands the profound nature of the United States. Miller's social drama mainly reflects the freedom of speech, freedom of belief, freedom from poverty, freedom from Confucianism and the freedom of American culture. In 1953, *The Witch of Salem* was written to reflect the state of political hysteria in the United States. *The Witch of Salem* reproduces the fear of witchcraft. Miller also twice won the New York Film Critics Award. Arthur Miller's creation highlights the unwavering pursuit of freedom in the Native American drama spirit. Arthur Miller, Eugene O'Neill and Tennessee Williams are regarded as the three great American dramatists in the 20th century.

Appreciation:

米勒的作品是现实主义手法的悲剧作品，他戏剧的主角多为普通人、小人物，通过平凡人、底层人物的“喜怒哀乐”的悲剧人生及不断挣扎的生存意识来反映残酷的社会现实。米勒最著名的作品——《推销员之死》，运用父子关系作为人物关系主线，讲述了美国经济大萧条时期一个家庭内部的矛盾冲突，同时也探讨了美国国家价值等更实际的问题。这部剧反映出对小人物美国梦的盲目追求。第二次世界大战后，美国面临着深刻而尖锐的内外矛盾：经济与社会的冲突、意识形态和文化观念的冲突、政治主张的冲突、物质财富与精神空虚的冲突、种族矛盾、成功的渴望等都加深了人们的焦虑与不满。美国内外环境的不安定，使得新一代的艺术家和作家受到存在主义哲学的影响，开始拿起手中的武器通过文字来表达个人、实现自我。米勒塑造的戏剧人物控诉了美国的资本主义鼓吹虚假的英雄主义和成功的神话，掩盖了个人真理和道德，违背了国家创始人所描述的最初的美国梦。在《推销员之死》中，米勒通过虚构人物威利美国梦的追求至其破灭，使人们感受到生存环境、社会环境和家庭环境对人的影响，对人性的考验。在该剧中，米勒成功地触及了国家精神及集体意识的深层意义。

这部剧的大部分情节和场景都设置在威利居住的布鲁克林社区家中。不同于纽约市的喧嚣，这个社区过去曾有着不断延伸的空间。当男女主人公威利和琳达买下它时，代表了威利对未来的希望。然而随着情节的发展，房子四周都被高楼、公寓楼包围，生存空间的不断挤压代表着威利梦想的逐渐破灭，威利的自我也被怀疑和否定所包围，将无法实现美国梦所承诺的名声和财富。米勒在剧中深刻描绘了威利的梦想与现实的冲突。在他的一生中，他构建了无数的幻想和期望，最初幻想失败时，威利会通过严重的自我欺骗来安慰自己，始终无法认清自我和现实，任自己生活在过去的幻想、自我想象及未来的白日梦中。由于心理需求无法满足，他的意识支离破碎，言行自相矛盾。戏剧中几个相关主题如下：

美国梦

受战后美国人对物质享受风气的影响，威利肤浅地认为美国梦的实现需要“魅力”和“亲和力”，这种错误的执着与对美国梦的更坚韧、更有益的理解背道而驰。个人努力和辛勤工作是美国梦成功的关键，而威利理解的成功在于是否获得上司的欣赏，个人野心是否实现。威利对美国梦的盲目信仰及不当理解导致他无法接受梦想与实际生活之间的差距，产生心理失落及痛苦。

家庭

威利幼时遭遇父亲的遗弃，这使得他想要自己家庭符合美国梦。然而，当他发现自己努力培养的完美儿子比夫在工作及生活上的不完美时，他陷入绝望之中。比夫在商业上的失败，使他与威利疏远。威利相信，他有权利期待比夫履行他所固有的承诺。当比夫无法实现威利的自我野心时，威利将这种拒绝视作对自身的侮辱，对他野心的背叛和作为父亲能力的失败。

神话

威利崇尚神话人物源于他对世界的理解及面临困境的自我欺骗。他认为传奇人物戴夫·辛格曼（Dave Singleman）的死一定是高尚的。威利提及希腊神话人物阿多尼斯和赫克勒斯，似乎他们是美国梦的化身，威利的神话信仰很盲目，连带对自己儿子比夫的个人魅力不切实际的假想，比夫事业的失败和缺乏雄心让威利深感绝望，野心落空，最终威利离想象中的快乐富足的生活及美国梦越来越远，徒留下悲惨的死亡及毫无意义的遗产。

米勒的社会剧大多呈现出悲剧的审美形态，存在着戏剧形式的传统与创新、本土与外来矛盾的冲突和融合，表现为对于人争取自我尊严及不断努力想要改变命运是给予肯定并赞扬的，但他同时指出人应当避免自我毁灭，适应自己在社会中的处境，而不是过度自负或追求无法实现的野心。米勒的戏剧创作关注社会问题，探究人的生命价值和意义，赞扬良知、责任感和正义感，这也是其社会剧的魅力所在。

Questions:

1. What evidence can we find to show that Willy may have chosen a profession that deviates from his natural inclinations?

2. Willy recalls his sons' teenage years as an idyllic past. Do you think the past is as idyllic as Willy imagines it to be?

3. How does Willy's interview with Howard reveal that Willy incorporates his professional and personal realms of his life?

4. What role does the fear of abandonment play in Willy's life? What evidence can we find ?

5. Are there any resemblance between Willy's desperate quest for the American Dream and a religious crusade?

6. Discuss the expressionistic elements in the play. How does it function as a way for Willy to move away from realism?

Part 6
Fiction

Novel

Definition of a Novel:

A novel is a long, fictional narrative which describes intimate human experiences. The novel in the modern era usually makes use of a literary prose style, and the development of the prose novel at this time was encouraged by innovations in printing, and the introduction of cheap paper, in the 15th century.

Elements of a Novel:

Like any other works of art, a novel is an organic whole. Its various elements are created simultaneously by novelists and cannot be separated without losing their perspectives. However, for the sake of focused analysis we can provisionally isolate some of its elements and give them due consideration. The major elements of a novel include: story, character, plot, theme, setting, style and point of view.

Origins of the Novel:

The genre has been described as having "a continuous and comprehensive history of about two thousand years," with its origins in classical Greece and Rome, in medieval and early modern romance, and in the tradition of the novella. The latter, an Italian word for a short story to distinguish it from a novel, has been used in English since the 18th century for a work that falls somewhere in between. Ian Watt, in *The Rise of the Novel*, suggested in 1957 that the novel first came into being in the early 18th century. Miguel de Cervantes, author of *Don Quixote* (the first part of which was published in 1605), is frequently cited as the first significant European novelist of the modern era.

How to Read a Novel:

While reading a novel, try to answer the following questions. These are the essential parts of the novel, and you need to grasp them before moving on to more difficult discussions.

(1) What does the main character(s) want?

(2) Who is telling the story?

(3) Where and when is the story set?

(4) What is the narrator's role in the story?

(5) What is the style of the story?

American Fiction

Young Goodman Brown (Excerpt)

Young Goodman Brown came forth, at sunset, into the street at Salem village; but put his head back, after crossing the threshold, to exchange a parting kiss with his young wife. And Faith, as the wife was aptly named, thrust her own pretty head into the street, letting the wind play with the pink ribbons of her cap, while she called to Goodman Brown.

"Dearest heart," whispered she, softly and rather sadly, when her lips were close to his ear, "pr'y thee, put off your journey until sunrise, and sleep in your own bed to-night. A lone woman is troubled with such dreams and such thoughts that she's afeard of herself, sometimes. Pray, tarry with me this night, dear husband, of all nights in the year!"

"My love and my Faith," replied young Goodman Brown, "of all nights in the year, this one night must I tarry away from thee. My journey, as thou callest it, forth and back again, must needs be done 'twixt now and sunrise. What, my sweet, pretty wife, dost thou doubt me already, and we but three months married!"

"Then God bless you!" said Faith, with the pink ribbons, "and may you find all well when you come back."

"Amen!" cried Goodman Brown. "Say thy prayers, dear Faith, and go to bed at dusk, and no harm will come to thee."

So they parted; and the young man pursued his way until, being about to turn the corner by the meeting-house, he looked back and saw the head of Faith still peeping after him with a melancholy air, in spite of her pink ribbons.

"Poor little Faith!" thought he, for his heart smote him. "What a wretch am I to leave her on such an errand! She talks of dreams, too. Methought, as she spoke, there was trouble in her face, as if a dream had warned her what work is to be done to-night. But no, no! 't would kill her to think it. Well, she's a blessed angel on earth; and after this one night, I'll cling to her skirts and follow her to heaven."

With this excellent resolve for the future, Goodman Brown felt himself justified in making more haste on his present evil purpose. He had taken a dreary road, darkened by all the gloomiest trees of the forest, which barely stood aside to let the narrow path creep through, and closed immediately behind. It was all as lonely as could be; and there is this peculiarity in such a solitude, that the traveller knows not who may be concealed by the innumerable trunks and the thick boughs overhead; so that with lonely footsteps he may yet be passing through an unseen multitude.

"There may be a devilish Indian behind every tree," said Goodman Brown to himself; and he glanced fearfully behind him as he added, "What if the devil himself should be at my very elbow!"

His head being turned back, he passed a crook of the road, and, looking forward again, beheld the figure of a man, in grave and decent attire, seated at the foot of an old tree. He arose at Goodman Brown's approach and walked onward side by side with him.

"You are late, Goodman Brown," said he. "The clock of the Old South was striking as I came through Boston, and that is full fifteen minutes agone."

"Faith kept me back a while," replied the young man, with a tremor in his voice, caused by the sudden appearance of his companion, though not wholly unexpected.

It was now deep dusk in the forest, and deepest in that part of it where these two were journeying. As nearly as could be discerned, the second traveller was about fifty years old, apparently in the same rank of life as Goodman Brown, and bearing a considerable resemblance to him, though perhaps more in expression than features. Still they might have been taken for father and son. And yet, though the elder person was as simply clad as the younger, and as simple in manner too, he had an indescribable air of one who knew the world, and who would not have felt abashed at the governor's dinner table or in King William's[1] court, were it possible that his affairs should call him thither. But the only thing about him that could be fixed upon as remarkable was his staff, which bore the likeness of a great black snake, so curiously wrought that it might almost be seen to twist and wriggle itself like a living serpent. This, of course, must have been an ocular deception, assisted by the uncertain light.

"Come, Goodman Brown," cried his fellow-traveller, "this is a dull pace for the beginning of a journey. Take my staff, if you are so soon weary."

"Friend," said the other, exchanging his slow pace for a full stop,"having kept covenant by meeting thee here, it is my purpose now to return whence I came. I have scruples touching the matter thou wot'st of."

"Sayest thou so?" replied he of the serpent, smiling apart. "Let us walk on, nevertheless, reasoning as we go; and if I convince thee not thou shalt turn back. We are but a little way in the forest yet."

"Too far! too far!" exclaimed the Goodman, unconsciously resuming his walk. "My father never went into the woods on such an errand, nor his father before him. We have been a race of honest men and good Christians since the days of the martyrs[2]. And shall I be the first of the name of Brown that ever took this path and kept"—

"Such company, thou wouldst say," observed the elder person, interpreting his pause. "Well said, Goodman Brown! I have been as well acquainted with your family as with ever a one among the Puritans; and that's no trifle to say. I helped your grandfather, the constable, when he lashed the Quaker woman so smartly through the streets of Salem; and it was I that brought your father a pitch-pine knot, kindled at my own hearth, to set fire to an Indian village, in King Philip's war[3]. They were my good friends, both; and many a pleasant walk have we had along this path, and returned merrily after midnight. I would fain be friends with you for their sake."

"If it be as thou sayest," replied Goodman Brown, "I marvel they never spoke of these matters; or, verily, I marvel not, seeing that the least rumor of the sort would have driven them from New England. We are a people of prayer, and good works to boot, and abide no such wickedness."

"Wickedness or not," said the traveller with the twisted staff, "I have a very general acquaintance here in New England. The deacons of many a church have drunk the communion wine with me; the selectmen of divers towns make me their chairman; and a majority of the Great and General Court[4] are firm supporters of my interest. The governor and I, too—But these are state secrets."

"Can this be so?" cried Goodman Brown, with a stare of amazement at his undisturbed companion. "Howbeit, I have nothing to do with the governor and council; they have their own ways, and are no rule for a simple husbandman[5] like me. But, were I to go on with thee, how should I meet the eye of that good old man, our minister, at Salem village? Oh, his voice would make me tremble both Sabbath day and lecture day[6]."

Thus far the elder traveller had listened with due gravity; but now burst into a fit of irrepressible mirth, shaking himself so violently that his snake-like staff actually seemed to wriggle in sympathy.

"Ha! ha! ha!" shouted he again and again; then composing himself, "Well, go on, Goodman Brown, go on; but, prithee, don't kill me with laughing."

"Well, then, to end the matter at once," said Goodman Brown, considerably nettled, "there is my wife, Faith. It would break her dear little heart; and I'd rather break my own."

"Nay, if that be the case," answered the other, "e'en go thy ways, Goodman Brown. I would not for twenty old women like the one hobbling before us that Faith should come to any harm."

As he spoke he pointed his staff at a female figure on the path, in whom Goodman Brown recognized a very pious and exemplary dame, who had taught him his catechism in youth, and was still his moral and spiritual adviser, jointly with the minister and Deacon Gookin.

"A marvel, truly, that Goody Cloyse[7] should be so far in the wilderness at nightfall," said he. "But with your leave, friend, I shall take a cut through the woods until we have left this Christian woman behind. Being a stranger to you, she might ask whom I was consorting with and whither I was going."

"Be it so," said his fellow-traveller. "Betake you to the woods, and let me keep the path."

Accordingly the young man turned aside, but took care to watch his companion, who advanced softly along the road until he had come within a staff's length of the old dame. She, meanwhile, was making the best of her way, with singular speed for so aged a woman, and mumbling some indistinct words—a prayer, doubtless—as she went. The traveller put forth his staff and touched her withered neck with what seemed the serpent's tail.

"The devil!" screamed the pious old lady.

"Then Goody Cloyse knows her old friend?" observed the traveller, confronting her and leaning on his writhing stick.

"Ah, forsooth, and is it your worship indeed?" cried the good dame. "Yea, truly is it, and in the very image of my old gossip, Goodman Brown, the grandfather of the silly fellow that now is. But—would your worship believe it?—my broomstick hath strangely disappeared, stolen, as I suspect, by that unhanged witch, Goody Cory, and that, too, when I was all anointed with the juice of smallage, and cinquefoil, and wolf's bane[8]"—

"Mingled with fine wheat and the fat of a new-born babe," said the shape of old Goodman Brown.

"Ah, your worship knows the recipe," cried the old lady, cackling aloud. "So, as I was saying, being all ready for the meeting, and no horse to ride on, I made up my mind to foot it; for they tell me there is a nice young man to be taken into communion to-night. But now your good worship will lend me your arm, and we shall be there in a twinkling."

"That can hardly be," answered her friend. "I may not spare you my arm, Goody Cloyse; but here is my staff, if you will."

So saying, he threw it down at her feet, where, perhaps, it assumed life, being one of the rods which its owner had formerly lent to the Egyptian magi[9]. Of this fact, however, Goodman Brown could not take cognizance. He had cast up his eyes in astonishment, and, looking down again, beheld neither Goody Cloyse nor the serpentine staff, but his fellow-traveller alone, who waited for him as calmly as if nothing had happened.

"That old woman taught me my catechism," said the young man; and there was a world of meaning in this simple comment.

They continued to walk onward, while the elder traveller exhorted his companion to make good speed and persevere in the path, discoursing so aptly that his arguments seemed rather to spring up in the bosom of his auditor than to be suggested by himself. As they went, he plucked a branch of maple to serve for a walking stick, and began to strip it of the twigs and little boughs, which were wet with evening dew. The moment his fingers touched them they became strangely withered and dried up as with a week's sunshine. Thus the pair proceeded, at a good free pace, until suddenly, in a gloomy hollow of the road, Goodman Brown sat himself down on the stump of a tree and refused to go any farther.

"Friend," said he, stubbornly, "my mind is made up. Not another step will I budge on this errand. What if a wretched old woman do choose to go to the devil when I thought she was going to heaven: is that any reason why I should quit my dear Faith and go after her?"

"You will think better of this by and by," said his acquaintance, composedly. "Sit here and rest yourself a while; and when you feel like moving again, there is my staff to help you along."

Without more words, he threw his companion the maple stick, and was as speedily out of sight as if he had vanished into the deepening gloom. The young man sat a few moments by the roadside, applauding himself greatly, and thinking with how clear a conscience he should meet the minister in his morning walk, nor shrink from the eye of good old Deacon Gookin. And what calm sleep would be his that very night, which was to have been spent so wickedly, but so purely and sweetly now, in the arms of Faith! Amidst these pleasant and praiseworthy meditations, Goodman Brown heard the tramp of horses along the road, and deemed it advisable to conceal himself within the verge of the forest, conscious of the guilty purpose that had brought him thither, though now so happily turned from it.

On came the hoof tramps and the voices of the riders, two grave old voices, conversing soberly as they drew near. These mingled sounds appeared to pass along the road, within a few yards of the young man's hiding-place; but, owing doubtless to the depth of the gloom at that particular spot, neither the travellers nor their steeds were visible. Though their figures brushed the small boughs by the wayside, it could not be seen that they intercepted, even for a moment, the faint gleam from the strip of bright sky athwart which they must have passed. Goodman Brown alternately crouched and stood on tiptoe, pulling aside the branches and thrusting forth his head as far as he durst without discerning so much as a shadow. It vexed him the more, because he could have sworn, were such a thing possible, that he recognized the voices of the minister and Deacon Gookin, jogging along quietly, as they were wont to do, when bound to some ordination or ecclesiastical council. While yet within hearing, one of the riders stopped to pluck a switch.

"Of the two, reverend sir," said the voice like the deacon's, "I had rather miss an ordination dinner than to-night's meeting. They tell me that some of our community are to be here from Falmouth and beyond, and others from Connecticut and Rhode Island, besides several of the Indian powows[10], who, after their fashion, know almost as much deviltry as the best of us. Moreover, there is a goodly young woman to be taken into communion."

"Mighty well, Deacon Gookin!" replied the solemn old tones of the minister. "Spur up, or we shall be late. Nothing can be done, you know, until I get on the ground."

The hoofs clattered again; and the voices, talking so strangely in the empty air, passed on through the forest, where no church had ever been gathered or solitary Christian prayed. Whither, then, could these holy men be journeying, so deep into the heathen wilderness? Young Goodman Brown caught hold of a tree for support, being ready to sink down on the ground, faint and overburdened with the heavy sickness of his heart. He looked up to the sky, doubting whether there really was a heaven above him. Yet there was the blue arch, and the stars brightening in it.

"With heaven above and Faith below, I will yet stand firm against the devil!" cried Goodman Brown.

While he still gazed upward into the deep arch of the firmament and had lifted his hands to pray, a cloud, though no wind was stirring, hurried across the zenith and hid the brightening stars. The blue sky was still visible, except directly overhead, where this black mass of cloud was sweeping swiftly northward. Aloft in the air, as if from the depths of the cloud, came a confused and doubtful sound of voices. Once the listener fancied that he could distinguish the accents of towns-people of his own, men and women, both pious and ungodly, many of whom he had met at the communion table, and had seen others rioting at the tavern. The next moment, so indistinct were the sounds, he doubted whether he had heard aught but the murmur of the old forest, whispering without a wind. Then came a stronger swell of those familiar tones, heard daily in the sunshine at Salem village, but never until now from a cloud of night. There was one voice of a young woman, uttering lamentations, yet with an uncertain sorrow, and entreating for some favor, which, perhaps, it would grieve her to obtain; and all the unseen multitude, both saints and sinners, seemed to encourage her onward.

"Faith!" shouted Goodman Brown, in a voice of agony and desperation; and the echoes of the forest mocked him, crying, "Faith! Faith!" as if bewildered wretches were seeking her, all through the wilderness.

The cry of grief, rage, and terror was yet piercing the night, when the unhappy husband held his breath for a response. There was a scream, drowned immediately in a louder murmur of voices, fading into far-off laughter, as the dark cloud swept away, leaving the clear and silent sky above Goodman Brown. But something fluttered lightly down through the air and caught on the branch of a tree. The young man seized it, and beheld a pink ribbon.

"My Faith is gone!" cried he, after one stupefied moment. "There is no good on earth; and sin is but a name. Come, devil; for to thee is this world given."

And, maddened with despair, so that he laughed loud and long, did Goodman Brown grasp his staff and set forth again, at such a rate that he seemed to fly along the forest path rather than to walk or run. The road grew wilder and drearier and more faintly traced, and vanished at length, leaving him in the heart of the dark wilderness, still rushing onward with the instinct that guides mortal man to evil. The whole forest was peopled with frightful sounds—the creaking of the trees, the howling of wild beasts, and the yell of Indians; while sometimes the wind tolled like a distant church bell, and sometimes gave a broad roar around the traveller, as if all Nature were laughing him to scorn. But he was himself the chief horror of the scene, and shrank not from its other horrors.

"Ha! ha! ha!" roared Goodman Brown when the wind laughed at him.

"Let us hear which will laugh loudest. Think not to frighten me with your deviltry. Come witch, come wizard, come Indian powwow, come devil himself, and here comes Goodman Brown. You may as well fear him as he fear you."

…

NOTES

1. 奥兰治亲王威廉为玛丽王后二世的丈夫也是其表兄，1689—1707 年期间他们共同统治英格兰。
2. 天主教的英格兰玛丽都铎王朝统治时期，由于女王对新教徒的迫害又被叫作血腥玛丽。
3. 瓦帕浓印第安人在 1675—1976 年对新英格兰殖民者发起了战争。
4. 立法机构。
5. 通常指农夫。此处指地位普通的人。
6. 指周三或周四的布道日。
7. 霍桑使用了塞勒姆女巫受审案中一些历史人物的名字。Goody 一词含有对地位卑微的已婚妇女的尊称的意思。

8. 与巫术有关的一些植物。
9. 参见《出埃及记》中亚伦在法老前砍下神杖，把它变成毒蛇之举。
10. 施巫术之人。

About the Author:

Nathaniel Hawthorne, born in 1804 in Salem, Massachusetts, was one of greatest Romantic novelists in the United States in the 19th century. He was a descendent of Puritan immigrants. One ancestor had been a judge in the Salem witchcraft trials. Much of Hawthorne's writing focuses on New England. Many works featured moral allegories with a Puritan inspiration. His themes often center on the inherent evil and sin of humanity, and his works often have moral messages and deep psychological complexity. His major works include *The House of the Seven Gables*, *Twice-Told Tales*, and *The Scarlet Letter*.

Appreciation:

《小伙子古德曼·布朗》是一篇关于承认邪恶和堕落是人的本性的寓言故事，是霍桑短篇小说中重要的一篇，被公认为是他的思想和艺术手法高度集中、完美结合的作品。这篇作品贯穿了霍桑创作思想中的一条主线，即试图以灵魂的罪恶来解释社会中种种黑暗与丑恶的现象，并竭力主张读者要认识这种人心的堕落，用自我忏悔的方式净化不洁的灵魂。每个人的内心都有一块黑暗的地方，罪恶与人类同在。霍桑旨在批判清教社会的理想化，表达自己的不屑。与霍桑的多数小说例如《红字》一样，这篇小说的故事背景也是设定在十七世纪殖民地时期的美国的塞勒姆镇。霍桑以具有特殊含义的名字为人物命名，赋予作品以寓意。如"年轻的古德曼·布朗"和"费丝"，在英文中分别表示"善者"和"信仰"的意思。两个人物可以看作是两种美德的化身。然而，人物的名字最终却与寓言故事的结论相悖，表达了鲜明的对比和讽刺。此外，在语言上，霍桑也使用了一些特定的措辞和口语化的表达等文学技巧来展现十七世纪的塞勒姆镇这一历史背景。

Questions:

1. What allegorical meanings may be given to Goodman Brown? His wife? The forest? Night (as opposed to day)? Brown's journey?

2. Does the story demonstrate the devil's claim that "Evil is the nature of mankind"? How?

The Purloined Letter (Excerpt)

At Paris, just after dark one gusty evening in the autumn of 18—, I was enjoying the twofold luxury of meditation and a meerschaum, in company with my friend, C. Auguste Dupin, in his little back library, or book-closet, au troisième[1], No. 33 Rue Dunôt, Faubourg St. Germain. For one hour at least we had maintained a profound silence; while each, to any casual observer, might have seemed intently and exclusively occupied with the curling eddies of smoke that oppressed the atmosphere of the chamber. For myself, however, I was mentally discussing certain topics which had formed matter for conversation between us at an earlier period of the evening; I mean the affair of the Rue Morgue, and the mystery attending the murder of Marie Rogêt. I looked upon it, therefore, as something of a coincidence, when the door of our apartment was thrown open and admitted our old acquaintance, Monsieur G—, the Prefect of the Parisian police.

We gave him a hearty welcome; for there was nearly half as much of the entertaining as of the contemptible about the man, and we had not seen him for several years. We had been sitting in the dark, and Dupin now arose for the purpose of lighting a lamp, but sat down again, without doing so, upon G.'s saying that he had called to consult us, or rather to ask the opinion of my friend, about some official business which had occasioned a great deal of trouble.

"If it is any point requiring reflection," observed Dupin, as he forbore to enkindle the wick, "we shall examine it to better purpose in the dark."

"That is another one of your odd notions," said the Prefect, who had the fashion of calling everything "odd" that was beyond his comprehension, and thus lived amid an absolute legion of "oddities."

"Very true," said Dupin, as he supplied his visitor with a pipe, and rolled toward him a comfortable chair.

"And what is the difficulty now?" I asked. "Nothing more in the assassination way I hope?"

"Oh, no; nothing of that nature. The fact is, the business is very simple indeed, and I make no doubt that we can manage it sufficiently well ourselves; but then I thought Dupin would like to hear the details of it because it is so excessively odd."

"Simple and odd," said Dupin.

"Why, yes; and not exactly that either. The fact is, we have all been a good deal puzzled because the affair is so simple, and yet baffles us altogether."

"Perhaps it is the very simplicity of the thing which puts you at fault," said my friend.

"What nonsense you do talk!" replied the Prefect, laughing heartily.

"Perhaps the mystery is a little too plain," said Dupin.

"Oh, good heavens! who ever heard of such an idea?"

"A little too self-evident."

"Ha! ha! ha!—ha! ha! ha!—ho! ho! ho!" roared our visitor, profoundly amused, "oh, Dupin, you will be the death of me yet!"

"And what, after all, is the matter on hand?" I asked.

"Why, I will tell you," replied the Prefect, as he gave a long, steady, and contemplative puff, and settled himself in his chair. "I will tell you in a few words; but, before I begin, let me caution you that this is an affair demanding the greatest secrecy, and that I should most probably lose the position I now hold, were it known that I confided it to any one."

"Proceed," said I.

"Or not," said Dupin.

"Well, then; I have received personal information, from a very high quarter, that a certain document of the last importance has been purloined from the royal apartments. The individual who purloined it is known; that beyond a doubt; he was seen to take it. It is known, also, that it still remains in his possession."

"How is this known?" asked Dupin.

"It is clearly inferred," replied the Prefect, "from the nature of the document, and from the non-appearance of certain results which would at once arise from its passing out of the robber's possession—that is to say, from his employing it as he must design in the end to employ it."

"Be a little more explicit," I said.

"Well, I may venture so far as to say that the paper gives its holder a certain power in a certain quarter where such power is immensely valuable." The Prefect was fond of the cant of diplomacy.

"Still I do not quite understand," said Dupin.

"No? Well; the disclosure of the document to a third person, who shall be nameless, would bring in question the honor of a personage of most exalted station; and this fact gives the holder of the document an ascendancy over the illustrious personage whose honor and peace are so jeopardized."

"But this ascendancy," I interposed, "would depend upon the robber's knowledge of the loser's knowledge of the robber. Who would dare—"

"The thief," said G., "is the Minister D—, who dares all things, those unbecoming as well as those becoming a man. The method of the theft was not less ingenious than bold. The document in question—a letter, to be frank—had been received by the personage robbed while alone in the royal boudoir. During its perusal she was suddenly interrupted by the entrance of the other exalted personage from whom especially it was her wish to conceal it. After a hurried and vain endeavor to thrust it in a drawer, she was forced to place it, open it was, upon a table. The address, however, was uppermost, and, the contents thus unexposed, the letter escaped notice. At this juncture enters the Minister D—. His lynx eye immediately perceives the paper, recognizes the handwriting of the address, observes the confusion of the personage addressed, and fathoms her secret. After some business transactions, hurried through in his ordinary manner, he produces a letter somewhat similar to the one in question, opens it, pretends to read it, and then places it in close juxtaposition to the other. Again he converses, for some fifteen minutes, upon the public affairs. At length, in taking leave, he takes also from the table the letter to which he has no claim. Its rightful owner saw, but, of course, dared not call attention to the act, in the presence of the third person who stood at her elbow. The minister decamped; leaving his own letter—of no importance—upon the table."

"Here, then," said Dupin to me, "you have precisely what you demand to make the ascendancy complete—the robber's knowledge of the loser's knowledge of the robber."

"Yes," replied the Prefect, "and the power thus attained has, for some months past, been wielded, for political purposes, to a very dangerous extent. The personage robbed is more thoroughly convinced, every day, of the necessity of reclaiming her letter. But this, of course, cannot be done openly. In fine, driven to despair, she has committed the matter to me."

"Than whom," said Dupin, amid a perfect whirlwind of smoke, "no more sagacious agent could, I suppose, be desired, or even imagined."

"You flatter me," replied the Prefect; "but it is possible that some such opinion may have been entertained."

"It is clear," said I, "as you observe, that the letter is still in the possession of the minister; since it is this possession, and not any employment of the letter, which bestows the power. With the employment the power departs."

"True," said G.; "and upon this conviction I proceeded. My first care was to make a thorough search of the minister's hotel; and here my chief embarrassment lay in the necessity of searching without his knowledge. Beyond all things, I have been warned of the danger which would result from giving him reason to suspect our design."

"But," said I, "you are quite au fait[2] in these investigations. The parisian police have done this thing often before."

"Oh, yes; and for this reason I did not despair. The habits of the minister gave me, too, a great advantage. He is frequently absent from home all night. His servants are no means numerous. They sleep at a distance from their master's apartment, and, being chiefly Neapolitans, are readily made drunk. I have keys, as you know, with which I can open any chamber or cabinet in Paris. For three months a night has not passed, during the greater part of which I have not been engaged, personally, in ransacking the D—Hotel. My honor is interested, and, to mention a great secret, the reward is enormous. So I did not abandon the search until I had become fully satisfied that the thief is a more astute man than myself. I fancy that I have investigated every nook and corner of the premises in which it is possible that the paper can be concealed."

"But is it not possible," I suggested, "that although the letter may be in possession of the minister, as it unquestionably is, he may have concealed it elsewhere than upon his own premises?"

"This is barely possible," said Dupin. "The present peculiar condition of affairs at court, and especially of those intrigues in which D—is known to be involved, would render the instant availability of the document—its susceptibility of being produced at a moments notice—a point of nearly equal importance with its possession."

"Its susceptibility of being produced?" said I.

"That is to say, of being destroyed," said Dupin.

"True," I observed; "the paper is clearly then upon the premises. As for its being upon the person of the minister, we may consider that as out of the question."

"Entirely," said the Prefect. "He has been twice waylaid, as if by footpads, and his person rigidly searched for my own inspection."

"You might have spared yourself this trouble," said Dupin. "D—, I presume, is not altogether a fool, and, if not, must have anticipated these waylayings, as a matter of course."

"Not altogether a fool," said G., "but then he is a poet, which I take to be only one removed from a fool."

"True," said Dupin, after a long and thoughtful whiff from his meerschaum, "although I have been guilty of certain doggerel myself."

"Suppose you detail," said I, "the particulars of your search."

"Why, the fact is, we took our time, and we searched everywhere. I have had long experience in these affairs. I took the entire building, room by room; devoting the nights of a whole week to each. We examined, first the furniture of each apartment. We opened every possible drawer; and I presume you know that, to a properly trained police-agent, such a thing as a "secret" drawer is impossible. Any man is a dolt who permits a "secret" drawer to escape him in a search of this kind. The thing is so plain. There is a certain amount of bulk—of space—to be accounted for in every cabinet. Then we have accurate rules. The fiftieth part of a line could not escape us. After the cabinets we took the chairs. The cushions we probed with the fine ling needles you have seen me employ. From the tables we removed the tops."

"Why so?"

"Sometimes the top of a table, or other similarly arranged piece of furniture, is removed by the person wishing to conceal an article; then the leg is excavated, the article deposited within the cavity, and the top replaced. The bottoms and tops of bedposts are employed in the same way."

"But could not the cavity be detected by sounding?" I asked.

"By no means, if, when the article is deposited, a sufficient wadding of cotton be placed around it. Besides, in our case, we were obliged to proceed without noise."

"But you could not have removed—you could not have taken to pieces all articles of furniture in which it would have been possible to make a deposit in the manner you mention. A letter may be compressed into a thin spiral roll, not differing much in shape or bulk from a large knitting-needle, and in this form it might be inserted into the rung of a chair, for example. You did not take to pieces all the chairs?"

"Certainly not; but we did better—we examined the rungs of every chair in the hotel, and, indeed, the jointings of every description of furniture, by the aid of a most powerful microscope[3]. Had there been any traces of recent disturbance we should not have failed to detect it instantly. A single grain of gimlet-dust, for example, would have been as obvious as an apple. Any disorder in the gluing—any unusual gap in the joints—would have sufficed to insure detection."

"Of course you looked to the mirrors, between the boards and the plates, and you probed the beds and the bedclothes, as well as the curtains and carpets."

"That of course; and when we had absolutely completed every particle of the furniture in this way, then we examined the house itself. We divided its entire surface into compartments, which we numbered, so that none might be missed; then we scrutinized each individual square inch throughout the premises, including the two houses immediately adjoining, with the microscope, as before."

"The two houses adjoining!" I exclaimed; "you must have had a great deal of trouble."

"We had; but the reward offered is prodigious."

"You included the grounds about the houses?"

"All the grounds are paved with brick. They give us comparatively little trouble. We examined the moss between the bricks, and found it undisturbed."

"You looked among D—'s papers, of course, and into the books of he library?"

"Certainly; we opened every package and parcel; we not only opened every book, but we turned over every leaf in each volume, not contenting ourselves with a mere shake, according to the fashion of some of our police officers. We also measured the thickness of every book cover, with the most accurate admeasurement, and applied to each the most jealous scrutiny of the microscope. Had any of the bindings been recently meddled with, it would have been utterly impossible that the fact should have escaped observation. Some five or six volumes, just from the hands of the binder, we carefully probed, longitudinally, with the needles."

"You explored the floors beneath the carpets?"

"Beyond doubt. We removed every carpet, and examined the boards with the microscope."

"And the paper on the walls?"

"Yes."

"You looked into the cellars?"

"We did."

"Then," I said, "you have been making a miscalculation, and the letter is not upon the premises, as you suppose."

"I fear you are right there," said the Prefect. "And now, Dupin, what would you advise me to do?"

"To make a thorough research of the premises."

"That is absolutely needless," replied G—. "I am not more sure that I breathe than I am that the letter is not at the hotel."

"I have no better advice to give you," said Dupin. "You have, of course, an accurate description of the letter?"

"Oh, yes!"—And here the Prefect, producing a memorandum-book, proceeded to read aloud a minute account of the internal, and especially of the external, appearance of the missing document. Soon after finishing the perusal of this description, he took his departure, more entirely depressed in spirits than I have ever known the good gentleman before.

In about a month afterward he paid another visit, and found us occupied very nearly as before. He took a pipe and a chair and entered into some ordinary conversation. At length I said:

"Well, but G., what of the purloined letter? I presume you have at last made up your mind that there is no such thing as overreaching the Minister?"

"Confound him, say I—yes; I made the re-examination, however, as Dupin suggested—but it was all labor lost, as I knew it would be."

"How much was the reward offered, did you say?" asked Dupin.

"Why, a very great deal—a very liberal reward—I don't like to say how much precisely; but one thing I will say, that I wouldn't mind giving my individual check for fifty thousand francs to any one who could obtain me that letter. The fact is, it is becoming of more and more importance every day; and the reward has been lately doubled. If it were trebled, however, I could do no more than I have done."

"Why, yes," said Dupin, drawlingly, between the whiffs of his meerschaum, "I really—think, G., you have not exerted yourself—to the utmost in the matter. You might—do a little more, I think, eh?"

"How?—in what way?"

"Why—puff, puff—you might—puff, puff—employ counsel in the matter, eh?—puff, puff, puff. Do you remember the story they tell of Abernethy?"

"No; hang Abernethy!"

"To be sure! hang him and welcome. But, once upon a time, a certain rich miser conceived the design of spunging upon this Abernethy for a medical opinion. Getting up, for this purpose, an ordinary conversation in a private company, he insinuated his case to the physician, as that of an imaginary individual.

"We will suppose," said the miser, "that his symptoms are such and such; now, doctor, what would you have directed him to take?"

"Take!" said Abernethy, "why, take advice, to be sure."

"But," said the Prefect, a little discomposed, "I am perfectly willing to take advice, and to pay for it. I would really give fifty thousand francs to any one who would aid me in the matter."

"In that case," replied Dupin, opening a drawer, and producing a check-book, "you may as well fill me up a check for the amount mentioned. When you have signed it, I will hand you the letter."

I was astonished. The Prefect appeared absolutely thunder-stricken. For some minutes he remained speechless and motionless, looking incredulously at my friend with open mouth, and eyes that seemed startling from their sockets; then apparently recovering himself in some measure, he seized a pen, and after several pauses and vacant stares, finally filled up and signed a check for fifty thousand francs, and handed it across the table to Dupin. The latter examined it carefully and deposited it in his pocket-book; then, unlocking an escritoire[4], took thence a letter and gave it to the Prefect. This functionary grasped it in a perfect agony of joy, opened it with a trembling hand, cast a rapid glance at its contents, and then, scrambling and struggling to the door, rushed at length unceremoniously from the room and from the house, without having uttered a syllable since Dupin had requested him to fill up the check.

…

NOTES

1. 三楼（法语），实际指第四楼。
2. 精通的（法语）。
3. 例如放大镜一类的。
4. 书桌（法语），现拼写为 ecritoire。

About the Author:

Edgar Allan Poe (1809–1849) was an American writer, editor, and literary critic. He is best known for his poetry and short stories, particularly his tales of mystery and the horror. He is generally considered as a leading figure of Romanticism in the United States and American literature as a whole. He was also one of America's earliest practitioners of the short story. Poe is widely regarded as the father of the detective fiction and a pioneer of science fiction. His notable poems are "To Helen," "The Raven" and "Annabel Lee." Stories like "The Fall of the House of Usher" reveal his talent in the genre of macabre.

Appreciation:

《失窃的信》是美国作家埃德加·爱伦·坡所写的短篇小说。这部小说首次出现于《礼物：给 1845 年》（1844），并很快被转载在了许多杂志和报纸上。这是他以虚构的 C. 奥古斯特·杜邦为主人公所著的三部侦探故事的第三部。这些故事被视为现代侦探小说的重要先驱。

《失窃的信》讲的是一桩盗信“奇案”，整个故事充满悬疑色彩。奇就奇在作案人的身份、作案的方法昭然若揭，但就是找不到作为证据的赃物 —— 信。为此，巴黎警察局长花了几个月的时间兴师动众，运用各种先进技术和手段，仔仔细细地搜查了作案人的房间，却徒劳无益。最后，还是小说的主人公 —— 业余侦探杜宾用他所说的“八岁小孩的推理能力”找到那封“失窃的信”。这令人啼笑皆非的破案方式简直是对巴黎警察的极大嘲弄。在侦探小说中，人物塑造往往是次要的，作家关注的核心似乎是故事本身和其中丝丝相扣的逻辑推理。《失窃的信》中的人物主要有四种角色：“受害者、罪犯、侦探，以及被罪案威胁又无力破案的人”，这包括证人、犯罪嫌疑人，还有能力平庸的警察和侦探的助手。爱伦·坡笔下的杜宾，这个性格怪异的业余侦探成了后世鼎鼎大名的福尔摩斯的前身。小说采用了第一人称的叙述手法。从叙事学意义上来看，它代表着一种叙事技巧的自觉性。

Questions:

1. How is Auguste Dupin, who appears in Edgar Allen Poe's so-called "detective" stories, different from ordinary people?

2. In "The Purloined Letter," explain how Poe characterizes Monsieur G of police.

3. Is "The Purloined Letter" a successful detective story? Why or why not?

The Awakening

I

A green and yellow parrot, which hung in a cage outside the door, kept repeating over and over:

"Allez vous-en! Allez vous-en! Sapristi [1]! That's all right!" He could speak a little Spanish, and also a language which nobody understood, unless it was the mocking-bird that hung on the other side of the door, whistling his fluty notes out upon the breeze with maddening persistence.

Mr. Pontellier, unable to read his newspaper with any degree of comfort, arose with an expression and an exclamation of disgust. He walked down the gallery and across the narrow "bridges" which connected the Lebrun cottages one with the other. He had been seated before the door of the main house. The parrot and the mockingbird were the property of Madame Lebrun, and they had the right to make all the noise they wished. Mr. Pontellier had the privilege of quitting their society when they ceased to be entertaining.

He stopped before the door of his own cottage, which was the fourth one from the main building and next to the last. Seating himself in a wicker rocker which was there, he once more applied himself to the task of reading the newspaper. The day was Sunday, the paper was a day old. The Sunday papers had not yet reached Grand Isle [2]. He was already acquainted with the market reports, and he glanced restlessly over the editorials and bits of news which he had not had time to read before quitting New Orleans the day before.

Mr. Pontellier wore eye-glasses. He was a man of forty, of medium height and rather slender build; he stooped a little. His hair was brown and straight, parted on one side. His beard was neatly and closely trimmed.

Once in a while he withdrew his glance from the newspaper and looked about him. There was more noise than ever over at the house. The main building was called "the house," to distinguish it from the cottages. The chattering and whistling birds were still at it. Two young girls, the Farival twins, were playing a duet from "Zampa[3]" upon the piano. Madame Lebrun was bustling in and out, giving orders in a high key to a yard-boy whenever she got inside the house, and directions in an equally high voice to a dining-room servant whenever she got outside. She was a fresh, pretty woman, clad always in white with elbow sleeves. Her starched skirts crinkled as she came and went. Farther down, before one of the cottages, a lady in black was walking demurely up and down, telling her beads. A good many persons of the pension had gone over to the Chénière Caminada in Beaudelet's lugger [4] to hear mass. Some young people were out under the wateroaks playing croquet. Mr. Pontellier's two children were there sturdy little fellows of four and five. A quadroon [5] nurse followed them about with a faraway, meditative air.

Mr. Pontellier finally lit a cigar and began to smoke, letting the paper drag idly from his hand. He fixed his gaze upon a white sunshade [6] that was advancing at snail's pace from the beach. He could see it plainly between the gaunt trunks of the water-oaks and across the stretch of yellow camomile. The gulf looked far away, melting hazily into the blue of the horizon. The sunshade continued to approach slowly. Beneath its pink-lined shelter were his wife, Mrs. Pontellier, and young Robert Lebrun. When they reached the cottage, the two seated themselves with some appearance of fatigue upon the upper step of the porch, facing each other, each leaning against a supporting post.

"What folly! to bathe at such an hour in such heat!" exclaimed Mr. Pontellier. He himself had taken a plunge at daylight. That was why the morning seemed long to him.

"You are burnt beyond recognition," he added, looking at his wife as one looks at a valuable piece of personal property which has suffered some damage. She held up her hands, strong, shapely hands, and surveyed them critically, drawing up her lawn [7] sleeves above the wrists. Looking at them reminded her of her rings, which she had given to her husband before leaving for the beach. She silently reached out to him, and he, understanding, took the rings from his vest pocket and dropped them into her open palm. She slipped them upon her fingers; then clasping her knees, she looked across at Robert and began to laugh. The rings sparkled upon her fingers. He sent back an answering smile.

"What is it?" asked Pontellier, looking lazily and amused from one to the other. It was some utter nonsense; some adventure out there in the water, and they both tried to relate it at once. It did not seem half so amusing when told. They realized this, and so did Mr. Pontellier. He yawned and stretched himself. Then he got up, saying he had half a mind to go over to Klein's hotel and play a game of billiards.

"Come go along, Lebrun," he proposed to Robert. But Robert admitted quite frankly that he preferred to stay where he was and talk to Mrs. Pontellier.

"Well, send him about his business when he bores you, Edna," instructed her husband as he prepared to leave.

"Here, take the umbrella," she exclaimed, holding it out to him. He accepted the sunshade, and lifting it over his head descended the steps and walked away.

"Coming back to dinner?" his wife called after him. He halted a moment and shrugged his shoulders. He felt in his vest pocket; there was a ten-dollar bill there. He did not know; perhaps he would return for the early dinner and perhaps he would not. It all depended upon the company which he found over at Klein's and the size of "the game." He did not say this, but she understood it, and laughed, nodding good-by to him.

Both children wanted to follow their father when they saw him starting out. He kissed them and promised to bring them back bonbons and peanuts.

II

Mrs. Pontellier's eyes were quick and bright; they were a yellowish brown, about the color of her hair. She had a way of turning them swiftly upon an object and holding them there as if lost in some inward maze of contemplation or thought.

Her eyebrows were a shade darker than her hair. They were thick and almost horizontal, emphasizing the depth of her eyes. She was rather handsome than beautiful. Her face was captivating by reason of a certain frankness of expression and a contradictory subtle play of features. Her manner was engaging.

Robert rolled a cigarette. He smoked cigarettes because he could not afford cigars, he said. He had a cigar in his pocket which Mr. Pontellier had presented him with, and he was saving it for his after-dinner smoke.

This seemed quite proper and natural on his part. In coloring he was not unlike his companion. A clean-shaved face made the resemblance more pronounced than it would otherwise have been. There rested no shadow of care upon his open countenance. His eyes gathered in and reflected the light and languor of the summer day.

Mrs. Pontellier reached over for a palm-leaf fan that lay on the porch and began to fan herself, while Robert sent between his lips light puffs from his cigarette. They chatted incessantly: about the things around them; their amusing adventure out in the water—it had again assumed its entertaining aspect; about the wind, the trees, the people who had gone to the Cheniere; about the children playing croquet under the oaks, and the Farival twins, who were now performing the overture to "The Poet and the Peasant[8]."

Robert talked a good deal about himself. He was very young, and did not know any better. Mrs. Pontellier talked a little about herself for the same reason. Each was interested in what the other said. Robert spoke of his intention to go to Mexico in the autumn, where fortune awaited him. He was always intending to go to Mexico, but some way never got there. Meanwhile he held on to his modest position in a mercantile house in New Orleans, where an equal familiarity with English, French and Spanish gave him no small value as a clerk and correspondent.

He was spending his summer vacation, as he always did, with his mother at Grand Isle. In former times, before Robert could remember, "the house" had been a summer luxury of the Lebruns. Now, flanked by its dozen or more cottages, which were always filled with exclusive visitors from the "Quartier Francais," it enabled Madame Lebrun to maintain the easy and comfortable existence which appeared to be her birthright.

Mrs. Pontellier talked about her father's Mississippi plantation and her girlhood home in the old Kentucky bluegrass country. She was an American woman, with a small infusion of French which seemed to have been lost in dilution. She read a letter from her sister, who was away in the East, and who had engaged herself to be married. Robert was interested, and wanted to know what manner of girls the sisters were, what the father was like, and how long the mother had been dead.

When Mrs. Pontellier folded the letter it was time for her to dress for the early dinner.

"I see Leonce isn't coming back," she said, with a glance in the direction whence her husband had disappeared. Robert supposed he was not, as there were a good many New Orleans club men over at Klein's.

When Mrs. Pontellier left him to enter her room, the young man descended the steps and strolled over toward the croquet players, where, during the half-hour before dinner, he amused himself with the little Pontellier children, who were very fond of him.

III

It was eleven o'clock that night when Mr. Pontellier returned from Klein's hotel. He was in an excellent humor, in high spirits, and very talkative. His entrance awoke his wife, who was in bed and fast asleep when he came in. He talked to her while he undressed, telling her anecdotes and bits of news and gossip that he had gathered during the day. From his trousers pockets he took a fistful of crumpled bank notes and a good deal of silver coin, which he piled on the bureau indiscriminately with keys, knife, handkerchief, and whatever else happened to be in his pockets. She was overcome with sleep, and answered him with little half utterances.

He thought it very discouraging that his wife, who was the sole object of his existence, evinced so little interest in things which concerned him, and valued so little his conversation.

Mr. Pontellier had forgotten the bonbons and peanuts for the boys. Notwithstanding he loved them very much, and went into the adjoining room where they slept to take a look at them and make sure that they were resting comfortably. The result of his investigation was far from satisfactory. He turned and shifted the youngsters about in bed. One of them began to kick and talk about a basket full of crabs.

Mr. Pontellier returned to his wife with the information that Raoul had a high fever and needed looking after. Then he lit a cigar and went and sat near the open door to smoke it.

Mrs. Pontellier was quite sure Raoul had no fever. He had gone to bed perfectly well, she said, and nothing had ailed him all day. Mr. Pontellier was too well acquainted with fever symptoms to be mistaken. He assured her the child was consuming [10] at that moment in the next room.

He reproached his wife with her inattention, her habitual neglect of the children. If it was not a mother's place to look after children, whose on earth was it? He himself had his hands full with his brokerage business. He could not be in two places at once; making a living for his family on the street, and staying at home to see that no harm befell them. He talked in a monotonous, insistent way.

Mrs. Pontellier sprang out of bed and went into the next room. She soon came back and sat on the edge of the bed, leaning her head down on the pillow. She said nothing, and refused to answer her husband when he questioned her. When his cigar was smoked out he went to bed, and in half a minute he was fast asleep.

Mrs. Pontellier was by that time thoroughly awake. She began to cry a little, and wiped her eyes on the sleeve of her peignoir. Blowing out the candle, which her husband had left burning, she slipped her bare feet into a pair of satin mules at the foot of the bed and went out on the porch, where she sat down in the wicker chair and began to rock gently to and fro.

It was then past midnight. The cottages were all dark. A single faint light gleamed out from the hallway of the house. There was no sound abroad except the hooting of an old owl in the top of a water-oak, and the everlasting voice of the sea, that was not uplifted at that soft hour. It broke like a mournful lullaby upon the night.

The tears came so fast to Mrs. Pontellier's eyes that the damp sleeve of her peignoir no longer served to dry them. She was holding the back of her chair with one hand; her loose sleeve had slipped almost to the shoulder of her uplifted arm. Turning, she thrust her face, steaming and wet, into the bend of her arm, and she went on crying there, not caring any longer to dry her face, her eyes, her arms. She could not have told why she was crying. Such experiences as the foregoing were not uncommon in her married life. They seemed never before to have weighed much against the abundance of her husband's kindness and a uniform devotion which had come to be tacit and self-understood.

An indescribable oppression, which seemed to generate in some unfamiliar part of her consciousness, filled her whole being with a vague anguish. It was like a shadow, like a mist passing across her soul's summer day. It was strange and unfamiliar; it was a mood. She did not sit there inwardly upbraiding her husband, lamenting at Fate, which had directed her footsteps to the path which they had taken. She was just having a good cry all to herself. The mosquitoes made merry over her, biting her firm, round arms and nipping at her bare insteps.

The little stinging, buzzing imps succeeded in dispelling a mood which might have held her there in the darkness half a night longer.

The following morning Mr. Pontellier was up in good time to take the rockaway [11] which was to convey him to the steamer at the wharf. He was returning to the city to his business, and they would not see him again at the Island till the coming Saturday. He had regained his composure, which seemed to have been somewhat impaired the night before. He was eager to be gone, as he looked forward to a lively week in Carondelet Street [12].

Mr. Pontellier gave his wife half of the money which he had brought away from Klein's hotel the evening before. She liked money as well as most women, and, accepted it with no little satisfaction.

"It will buy a handsome wedding present for Sister Janet!" she exclaimed, smoothing out the bills as she counted them one by one. "Oh! we'll treat Sister Janet better than that, my dear," he laughed, as he prepared to kiss her good-by.

The boys were tumbling about, clinging to his legs, imploring that numerous things be brought back to them. Mr. Pontellier was a great favorite, and ladies, men, children, even nurses, were always on hand to say good-by to him. His wife stood smiling and waving, the boys shouting, as he disappeared in the old rockaway down the sandy road.

A few days later a box arrived for Mrs. Pontellier from New Orleans. It was from her husband. It was filled with friandises, with luscious and toothsome bits—the finest of fruits, pates, a rare bottle or two, delicious syrups, and bonbons in abundance.

Mrs. Pontellier was always very generous with the contents of such a box; she was quite used to receiving them when away from home. The pates and fruit were brought to the dining-room; the bonbons were passed around. And the ladies, selecting with dainty and discriminating fingers and a little greedily, all declared that Mr. Pontellier was the best husband in the world.

Mrs. Pontellier was forced to admit that she knew of none better.

…

NOTES

1. 法语，意为：走开！走开！看在老天的分上！
2. 一观光海岛，距离新奥尔良 50 英里，位于墨西哥湾和卡米纳达湾之间。
3. Louis Hérold（1791—1833）的浪漫歌剧。
4. 指客船。pension 指的是旅馆。Chénière Caminada 位于格兰德岛和路易斯安那海岸的海岛。
5. 有四分之一黑人血统的人。
6. 即太阳伞。
7. 上等的亚麻或是细棉布。
8. Franz von Suppé（1819—1895）的轻歌剧。
9. 新奥尔良的法语区。
10. 发热、发烧的。
11. 四轮马车，产于新泽西的 Rockaway。
12. 即新奥尔良的华尔街。

About the Author:

Kate Chopin (1850–1904), born in St. Louis, Missouri, was an American author. She is now considered to have been a forerunner of American 20th-century feminist authors of Southern or Catholic background.

Her father was an Irish immigrant. Her mother, grandmother and great-grandmother were active and pious Catholics of French heritage. The family enjoyed a high place in St. Louis society. She married and moved with her husband to New Orleans. They later lived in the country in Cloutierville, Louisiana.

Her major works included two short story collections: *Bayou Folk* (1894) and *A Night in Acadie* (1897). She also wrote two novels: *At Fault* (1890) and *The Awakening* (1899), which are set in New Orleans and Grand Isle, respectively. When it was published, *The Awakening* aroused hostility among reviewers. Though the novel and its author fell into obscurity for half a century, they have now secured an honored place in American literary history. Chopin is widely recognized as one of the leading writers of her time.

Appreciation:

《觉醒》自1899年发表之后，有好几十年遭受谴责，圣路易斯等地的图书馆甚至把它列为禁书。它从20世纪50年代起开始受到重视，如今已是经典美国文学作品。小说场景设置在19世纪末新奥尔良和路易斯安那湾沿岸。故事围绕主人公Edna Pontellier，以及她日趋非传统的女性和母性观与当时美国南方社会普遍的社会态度之间的冲突而展开。这是一部关注女性问题最早的美国小说之一。它也被广泛认为是一部早期女权主义里程碑式的作品，在当代读者和评论家中产生了各种反响。小说融合了现实主义叙事、尖锐的社会评论和复杂的心理分析性，这使得该小说成为美国现代主义文学的先驱。它预示着像福克纳、海明威这样的美国作家的作品的出现，同时与同时代的伊迪丝·华顿和亨利·詹姆斯的作品形成呼应，也是美国南方文学较早的巅峰之作。

Questions:

1. Throughout the novel, Edna feels caught between the way others see her and the way she sees herself. Identify several moments in which this struggle is apparent. How does the writer portray Edna's growing awareness of these contradicting views?

2. Of the many awakenings Edna undergoes in the novel, which are most important to her progress? Which may be considered "rude" or unexpected awakenings?

3. Some critics view Edna's suicide at the end of the novel as a failure to complete her escape from convention—an inability to defy society once stripped of the motivation of a man by her side, while others view her suicide as a final awakening, a decision to give herself to the sea in a show of strength and independence that defies social expectation. Which interpretation do you find more compelling, and why?

Martin Eden (Excerpt)

"Say, Joe," was his greeting to his old-time working-mate next morning, "there's a Frenchman out on Twenty-eighth Street. He's made a pot of money, and he's going back to France. It's a dandy, well-appointed, small steam laundry. There's a start for you if you want to settle down. Here, take this; buy some clothes with it and be at this man's office by ten o'clock. He looked up the laundry for me, and he'll take you out and show you around. If you like it, and think it is worth the price—twelve thousand—let me know and it is yours. Now run along. I'm busy. I'll see you later."

"Now look here, Mart," the other said slowly, with kindling anger, "I come here this mornin' to see you. Savve[1]? I didn't come here to get no laundry. I come a here for a talk for old friends' sake, and you shove a laundry at me. I tell you, what you can do. You can take that laundry an' go to hell."

He was starting to fling out of the room when Martin caught him and whirled him around.

"Now look here, Joe," he said; "if you act that way, I'll punch your head. An for old friends' sake I'll punch it hard. Savve?—you will, will you?"

Joe had clinched and attempted to throw him, and he was twisting and writhing out of the advantage of the other's hold. They reeled about the room, locked in each other's arms, and came down with a crash across the splintered wreckage of a wicker chair. Joe was underneath, with arms spread out and held and with Martin's knee on his chest. He was panting and gasping for breath when Martin released him.

"Now we'll talk a moment," Martin said. "You can't get fresh with me. I want that laundry business finished first of all. Then you can come back and we'll talk for old sake's sake. I told you I was busy. Look at that."

A servant had just come in with the morning mail, a great mass of letters and magazines.

"How can I wade through that and talk with you? You go and fix up that laundry, and then we'll get together."

"All right," Joe admitted reluctantly. "I thought you was turnin' me down, but I guess I was mistaken. But you can't lick me, Mart, in a stand-up fight. I've got the reach on you."

"We'll put on the gloves sometime and see," Martin said with a smile.

"Sure; as soon as I get that laundry going." Joe extended his arm. "You see that reach? It'll make you go a few."

Martin heaved a sigh of relief when the door closed behind the laundryman. He was becoming anti-social. Daily he found it a severer strain to be decent with people. Their presence perturbed him, and the effort of conversation irritated him. They made him restless, and no sooner was he in contact with them than he was casting about for excuses to get rid of them.

He did not proceed to attack his mail, and for a half hour he lolled in his chair, doing nothing, while no more than vague, half-formed thoughts occasionally filtered through his intelligence, or rather, at wide intervals, themselves constituted the flickering of his intelligence.

He roused himself and began glancing through his mail. There were a dozen requests for autographs—he knew them at sight; there were professional begging letters; and there were letters from cranks, ranging from the man with a working model of perpetual motion, and the man who demonstrated that the surface of the earth was the inside of a hollow sphere, to the man seeking financial aid to purchase the Peninsula of Lower California for the purpose of communist colonization. There were letters from women seeking to know him, and over one such he smiled, for enclosed was her receipt for pew-rent, sent as evidence of her good faith and as proof of her respectability.

Editors and publishers contributed to the daily heap of letters, the former on their knees for his manuscripts, the latter on their knees for his books—his poor disdained manuscripts that had kept all he possessed in pawn for so many dreary months in order to find them in postage. There were unexpected checks for English serial rights and for advance payments on foreign translations. His English agent announced the sale of German translation rights in three of his books, and informed him that Swedish editions, from which he could expect nothing because Sweden was not a party to the Berne Convention[2], were already on the market. Then there was a nominal request for his permission for a Russian translation, that country being likewise outside the Berne Convention.

He turned to the huge bundle of clippings which had come in from his press bureau, and read about himself and his vogue, which had become a furore. All his creative output had been flung to the public in one magnificent sweep. That seemed to account for it. He had taken the public off its feet, the way Kipling [3] had, that time when he lay near to death and all the mob, animated by a mob-mind thought, began suddenly to read him. Martin remembered how that same world-mob, having read him and acclaimed him and not understood him in the least, had, abruptly, a few months later, flung itself upon him and torn him to pieces. Martin grinned at the thought. Who was he that he should not be similarly treated in a few more months? Well, he would fool the mob. He would be away, in the South Seas, building his grass house, trading for pearls and copra, jumping reefs in frail outriggers, catching sharks and bonitas, hunting wild goats among the cliffs of the valley that lay next to the valley of Taiohae[4].

In the moment of that thought the desperateness of his situation dawned upon him. He saw, cleared eyed, that he was in the Valley of the Shadow[5]. All the life that was in him was fading, fainting, making toward death. He realized how much he slept, and how much he desired to sleep. Of old, he had hated sleep. It had robbed him of precious moments of living. Four hours of sleep in the twenty-four had meant being robbed of four hours of life. How he had grudged sleep! Now it was life he grudged. Life was not good; its taste in his mouth was without tang, and bitter. This was his peril. Life that did not yearn toward life was in fair way toward ceasing. Some remote instinct for preservation stirred in him, and he knew he must get away. He glanced about the room, and the thought of packing was burdensome. Perhaps it would be better to leave that to the last. In the meantime he might be getting an outfit.

He put on his hat and went out, stopping in at a gun-store, where he spent the remainder of the morning buying automatic rifles, ammunition, and fishing tackle. Fashions changed in trading, and he knew he would have to wait till he reached Tahiti [6] before ordering his trade-goods. They could come up from Australia, anyway. This solution was a source of pleasure. He had avoided doing something, and the doing of anything just now was unpleasant. He went back to the hotel gladly, with a feeling of satisfaction in that the comfortable Morris chair was waiting for him; and he groaned inwardly, on entering his room, at sight of Joe in the Morris chair.

Joe was delighted with the laundry. Everything was settled, and he would enter into possession next day. Martin lay on the bed, with closed eyes, while the other talked on. Martin's thoughts were far away—so far away that he was rarely aware that he was thinking. It was only by an effort that he occasionally responded. And yet this was Joe, whom he had always liked. But Joe was too keen with life. The boisterous impact of it on Martin's jaded mind was a hurt. It was an aching probe to his tired sensitiveness. When Joe reminded him that sometime in the future they were going to put on the gloves together, he could almost have screamed.

"Remember, Joe, you're to run the laundry according to those old rules you used to lay down at Shelly Hot Springs," he said. "No overworking. No working at night. And no children at the mangles. No children anywhere. And a fair wage."

Joe nodded and pulled out a note-book.

"Look at here. I was workin' out them rules before breakfast this A.M. What d'ye think of them?"

He read them aloud, and Martin approved, worrying at the same time as to when Joe would take himself off.

It was late afternoon when he awoke. Slowly the fact of life came back to him. He glanced about the room. Joe had evidently stolen away after he had dozed off. That was considerate of Joe, he thought. Then he closed his eyes and slept again.

In the days that followed Joe was too busy organizing and taking hold of the laundry to bother him much; and it was not until the day before sailing that the newspapers made the announcement that he had taken passage on the Mariposa. Once, when the instinct of preservation fluttered, he went to a doctor and underwent a searching physical examination. Nothing could be found the matter with him. His heart and lungs were pronounced magnificent. Every organ, so far as the doctor could know, was normal and was working normally.

"There is nothing the matter with you, Mr. Eden," he said, "positively nothing the matter with you. You are in the pink of condition. Candidly, I envy you your health. It is superb. Look at that chest. There, and in your stomach, lies the secret of your remarkable constitution. Physically, you are a man in a thousand—in ten thousand. Barring accidents, you should live to be a hundred."

And Martin knew that Lizzie's diagnosis had been correct. Physically he was all right. It was his "think-machine" that had gone wrong, and there was no cure for that except to get away to the South Seas. The trouble was that now, on the verge of departure, he had no desire to go. The South Seas charmed him no more than did bourgeois civilization. There was no zest in the thought of departure, while the act of departure appalled him as a weariness of the flesh. He would have felt better if he were already on board and gone.

The last day was a sore trial. Having read of his sailing in the morning papers, Bernard Higginbotham, Gertrude, and all the family came to say good-by, as did Hermann von Schmidt and Marian. Then there was business to be transacted, bills to be paid, and everlasting reporters to be endured. He said good-by to Lizzie Connolly, abruptly, at the entrance to night school, and hurried away. At the hotel he found Joe, too busy all day with the laundry to have come to him earlier. It was the last straw, but Martin gripped the arms of his chair and talked and listened for half an hour.

"You know, Joe," he said, "that you are not tied down to that laundry. There are no strings on it. You can sell it any time and blow the money. Any time you get sick of it and want to hit the road, just pull out. Do what will make you the happiest."

Joe shook his head.

"No more road in mine, thank you kindly. Hoboin[7]'s all right, exceptin' for one thing — the girls. I can't help it, but I'm a ladies' man. I can't get along without 'em, and you've got to get along without 'em when you're hoboin'. The times I've passed by houses where dances an' parties was goin' on, an' heard the women laugh, an' saw their white dresses and smiling faces through the windows—Gee! I tell you them moments was plain hell. I like dancin' an' picnics, an' walking in the moonlight, an' all the rest too well. Me for the laundry, and a good front, with big iron dollars clinkin' in my jeans. I seen a girl already, just yesterday, and, d'ye know, I'm feelin' already I'd just as soon marry her as not. I've ben whistlin' all day at the thought of it. She's a beaut, with the kindest eyes and softest voice you ever heard. Me for her, you can stack on that. Say, why don't you get married with all this money to burn? You could get the finest girl in the land."

Martin shook his head with a smile, but in his secret heart he was wondering why any man wanted to marry. It seemed an amazing and incomprehensible thing.

From the deck of the Mariposa, at the sailing hour, he saw Lizzie Connolly hiding in the skirts of the crowd on the wharf. Take her with you, came the thought. It is easy to be kind. She will be supremely happy. It was almost a temptation one moment, and the succeeding moment it became a terror. He was in a panic at the thought of it. His tired soul cried out in protest. He turned away from the rail with a groan, muttering, "Man, you are too sick, you are too sick."

He fled to his stateroom, where he lurked until the steamer was clear of the dock. In the dining saloon, at luncheon, he found himself in the place of honor, at the captain's right; and he was not long in discovering that he was the great man on board. But no more unsatisfactory great man ever sailed on a ship. He spent the afternoon in a deck-chair, with closed eyes, dozing brokenly most of the time, and in the evening went early to bed.

After the second day, recovered from seasickness, the full passenger list was in evidence, and the more he saw of the passengers the more he disliked them. Yet he knew that he did them injustice. They were good and kindly people, he forced himself to acknowledge, and in the moment of acknowledgment he qualified—good and kindly like all the bourgeoisie, with all the psychological cramp and intellectual futility of their kind, they bored him when they talked with him, their little superficial minds were so filled with emptiness; while the boisterous high spirits and the excessive energy of the younger people shocked him. They were never quiet, ceaselessly playing deck-quoits, tossing rings, promenading, or rushing to the rail with loud cries to watch the leaping porpoises and the first schools of flying fish.

He slept much. After breakfast he sought his deck-chair with a magazine he never finished. The printed pages tired him. He puzzled that men found so much to write about, and, puzzling, dozed in his chair. When the gong awoke him for luncheon, he was irritated that he must awaken. There was no satisfaction in being awake.

Once, he tried to arouse himself from his lethargy, and went forward into the forecastle with the sailors. But the breed of sailors seemed to have changed since the days he had lived in the forecastle. He could find no kinship with these stolid-faced, ox- minded bestial creatures. He was in despair. Up above nobody had wanted Martin Eden for his own sake, and he could not go back to those of his own class who had wanted him in the past. He did not want them. He could not stand them any more than he could stand the stupid first-cabin passengers and the riotous young people.

Life was to him like strong, white light that hurts the tired eyes of a sick person. During every conscious moment life blazed in a raw glare around him and upon him. It hurt. It hurt intolerably. It was the first time in his life that Martin had travelled first class. On ships at sea he had always been in the forecastle, the steerage, or in the black depths of the coal-hold, passing coal. In those days, climbing up the iron ladders out the pit of stifling heat, he had often caught glimpses of the passengers, in cool white, doing nothing but enjoy themselves, under awnings spread to keep the sun and wind away from them, with subservient stewards taking care of their every want and whim, and it had seemed to him that the realm in which they moved and had their being was nothing else than paradise. Well, here he was, the great man on board, in the midmost centre of it, sitting at the captain's right hand, and yet vainly harking back to forecastle and stoke-hole in quest of the Paradise he had lost. He had found no new one, and now he could not find the old one.

He strove to stir himself and find something to interest him. He ventured the petty officers' mess, and was glad to get away. He talked with a quartermaster off duty, an intelligent man who promptly prodded him with the socialist propaganda and forced into his hands a bunch of leaflets and pamphlets. He listened to the man expounding the slave-morality, and as he listened, he thought languidly of his own Nietzsche [8] philosophy. But what was it worth, after all? He remembered one of Nietzsche's mad utterances wherein that madman had doubted truth. And who was to say? Perhaps Nietzsche had been right. Perhaps there was no truth in anything, no truth in truth—no such thing as truth. But his mind wearied quickly, and he was content to go back to his chair and doze.

NOTES

1. 知道，明白（俚语），savve=savvy。
2. 《伯尔尼公约》，1887 年生效。该公约规定，所有签字国都应遵守有关版权的规定。
3. Rudyard Kipling (1865—1933)，英国诗人、小说家。
4. 位于太平洋。
5. 死荫的幽谷。参见《旧约 · 诗篇》23:4（Yea, though I walk through the valley of the shadow of death, I will fear no evil.）
6. 大溪地，南太平洋法属社会群岛之一。
7. Hoboin=hoboing。
8. Friedrich Wilhelm Nietzsche (1844—1900)，尼采，德国哲学家。one of Nietzsche's mad utterances 可能是指尼采所讲 "We cannot believe the dogmas of religion and metaphysics if we have the strict methods of truth in heart and head。"

About the Author:

John Griffith London (1876–1916) was an American novelist, journalist and social activist.

He was the first American writer to become a millionaire only by virtue of his earnings as an author. Some of his most famous works include *The Call of the Wild*, *White Fang*, *The Sea Wolf* and the autobiographical novel *Martin Eden*, as well as the short stories "To Build a Fire," "An Odyssey of the North" and "Love of Life." His vigorous stories of men and animals against the environment, and survival against hardships were drawn mainly from his own experience.

Appreciation:

《马丁·伊登》是一部著名的自传体小说。马丁·伊登是一个有追求的年轻人。他出身低微，身体结实，意志坚强。他在一个偶然的机会结识了贵族小姐罗丝，并爱上了她。罗丝也被他所吸引。阶级的差异让马丁自惭形秽，但他发愤图强开始自学写作，不料投稿屡试屡败，生活随之变得很拮据。罗丝也断绝了和他来往。后来马丁·伊登获得了成功，名利双收，也因此受到了上层社会所谓"精英们"的盛情邀请，甚至罗丝小姐又回到了他的怀抱。但他已看透世态炎凉，在万念俱灰中投入大海怀抱。人性的虚伪在小说中被一针见血地表现出来。

在作者杰克·伦敦所生活的美国现实社会中，美国已经进入了垄断资本主义时期，资产阶级不仅仅垄断了整个社会的物质财富，也垄断了精神财富。面对社会下层人群他们嗤之以鼻，不屑一顾。小说对于资本主义制度腐朽性、资产阶级的虚伪和不平等的阶级等级划分进行了批判。

Questions:

1. What leads to Martin's tragedy?
2. Try to analyze such themes in the novel as machinery, social class and individualism vs. socialism.

British Fiction

David Copperfield (Excerpt)

What an amazing place London was to me when I saw it in the distance, and how I believed all the adventures of all my favourite heroes to be constantly enacting and re-enacting there, and how I vaguely made it out in my own mind to be fuller of wonders and wickedness than all the cities of the earth, I need not stop here to relate. We approached it by degrees, and got, in due time, to the inn in the Whitechapel district, for which we were bound. I forget whether it was the Blue Bull, or the Blue Boar; but I know it was the Blue Something, and that its likeness was painted up on the back of the coach.

The guard's eye lighted on me as he was getting down, and he said at the booking-office door:

"Is there anybody here for a yoongster booked in the name of Murdstone, from Bloonderstone, Sooffolk[1], to be left till called for?"

Nobody answered.

"Try Copperfield, if you please, sir," said I, looking helplessly down.

"Is there anybody here for a yoongster, booked in the name of Murdstone, from Bloonderstone, Sooffolk, but owning to the name of Copperfield, to be left till called for?" said the guard. "Come! IS there anybody?"

No. There was nobody. I looked anxiously around; but the inquiry made no impression on any of the bystanders, if I except a man in gaiters, with one eye, who suggested that they had better put a brass collar round my neck, and tie me up in the stable.

A ladder was brought, and I got down after the lady, who was like a haystack, not daring to stir, until her basket was removed. The coach was clear of passengers by that time, the luggage was very soon cleared out, the horses had been taken out before the luggage, and now the coach itself was wheeled and backed off by some hostlers, out of the way. Still, nobody appeared, to claim the dusty youngster from Blunderstone, Suffolk.

More solitary than Robinson Crusoe, who had nobody to look at him and see that he was solitary, I went into the booking-office, and, by invitation of the clerk on duty, passed behind the counter, and sat down on the scale at which they weighed the luggage. Here, as I sat looking at the parcels, packages, and books, and inhaling the smell of stables (ever since associated with that morning), a procession of most tremendous considerations began to march through my mind. Supposing nobody should ever fetch me, how long would they consent to keep me there? Would they keep me long enough to spend seven shillings? Should I sleep at night in one of those wooden bins, with the other luggage, and wash myself at the pump in the yard in the morning; or should I be turned out every night, and expected to come again to be left till called for, when the office opened next day? Supposing there was no mistake in the case, and Mr. Murdstone had devised this plan to get rid of me, what should I do? If they allowed me to remain there until my seven shillings were spent, I couldn't hope to remain there when I began to starve. That would obviously be inconvenient and unpleasant to the customers, besides entailing on the Blue

Whatever-it-was, the risk of funeral expenses. If I started off at once, and tried to walk back home, how could I ever find my way, how could I ever hope to walk so far, how could I make sure of anyone but Peggotty, even if I got back? If I found out the nearest proper authorities, and offered myself to go for a soldier, or a sailor, I was such a little fellow that it was most likely they wouldn't take me in. These thoughts, and a hundred other such thoughts, turned me burning hot, and made me giddy with apprehension and dismay. I was in the height of my fever when a man entered and whispered to the clerk, who presently slanted me off the scale, and pushed me over to him, as if I were weighed, bought, delivered, and paid for.

As I went out of the office, hand in hand with this new acquaintance, I stole a look at him. He was a gaunt, sallow young man, with hollow cheeks, and a chin almost as black as Mr. Murdstone's; but there the likeness ended, for his whiskers were shaved off, and his hair, instead of being glossy, was rusty and dry. He was dressed in a suit of black clothes which were rather rusty and dry too, and rather short in the sleeves and legs; and he had a white neck-kerchief on, that was not over-clean. I did not, and do not, suppose that this neck-kerchief was all the linen he wore[2], but it was all he showed or gave any hint of.

"You're the new boy?" he said. "Yes, sir," I said.

I supposed I was. I didn't know.

"I'm one of the masters at Salem House," he said.

I made him a bow and felt very much overawed. I was so ashamed to allude to a commonplace thing like my box, to a scholar and a master at Salem House, that we had gone some little distance from the yard before I had the hardihood to mention it. We turned back, on my humbly insinuating that it might be useful to me hereafter; and he told the clerk that the carrier had instructions to call for it at noon.

"If you please, sir," I said, when we had accomplished about the same distance as before, "is it far?"

"It's down by Blackheath," he said.

"Is that far, sir?" I diffidently asked.

"It's a good step," he said. "We shall go by the stage-coach. It's about six miles."

I was so faint and tired, that the idea of holding out for six miles more, was too much for me. I took heart to tell him that I had had nothing all night, and that if he would allow me to buy something to eat, I should be very much obliged to him. He appeared surprised at this—I see him stop and look at me now—and after considering for a few moments, said he wanted to call on an old person who lived not far off, and that the best way would be for me to buy some bread, or whatever I liked best that was wholesome, and make my breakfast at her house, where we could get some milk.

Accordingly we looked in at a baker's window, and after I had made a series of proposals to buy everything that was bilious in the shop, and he had rejected them one by one, we decided in favour of a nice little loaf of brown bread, which cost me three pence. Then, at a grocer's shop, we bought an egg and a slice of streaky bacon; which still left what I thought a good deal of change, out of the second of the bright shillings, and made me consider London a very cheap place. These provisions laid in, we went on through a great noise and uproar that confused my weary head beyond description, and over a bridge which, no doubt, was London Bridge (indeed I think he told me so, but I was half asleep), until we came to the poor person's house, which was a part of some alms-houses, as I knew by their look, and by an inscription on a stone over the gate which said they were established for twenty-five poor women.

The Master at Salem House lifted the latch of one of a number of little black doors that were all alike, and had each a little diamond-paned window on one side, and another little diamond-paned window above; and we went into the little house of one of these poor old women, who was blowing a fire to make a little saucepan boil. On seeing the master enter, the old woman stopped with the bellows on her knee, and said something that I thought sounded like "My Charley!" but on seeing me come in too, she got up, and rubbing her hands made a confused sort of half curtsey.

"Can you cook this young gentleman's breakfast for him, if you please?" said the Master at Salem House.

"Can I?" said the old woman. "Yes can I, sure!"

"How's Mrs. Fibbitson today?" said the Master, looking at another old woman in a large chair by the fire, who was such a bundle of clothes that I feel grateful to this hour for not having sat upon her by mistake.

"Ah, she's poorly," said the first old woman. "It's one of her bad days. If the fire was to go out, through any accident, I verily believe she'd go out too, and never come to life again."

As they looked at her, I looked at her also. Although it was a warm day, she seemed to think of nothing but the fire. I fancied she was jealous even of the saucepan on it; and I have reason to know that she took its impressment into the service of boiling my egg and broiling my bacon, in dudgeon; for I saw her, with my own discomfited eyes, shake her fist at me once, when those culinary operations were going on, and no one else was looking. The sun streamed in at the little window, but she sat with her own back and the back of the large chair towards it, screening the fire as if she were sedulously keeping it warm, instead of it keeping her warm, and watching it in a most distrustful manner. The completion of the preparations for my breakfast, by relieving the fire, gave her such extreme joy that she laughed aloud—and a very unmelodious laugh she had, I must say.

I sat down to my brown loaf, my egg, and my rasher of bacon, with a basin of milk besides, and made a most delicious meal. While I was yet in the full enjoyment of it, the old woman of the house said to the Master:

"Have you got your flute with you?"

"Yes," he returned.

"Have a blow at it," said the old woman, coaxingly. "Do!"

The Master, upon this, put his hand underneath the skirts of his coat, and brought out his flute in three pieces, which he screwed together, and began immediately to play. My impression is, after many years of consideration, that there never can have been anybody in the world who played worse. He made the most dismal sounds I have ever heard produced by any means, natural or artificial. I don't know what the tunes were—if there were such things in the performance at all, which I doubt—but the influence of the strain upon me was, first, to make me think of all my sorrows until I could hardly keep my tears back; then to take away my appetite; and lastly, to make me so sleepy that I couldn't keep my eyes open. They begin to close again, and I begin to nod, as the recollection rises fresh upon me. Once more the little room, with its open corner cupboard, and its square-backed chairs, and its angular little staircase leading to the room above, and its three peacock's feathers displayed over the mantelpiece—I remember wondering when I first went in, what that peacock would have thought if he had known what his finery was doomed to come to—fades from before me, and I nod, and sleep. The flute becomes inaudible, the wheels of the coach are heard instead, and I am on my journey. The coach jolts, I wake with a start, and the flute has come back again, and the Master at Salem House is sitting with his legs crossed, playing it dolefully, while the old woman of the house looks on delighted. She fades in her turn, and he fades, and all fades, and there is no flute, no Master, no Salem House, no David Copperfield, no anything but heavy sleep.

I dreamed, I thought, that once while he was blowing into this dismal flute, the old woman of the house, who had gone nearer and nearer to him in her ecstatic admiration, leaned over the back of his chair and gave him an affectionate squeeze round the neck, which stopped his playing for a moment. I was in the middle state between sleeping and waking, either then or immediately afterwards; for, as he resumed—it was a real fact that he had stopped playing—I saw and heard the same old woman ask Mrs. Fibbitson if it wasn't delicious (meaning the flute), to which Mrs. Fibbitson replied, "Ay, ay! yes!" and nodded at the fire: to which, I am persuaded, she gave the credit of the whole performance.

When I seemed to have been dozing a long while, the Master at Salem House unscrewed his flute into the three pieces, put them up as before, and took me away. We found the coach very near at hand, and got upon the roof; but I was so dead sleepy, that when we stopped on the road to take up somebody else, they put me inside where there were no passengers, and where I slept profoundly, until I found the coach going at a footpace up a steep hill among green leaves. Presently, it stopped, and had come to its destination.

A short walk brought us—I mean the Master and me—to Salem House, which was enclosed with a high brick wall, and looked very dull. Over a door in this wall was a board with Salem House upon it; and through a grating in this door we were surveyed when we rang the bell by a surly face, which I found, on the door being opened, belonged to a stout man with a bull-neck, a wooden leg, overhanging temples, and his hair cut close all round his head.

"The new boy," said the Master.

The man with the wooden leg eyed me all over—it didn't take long, for there was not much of me—and locked the gate behind us, and took out the key. We were going up to the house, among some dark heavy trees, when he called after my conductor. "Hallo!"

We looked back, and he was standing at the door of a little lodge, where he lived, with a pair of boots in his hand.

"Here! The cobbler's been," he said, "since you've been out, Mr. Mell, and he says he can't mend 'em any more. He says there ain't a bit of the original boot left, and he wonders you expect it."

With these words he threw the boots towards Mr. Mell, who went back a few paces to pick them up, and looked at them (very disconsolately, I was afraid), as we went on together. I observed then, for the first time, that the boots he had on were a good deal the worse for wear, and that his stocking was just breaking out in one place, like a bud.

Salem House was a square brick building with wings; of a bare and unfurnished appearance. All about it was so very quiet, that I said to Mr. Mell I supposed the boys were out; but he seemed surprised at my not knowing that it was holiday-time. That all the boys were at their several homes. That Mr. Creakle, the proprietor, was down by the sea-side with Mrs. and Miss Creakle; and that I was sent in holiday-time as a punishment for my misdoing, all of which he explained to me as we went along.

I gazed upon the schoolroom into which he took me, as the most forlorn and desolate place I had ever seen. I see it now. A long room with three long rows of desks, and six of forms, and bristling all round with pegs for hats and slates. Scraps of old copy-books and exercises litter the dirty floor. Some silkworms' houses, made of the same materials, are scattered over the desks. Two miserable little white mice, left behind by their owner, are running up and down in a fusty castle made of pasteboard and wire, looking in all the corners with their red eyes for anything to eat. A bird, in a cage very little bigger than himself, makes a mournful rattle now and then in hopping on his perch, two inches high, or dropping from it; but neither sings nor chirps. There is a strange unwholesome smell upon the room, like mildewed corduroys, sweet apples wanting air, and rotten books. There could not well be more ink splashed about it, if it had been roofless from its first construction, and the skies had rained, snowed, hailed, and blown ink through the varying seasons of the year.

Mr. Mell having left me while he took his irreparable boots upstairs, I went softly to the upper end of the room, observing all this as I crept along. Suddenly I came upon a pasteboard placard, beautifully written, which was lying on the desk, and bore these words: "TAKE CARE OF HIM. HE BITES."

I got upon the desk immediately, apprehensive of at least a great dog underneath. But, though I looked all round with anxious eyes, I could see nothing of him. I was still engaged in peering about, when Mr. Mell came back, and asked me what I did up there?

"I beg your pardon, sir," says I, "if you please, I'm looking for the dog."

"Dog?" he says. "What dog?"

"Isn't it a dog, sir?"

"Isn't what a dog?"

"That's to be taken care of, sir; that bites."

"No, Copperfield," says he, gravely, "that's not a dog. That's a boy. My instructions are, Copperfield, to put this placard on your back. I am sorry to make such a beginning with you, but I must do it." With that he took me down, and tied the placard, which was neatly constructed for the purpose, on my shoulders like a knapsack; and wherever I went, afterwards, I had the consolation of carrying it.

What I suffered from that placard, nobody can imagine. Whether it was possible for people to see me or not, I always fancied that somebody was reading it. It was no relief to turn round and find nobody; for wherever my back was, there I imagined somebody always to be. That cruel man with the wooden leg aggravated my sufferings. He was in authority; and if he ever saw me leaning against a tree, or a wall, or the house, he roared out from his lodge door in a stupendous voice, "Hallo, you sir! You Copperfield! Show that badge conspicuous, or I'll report you!" The playground was a bare gravelled yard, open to all the back of the house and the offices; and I knew that the servants read it, and the butcher read it, and the baker read it; that everybody, in a word, who came backwards and forwards to the house, of a morning when I was ordered to walk there, read that I was to be taken care of, for I bit, I recollect that I positively began to have a dread of myself, as a kind of wild boy who did bite.

There was an old door in this playground, on which the boys had a custom of carving their names. It was completely covered with such inscriptions. In my dread of the end of the vacation and their coming back, I could not read a boy's name, without inquiring in what tone and with what emphasis he would read, "Take care of him. He bites." There was one boy—a certain J. Steerforth—who cut his name very deep and very often, who, I conceived, would read it in a rather strong voice, and afterwards pull my hair. There was another boy, one Tommy Traddles, who I dreaded would make game of it, and pretend to be dreadfully frightened of me. There was a third, George Demple, who I fancied would sing it. I have looked, a little shrinking creature, at that door, until the owners of all the names—there were five-and-forty of them in the school then, Mr. Mell said—seemed to send me to Coventry by general acclamation, and to cry out, each in his own way, "Take care of him. He bites!"

It was the same with the places at the desks and forms. It was the same with the groves of deserted bedsteads I peeped at, on my way to, and when I was in, my own bed. I remember dreaming night after night, of being with my mother as she used to be, or of going to a party at Mr. Peggotty's, or of travelling outside the stage-coach, or of dining again with my unfortunate friend the waiter, and in all these circumstances making people scream and stare, by the unhappy disclosure that I had nothing on but my little night-shirt, and that placard.

NOTES

1. 看车的人没有读准地名。
2. 此处暗示该人未穿衬衣。

About the Author

Charles John Huffam Dickens (1812–1870), an English novelist and critic, was born on February 7, 1812, in Portsmouth, England. When his father, John Dickens, a clerk at the Navy Pay Office, was imprisoned for debt in the Marshalsea in 1824, Charles was 12 years old and had to be removed from school and sent to work at a boot-blacking factory with only 6 shillings a week to help support the family. Without doubt, this experience would be a heavy influence on Dickens' later views reflected in his fiction.

Dickens wrote 15 major novels and countless short stories and articles. Having created some of the world's best-known fictional characters, he is regarded by many as the greatest novelist of the Victorian era. Over the course of his writing career, the beloved classic novels he wrote include *Oliver Twist*, *A Christmas Carol*, *Nicholas Nickleby*, *David Copperfield*, *A Tale of Two Cities* and *Great Expectations*. On June 9, 1870, Dickens died of a stroke in Kent, England, leaving his final novel, *The Mystery of Edwin Drood*, unfinished. He was laid to rest in Poet's Corner, Westminster Abbey.

Appreciation:

狄更斯在《大卫·科波菲尔》（1850）的序言中这样写道："在我所有的书里，我最喜欢的就是这本。对于我想象中创造出的所有孩子，我都是个溺爱的父亲，从没人像我这样对他们深深爱着。可是，正如许多溺爱的父母一样，在我心底深处有一个孩子最受我宠爱，他的名字就叫大卫·科波菲尔。"本书是狄更斯最重要且耗费心血最多、篇幅最长的一部半自传体著作，被称为他"心中最宠爱的孩子"。本书于 1849 至 1850 年间，分 20 个部分逐月发表。

《大卫·科波菲尔》描写的是一个小资产阶级知识分子在资本主义社会寻求出路的故事。孤儿大卫·科波菲尔经受了许多磨难，饱尝人生辛酸，在一些善良的人们多方救助下，经过不屈不挠的奋斗，最后终于获得了事业上的成就和家庭的幸福。作者通过对主人公一生悲欢离合的多层次描写，揭示了当时社会的真实面貌，表现了金钱对婚姻、家庭和社会的腐蚀作用。评论家们认为，《大卫·科波菲尔》的成就，超过了狄更斯所有的其他作品。列夫·托尔斯泰誉之为"一切英国小说中最好的一部"。在这部具有强烈自传色彩的小说里，狄更斯借用大卫自身的历史和经验，从不少方面回顾了自己的生活道路和经验，表现了他的人生哲学和道德理想。

大卫·科波菲尔是遗腹子，在母亲及女仆辟果提（Peggotty）的照管下长大。不久，母亲改嫁，继父摩德斯东凶狠贪婪，他把大卫看作累赘，不但常常在肉体上责打他，还剥夺了母亲对他的关怀和爱抚，让他饱受精神上的折磨。选文出自第五章，继父要把小大卫送到一所寄宿学校，他离开家，独自一人上路，心中满怀悲伤，路上受到车夫和旅店伙计的欺凌，到学校后又遭到不公正的待遇。

Questions:

1. The tone of *David Copperfield* is often melodramatic and emotional, but the language of the novel is actually pretty realistic. Find out examples to illustrate this.

2. Why did Mr. Mell put the placard with the words "TAKE CARE OF HIM. HE BITES." on David's back? How did this trouble him?

Frankenstein (Excerpt)

From this day natural philosophy, and particularly chemistry, in the most comprehensive sense of the term, became nearly my sole occupation. I read with ardour those works, so full of genius and discrimination, which modern inquirers have written on these subjects. I attended the lectures and cultivated the acquaintance of the men of science of the university, and I found even in M. Krempe a great deal of sound sense and real information, combined, it is true, with a repulsive physiognomy and manners, but not on that account the less valuable. In M. Waldman I found a true friend. His gentleness was never tinged by dogmatism, and his instructions were given with an air of frankness and good nature that banished every idea of pedantry. In a thousand ways he smoothed for me the path of knowledge and made the most abstruse inquiries clear and facile to my apprehension. My application was at first fluctuating and uncertain; it gained strength as I proceeded and soon became so ardent and eager that the stars often disappeared in the light of morning whilst I was yet engaged in my laboratory.

As I applied so closely, it may be easily conceived that my progress was rapid. My ardour was indeed the astonishment of the students, and my proficiency that of the masters. Professor Krempe often asked me, with a sly smile, how Cornelius Agrippa[1] went on, whilst M. Waldman expressed the most heartfelt exultation in my progress. Two years passed in this manner, during which I paid no visit to Geneva, but was engaged, heart and soul, in the pursuit of some discoveries which I hoped to make. None but those who have experienced them can conceive of the enticements of science. In other studies you go as far as others have gone before you, and there is nothing more to know; but in a scientific pursuit there is continual food for discovery and wonder. A mind of moderate capacity which closely pursues one study must infallibly arrive at great proficiency in that study; and I, who continually sought the attainment of one object of pursuit and was solely wrapped up in this, improved so rapidly that at the end of two years I made some discoveries in the improvement of some chemical instruments, which procured me great esteem and admiration at the university. When I had arrived at this point and had become as well acquainted with the theory and practice of natural philosophy as depended on the lessons of any of the professors at Ingolstadt, my residence there being no longer conducive to my improvements, I thought of returning to my friends and my native town, when an incident happened that protracted my stay.

One of the phenomena which had peculiarly attracted my attention was the structure of the human frame, and, indeed, any animal endued with life. Whence, I often asked myself, did the principle of life proceed? It was a bold question, and one which has ever been considered as a mystery; yet with how many things are we upon the brink of becoming acquainted, if cowardice or carelessness did not restrain our inquiries. I revolved these circumstances in my mind and determined thenceforth to apply myself more particularly to those branches of natural philosophy which relate to physiology. Unless I had been animated by an almost supernatural enthusiasm, my application to this study would have been irksome and almost intolerable. To examine the causes of life, we must first have recourse to death. I became acquainted with the science of anatomy, but this was not sufficient; I must also observe the natural decay and corruption of the human body. In my education my father had taken the greatest precautions that my mind should be impressed with no supernatural horrors. I do not ever remember to have trembled at a tale of superstition or to have feared the apparition of a spirit. Darkness had no effect upon my fancy, and a churchyard was to me merely the receptacle of bodies deprived of life, which, from being the seat of beauty and strength, had become food for the worm. Now I was led to examine the cause and progress of this decay and forced to spend days and nights in vaults and charnel-houses[2]. My attention was fixed upon every object the most insupportable to the delicacy of the human feelings. I saw how the fine form of man was degraded and wasted; I beheld the corruption of death succeed to the blooming cheek of life; I saw how the worm inherited the wonders of the eye and brain. I paused, examining and analysing all the minutiae of causation, as exemplified in the change from life to death, and death to life, until from the midst of this darkness a sudden light broke in upon me—a light so brilliant and wondrous, yet so simple, that while I became dizzy with the immensity of the prospect which it illustrated, I was surprised that among so many men of genius who had directed their inquiries towards the same science, that I alone should be reserved to discover so astonishing a secret.

Remember, I am not recording the vision of a madman. The sun does not more certainly shine in the heavens than that which I now affirm is true. Some miracle might have produced it, yet the stages of the discovery were distinct and probable. After days and nights of incredible labour and fatigue, I succeeded in discovering the cause of generation and life; nay, more, I became myself capable of bestowing animation upon lifeless matter.

The astonishment which I had at first experienced on this discovery soon gave place to delight and rapture. After so much time spent in painful labour, to arrive at once at the summit of my desires was the most gratifying consummation of my toils. But this discovery was so great and overwhelming that all the steps by which I had been progressively led to it were obliterated, and I beheld only the result. What had been the study and desire of the wisest men since the creation of the world was now within my grasp. Not that, like a magic scene, it all opened upon me at once: the information I had obtained was of a nature rather to direct my endeavours so soon as I should point them towards the object of my search than to exhibit that object already accomplished. I was like the Arabian who had been buried with the dead and found a passage to life, aided only by one glimmering and seemingly ineffectual light.

I see by your eagerness and the wonder and hope which your eyes express, my friend, that you expect to be informed of the secret with which I am acquainted; that cannot be; listen patiently until the end of my story, and you will easily perceive why I am reserved upon that subject. I will not lead you on, unguarded and ardent as I then was, to your destruction and infallible misery. Learn from me, if not by my precepts, at least by my example, how dangerous is the acquirement of knowledge and how much happier that man is who believes his native town to be the world, than he who aspires to become greater than his nature will allow.

When I found so astonishing a power placed within my hands, I hesitated a long time concerning the manner in which I should employ it. Although I possessed the capacity of bestowing animation, yet to prepare a frame for the reception of it, with all its intricacies of fibres, muscles, and veins, still remained a work of inconceivable difficulty and labour. I doubted at first whether I should attempt the creation of a being like myself, or one of simpler organization; but my imagination was too much exalted by my first success to permit me to doubt of my ability to give life to an animal as complete and wonderful as man. The materials at present within my command hardly appeared adequate to so arduous an undertaking, but I doubted not that I should ultimately succeed. I prepared myself for a multitude of reverses; my operations might be incessantly baffled, and at last my work be imperfect, yet when I considered the improvement which every day takes place in science and mechanics, I was encouraged to hope my present attempts would at least lay the foundations of future success. Nor could I consider the magnitude and complexity of my plan as any argument of its impracticability. It was with these feelings that I began the creation of a human being. As the minuteness of the parts formed a great hindrance to my speed, I resolved, contrary to my first intention, to make the being of a gigantic stature, that is to say, about eight feet in height, and proportionably large. After having formed this determination and having spent some months in successfully collecting and arranging my materials, I began.

No one can conceive the variety of feelings which bore me onwards, like a hurricane, in the first enthusiasm of success. Life and death appeared to me ideal bounds, which I should first break through, and pour a torrent of light into our dark world. A new species would bless me as its creator and source; many happy and excellent natures would owe their being to me. No father could claim the gratitude of his child so completely as I should deserve theirs. Pursuing these reflections, I thought that if I could bestow animation upon lifeless matter, I might in process of time (although I now found it impossible) renew life where death had apparently devoted the body to corruption.

These thoughts supported my spirits, while I pursued my undertaking with unremitting ardour. My cheek had grown pale with study, and my person had become emaciated with confinement. Sometimes, on the very brink of certainty, I failed; yet still I clung to the hope which the next day or the next hour might realize. One secret which I alone possessed was the hope to which I had dedicated myself; and the moon gazed on my midnight labours, while, with unrelaxed and breathless eagerness, I pursued nature to her hiding-places. Who shall conceive the horrors of my secret toil as I dabbled among the unhallowed damps of the grave or tortured the living animal to animate the lifeless clay? My limbs now tremble, and my eyes swim with the remembrance; but then a resistless and almost frantic impulse urged me forward; I seemed to have lost all soul or sensation but for this one pursuit. It was indeed but a passing trance, that only made me feel with renewed acuteness so soon as, the unnatural stimulus ceasing to operate, I had returned to my old habits. I collected bones from charnel-houses and disturbed, with profane fingers, the tremendous secrets of the human frame. In a solitary chamber, or rather cell, at the top of the house, and separated from all the other apartments by a gallery and staircase, I kept my workshop of filthy creation; my eyeballs were starting from their sockets in attending to the details of my employment. The dissecting room and the slaughter-house furnished many of my materials; and often did my human nature turn with loathing from my occupation, whilst, still urged on by an eagerness which perpetually increased, I brought my work near to a conclusion.

The summer months passed while I was thus engaged, heart and soul, in one pursuit. It was a most beautiful season; never did the fields bestow a more plentiful harvest or the vines yield a more luxuriant vintage, but my eyes were insensible to the charms of nature. And the same feelings which made me neglect the scenes around me caused me also to forget those friends who were so many miles absent, and whom I had not seen for so long a time. I knew my silence disquieted them, and I well remembered the words of my father: "I know that while you are pleased with yourself you will think of us with affection, and we shall hear regularly from you. You must pardon me if I regard any interruption in your correspondence as a proof that your other duties are equally neglected."

I knew well therefore what would be my father's feelings, but I could not tear my thoughts from my employment, loathsome in itself, but which had taken an irresistible hold of my imagination. I wished, as it were, to procrastinate all that related to my feelings of affection until the great object, which swallowed up every habit of my nature, should be completed.

I then thought that my father would be unjust if he ascribed my neglect to vice or faultiness on my part, but I am now convinced that he was justified in conceiving that I should not be altogether free from blame. A human being in perfection ought always to preserve a calm and peaceful mind and never to allow passion or a transitory desire to disturb his tranquillity. I do not think that the pursuit of knowledge is an exception to this rule. If the study to which you apply yourself has a tendency to weaken your affections and to destroy your taste for those simple pleasures in which no alloy can possibly mix, then that study is certainly unlawful, that is to say, not befitting the human mind. If this rule were always observed; if no man allowed any pursuit whatsoever to interfere with the tranquillity of his domestic affections, Greece had not been enslaved, Caesar would have spared his country, America would have been discovered more gradually, and the empires of Mexico and Peru had not been destroyed.

But I forget that I am moralizing in the most interesting part of my tale, and your looks remind me to proceed. My father made no reproach in his letters and only took notice of my science by inquiring into my occupations more particularly than before. Winter, spring, and summer passed away during my labours; but I did not watch the blossom or the expanding leaves—sights which before always yielded me supreme delight—so deeply was I engrossed in my occupation. The leaves of that year had withered before my work drew near to a close, and now every day showed me more plainly how well I had succeeded. But my enthusiasm was checked by my anxiety, and I appeared rather like one doomed by slavery to toil in the mines, or any other unwholesome trade than an artist occupied by his favourite employment. Every night I was oppressed by a slow fever, and I became nervous to a most painful degree; the fall of a leaf startled me, and I shunned my fellow creatures as if I had been guilty of a crime. Sometimes I grew alarmed at the wreck I perceived that I had become; the energy of my purpose alone sustained me: my labours would soon end, and I believed that exercise and amusement would then drive away incipient disease; and I promised myself both of these when my creation should be complete.

NOTES

1. Cornelius Agrippa: 科尼利厄斯·阿格里帕 (1486—1535)，文艺复兴时期秘教中最有影响的作家。雪莱在牛津期间曾读过他的很多作品。
2. Charnel-houses 停尸所。

About the Author:

Mary Shelley（1797–1851）was born as Mary Wollstonecraft Godwin on August 30, 1797, in Somers Town, London, England. Her mother is the feminist philosopher, educator, and writer Mary Wollstonecraft, and her father, the philosopher, novelist, and journalist William Godwin. In 1814, Mary began a romance with one of her father's political followers, Percy Bysshe Shelley. The two married in late 1816, after the suicide of Harriet, the wife of Percy Bysshe Shelley. Two years later, she published her most famous novel, *Frankenstein*, which is considered as the first science fiction, and she is regarded as the mother of science fiction. She died of brain cancer on February 1, 1851, in London, England. Some other books she wrote are *Valperga* (1823), *The Last Man* (1826), *Lodore* (1835) and *Mathilde* (posthumously published).

Appreciation:

《弗兰肯斯坦》全名《弗兰肯斯坦——现代普罗米修斯的故事》，是英国诗人雪莱的妻子玛丽·雪莱在 1818 年创作的小说，被认为是世界第一部真正意义上的科幻小说。

主人公年轻的科学家弗兰肯斯坦痴迷科学研究，力图用人工创造出生命。他利用当时的生物学知识，在他的实验室里，通过无数次的探索，利用从停尸房等处取得不同人体的器官和组织，拼合成一个人体，并利用雷电使这个人体拥有了生命。然而这怪物甫一造成，他便觉其面目可憎，奇丑无比，于是仓皇逃离现场，随之大病一场。刚开始之时，怪物天性善良，向往美好，渴望感情，但是，由于其面貌丑陋，被社会视为怪物，被当作巨大的威胁，处处碰壁。于是，他要求弗兰肯斯坦为自己制造一个配偶，答应事成后与其双双远离人间。弗兰肯斯坦最初应允了怪物，但在接近成功之时，由于担心怪物种族从此危害社会，他又毁去了女性怪物。苦苦企盼的怪物开始疯狂地报复，他憎恨一切，想毁灭一切，杀害了弗兰肯斯坦的弟弟威廉等几个亲人。于是弗兰肯斯坦发誓毁掉自己的作品，怀着满腔怒火追捕他所创造的恶魔般的怪物一直到北极地带，受尽折磨后病逝，而怪物亦自焚而死。节选的第四章主要叙述主人公弗兰肯斯坦对科学的狂热，其创造怪物的缘起和过程。

Questions:

1. "…how dangerous is the acquirement of knowledge and how much happier that man is who believes his native town to be the world, than he who aspires to become greater than his nature will allow" (Para.7). How do you understand these words? Do you agree that the acquirement of knowledge is dangerous? Why or why not?

2. What's your opinion about the fast development of science and technology nowadays?

Heart of Darkness (Excerpt)

The sun set; the dusk fell on the stream, and lights began to appear along the shore. The Chapman light-house, a three-legged thing erect on a mud-flat, shone strongly. Lights of ships moved in the fairway—a great stir of lights going up and going down. And farther west on the upper reaches the place of the monstrous town was still marked ominously on the sky, a brooding gloom in sunshine, a lurid glare under the stars.

"And this also," said Marlow suddenly, "has been one of the dark places of the earth."

He was the only man of us who still "followed the sea." The worst that could be said of him was that he did not represent his class. He was a seaman, but he was a wanderer, too, while most seamen lead, if one may so express it, a sedentary life. Their minds are of the stay-at-home order, and their home is always with them—the ship; and so is their country—the sea. One ship is very much like another, and the sea is always the same. In the immutability of their surroundings the foreign shores, the foreign faces, the changing immensity of life, glide past, veiled not by a sense of mystery but by a slightly disdainful ignorance; for there is nothing mysterious to a seaman unless it be the sea itself, which is the mistress of his existence and as inscrutable as Destiny. For the rest, after his hours of work, a casual stroll or a casual spree on shore suffices to unfold for him the secret of a whole continent, and generally he finds the secret not worth knowing. The yarns of seamen have a direct simplicity, the whole meaning of which lies within the shell of a cracked nut. But Marlow was not typical (if his propensity to spin yarns be excepted), and to him the meaning of an episode was not inside like a kernel but outside, enveloping the tale which brought it out only as a glow brings out a haze, in the likeness of one of these misty halos that sometimes are made visible by the spectral illumination of moonshine.

His remark did not seem at all surprising. It was just like Marlow. It was accepted in silence. No one took the trouble to grunt even; and presently he said, very slow—"I was thinking of very old times, when the Romans first came here, nineteen hundred years ago—the other day ... Light came out of this river since—you say Knights? Yes; but it is like a running blaze on a plain, like a flash of lightning in the clouds. We live in the flicker—may it last as long as the old earth keeps rolling! But darkness was here yesterday. Imagine the feelings of a commander of a fine—what d'ye call 'em?—trireme in the Mediterranean, ordered suddenly to the north; run overland across the Gauls in a hurry; put in charge of one of these craft the legionaries—a wonderful lot of handy men they must have been, too—used to build, apparently by the hundred, in a month or two, if we may believe what we read. Imagine him here—the very end of the world, a sea the colour of lead, a sky the colour of smoke, a kind of ship about as rigid as a concertina—and going up this river with stores, or orders, or what you like. Sand-banks, marshes, forests, savages, —precious little to eat fit for a civilized man, nothing but Thames water to drink. No Falernian wine here, no going ashore. Here and there a military camp lost in a wilderness, like a needle in a bundle of hay—cold, fog, tempests, disease, exile, and death—death skulking in the air, in the water, in the bush. They must have been dying like flies here. Oh, yes—he did it. Did it very well, too, no doubt, and without thinking much about it either, except afterwards to brag of what he had gone through in his time, perhaps. They were men enough to face the darkness. And perhaps he was cheered by keeping his eye on a chance of promotion to the fleet at Ravenna[1] by and by, if he had good friends in Rome and survived the awful climate. Or think of a decent young citizen in a toga—perhaps too much dice, you know—coming out here in the train of some prefect, or tax-gatherer, or trader even, to mend his fortunes. Land in a swamp, march through the woods, and in some inland post feel the savagery, the utter savagery, had closed round him—all that mysterious life of the wilderness that stirs in the forest, in the jungles, in the hearts of wild men. There's no initiation either into such mysteries. He has to live in the midst of the incomprehensible, which is also detestable. And it has a fascination, too, that goes to work upon him. The fascination of the abomination—you know, imagine the growing regrets, the longing to escape, the powerless disgust, the surrender, the hate."

He paused.

"Mind," he began again, lifting one arm from the elbow, the palm of the hand outwards, so that, with his legs folded before him, he had the pose of a Buddha preaching in European clothes and without a lotus-flower—"Mind, none of us would feel exactly like this. What saves us is efficiency—the devotion to efficiency. But these chaps were not much account, really. They were no colonists; their administration was merely a squeeze, and nothing more, I suspect. They were conquerors, and for that you want only brute force—nothing to boast of, when you have it, since your strength is just an accident arising from the weakness of others. They grabbed what they could get for the sake of what was to be got. It was just robbery with violence, aggravated murder on a great scale, and men going at it blind—as is very proper for those who tackle a darkness. The conquest of the earth, which mostly means the taking it away from those who have a different complexion or slightly flatter noses than ourselves, is not a pretty thing when you look into it too much. What redeems it is the idea only. An idea at the back of it; not a sentimental pretence but an idea; and an unselfish belief in the idea—something you can set up, and bow down before, and offer a sacrifice to ..."

He broke off. Flames glided in the river, small green flames, red flames, white flames, pursuing, overtaking, joining, crossing each other—then separating slowly or hastily. The traffic of the great city went on in the deepening night upon the sleepless river. We looked on, waiting patiently—there was nothing else to do till the end of the flood; but it was only after a long silence, when he said, in a hesitating voice, "I suppose you fellows remember I did once turn fresh-water sailor for a bit," that we knew we were fated, before the ebb began to run, to hear about one of Marlow's inconclusive experiences.

"I don't want to bother you much with what happened to me personally," he began, showing in this remark the weakness of many tellers of tales who seem so often unaware of what their audience would like best to hear; "yet to understand the effect of it on me you ought to know how I got out there, what I saw, how I went up that river to the place where I first met the poor chap. It was the farthest point of navigation and the culminating point of my experience. It seemed somehow to throw a kind of light on everything about me—and into my thoughts. It was sombre enough, too—and pitiful—not extraordinary in any way—not very clear either. No, not very clear. And yet it seemed to throw a kind of light.

I had then, as you remember, just returned to London after a lot of Indian Ocean, Pacific, China Seas—a regular dose of the East—six years or so, and I was loafing about, hindering you fellows in your work and invading your homes, just as though I had got a heavenly mission to civilize you. It was very fine for a time, but after a bit I did get tired of resting. Then I began to look for a ship—I should think the hardest work on earth. But the ships wouldn't even look at me. And I got tired of that game, too.

Now when I was a little chap I had a passion for maps. I would look for hours at South America, or Africa, or Australia, and lose myself in all the glories of exploration. At that time there were many blank spaces on the earth, and when I saw one that looked particularly inviting on a map (but they all look that) I would put my finger on it and say, "When I grow up I will go there." The North Pole was one of these places, I remember. Well, I haven't been there yet, and shall not try now. The glamour's off. Other places were scattered about the hemispheres. I have been in some of them, and ... well, we won't talk about that. But there was one yet—the biggest, the most blank, so to speak—that I had a hankering after.

True, by this time it was not a blank space any more. It had got filled since my boyhood with rivers and lakes and names. It had ceased to be a blank space of delightful mystery—a white patch for a boy to dream gloriously over. It had become a place of darkness. But there was in it one river especially, a mighty big river, that you could see on the map, resembling an immense snake uncoiled, with its head in the sea, its body at rest curving afar over a vast country, and its tail lost in the depths of the land. And as I looked at the map of it in a shop-window, it fascinated me as a snake would a bird—a silly little bird. Then I remembered there was a big concern, a Company for trade on that river. Dash it all! I thought to myself, they can't trade without using some kind of craft on that lot of fresh water—steamboats! Why shouldn't I try to get charge of one? I went on along Fleet Street[2], but could not shake off the idea. The snake had charmed me.

You understand it was a Continental concern, that Trading society; but I have a lot of relations living on the Continent, because it's cheap and not so nasty as it looks, they say.

I am sorry to own I began to worry them. This was already a fresh departure for me. I was not used to get things that way, you know. I always went my own road and on my own legs where I had a mind to go. I wouldn't have believed it of myself; but, then—you see—I felt somehow I must get there by hook or by crook. So I worried them. The men said "My dear fellow," and did nothing. Then—would you believe it?—I tried the women. I, Charlie Marlow, set the women to work—to get a job. Heavens! Well, you see, the notion drove me. I had an aunt, a dear enthusiastic soul. She wrote: "It will be delightful. I am ready to do anything, anything for you. It is a glorious idea. I know the wife of a very high personage in the Administration, and also a man who has lots of influence with," etc. She was determined to make no end of fuss to get me appointed skipper of a river steamboat, if such was my fancy.

I got my appointment—of course; and I got it very quick. It appears the Company had received news that one of their captains had been killed in a scuffle with the natives. This was my chance, and it made me the more anxious to go. It was only months and months afterwards, when I made the attempt to recover what was left of the body, that I heard the original quarrel arose from a misunderstanding about some hens. Yes, two black hens. Fresleven—that was the fellow's name, a Dane—thought himself wronged somehow in the bargain, so he went ashore and started to hammer the chief of the village with a stick. Oh, it didn't surprise me in the least to hear this, and at the same time to be told that Fresleven was the gentlest, quietest creature that ever walked on two legs. No doubt he was; but he had been a couple of years already out there engaged in the noble cause, you know, and he probably felt the need at last of asserting his self-respect in some way. Therefore he whacked the old nigger mercilessly, while a big crowd of his people watched him, thunderstruck, till some man—I was told the chief's son—in desperation at hearing the old chap yell, made a tentative jab with a spear at the white man—and of course it went quite easy between the shoulder-blades. Then the whole population cleared into the forest, expecting all kinds of calamities to happen, while, on the other hand, the steamer Fresleven commanded left also in a bad panic, in charge of the engineer, I believe. Afterwards nobody seemed to trouble much about Fresleven's remains, till I got out and stepped into his shoes. I couldn't let it rest, though; but when an opportunity offered at last to meet my predecessor, the grass growing through his ribs was tall enough to hide his bones. They were all there. The supernatural being had not been touched after he fell. And the village was deserted, the huts gaped black, rotting, all askew within the fallen enclosures. A calamity had come to it, sure enough. The people had vanished. Mad terror had scattered them, men, women, and children, through the bush, and they had never returned. What became of the hens I don't know either. I should think the cause of progress got them, anyhow. However, through this glorious affair I got my appointment, before I had fairly begun to hope for it.

I flew around like mad to get ready, and before forty-eight hours I was crossing the Channel to show myself to my employers, and sign the contract. In a very few hours I arrived in a city that always makes me think of a whited sepulchre. Prejudice no doubt. I had no difficulty in finding the Company's offices. It was the biggest thing in the town, and everybody I met was full of it. They were going to run an over-sea empire, and make no end of coin by trade.

…

NOTES

1. Ravenna：拉文纳，意大利东北部的一个港口城市。
2. Fleet Street：舰队街，英国伦敦市内一条著名的街道，以邻近舰队河而命名。直到20世纪80年代舰队街都是传统上英国媒体的总部，鼎盛时期的舰队街共有100多家全国或地区性报馆，因此被称为英国报纸的老家。今日舰队街依旧是英国媒体的代名词。

About the Author:

Joseph Conrad（1857–1924）grew up in the Polish Ukraine. Spending a few years in France, he mastered his second language and the fundamentals of seamanship. By 1878, Joseph had made his way to England with the intention of becoming an officer on a British ship. After spending twenty years at sea, he became an English citizen in 1886.

In the summer of 1889, Conrad began his crucial transition from sailor to writer by starting his first novel *Almayer's Folly* in English, his third language. In 1894, his first novel was published. The major productive phase of Conrad's career spanned from 1897 to 1911, during which time he composed *The Nigger of the Narcissus*, *Youth*, *Heart of Darkness*, *Lord Jim*, *Nostromo*, *The Secret Agent, and Under Western Eyes*, among other works.

In 1924, he died of a heart attack at the age of 67 when he then traveled in America.

Appreciation:

《黑暗的心》(1902)是英籍波兰作家约瑟夫·康拉德的主要作品之一。这部中篇小说记录了船长马洛在一艘停靠于泰晤士河上的海船上所讲的深入非洲腹地的故事。马洛的故事除了涉及马洛自己年轻时在非洲的所见所闻外，主要讲述了他在非洲期间所认识的一个叫库尔兹的白人殖民者的故事：库尔兹最初是一位矢志将“文明进步”带到非洲的理想主义者，最后却堕落为一个贪婪的殖民者。

“黑暗的心”作为小说的题目，也是该小说中的主要意象，既是指地理意义上的黑色的非洲腹地，也是指欧洲殖民主义者黑暗的内心。主人公马洛的刚果之行，不仅是进入非洲腹地的航程，同时也是一个探索自我、发现人的内心黑暗世界的历程。

康拉德在小说中采用两个叙述者：一个是无名氏叙述者，为小说提供总体故事的框架；另一个则是叙述者马洛。后者在叙述过程中，不时地停下来与无名氏叙述者进行对话。在某种程度上，这也是马洛与作者的一种对话。作者借无名氏叙述者之口，传递了马洛的形象。马洛又在不断地否定无名氏的叙述，并与不同主体进行互动和对话，从而使读者从多侧面对所讲的故事做出评判，进行思考。选文出自小说的第一章，故事的框架叙述者开篇便引起读者对马洛要讲的故事产生兴趣。

Questions:

1. How does the frame narrator distinguish Marlow from other sailors? How is this distinction significant with respect to the adventure that Marlow recounts?

2. This story begins as a quest. What sort of difficulties does the protagonist face?

3. What effect does having a double audience (those listening to the narrator as well as the reader) create?

The Mark on the Wall (Excerpt)

Perhaps it was the middle of January in the present year that I first looked up and saw the mark on the wall. In order to fix a date it is necessary to remember what one saw. So now I think of the fire; the steady film of yellow light upon the page of my book; the three chrysanthemums in the round glass bowl on the mantelpiece. Yes, it must have been the winter time, and we had just finished our tea, for I remember that I was smoking a cigarette when I looked up and saw the mark on the wall for the first time. I looked up through the smoke of my cigarette and my eye lodged for a moment upon the burning coals, and that old fancy of the crimson flag flapping from the castle tower came into my mind, and I thought of the cavalcade of red knights riding up the side of the black rock. Rather to my relief the sight of the mark interrupted the fancy, for it is an old fancy, an automatic fancy, made as a child perhaps. The mark was a small round mark, black upon the white wall, about six or seven inches above the mantelpiece.

How readily our thoughts swarm upon a new object, lifting it a little way, as ants carry a blade of straw so feverishly, and then leave it ... if that mark was made by a nail, it can't have been for a picture, it must have been for a miniature—the miniature of a lady with white powdered curls, powder-dusted cheeks, and lips like red carnations. A fraud of course, for the people who had this house before us would have chosen pictures in that way—an old picture for an old room. That is the sort of people they were very interesting people, and I think of them so often, in such queer places, because one will never see them again, never know what happened next. They wanted to leave this house because they wanted to change their style of furniture, so he said, and he was in process of saying that in his opinion art should have ideas behind it when we were torn asunder, as one is torn from the old lady about to pour out tea and the young man about to hit the tennis ball in the back garden of the suburban villa as one rushes past in the train.

But as for that mark, I'm not sure about it; I don't believe it was made by a nail after all; it's too big, too round, for that. I might get up, but if I got up and looked at it, ten to one I shouldn't be able to say for certain; because once a thing's done, no one ever knows how it happened. Oh! dear me, the mystery of life! The inaccuracy of thought! The ignorance of humanity! To show how very little control of our possessions we have—what an accidental affair this living is after all our civilisation—let me just count over a few of the things lost in our lifetime, beginning, for that seems always the most mysterious of losses—what cat would gnaw, what rat would nibble—three pale blue canisters of book-binding tools? Then there were the bird cages, the iron hoops, the steel skates, the Queen Anne coal-scuttle, the bagatelle board, the hand organ—all gone, and jewels too. Opals and emeralds, they lie about the roots of turnips. What a scraping paring affair it is to be sure! The wonder is that I've any clothes on my back, that I sit surrounded by solid furniture at this moment. Why, if one wants to compare life to anything, one must liken it to being blown through the Tube at fifty miles an hour—landing at the other end without a single hairpin in one's hair! Shot out at the feet of God entirely naked! Tumbling head over heels in the asphodel meadows like brown paper parcels pitched down a shoot in the post office! With one's hair flying back like the tail of a racehorse. Yes, that seems to express the rapidity of life, the perpetual waste and repair; all so casual, all so haphazard ...

But after life. The slow pulling down of thick green stalks so that the cup of the flower, as it turns over, deluges one with purple and red light. Why, after all, should one not be born there as one is born here, helpless, speechless, unable to focus one's eyesight, groping at the roots of the grass, at the toes of the Giants ? As for saying which are trees, and which are men and women, or whether there are such things, that one won't be in a condition to do for fifty years or so. There will be nothing but spaces of light and dark, intersected by thick stalks, and rather higher up perhaps, rose-shaped blots of an indistinct colour—dim pinks and blues—which will, as time goes on, become more definite, become—I don't know what ...

And yet the mark on the wall is not a hole at all. It may even be caused by some round black substance, such as a small rose leaf, left over from the summer, and I, not being a very vigilant housekeeper—look at the dust on the mantelpiece, for example, the dust which, so they say, buried Troy three times over, only fragments of pots utterly refusing annihilation, as one can believe.

The tree outside the window taps very gently on the pane ... I want to think quietly, calmly, spaciously, never to be interrupted, never to have to rise from my chair, to slip easily from one thing to another, without any sense of hostility, or obstacle. I want to sink deeper and deeper, away from the surface, with its hard separate facts. To steady myself, let me catch hold of the first idea that passes ... Shakespeare ... Well, he will do as well as another. A man who sat himself solidly in an arm-chair, and looked into the fire, so—A shower of ideas fell perpetually from some very high Heaven down through his mind. He leant his forehead on his hand, and people, looking in through the open door—for this scene is supposed to take place on a summer's evening—But how dull this is, this historical fiction! It doesn't interest me at all. I wish I could hit upon a pleasant track of thought, a track indirectly reflecting credit upon myself, for those are the pleasantest thoughts, and very frequent even in the minds of modest mouse-coloured people, who believe genuinely that they dislike to hear their own praises. They are not thoughts directly praising oneself; that is the beauty of them; they are thoughts like this:

"And then I came into the room. They were discussing botany. I said how I'd seen a flower growing on a dust heap on the site of an old house in Kingsway. The seed, I said, must have been sown in the reign of Charles the First. What flowers grew in the reign of Charles the First?" I asked—(but I don't remember the answer). Tall flowers with purple tassels to them perhaps. And so it goes on. All the time I'm dressing up the figure of myself in my own mind, lovingly, stealthily, not openly adoring it, for if I did that, I should catch myself out, and stretch my hand at once for a book in self-protection. Indeed, it is curious how instinctively one protects the image of oneself from idolatry or any other handling that could make it ridiculous, or too unlike the original to be believed in any longer. Or is it not so very curious after all? It is a matter of great importance. Suppose the looking-glass smashes, the image disappears, and the romantic figure with the green of forest depths all about it is there no longer, but only that shell of a person which is seen by other people—what an airless, shallow, bald, prominent world it becomes! A world not to be lived in. As we face each other in omnibuses and underground railways we are looking into the mirror; that accounts for the vagueness, the gleam of glassiness, in our eyes. And the novelists in future will realise more and more the importance of these reflections, for of course there is not one reflection but an almost infinite number; those are the depths they will explore, those the phantoms they will pursue, leaving the description of reality more and more out of their stories, taking a knowledge of it for granted, as the Greeks did and Shakespeare perhaps—but these generalisations are very worthless. The military sound of the word is enough. It recalls leading articles, cabinet ministers—a whole class of things indeed which as a child one thought the thing itself, the standard thing, the real thing, from which one could not depart save at the risk of nameless damnation. Generalisations bring back somehow Sunday in London, Sunday afternoon walks, Sunday luncheons, and also ways of speaking of the dead, clothes, and habits—like the habit of sitting all together in one room until a certain hour, although nobody liked it. There was a rule for everything. The rule for tablecloths at that particular period was that they should be made of tapestry with little yellow compartments marked upon them, such as you may see in photographs of the carpets in the corridors of the royal palaces. Tablecloths of a different kind were not real tablecloths. How shocking, and yet how wonderful it was to discover that these real things, Sunday luncheons, Sunday walks, country houses, and tablecloths were not entirely real, were indeed half phantoms, and the damnation which visited the disbeliever in them was only a sense of illegitimate freedom. What now takes the place of those things I wonder, those real standard things? Men perhaps, should you be a woman; the masculine point of view which governs our lives, which sets the standard, which establishes Whitaker's Table of Precedency[1], which has become, I suppose, since the war half a phantom to many men and women, which soon, one may hope, will be laughed into the dustbin where the phantoms go, the mahogany sideboards and the Landseer prints, Gods and Devils, Hell and so forth, leaving us all with an intoxicating sense of illegitimate freedom—if freedom exists ...

In certain lights that mark on the wall seems actually to project from the wall. Nor is it entirely circular. I cannot be sure, but it seems to cast a perceptible shadow, suggesting that if I ran my finger down that strip of the wall it would, at a certain point, mount and descend a small tumulus, a smooth tumulus like those barrows on the South Downs which are, they say, either tombs or camps. Of the two I should prefer them to be tombs, desiring melancholy like most English people, and finding it natural at the end of a walk to think of the bones stretched beneath the turf ... There must be some book about it. Some antiquary must have dug up those bones and given them a name ... What sort of a man is an antiquary, I wonder? Retired Colonels for the most part, I dare say, leading parties of aged labourers to the top here, examining clods of earth and stone, and getting into correspondence with the neighbouring clergy, which, being opened at breakfast time, gives them a feeling of importance, and the comparison of arrowheads necessitates cross-country journeys to the country towns, an agreeable necessity both to them and to their elderly wives, who wish to make plum jam or to clean out the study, and have every reason for keeping that great question of the camp or the tomb in perpetual suspension, while the Colonel himself feels agreeably philosophic in accumulating evidence on both sides of the question. It is true that he does finally incline to believe in the camp; and, being opposed, indites a pamphlet which he is about to read at the quarterly meeting of the local society when a stroke lays him low, and his last conscious thoughts are not of wife or child, but of the camp and that arrowhead there, which is now in the case at the local museum, together with the foot of a Chinese murderess, a handful of Elizabethan nails, a great many Tudor clay pipes, a piece of Roman pottery, and the wine-glass that Nelson drank out of—proving I really don't know what.

No, no, nothing is proved, nothing is known. And if I were to get up at this very moment and ascertain that the mark on the wall is really—what shall I say?—the head of a gigantic old nail, driven in two hundred years ago, which has now, owing to the patient attrition of many generations of housemaids, revealed its head above the coat of paint, and is taking its first view of modern life in the sight of a white-walled fire-lit room, what should I gain? Knowledge? Matter for further speculation? I can think sitting still as well as standing up. And what is knowledge? What are our learned men save the descendants of witches and hermits who crouched in caves and in woods brewing herbs, interrogating shrew-mice and writing down the language of the stars? And the less we honour them as our superstitions dwindle and our respect for beauty and health of mind increases ... Yes, one could imagine a very pleasant world. A quiet spacious world, with the flowers so red and blue in the open fields. A world without professors or specialists or house-keepers with the profiles of policemen, a world which one could slice with one's thought as a fish slices the water with his fin, grazing the stems of the water-lilies, hanging suspended over nests of white sea eggs ... How peaceful it is down here, rooted in the centre of the world and gazing up through the grey waters, with their sudden gleams of light, and their reflections—if it were not for Whitaker's Almanack—if it were not for the Table of Precedency!

I must jump up and see for myself what that mark on the wall really is—a nail, a rose-leaf, a crack in the wood?

Here is Nature once more at her old game of self-preservation. This train of thought, she perceives, is threatening mere waste of energy, even some collision with reality, for who will ever be able to lift a finger against Whitaker's Table of Precedency? The Archbishop of Canterbury is followed by the Lord High Chancellor; the Lord High Chancellor is followed by the Archbishop of York. Everybody follows somebody, such is the philosophy of Whitaker; and the great thing is to know who follows whom. Whitaker knows, and let that, so Nature counsels, comfort you, instead of enraging you; and if you can't be comforted, if you must shatter this hour of peace, think of the mark on the wall.

I understand Nature's game—her prompting to take action as a way of ending any thought that threatens to excite or to pain. Hence, I suppose, comes our slight contempt for men of action—men, we assume, who don't think. Still, there's no harm in putting a full stop to one's disagreeable thoughts by looking at a mark on the wall.

Indeed, now that I have fixed my eyes upon it, I feel that I have grasped a plank in the sea; I feel a satisfying sense of reality which at once turns the two Archbishops and the Lord High Chancellor to the shadows of shades. Here is something definite, something real. Thus, waking from a midnight dream of horror, one hastily turns on the light and lies quiescent, worship ping the chest of drawers, worship ping solidity, worship ping reality, worship ping the impersonal world which is proof of some existence other than ours. That is what one wants to be sure of ... Wood is a pleasant thing to think about. It comes from a tree; and trees grow, and we don't know how they grow. For years and years they grow, without paying any attention to us, in meadows, in forests, and by the side of rivers—all things one likes to think about The cows swish their tails beneath them on hot afternoons; they paint rivers so green that when a moor hen dives one expects to see its feathers all green when it comes up again. I like to think of the fish balanced against the stream like flags blown out; and of water-beetles slowly raising domes of mud upon the bed of the river. I like to think of the tree itself: first the dose dry sensation of being wood; then the grinding of the storm; then the slow, delicious ooze of sap. I like to think of it, too, on winter's nights standing in the empty field with all leaves close-furled, nothing tender exposed to the iron bullets of the moon, a naked mast upon an earth that goes tumbling, tumbling all night long. The song of birds must sound very loud and strange in June; and how cold the feet of insects must feel upon it, as they make laborious progresses up the creases of the bark, or sun themselves upon the thin green awning of the leaves, and look straight in front of them with diamond-cut red eyes ... One by one the fibres snap beneath the immense cold pressure of the earth, then the last storm comes and, falling, the highest branches drive deep into the ground again. Even so, life isn't done with; there are a million patient, watchful lives still for a tree, all over the world, in bedrooms, in ships, on the pavement, lining rooms, where men and women sit after tea, smoking cigarettes. It is full of peaceful thoughts, happy thoughts, this tree. I should like to take each one separately—but something is getting in the way ... Where was I? What has it all been about? A tree? A river? The Downs? Whitaker's Almanack? The fields of asphodel? I can't remember a thing. Everything's moving, falling, slipping, vanishing ... There is a vast upheaval of matter. Someone is standing over me and saying—

"I'm going out to buy a newspaper."

"Yes?"

"Though it's no good buying newspapers ... Nothing ever happens. Curse this war; God damn this war! ... All the same, I don't see why we should have a snail on our wall."

Ah, the mark on the wall! It was a snail.

NOTES

1. Whitaker：惠特克 (1820—1895)，英国出版商，创办过《书商》杂志，于 1868 年开始编纂惠特克年鉴。

About the Author

Virginia Woolf (1882–1941) was an English novelist, essayist, biographer, and feminist. She began writing as a young girl and published her first novel, *The Voyage Out*, in 1915. Woolf was a prolific writer. In her great writing, there are modernist classics including *Mrs. Dallowa*y (1925), *To the Lighthouse* (1927) and *Orlando* (1928), as well as the pioneering feminist works, *A Room of One's Own* (1929) and *Three Guineas*.

As a significant figure in London literary society and a member of the Bloomsbury Group, Virginia Woolf is considered to be one of the foremost modernist/feminist literary figures of the twentieth century. In the book-length essay *A Room of One's Own*, she wrote the famous dictum, "A woman must have money and a room of her own if she is to write fiction."

In his obituary for Virginia, T.S. Eliot writes: "Without Virginia Woolf at the center of it, it would have remained formless or marginal ... With the death of Virginia Woolf, a whole pattern of culture is broken."

Appreciation:

《墙上的斑点》是弗吉尼亚·沃尔夫的第一部意识流小说。主要讲述了主人公在一个普通日子的平常瞬间，抬头看见墙上的斑点，由此引发意识的发散，产生了一系列的幻觉和遐想：想到生命的神秘、人生的无常、想到莎士比亚，法庭上的诉讼程序等，最后又回到那个斑点本身，原来那个斑点不过是只爬在墙上的蜗牛。通过这种自由的联想，人物头脑中意识流动的状况得到呈现，细致地摹写了人物内心的隐微活动。

小说围绕着墙上的这个斑点展开，更确切地说，是围绕着作家对这个斑点的思绪展开。整个作品没有像传统小说那样按照开端、发展、高潮、结局的“情节结构”来展开，而完全是由墙上的那个斑点所引起的一连串联想。《墙上的斑点》比较典型地采用了内心独白和自由联想两种技巧。作品中的种种联想，充分体现了意识流小说的意识“流”的特点。

Questions:

1. What's the function of "the mark" in the story? How about the structure of the story?
2. How do you understand the main idea of the story?
3. What are the features of the stream-of-consciousness novel?

Short Stories

Definition of Short Stories:

A short story is a piece of prose fiction whose volume ranges from 1, 600 to 20, 000 words. It often concentrates on one character and a single subject. Normally, there is little development of the character throughout the story because it catches a snapshot of life, a decisive moment more often. It aims to show a decisive moment of the character's life and create an emphasis on the theme by using as few means and words as possible.

Elements of a Short Story:

Just like novels, a short story also includes the elements like setting, plot, character, point of view, and theme. Setting tells the place, time, weather conditions, social background and even mood of the story. Even though short stories are short in size, their plot still follows the basic steps: introduction /orientation, rising action, climax, falling action, and resolution/denouement. Compared to longer novels, short stories have limited number of characters. Often times, only one or couple of characters are given special attention. And they are usually not fully developed due to the brief time period of the story. As to the point of view, short story writers use first, second (very rarely), and third person point of view to tell their stories. The third person omniscient is the mostly used point of view. When it comes to main ideas the writers want to deliver, they often focus on a single theme once again due to the volume of the story.

The Origins of Short Stories:

Short stories may find their early form in the oral storytelling tradition, like anecdotes, fables, fairy tales, and parables. "Aesop's Fables," first collected in the 4th century B.C., may have been the first anthology of short stories in Western literature. Over time, genres and writers all around the world have influenced the development of the short story. For example, Norse legends, Irish ballads, and Gothic ghost stories have all helped to shape the form of short stories on the aspects like structure, characterization, setting and subject matter.

What Makes a Great Short Story:

Edgar Allan Poe claimed that the perfect short story should adhere to the following rules: Length: the story can be read in one sitting; Ending: the story should end in its climax; Unity of effect: the story should only have one mood. According to Milton Crane, a great short story should convey at least one of these: "The sudden unforgettable revelation of character; the vision of a world through another's eyes; the glimpse of truth; the capture of a moment in time."

A Sunrise on the Veld[1]

Every night that winter he said aloud into the dark of the pillow: Half-past four! Half-past four! till his brain had gripped the words and held them fast. Then he fell asleep at once, as if a shutter had fallen; and lay with his face turned to the clock so that he could see it first thing when he woke.

It was half-past four to the minute, every morning. Triumphantly pressing down the alarm-knob of the clock, which the dark half of his mind had outwitted, remaining vigilant all night and counting the hours as he lay relaxed in sleep, he huddled down for a last warm moment under the clothes, playing with the idea of lying abed for this once only. But he played with it for the fun of knowing that it was a weakness he could defeat without effort; just as he set the alarm each night for the delight of the moment when he woke and stretched his limbs, feeling the muscles tighten, and thought: Even my brain—even that! I can control every part of myself.

Luxury of warm rested body, with the arms and legs and fingers waiting like soldiers for a word of command! Joy of knowing that the precious hours were given to sleep voluntarily! —for he had once stayed awake three nights running, to prove that he could, and then worked all day, refusing even to admit that he was tired; and now sleep seemed to him a servant to be commanded and refused.

The boy stretched his frame full-length, touching the wall at his head with his hands, and the bedfoot with his toes; then he sprung out, like a fish leaping from water. And it was cold, cold.

He always dressed rapidly, so as to try and conserve his night-warmth till the sun rose two hours later; but by the time he had on his clothes his hands were numbed and he could scarcely hold his shoes. These he could not put on for fear of waking his parents, who never came to know how early he rose.

As soon as he stepped over the lintel, the flesh of his soles contracted on the chilled earth, and his legs began to ache with cold. It was night: the stars were glittering, the trees standing black and still. He looked for signs of day, for the greying of the edge of a stone, or a lightening in the sky where the sun would rise, but there was nothing yet. Alert as an animal he crept past the dangerous window, standing poised with his hand on the sill for one proudly fastidious moment, looking in at the stuffy blackness of the room where his parents lay.

Feeling for the grass-edge of the path with his toes, he reached inside another window further along the wall, where his gun had been set in readiness the night before. The steel was icy, and numbed fingers slipped along it, so that he had to hold it in the crook of his arm for safety. Then he tiptoed to the room where the dogs slept, and was fearful that they might have been tempted to go before him; but they were waiting, their haunches crouched in reluctance at the cold, but ears and swinging tails greeting the gun ecstatically. His warning undertone kept them secret and silent till the house was a hundred yards back: then they bolted off into the bush, yelping excitedly. The boy imagined his parents turning in their beds and muttering: Those dogs again! before they were dragged back in sleep; and he smiled scornfully. He always looked back over his shoulder at the house before he passed a wall of trees that shut it from sight. It looked so low and small, crouching there under a tall and brilliant sky. Then he turned his back on it.

He would have to hurry. Before the light grew strong he must be miles away; and already a tint of green stood in the hollow of a leaf, and the air smelled of morning and the stars were dimming.

He slung the shoes over his shoulder, veld skoen[2] that were crinkled and hard with the dews of a hundred mornings. They would be necessary when the ground became too hot to bear. Now he felt the chilled dust push up between his toes, and he let the muscles of his feet spread and settle into the shapes of the earth; and he thought: I could walk a hundred miles on feel like these! I could walk all day, and never tire!

He was walking swiftly through the dark tunnel of foliage that in day-time was a road. The dogs were invisibly ranging the lower travelways of the bush, and he heard them panting. Sometimes he felt a cold muzzle on his leg before they were off again, scouting for a trail to follow. They were not trained, but free-running companions of the hunt, who often tired of the long stalk before the final shots, and went off on their own pleasure. Soon he could see them, small and wild-looking in a wild strange light, now that the bush stood trembling on the verge of colour, waiting for the sun to paint earth and grass afresh.

The grass stood to his shoulders; and the trees were showering a faint silvery rain. He was soaked; his whole body was clenched in a steady shiver.

Once he bent to the road that was newly scored with animal trails, and regretfully straightened, reminding himself that the pleasure of tracking must wait till another day.

He began to run along the edge of a field, noting jerkily how it was filmed over with fresh spiderweb, so that the long reaches of great black clods seemed netted in glistening grey. He was using the steady lope he had learned by watching the natives, the run that is a dropping of the weight of the body from one foot to the next in a slow balancing movement that never tires, nor shortens the breath; and he felt the blood pulsing down his legs and along his arms, and the exultation and pride of body mounted in him till he was shutting his teeth hard against a violent desire to shout his triumph.

Soon he had left the cultivated part of the farm. Behind him the bush was low and black. In front was a long vlei[3], acres of long pale grass that sent back a hollowing gleam of light to a satiny sky. Near him thick swathes of grass were bent with the weight of water, and diamond drops sparkled on each frond.

The first bird woke at his feet and at once a flock of them sprang into the air calling shrilly that day had come; and suddenly, behind him, the bush woke into song, and he could hear the guinea fowl calling far ahead of him. That meant they would now be sailing down from their trees into thick grass, and it was for them he had come: he was too late. But he did not mind. He forgot he had come to shoot. He set his legs wide, and balanced from foot to foot, and swung his gun up and down in both hands horizontally, in a kind of improvised exercise, and let his head sink back till it was pillowed in his neck muscles and watched how above him small rosy clouds floated in a lake of gold.

Suddenly it all rose in him: it was unbearable, and he leapt up into the air, shouting and yelling wild, unrecognisable noises. Then he began to run, not carefully, as he had before, but madly, like a wild thing. He was clean crazy, yelling mad with the joy of living and a superfluity of youth. He rushed down the vlei under a tumult of crimson and gold, while all the birds of the world sang around him. He ran in great, leaping strides, and shouted as he ran, feeling his body rise into the crisp rushing air and fall back surely on to sure feet; and thought briefly, not believing that such a thing could happen to him, that he could break his ankle any moment, in this thick tangled grass. He cleared bushes like a duiker, leapt over rocks; and finally came to a dead stop at a place where the ground fell abruptly away below him to the river. It had been a two-mile-long dash through waist-high growth, and he was breathing hoarsely and could no longer sing. But he poised on a rock and looked down at stretches of water that gleamed through stooping trees, and thought suddenly, I am fifteen! Fifteen! The words came new to him; so that he kept repeating them wonderingly, with swelling excitement; and he felt the years of his life with his hands, as if he were counting marbles, each one hard and separate and compact, each one a wonderful shining thing. That was what he was: fifteen years of this rich soil, and this slow-moving water, and air that smelt like a challenge whether it was warm and sultry at noon, or as brisk as cold water, like it was now.

There was nothing he couldn't do, nothing! A vision came to him, as he stood there, like when a child hears the word "eternity" and tries to understand it, and time takes possession of the mind. He felt his life ahead of him as a great and wonderful thing, something that was his; and he said aloud, with the blood rushing to his head: all the great men of the world have been as I am now, and there is nothing I can't become, nothing I can't do; there is no country in the world I cannot make part of myself, if I choose. I contain the world. I can make of it what I want. If I choose, I can change everything that is going to happen: it depends on me, and what I decide now.

The urgency and the truth and the courage of what his voice was saying exulted him so that he began to sing again, at the top of his voice, and the sound went echoing down the river gorge. He stopped for the echo, and sang again: stopped and shouted. That was what he was! —he sang, if he chose; and the world had to answer him.

And for minutes he stood there, shouting and singing and waiting for the lovely eddying sound of the echo; so that his own new strong thoughts came back and washing round his head, as if someone were answering him and encouraging him; till the gorge was full of soft voices clashing back and forth from rock to rock over the river. And then it seemed as if there was a new voice. He listened, puzzled, for it was not his own. Soon he was leaning forward, all his nerves alert, quite still: somewhere close to him there was a noise that was no joyful bird, nor tinkle of falling water, nor ponderous movement of cattle.

There it was again. In the deep morning hush that held his future and his past, was a sound of pain, and repeated over and over: it was a kind of shortened scream, as if someone, something, had no breath to scream. He came to himself, looked about him, and called for the dogs. They did not appear; they had gone off on their own business, and he was alone. Now he was clean sober, all the madness gone. His heart beating fast, because of that frightened screaming, he stepped carefully off the rock and went towards a belt of trees. He was moving cautiously, for not so long ago he had seen a leopard in just this spot.

At the edge of the trees he stopped and peered, holding his gun ready; he advanced, looking steadily about him, his eyes narrowed. Then all at once, in the middle of a step, he faltered, and his face was puzzled. He shook his head impatiently, as if he doubted his own sight.

There, between two trees, against a background of gaunt black rocks, was a figure from a dream, a strange beast that was horned and drunken-legged, but like something he had never even imagined. It seemed to be ragged. It looked like a small buck that had black ragged tufts of fur standing up irregularly all over it, with patches of raw flesh beneath ... but the patches of rawness were disappearing under moving black and came again elsewhere; and all the time the creature screamed, in small gasping screams, and leaped drunkenly from side to side, as if it were blind.

Then the boy understood: it *was* a buck. He ran closer, and again stood still, stopped by a new fear. Around him the grass was whispering and alive. He looked wildly about, and then down. The ground was black with ants, great energetic ants that took no notice of him, but hurried and scurried towards the fighting shape, like glistening black water flowing through the grass.

And, as he drew in his breath and pity and terror seized him, the beast fell and the screaming stopped. Now he could hear nothing but one bird singing, and the sound of the rustling, whispering ants.

He peered over at the writhing blackness that jerked convulsively with the jerking nerves. It grew quieter. There were small twitches from the mass that still looked vaguely like the shape of a small animal.

It came into his mind that he should shoot it and end its pain; and he raised the gun. Then he lowered it again. The buck could no longer feel; its fighting was a mechanical protest of the nerves. But it was not that which made him put down the gun. It was a swelling feeling of rage and misery and protest that expressed itself in the thought: if I had not come it would have died like this: so why should I interfere? All over the bush things like this happen; they happen all the time; this is how life goes on, by living things dying in anguish. He gripped the gun between his knees and felt in his own limbs the myriad swarming pain of the twitching animal that could no longer feel, and set his teeth, and said over and over under his breath: I can't stop it. I can't stop it. There is nothing I can do.

He was glad that he did not have to make a decision to kill it even when he was feeling with his whole body: this is what happens, this is how things work.

It was right—that was what he was feeling. It was right and nothing could alter it.

The knowledge of fatality, of what has to be, had gripped him and for the first time in his life; and he was left unable to make any movement of brain or body, except to say: "Yes, yes. That is what living is." It had entered his flesh and his bones and grown in to the furthest corners of his brain and would never leave him. And at that moment he could not have performed the smallest action of mercy, knowing as he did, having lived on it all his life, the vast, unalterable, cruel veld, where at any moment one night stumble over a skull or crush the skeleton of some small creature.

Suffering, sick, and angry, but also grimly satisfied with his new stoicism, he stood there leaning on his rifle, and watched the seething black mound grown smaller. At his feet, now, were ants trickling back with pink fragments in their mouths, and there was a fresh acid smell in his nostrils. He sternly controlled the uselessly convulsing muscles of his empty stomach, and reminded himself: the ants must eat too! At the same time he found that the tears were streaming down his face, and his clothes were soaked with the sweat of that other creature's pain.

The shape had grown small. Now it looked like nothing recognisable. He did not know how long it was before he saw the blackness thin, and bits of white showed through, shining in the sun—yes, there was the sun, just up, glowing over the rocks. Why, the whole thing could not have taken longer than a few minutes.

He began to swear, as if the shortness of the time was in itself unbearable, using the words he had heard his father say. He strode forward, crushing ants with each step, and brushing them off his clothes, till he stood above the skeleton, which lay sprawled under a small bush. It was clean-picked. It might have been lying there years, save that on the white bone were pink fragments of gristle. About the bones ants were ebbing away, their pincers full of meat.

The boy looked at them, big black ugly insects. A few were standing and gazing up at him with small glittering eyes.

"Go away!" he said to the ants, very coldly. "I am not for you—not just yet, at any rate. Go away." And he fancied that the ants turned and went away.

He bent over the bones and touched the sockets in the skull, that was where the eyes were, he thought incredulously, remembering the liquid dark eyes of a buck. And then he bent the slim foreleg bone, swinging it horizontally in his palm.

That morning, perhaps an hour ago, this small creature had been stepping proudly and free through the bush, feeling the chill on its hide even as he himself had done, exhilarated by it. Proudly stepping the earth, tossing its horns, frisking a pretty white tail, it had sniffed the cold morning air. Walking like kings and conquerors it had moved through this fee-held bush, where each blade of grass grew for it alone, and where the river ran pure sparkling water for its slaking.

And then—what had happened? Such a swift surefooted thing could surely not be trapped by a swarm of ants?

The boy bent curiously to the skeleton. Then he saw that the back leg that lay uppermost and strained out in the tension of death, was snapped midway in the thigh, so that broken bones jutted over each other uselessly. So that was it! Limping into the ant-masses it could not escape, once it had sensed the danger. Yes, but how had the leg been broken? Had it fallen, perhaps? Impossible, a buck was too light and graceful. Had some jealous rival horned it?

What could possibly have happened? Perhaps some Africans had thrown stones at it, as they do, trying to kill it for meat, and had broken its leg. Yes, that must be it.

Even as he imagined the crowd of running, shouting natives, and the flying stones, and the leaping buck, another picture came into his mind. He saw himself, on any one of these bright ringing mornings, drunk with excitement, taking a snap shot at some half-seen buck. He saw himself with the gun lowered, wondering whether he had missed or not; and thinking at last that it was late, and he wanted his breakfast, and it was not worth while to track miles after an animal that would very likely get away from him in any case.

For a moment he would not face it. He was a small boy again, kicking sulkily at the skeleton, hanging his head, refusing to accept the responsibility.

Then he straightened up, and looked down at the bones with an odd expression of dismay, all the anger gone out of him. His mind went quite empty; all around him he could see trickles of ants disappearing into the grass. The whispering noise was faint and dry, like the rustling of a cast snakeskin.

At last he picked up his gun and walked homewards. He was telling himself half defiantly that he wanted his breakfast. He was telling himself that it was getting very hot, much too hot to be out roaming the bush.

Really, he was tired. He walked heavily, not looking where he put his feet. When he came without sight of his home he stopped, knitting his brows. There was something he had to think out. The death of that small animal was a thing that concerned him, and was by no means finished with it. It lay at the back of his mind uncomfortably.

Soon, the very next morning, he would get clear of everybody and go to the bush and think about it.

NOTES

1. Flat treeless open grassland of the South African plateau.
2. Southern African walking shoes made from vegetable-tanned leather or soft rawhide uppers attached to a leather footbed and rubber sole without tacks or nails. The name comes from Afrikaans vel ("skin") (later assimilated to veld ("field")) and skoen ("shoe").
3. An area of low marshy ground, especially one that feeds a stream in South Africa.

About the Author:

Doris Lessing was born to a British family in Persia (present-day Iran) in 1919. Her family moved to British colony Southern Rhodesia (now Zimbabwe) in 1925. There, Lessing explored the natural world with her brother, Harry, which provided the materials for her later stories. Lessing is a self-made writer. Her novels are often autobiographical, which include *The Grass is Singing* (1950), *Children of Violence* (1952–1969), *The Golden Notebook* (1962), *The Good Terrorist* (1985), *Canopus in Argos: Archives* (1979–1983), the themes of which range from colonialism and political repression to gender inequality and feminism.

When she received the 2007 Nobel Prize in Literature from the Swedish Academy, Doris Lessing was introduced as "that epicist of the female experience, who with skepticism, fire and visionary power has subjected a divided civilization to scrutiny." By then, Lessing was the eleventh woman and the oldest person ever to receive the Nobel Prize in Literature. In 2008, *The Times* ranked her fifth on a list of "The 50 greatest British writers since 1945."

Appreciation:

从她第一本小说《草原在歌唱》发表开始，多丽丝·莱辛的创作生涯持续了将近半个世纪。其作品讨论的主题可谓包罗万象，有对非洲殖民的控诉，也有对大自然的赞颂；有对女性解放的支持，也有对种族矛盾的思考。该短篇小说将视角对准了一个刚满十五岁的男孩，一开始他认为自己无所不能；但在目睹了一只受伤的雄鹿被蚁群残忍吞噬之后，小男孩意识到了雄鹿的受伤有可能与自己的打猎有关；更认识到了自己并非无所不能，比如他无法改变雄鹿被吞噬的命运。因此，这个故事是有关学习与成长的故事（story of coming-of-age）。在阅读过程中，注意小男孩在目睹雄鹿被吞噬前后的心态变化以及文中诸多类比与隐喻，比如闹钟、日出、雄鹿等等的隐喻。

Questions:

1. How does the author employ symbols to show the boy's seemingly omnipotence?
2. The young boy goes on a journey in this short story, both literally and metaphorically. Explain the metaphorical side of the journey.

The Garden Party (Excerpt)

And after all the weather was ideal. They could not have had a more perfect day for a garden-party if they had ordered it. Windless, warm, the sky without a cloud. Only the blue was veiled with a haze of light gold, as it is sometimes in early summer. The gardener had been up since dawn, mowing the lawns and sweeping them, until the grass and the dark flat rosettes where the daisy plants had been seemed to shine. As for the roses, you could not help feeling they understood that roses are the only flowers that impress people at garden-parties; the only flowers that everybody is certain of knowing. Hundreds, yes, literally hundreds, had come out in a single night; the green bushes bowed down as though they had been visited by archangels[1].

Breakfast was not yet over before the men came to put up the marquee[2].

"Where do you want the marquee put, mother?"

"My dear child, it's no use asking me. I'm determined to leave everything to you children this year. Forget I am your mother. Treat me as an honoured guest."

But Meg could not possibly go and supervise the men. She had washed her hair before breakfast, and she sat drinking her coffee in a green turban, with a dark wet curl stamped on each cheek. Jose, the butterfly, always came down in a silk petticoat and a kimono[3] jacket.

"You'll have to go, Laura; you're the artistic one."

Away Laura flew, still holding her piece of bread-and-butter. It's so delicious to have an excuse for eating out of doors, and besides, she loved having to arrange things; she always felt she could do it so much better than anybody else.

…

"Laura, Laura, where are you? Telephone, Laura!" a voice cried from the house.

"Coming!" Away she skimmed, over the lawn, up the path, up the steps, across the veranda, and into the porch. In the hall her father and Laurie were brushing their hats ready to go to the office.

"I say, Laura," said Laurie very fast, "you might just give a squiz at my coat before this afternoon. See if it wants pressing."

"I will," said she. Suddenly she couldn't stop herself. She ran at Laurie and gave him a small, quick squeeze. "Oh, I do love parties, don't you?" gasped Laura.

"Ra-ther," said Laurie's warm, boyish voice, and he squeezed his sister too, and gave her a gentle push. "Dash off to the telephone, old girl."

The telephone. "Yes, yes; oh yes. Kitty? Good morning, dear. Come to lunch? Do, dear. Delighted of course. It will only be a very scratch meal—just the sandwich crusts and broken meringue-shells and what's left over. Yes, isn't it a perfect morning? Your white? Oh, I certainly should. One moment—hold the line. Mother's calling." And Laura sat back. "What, mother? Can't hear."

Mrs. Sheridan's voice floated down the stairs. "Tell her to wear that sweet hat she had on last Sunday."

"Mother says you're to wear that sweet hat you had on last Sunday. Good. One o'clock. Bye-bye."

…

The front door bell pealed, and there sounded the rustle of Sadie's print skirt on the stairs.

…

"Godber's has come," announced Sadie, issuing out of the pantry. She had seen the man pass the window.

That meant the cream puffs had come. Godber's were famous for their cream puffs. Nobody ever thought of making them at home.

"Bring them in and put them on the table, my girl," ordered Cook.

Sadie brought them in and went back to the door. Of course Laura and Jose were far too grown-up to really care about such things. All the same, they couldn't help agreeing that the puffs looked very attractive. Very. Cook began arranging them, shaking off the extra icing sugar.

"Don't they carry one back to all one's parties?" said Laura.

"I suppose they do," said practical Jose, who never liked to be carried back. "They look beautifully light and feathery, I must say."

"Have one each, my dears," said Cook in her comfortable voice. "Yer ma won't know."

Oh, impossible. Fancy cream puffs so soon after breakfast. The very idea made one shudder. All the same, two minutes later Jose and Laura were licking their fingers with that absorbed inward look that only comes from whipped cream.

"Let's go into the garden, out by the back way," suggested Laura. "I want to see how the men are getting on with the marquee. They're such awfully nice men."

But the back door was blocked by cook, Sadie, Godber's man and Hans.

Something had happened.

"Tuk-tuk-tuk," clucked Cook like an agitated hen. Sadie had her hand clapped to her cheek as though she had toothache. Hans's face was screwed up in the effort to understand. Only Godber's man seemed to be enjoying himself; it was his story.

"What's the matter? What's happened?"

"There's been a horrible accident," said Cook. "A man killed."

"A man killed! Where? How? When?"

But Godber's man wasn't going to have his story snatched from under his very nose.

"Know those little cottages just below here, miss?" Know them? Of course, she knew them. "Well, there's a young chap living there, name of Scott, a carter. His horse shied at a traction-engine, corner of Hawke Street this morning, and he was thrown out on the back of his head. Killed."

"Dead!" Laura stared at Godber's man.

"Dead when they picked him up," said Godber's man with relish. "They were taking the body home as I come up here." And he said to the Cook, "He's left a wife and five little ones."

"Jose, come here." Laura caught hold of her sister's sleeve and dragged her through the kitchen to the other side of the green baize door. There she paused and leaned against it. "Jose!" she said, horrified, "however are we going to stop everything?"

"Stop everything, Laura!" cried Jose in astonishment. "What do you mean?"

"Stop the garden-party, of course." Why did Jose pretend?

But Jose was still more amazed. "Stop the garden-party? My dear Laura, don't be so absurd. Of course we can't do anything of the kind. Nobody expects us to. Don't be so extravagant."

"But we can't possibly have a garden-party with a man dead just outside the front gate."

That really was extravagant, for the little cottages were in a lane to themselves at the very bottom of a steep rise that led up to the house. A broad road ran between. True, they were far too near. They were the greatest possible eyesore, and they had no right to be in that neighbourhood at all. They were little mean dwellings painted a chocolate brown. In the garden patches there was nothing but cabbage stalks, sick hens and tomato cans. The very smoke coming out of their chimneys was poverty-stricken. Little rags and shreds of smoke, so unlike the great silvery plumes that uncurled from the Sheridans' chimneys. Washerwomen lived in the lane and sweeps and a cobbler, and a man whose house-front was studded all over with minute bird-cages. Children swarmed. When the Sheridans were little they were forbidden to set foot there because of the revolting language and of what they might catch. But since they were grown up, Laura and Laurie on their prowls sometimes walked through. It was disgusting and sordid. They came out with a shudder. But still one must go everywhere; one must see everything. So through they went.

"And just think of what the band would sound like to that poor woman," said Laura.

"Oh, Laura!" Jose began to be seriously annoyed. "If you're going to stop a band playing every time some one has an accident, you'll lead a very strenuous life. I'm every bit as sorry about it as you. I feel just as sympathetic." Her eyes hardened. She looked at her sister just as she used to when they were little and fighting together. "You won't bring a drunken workman back to life by being sentimental," she said softly.

"Drunk! Who said he was drunk?" Laura turned furiously on Jose. She said, just as they had used to say on those occasions, "I'm going straight up to tell mother."

"Do, dear," cooed Jose.

"Mother, can I come into your room?" Laura turned the big glass door-knob.

"Of course, child. Why, what's the matter? What's given you such a colour?" And Mrs. Sheridan turned round from her dressing-table. She was trying on a new hat.

"Mother, a man's been killed," began Laura.

"Not in the garden?" interrupted her mother.

"No, no!"

"Oh, what a fright you gave me!" Mrs. Sheridan sighed with relief, and took off the big hat and held it on her knees.

"But listen, mother," said Laura. Breathless, half-choking, she told the dreadful story. "Of course, we can't have our party, can we?" she pleaded. "The band and everybody arriving. They'd hear us, mother; they're nearly neighbours!"

To Laura's astonishment her mother behaved just like Jose; it was harder to bear because she seemed amused. She refused to take Laura seriously.

"But, my dear child, use your common sense. It's only by accident we've heard of it. If some one had died there normally—and I can't understand how they keep alive in those poky little holes—we should still be having our party, shouldn't we?"

Laura had to say "yes" to that, but she felt it was all wrong. She sat down on her mother's sofa and pinched the cushion frill.

"Mother, isn't it terribly heartless of us?" she asked.

"Darling!" Mrs. Sheridan got up and came over to her, carrying the hat. Before Laura could stop her she had popped it on. "My child!" said her mother, "the hat is yours. It's made for you. It's much too young for me. I have never seen you look such a picture. Look at yourself!" And she held up her hand-mirror.

"But, mother," Laura began again. She couldn't look at herself; she turned aside.

This time Mrs. Sheridan lost patience just as Jose had done.

"You are being very absurd, Laura," she said coldly. "People like that don't expect sacrifices from us. And it's not very sympathetic to spoil everybody's enjoyment as you're doing now."

…

Soon after that people began coming in streams. The band struck up; the hired waiters ran from the house to the marquee. Wherever you looked there were couples strolling, bending to the flowers, greeting, moving on over the lawn. They were like bright birds that had alighted in the Sheridans' garden for this one afternoon, on their way to—where? Ah, what happiness it is to be with people who all are happy, to press hands, press cheeks, smile into eyes.

"Darling Laura, how well you look!"

"What a becoming hat, child!"

"Laura, you look quite Spanish. I've never seen you look so striking."

And Laura, glowing, answered softly, "Have you had tea? Won't you have an ice? The passion-fruit ices really are rather special." She ran to her father and begged him. "Daddy darling, can't the band have something to drink?"

And the perfect afternoon slowly ripened, slowly faded, slowly its petals closed.

"Never a more delightful garden-party ..." "The greatest success ... " "Quite the most ..."

Laura helped her mother with the good-byes. They stood side by side in the porch till it was all over.

"All over, all over, thank heaven," said Mrs. Sheridan. "Round up the others, Laura. Let's go and have some fresh coffee. I'm exhausted. Yes, it's been very successful. But oh, these parties, these parties! Why will you children insist on giving parties!" And they all of them sat down in the deserted marquee.

"Have a sandwich, daddy dear. I wrote the flag."

"Thanks." Mr. Sheridan took a bite and the sandwich was gone. He took another. "I suppose you didn't hear of a beastly accident that happened today?" he said.

"My dear," said Mrs. Sheridan, holding up her hand, "we did. It nearly ruined the party. Laura insisted we should put it off."

"Oh, mother!" Laura didn't want to be teased about it.

"It was a horrible affair all the same," said Mr. Sheridan. "The chap was married too. Lived just below in the lane, and leaves a wife and half a dozen kiddies, so they say."

An awkward little silence fell. Mrs. Sheridan fidgeted with her cup. Really, it was very tactless of father ...

Suddenly she looked up. There on the table were all those sandwiches, cakes, puffs, all uneaten, all going to be wasted. She had one of her brilliant ideas.

"I know," she said. "Let's make up a basket. Let's send that poor creature some of this perfectly good food. At any rate, it will be the greatest treat for the children. Don't you agree? And she's sure to have neighbours calling in and so on. What a point to have it all ready prepared.

Laura!" She jumped up. "Get me the big basket out of the stairs cupboard."

"But, mother, do you really think it's a good idea?" said Laura.

Again, how curious, she seemed to be different from them all. To take scraps from their party. Would the poor woman really like that?

"Of course! What's the matter with you today? An hour or two ago you were insisting on us being sympathetic, and now—"

Oh well! Laura ran for the basket. It was filled, it was heaped by her mother.

"Take it yourself, darling," said she. "Run down just as you are. No, wait, take the arum lilies too. People of that class are so impressed by arum lilies."

"The stems will ruin her lace frock," said practical Jose.

So they would. Just in time. "Only the basket, then. And, Laura!" —her mother followed her out of the marquee—"don't on any account—"

"What mother?"

No, better not put such ideas into the child's head! "Nothing! Run along."

It was just growing dusky as Laura shut their garden gates. A big dog ran by like a shadow. The road gleamed white, and down below in the hollow the little cottages were in deep shade. How quiet it seemed after the afternoon. Here she was going down the hill to somewhere where a man lay dead, and she couldn't realize it. Why couldn't she? She stopped a minute. And it seemed to her that kisses, voices, tinkling spoons, laughter, the smell of crushed grass were somehow inside her. She had no room for anything else. How strange! She looked up at the pale sky, and all she thought was, "Yes, it was the most successful party."

Now the broad road was crossed. The lane began, smoky and dark. Women in shawls and men's tweed caps hurried by. Men hung over the palings; the children played in the doorways. A low hum came from the mean little cottages. In some of them there was a flicker of light, and a shadow, crab-like, moved across the window. Laura bent her head and hurried on. She wished now she had put on a coat. How her frock shone! And the big hat with the velvet streamer—if only it was another hat! Were the people looking at her? They must be. It was a mistake to have come; she knew all along it was a mistake. Should she go back even now?

No, too late. This was the house. It must be. A dark knot of people stood outside. Beside the gate an old, old woman with a crutch sat in a chair, watching. She had her feet on a newspaper. The voices stopped as Laura drew near. The group parted. It was as though she was expected, as though they had known she was coming here.

Laura was terribly nervous. Tossing the velvet ribbon over her shoulder, she said to a woman standing by, "Is this Mrs. Scott's house?" and the woman, smiling queerly, said, "It is, my lass."

Oh, to be away from this! She actually said, "Help me, God," as she walked up the tiny path and knocked. To be away from those staring eyes, or to be covered up in anything, one of those women's shawls even. I'll just leave the basket and go, she decided. I shan't even wait for it to be emptied.

Then the door opened. A little woman in black showed in the gloom.

Laura said, "Are you Mrs. Scott?" But to her horror the woman answered, "Walk in please, miss," and she was shut in the passage.

"No," said Laura, "I don't want to come in. I only want to leave this basket. Mother sent—"

The little woman in the gloomy passage seemed not to have heard her. "Step this way, please, miss," she said in an oily voice, and Laura followed her.

She found herself in a wretched little low kitchen, lighted by a smoky lamp. There was a woman sitting before the fire.

"Em," said the little creature who had let her in. "Em! It's a young lady." She turned to Laura. She said meaningly, "I'm her sister, miss. You'll excuse her, won't you?"

< 16 >

"Oh, but of course!" said Laura. "Please, please don't disturb her. I—I only want to leave—"

But at that moment the woman at the fire turned round. Her face, puffed up, red, with swollen eyes and swollen lips, looked terrible. She seemed as though she couldn't understand why Laura was there. What did it mean? Why was this stranger standing in the kitchen with a basket? What was it all about? And the poor face puckered up again.

"All right, my dear," said the other. "I'll thenk the young lady."

And again she began, "You'll excuse her, miss, I'm sure," and her face, swollen too, tried an oily smile.

Laura only wanted to get out, to get away. She was back in the passage. The door opened. She walked straight through into the bedroom, where the dead man was lying.

"You'd like a look at 'im, wouldn't you?" said Em's sister, and she brushed past Laura over to the bed. "Don't be afraid, my lass,"—and now her voice sounded fond and sly, and fondly she drew down the sheet—"'e looks a picture. There's nothing to show. Come along, my dear."

Laura came.

There lay a young man, fast asleep—sleeping so soundly, so deeply, that he was far, far away from them both. Oh, so remote, so peaceful. He was dreaming. Never wake him up again. His head was sunk in the pillow, his eyes were closed; they were blind under the closed eyelids. He was given up to his dream. What did garden-parties and baskets and lace frocks matter to him? He was far from all those things. He was wonderful, beautiful. While they were laughing and while the band was playing, this marvel had come to the lane. Happy ... happy ... All is well, said that sleeping face. This is just as it should be. I am content.

But all the same you had to cry, and she couldn't go out of the room without saying something to him. Laura gave a loud childish sob.

"Forgive my hat," she said.

And this time she didn't wait for Em's sister. She found her way out of the door, down the path, past all those dark people. At the corner of the lane she met Laurie.

He stepped out of the shadow. "Is that you, Laura?"

"Yes."

"Mother was getting anxious. Was it all right?"

"Yes, quite. Oh, Laurie!" She took his arm, she pressed up against him.

"I say, you're not crying, are you?" asked her brother.

Laura shook her head. She was.

Laurie put his arm round her shoulder. "Don't cry," he said in his warm, loving voice. "Was it awful?"

"No," sobbed Laura. "It was simply marvellous. But Laurie—" She stopped, she looked at her brother. "Isn't life," she stammered, "isn't life—" But what life was she couldn't explain. No matter. He quite understood.

"Isn't it, darling?" said Laurie.

NOTES

1. Angel of the highest rank.
2. Large tent used for garden parties, flower shows, circuses, etc.
3. Long loose Japanese robe with wide sleeves, worn with a sash.

About the Author:

Kathleen Mansfield Murry (penname, Katherine Mansfield) was born in 1888, to a socially prominent family in Wellington, New Zealand. After moving to England at age 19, she published her collection *Bliss* (1920), which helped her land a place in the literary world. When her short story collection *The Garden Party* came out, she reached the highest point in her writing career. She died of tuberculosis at the age of 34. Mansfield is considered one of the best short story writers in her time. Her works like "Miss Brill," "Prelude," "The Garden Party," "The Doll's

House," and later works such as "The Fly" are often chosen in short story anthologies.

The plot of Mansfield's stories is also conventional. Instead of following the traditional sequence of events, she focuses more on a crisis or a turning point, which was influenced by Russian writer Anton Chekov. Her use of symbolism is prevalent, and these symbols are often inspired by nature. The themes of her stories include: gender roles, inequality caused by class, human isolation, hypocrisy of the middle and upper society.

Appreciation:

该短篇小说最早发表于 1922 年，讲述了一个富裕家庭在准备园会时邻居意外身亡时家庭成员，尤其是母女的不同反应：女儿罗拉希望暂停园会以示哀悼；罗拉的母亲谢里丹夫人则执意照常举办园会。最终园会照常举行，罗拉则按照母亲的吩咐带着园会剩下的食物拜访了逝者家属。罗拉回来的时候显得困惑，又似乎对生命有了新的理解。阅读小说时注意谢里丹家庭的环境与死者斯科特家庭环境的对比，以及小罗拉的心理变化。同时，作者很明显地将希腊神话中的丰收女神得墨忒耳与其女儿珀尔塞福涅的故事融入小说当中，增强了小说的趣味性，阅读时注意将两者联系起来。另外，该小说表达的主题很丰富，其中之一就是成长。与《草原日出》相似，罗拉最后对死者家属的拜访也是一次成长之旅，可将两篇小说对比阅读与讨论。

Questions:

1. How is this story related to the Greek mythology story of Demeter and Persephone?
2. In the end, Laura stammered, "isn't life—", but didn't finish her words. What did she want to say ?

The Heart of a Broken Story

Every day Justin Horgenschlag, thirty-dollar-a-week printer's assistant, saw at close quarters approximately sixty women whom he had never seen before. Thus in the few years he had lived in New York, Horgenschlag had seen at close quarters about 75,120 different women. Of these 75,120 women, roughly 25,000 were under thirty years of age and over fifteen years of age. Of the 25,000 only 5,000 weighed between one hundred five and one hundred twenty-five pounds. Of these 5,000 only 1,000 were not ugly. Only 500 were reasonably attractive; only 100 of these were quite attractive; only 25 could have inspired a long, slow whistle. And with only 1 did

Horgenschlag fall in love at first sight.

Now, there are two kinds of femme fatale[1]. There is the femme fatale who is a femme fatale in every sense of the word, and there is the femme fatale who is not a femme fatale in every sense of the word.

Her name was Shirley Lester. She was twenty years old (eleven years younger than Horgenschlag), was five-foot-four (bringing her head to the level of Horgenschlag's eyes), weighed 117 pounds (light as a feather to carry). Shirley was a stenographer[2], lived with and supported her mother, Agnes Lester, an old Nelson Eddy fan. In reference to Shirley's looks people often put it this way: "Shirley's as pretty as a picture."

And in the Third Avenue bus early one morning, Horgenschlag stood over Shirley Lester, and was a dead duck. All because Shirley's mouth was open in a peculiar way. Shirley was reading a cosmetic advertisement in the wall panel of the bus; and when Shirley read, Shirley relaxed slightly at the jaw. And in that short moment while Shirley's mouth was open, lips were parted, Shirley was probably the most fatal one in all Manhattan. Horgenschlag saw in her a positive cure-all for a gigantic monster of loneliness which had been stalking around his heart since he had come to New York. Oh, the agony of it! The agony of standing over Shirley Lester and not being able to bend down and kiss Shirley's parted lips. The inexpressible agony of it!

That was the beginning of the story I started to write for *Collier's*[3]. I was going to write a lovely tender boy-meets-girl story. What could be finer, I thought. The world needs boy-meets-girl stories. But to write one, unfortunately, the writer must go about the business of having the boy meet the girl. I couldn't do it with this one. Not and have it make sense. I couldn't get Horgenschlag and Shirley together properly. And here are the reasons:

Certainly it was impossible for Horgenschlag to bend over and say in all sincerity:

"I beg your pardon. I love you very much. I'm nuts about you. I know it. I could love you all my life. I'm a printer's assistant and I make thirty dollars a week. Gosh, how I love you. Are you busy tonight?"

This Horgenschlag may be a goof, but not that big a goof. He may have been born yesterday, but not today. You can't expect *Collier's* readers to swallow that kind of bilge[4]. A nickel's a nickel, after all.

I couldn't, of course, all of a sudden give Horgenschlag a suave serum[5], mixed from William Powell[6]'s old cigarette case and Fred Astaire[7]'s old top hat.

"Please don't misunderstand me, Miss. I'm a magazine illustrator. My card. I'd like to sketch you more than I've ever wanted to sketch anyone in my life. Perhaps such an undertaking would be to a mutual advantage. May I telephone you this evening, or in the very near future? (Short, debonair laugh.) I hope I don't sound too desperate. (Another one.) I suppose I am, really."

Oh, boy. Those lines delivered with a weary, yet gay, yet reckless smile. If only Horgenschlag had delivered them. Shirley, of course, was an old Nelson Eddy[8] fan herself, and an active member of the Keystone Circulating Library.

Maybe you're beginning to see what I was up against.

True, Horgenschlag might have said the following:

"Excuse me, but aren't you Wilma Pritchard?"

To which Shirley would have replied coldly, and seeking a neutral point on the other side of the bus:

"No."

"That's funny," Horgenschlag could have gone on, "I was willing to swear you were Wilma Pritchard. Uh. You don't by any chance come from Seattle?"

"No."—More ice where that came from.

"Seattle's my home town."

Neutral point.

"Great little town, Seattle. I mean it's really a great little town. I've only been here—I mean in New York—four years. I'm a printer's assistant. Justin Horgenschlag is my name."

"I'm really not interested."

Oh, Horgenschlag wouldn't have got anywhere with that kind of line. He had neither the looks, personality, or good clothes to gain Shirley's interest under the circumstances. He didn't have a chance. And, as I said before, to write a really good boy-meets-girl story it's wise to have the boy meet the girl.

Maybe Horgenschlag might have fainted, and in doing so grabbed for support: the support being Shirley's ankle. He could have torn the stocking that way, or succeeded in ornamenting it with a fine long run. People would have made room for the stricken Horgenschlag, and he would have got to his feet, mumbling: "I'm all right, thanks," then, "Oh, say! I'm terribly sorry, Miss. I've torn your stocking. You must let me pay for it. I'm short of cash right now, but just give me your address."

Shirley wouldn't have given him her address. She just would have become embarrassed and inarticulate. "It's all right," she would have said, wishing Horgenschlag hadn't been born. And besides, the whole idea is illogical. Horgenschlag, a Seattle boy, wouldn't have dreamed of clutching at Shirley's ankle. Not in the Third Avenue Bus.

But what is more logical is the possibility that Horgenschlag might have got desperate. There are still a few men who love desperately. Maybe Horgenschlag was one. He might have snatched

Shirley's handbag and run with it toward the rear exit door. Shirley would have screamed. Men would have heard her, and remembered the Alamo or something. Horgenschlag's flight, let's say, is now arrested. The bus is stopped. Patrolman Wilson, who hasn't made a good arrest in a long time, reports on the scene. What's going on here? Officer, this man tried to steal my purse.

Horgenschlag is hauled into court. Shirley, of course, must attend session. They both give their addresses; thereby Horgenschlag is informed of the location of Shirley's divine abode.

Judge Perkins, who can't even get a good, really good cup of coffee in his own house, sentences Horgenschlag to a year in jail. Shirley bites her lip, but Horgenschlag is marched away.

In prison, Horgenschlag writes the following letter to Shirley Lester:

"Dear Miss Lester:

"I did not really mean to steal your purse. I just took it because I love you. You see I only wanted to get to know you. Will you please write me a letter sometime when you get the time? It gets pretty lonely here and I love you very much and maybe even you would come to see me some time if you get the time.

Your friend,

Justin Horgenschlag"

Shirley shows the letter to all her friends. They say, "Ah, it's cute, Shirley." Shirley agrees that it's kind of cute in a way. Maybe she'll answer it. "Yes! Answer it. Give'm a break. What've ya got t'lose?" So Shirley answers Horgenschlag's letter.

"Dear Mr. Horgenschlag:

"I received your letter and really feel very sorry about what has happened. Unfortunately there is very little we can do about it at this time, but I do feel abominable concerning the turn of events. However, your sentence is a short one and soon you will be out. The best of luck to you.

Sincerely yours,

Shirley Lester"

"Dear Miss Lester:

"You will never know how cheered up you made me feel when I received your letter. You should not feel abominable at all. It was all my fault for being so crazy so don't feel that way at all. We get movies here once a week and it really is not so bad. I am 31 years of age and come from Seattle. I have been in New York 4 years and think it is a great town only once in a while you get pretty lonesome. You are the prettiest girl I have ever seen even in Seattle. I wish you would come to see me some Saturday afternoon during visiting hours 2 to 4 and I will pay your train fare.

Your friend,

Justin Horgenschlag"

Shirley would have shown this letter, too, to all her friends. But she would not answer this one. Anyone could see that this Horgenschlag was a goof. And after all. She had answered the first letter. If she answered this silly letter the thing might drag on for months and everything. She did all she could do for the man. And what a name. Horgenschlag.

Meanwhile, in prison Horgenschlag is having a terrible time, even though they have movies once a week. His cellmates are Snipe Morgan and Slicer Burke, two boys from the back room, who see in Horgenschlag's face a resemblance to a chap in Chicago who once ratted on them. They are convinced that Ratface Ferrero and Justin Horgenschlag are one and the same person.

"But I'm not Ratface Ferrero," Horgenschlag tells them.

"Don't gimme that," says Slicer, knocking Horgenschlag's meager food rations to the floor.

"Bash his head in," says Snipe.

"I tell ya I'm just here because I stole a girl's purse on the Third Avenue Bus," pleads Horgenschlag. "Only I didn't really steal it. I fell in love with her, and it was the only way I could get to know her."

"Don't gimme that," says Slicer.

"Bash his head in," says Snipe.

Then there is the day when seventeen prisoners try to make an escape. During play period in the recreation yard, Slicer Burke lures the warden's niece, eight-year-old Lisbeth Sue, into his clutches. He puts his eight-by-twelve hands around the child's waist and holds her up for the warden to see.

"Hey, warden!" yells Slicer. "Open up them gates or it's curtains for the kid!"

"I'm not afraid, Uncle Bert!" calls out Lisbeth Sue.

"Put down that child, Slicer!" commands the warden, with all the impotence at his command.

But Slicer knows he has the warden just where he wants him. Seventeen men and a small blonde child walk out the gates. Sixteen men and a small blonde child walk out safely. A guard in the high tower thinks he sees a wonderful opportunity to shoot Slicer in the head, and thereby destroy the unity of the escaping group. But he misses, and succeeds only in shooting the small man walking nervously behind Slicer, killing him instantly.

Guess who?

And, thus, my plan to write a boy-meets-girl story for *Collier's*, a tender, memorable love story, is thwarted by the death of my hero.

Now, Horgenschlag never would have been among those seventeen desperate men if only he had not been made desperate and panicky by Shirley's failure to answer his second letter. But the fact remains that she did not answer his second letter. She never in a hundred years would have answered it. I can't alter facts.

And what a shame. What a pity that Horgenschlag, in prison, was unable to write the following letter to Shirley Lester:

"Dear Miss Lester:

"I hope a few lines will not annoy or embarrass you. I'm writing, Miss Lester, because I'd like you to know that I am not a common thief. I stole your bag, I want you to know, because I fell in love with you the moment I saw you on the bus. I could think of no way to become acquainted with you except by acting rashly—foolishly, to be accurate. But then, one is a fool when one is in love.

"I loved the way your lips were so slightly parted. You represented the answer to everything to me. I haven't been unhappy since I came to New York four years ago, but neither have I been happy. Rather, I can best describe myself as having been one of the thousands of young men in New York who simply exist.

"I came to New York from Seattle. I was going to become rich and famous and well-dressed and suave. But in four years I've learned that I am not going to become rich and famous and well-dressed and suave. I'm a good printer's assistant, but that's all I am. One day the printer got sick, and I had to take his place. What a mess I made of things, Miss Lester. No one would take my orders. The typesetters just sort of giggled when I would tell them to get to work. And I don't blame them. I'm a fool when I give orders. I suppose I'm just one of the millions who was never meant to give orders. But I don't mind anymore. There's a twenty-three-year-old kid my boss just hired. He's only twenty-three, and I am thirty-one and have worked at the same place for four years. But I know that one day he will become head printer, and I will be his assistant. But I don't mind knowing this anymore.

"Loving you is the important thing, Miss Lester. There are some people who think love is sex and marriage and six o'clock-kisses and children, and perhaps it is, Miss Lester. But do you know what I think? I think love is a touch and yet not a touch.

"I suppose it's important to a woman that other people think of her as the wife of a man who is either rich, handsome, witty or popular. I'm not even popular. I'm not even hated. I'm just—I'm just—Justin Horgenschlag. I never make people gay, sad, angry, or even disgusted. I think people regard me as a nice guy, but that's all.

"When I was a child no one pointed me out as being cute or bright or good-looking. If they had to say something they said I had sturdy little legs.

"I don't expect an answer to this letter, Miss Lester. I would like an answer more than anything else in the world, but truthfully I don't expect one. I merely wanted you to know the truth. If my love for you has only led me to a new and great sorrow, only I am to blame.

"Perhaps one day you will understand and forgive your blundering admirer, Justin Horgenschlag."

Such a letter would be no more unlikely than the following:

"Dear Mr. Horgenschlag:

"I got your letter and loved it. I feel guilty and miserable that events have taken the turn they have. If only you had spoken to me instead of taking my purse! But then, I suppose I should have turned the conversational chill on you.

"It's lunch hour at the office, and I'm alone here writing to you. I felt that I wanted to be alone today at lunch hour. I felt that if I had to go have lunch with the girls at the Automat and they jabbered through the meal as usual, I'd suddenly scream.

"I don't care if you're not a success, or that you're not handsome, or rich, or famous or suave. Once upon a time I would have cared. When I was in high school I was always in love with the Joe Glamor boys. Donald Nicolson, the boy who walked in the rain and knew all Shakespeare's sonnets backwards. Bob Lacey, the handsome gink who could shoot a basket from the middle of the floor, with the score tied and the chukker[9] almost over. Harry Miller, who was so shy and had such nice, durable brown eyes.

"But that crazy part of my life is over.

"The people in your office who giggled when you gave them orders are on my black list. I hate them as I've never hated anybody.

"You saw me when I had all my make-up on. Without it, believe me, I'm no raving beauty. Please write me when you're allowed to have visitors. I'd like you to take a second look at me. I'd like to be sure that you didn't catch me at a phony best.

"Oh, how I wish you'd told the judge why you stole my purse! We might be together and able to talk over all the many things I think we have in common.

"Please let me know when I may come to see you.

Yours sincerely,

Shirley Lester"

But Justin Horgenschlag never got to know Shirley Lester. She got off at Fifty-Sixth Street, and he got off at Thirty-Second Street. That night Shirley Lester went to the movies with Howard Lawrence with whom she was in love. Howard thought Shirley was a darn good sport, but that was as far as it went. And Justin Horgenschlag that night stayed home and listened to the Lux

Toilet Soap radio play. He thought about Shirley all night, all the next day, and very often during that month. Then all of a sudden he was introduced to Doris Hillman who was beginning to be afraid she wasn't going to get a husband. And then before Justin Horgenschlag knew it, Doris Hillman and things were filing away Shirley Lester in the back of his mind. And Shirley Lester, the thought of her, no longer was available.

And that's why I never wrote a boy-meets-girl story for *Collier's*. In a boy-meets-girl story the boy should always meet the girl.

NOTES

1. French phrase which means a stock character of a mysterious and seductive woman whose charms ensnare her lovers, often leading them into compromising, dangerous, and deadly situations. She is an archetype of literature and art.
2. Stenographer is a person whose job is to write down what somebody else says, using a quick system of signs or abbreviations.
3. *Collier's* was an American magazine, founded in 1888 by Peter Fenelon Collier. It was initially launched as *Collier's Once a Week*, then changed in 1895 to *Collier's Weekly: An Illustrated Journal*, and finally shortened in 1905 to simply *Collier's*. The magazine ceased publication with the issue dated January 4, 1957, though a brief, failed attempt was made to revive the Collier's name with a new magazine in 2012.
4. worthless ideas or talk; nonsense
5. Suave means confident, elegant and polite, sometimes in a way that does not seem sincere. Serum is liquid taken from an animal that is immune to a disease, used for inoculations.
6. William Horatio Powell (July 29, 1892–March 5, 1984) was an American actor. A major star at Metro-Goldwyn-Mayer, he was paired with Myrna Loy in 14 films, including the popular *Thin Man*. Powell was nominated for the Academy Award for Best Actor three times.
7. Fred Astaire (born Frederick Austerlitz; May 10, 1899–June 22, 1987) was an American dancer, singer, actor, choreographer and television presenter.
8. Nelson Ackerman Eddy (June 29, 1901–March 6, 1967) was an American singer and actor who appeared in 19 musical films during the 1930s and 1940s, as well as in opera and on the concert stage, radio, television, and in nightclubs.
9. One of the six playing periods into which a polo match is divided. Here it means one game in a basketball match.

About the Author:

Jerome David Salinger was born to a family in New York City on January 1, 1919. He started writing short stories while in secondary school. Several were published in *Story* magazine in the early 1940s, after which he served in World War II. In 1951, his novel *The Catcher in the Rye* was published and enjoyed an immediate popular success. As his fame shot up, Salinger gradually became a recluse, cutting himself from the public attention, and living a private life in Cornish, New Hampshire. Salinger died on January 27, 2010. His books also include *Nine Stories* (1953), *Franny and Zooey* (1961) and *Raise High the Roof Beam, Carpenters and Seymour: An Introduction* (1963).

Appreciation:

《破碎故事之心》最早于 1941 年发表在《绅士》杂志上。故事一开始描写了一个浪漫爱情故事的典型开端：贾斯汀·豪根斯拉格 (Justin Horgenshlag) 和雪莉·莱斯特 (Shirley Lester) 由于一同乘坐第三大道的公交车而相识。等读者正在期待故事如何发展的时候塞林格笔锋一转，交代说，普通的贾斯汀没法鼓起勇气去认识漂亮的雪莉，读者本以为的浪漫故事连开端都没有。即使贾斯汀对雪莉一见钟情，但爱慕之情难以言表最终使得他们只能像两条平行线各自继续各自的生活。而男主人公最后也会踏入婚姻生活而将曾经钟情的雪莉遗忘。塞林格在告诉我们现实并非充满玫瑰花瓣和五彩的泡泡，现实与理想总是会有差距。作者对“爱情是什么”的讨论也值得深思。另外，塞林格传记的作者表示该故事本意是讽刺 *Collier's* 这类杂志的商业化。这类杂志往往广告成堆，喜欢采用一些写着陈词滥调内容、刻意迎合读者的故事。塞林格一改浪漫故事甜腻的风格，把残酷事实的现实摆出来给读者。这也体现出塞林格不拘一格的态度。语言上来看，作者多处运用虚拟语气，比如 should/could have done，不断提醒读者男主人公本可以这样做实际上却没有，那些偶遇的桥段、调情的伎俩、来往的信件都是作者虚拟出来的，我们在阅读的时候要仔细判断，不要被作者欺骗。

Questions:

1. What should a “boy-meets-girl story” be like? In the end, why does the author say “In a boy-meets-girl story the boy should always meet the girl” ?
2. How do you understand this sentence, “love is a touch yet not a touch” ?

Eveline[1]

She sat at the window watching the evening invade the avenue. Her head was leaned against the window curtains and in her nostrils was the odour of dusty cretonne. She was tired.

Few people passed. The man out of the last house passed on his way home; she heard his footsteps clacking along the concrete pavement and afterwards crunching on the cinder path before the new red houses. One time there used to be a field there in which they used to play every evening with other people's children. Then a man from Belfast[2] bought the field and built houses in it—not like their little brown houses but bright brick houses with shining roofs. The children of the avenue used to play together in that field—the Devines, the Waters, the Dunns, little Keogh the cripple, she and her brothers and sisters. Ernest, however, never played: he was too grown up. Her father used often to hunt them in out of the field with his blackthorn stick; but usually little Keogh used to keep nix[3] and call out when he saw her father coming. Still they seemed to have been rather happy then. Her father was not so bad then; and besides, her mother was alive. That was a long time ago; she and her brothers and sisters were all grown up her mother was dead. Tizzie Dunn was dead, too, and the Waters had gone back to England. Everything changes. Now she was going to go away like the others, to leave her home.

Home! She looked round the room, reviewing all its familiar objects which she had dusted once a week for so many years, wondering where on earth all the dust came from. Perhaps she would never see again those familiar objects from which she had never dreamed of being divided. And yet during all those years she had never found out the name of the priest whose yellowing photograph hung on the wall above the broken harmonium beside the coloured print of the promises made to Blessed Margaret Mary Alacoque. He had been a school friend of her father. Whenever he showed the photograph to a visitor her father used to pass it with a casual word:

"He is in Melbourne now."

She had consented to go away, to leave her home. Was that wise? She tried to weigh each side of the question. In her home anyway she had shelter and food; she had those whom she had known all her life about her. Of course she had to work hard, both in the house and at business. What would they say of her in the Stores when they found out that she had run away with a fellow? Say she was a fool, perhaps; and her place would be filled up by advertisement. Miss Gavan would be glad. She had always had an edge on[4] her, especially whenever there were people listening.

"Miss Hill, don't you see these ladies are waiting?"

"Look lively, Miss Hill, please."

She would not cry many tears at leaving the Stores.

But in her new home, in a distant unknown country, it would not be like that. Then she would be married—she, Eveline. People would treat her with respect then. She would not be treated as her mother had been. Even now, though she was over nineteen, she sometimes felt herself in danger of her father's violence. She knew it was that that had given her the palpitations. When they were growing up he had never gone for her like he used to go for Harry and Ernest, because she was a girl but latterly he had begun to threaten her and say what he would do to her only for her dead mother's sake. And she had nobody to protect her. Ernest was dead and Harry, who was in the church decorating business, was nearly always down somewhere in the country. Besides, the invariable squabble for money on Saturday nights had begun to weary her unspeakably. She always gave her entire wages—seven shillings—and Harry always sent up what he could but the trouble was to get any money from her father. He said she used to squander the money, that she had no head, that he wasn't going to give her his hard-earned money to throw about the streets, and much more, for he was usually fairly bad on Saturday night. In the end he would give her the money and ask her had she any intention of buying Sunday's dinner. Then she had to rush out as quickly as she could and do her marketing, holding her black leather purse tightly in her hand as she elbowed her way through the crowds and returning home late under her load of provisions. She had hard work to keep the house together and to see that the two young children who had been left to her charge went to school regularly and got their meals regularly. It was hard work—a hard life—but now that she was about to leave it she did not find it a wholly undesirable life.

She was about to explore another life with Frank. Frank was very kind, manly, open-hearted. She was to go away with him by the night-boat to be his wife and to live with him in Buenos Ayres[5] where he had a home waiting for her. How well she remembered the first time she had seen him; he was lodging[6] in a house on the main road where she used to visit. It seemed a few weeks ago. He was standing at the gate, his peaked cap pushed back on his head and his hair tumbled forward over a face of bronze. Then they had come to know each other. He used to meet her outside the Stores every evening and see her home. He took her to see The Bohemian Girl and she felt elated as she sat in an unaccustomed part of the theatre with him. He was awfully fond of music and sang a little. People knew that they were courting and, when he sang about the lass that loves a sailor, she always felt pleasantly confused. He used to call her Poppens out of fun. First of all it had been an excitement for her to have a fellow and then she had begun to like him. He had tales of distant countries. He had started as a deck boy at a pound a month on a ship of the Allan

Line going out to Canada. He told her the names of the ships he had been on and the names of the different services. He had sailed through the Straits of Magellan and he told her stories of the terrible Patagonians. He had fallen on his feet in Buenos Ayres, he said, and had come over to the old country just for a holiday. Of course, her father had found out the affair and had forbidden her to have anything to say to him.

"I know these sailor chaps," he said.

One day he had quarrelled with Frank and after that she had to meet her lover secretly.

The evening deepened in the avenue. The white of two letters in her lap grew indistinct. One was to Harry; the other was to her father. Ernest had been her favourite but she liked Harry too. Her father was becoming old lately, she noticed; he would miss her. Sometimes he could be very nice. Not long before, when she had been laid up for a day, he had read her out a ghost story and made toast for her at the fire. Another day, when their mother was alive, they had all gone for a picnic to the Hill of Howth. She remembered her father putting on her mother's bonnet to make the children laugh.

Her time was running out but she continued to sit by the window, leaning her head against the window curtain, inhaling the odour of dusty cretonne. Down far in the avenue she could hear a street organ playing. She knew the air Strange that it should come that very night to remind her of the promise to her mother, her promise to keep the home together as long as she could. She remembered the last night of her mother's illness; she was again in the close dark room at the other side of the hall and outside she heard a melancholy air of Italy. The organ-player had been ordered to go away and given sixpence. She remembered her father strutting back into the sickroom saying:

"Damned Italians! coming over here!"

As she mused the pitiful vision of her mother's life laid its spell on the very quick of her being—that life of commonplace sacrifices closing in final craziness. She trembled as she heard again her mother's voice saying constantly with foolish insistence:

"Derevaun Seraun! Derevaun Seraun[7]!"

She stood up in a sudden impulse of terror. Escape! She must escape! Frank would save her. He would give her life, perhaps love, too. But she wanted to live. Why should she be unhappy? She had a right to happiness. Frank would take her in his arms, fold her in his arms. He would save her.

She stood among the swaying crowd in the station at the North Wall. He held her hand and she knew that he was speaking to her, saying something about the passage over and over again. The station was full of soldiers with brown baggages. Through the wide doors of the sheds she caught a glimpse of the black mass of the boat, lying in beside the quay wall, with illumined portholes. She answered nothing. She felt her cheek pale and cold and, out of a maze of distress, she prayed to God to direct her, to show her what was her duty. The boat blew a long mournful whistle into the mist. If she went, tomorrow she would be on the sea with Frank, steaming towards Buenos Ayres. Their passage had been booked. Could she still draw back after all he had done for her? Her distress awoke a nausea in her body and she kept moving her lips in silent fervent prayer.

A bell clanged upon her heart. She felt him seize her hand:

"Come!"

All the seas of the world tumbled about her heart. He was drawing her into them: he would drown her. She gripped with both hands at the iron railing.

"Come!"

No! No! No! It was impossible. Her hands clutched the iron in frenzy. Amid the seas she sent a cry of anguish.

"Eveline! Evvy!"

He rushed beyond the barrier and called to her to follow. He was shouted at to go on but he still called to her. She set her white face to him, passive, like a helpless animal. Her eyes gave him no sign of love or farewell or recognition.

NOTES

1. "Eveline" is a short story by the Irish writer James Joyce. It was first published in 1904 by the journal *Irish Homestead* and later featured in his 1914 collection of short stories *Dubliners*.
2. Capital and largest city of Northern Ireland, the second largest on the island of Ireland.
3. Keep watch or be on the lookout, in Chinese, " 望风 ".
4. Have an edge on somebody means have a slight advantage over somebody.
5. Capital city of Argentina.
6. Live for payment in somebody's house.
7. Some nonsense mumbled by Eveline's mother.

About the Author:

James Joyce was born in Dublin, on February 2, 1882, to a middle-class family on the way down. Joyce had been well educated since he was young. From the age of six Joyce was educated at Clongowes Wood College, Belvedere College and University College, Dublin. He went to Paris after graduation in 1902. Two years later, Joyce emigrated permanently to Trieste, Paris. Like many writers, Joyce's works are often based on his life. Even though he left his hometown in his early twenties, Joyce's stories centre on Dublin. He once said, "For myself, I always write about Dublin, because if I can get to the heart of Dublin I can get to the heart of all the cities of the world. In the particular is contained the universal." Readers may find his works characteristic of expansive use of puns, allusions, metaphors, and stream of consciousness.

Appreciation:

该短篇故事取自詹姆斯·乔伊斯的早期作品《都柏林人》。《都柏林人》这个故事集一共由 15 个故事组成，每个故事集中有一个主角。虽然故事各不相同，但都选择了以 19 世纪末 20 世纪初的爱尔兰首都都柏林为背景。在乔伊斯看来，都柏林是"瘫痪（Paralysis）的中心"。这些故事中的人物都或多或少经历着情感的瘫痪，他们无力交流、封闭自我、无法实现爱情、无法逃脱生活的禁锢。伊芙琳也是这样一个人物。她希望逃离酗酒且有着暴力倾向的父亲，跟随男友到一个新的国度开始新的生活。但想到在母亲临终时许下照顾好家庭的承诺，想到父亲时不时表现出来的慈爱，想到周围熟悉的人、事以及新环境的陌生，她出走的心又动摇了。虽然她跟着男友到了港口，貌似做好了离开的决定，但最后随着一声拖沓的汽笛声，她的勇气又软弱下来。最后她面无表情地看着载着男友的船驶出港口。伊芙琳在权衡离开的利弊时的纠结最吸引读者的注意力，我们都想知道最终她做出了什么样的决定。这样的心情也最能被我们感同身受，因为当我们在做出一个重大决定时，我们是审慎的、迷惑的，甚至是无助的。乔伊斯善于精雕细琢，对人物内心活动的描写细致入微，阅读过程中仔细体会他的遣词造句以及从词句中传达出来的细腻情感。另外，值得一提的是美国作家理查德·耶茨（Richard Yates）的作品《十一种孤独》。这本故事集讲述了 20 世纪五六十年代纽约十一个普通人的孤独人生。无论从故事的编排、主题的表达都与《都柏林人》相似，被《纽约时报》称为"《都柏林人》的纽约版本"。

Questions:

1. In the end why did Eveline decide not to board with Frank?
2. What if Eveline actually did escape Dublin? Based on what you know about her, how would Eveline handle Buenos Ayres?

Bibliography

Abrams, M. H., et al., eds. *The Norton Anthology of English Literature: The Major Authors*. 7th Edition. New York: W. W. Norton & Company, Inc., 2001.

Barnet, Sylvan, ed. *Types of Drama: Plays and Essays*. 6th ed. New York: Harper, 1993.

Barnet, Sylvan, Morton Berman, and William Burto, eds. *An Introduction to Literature*. Exp. Edi. New York: Harper, 1994.

Brook, Peter. *The Empty Space*. Trans. Dong, Dao Ming. Beijing: China Drama Press, 1988.

Bulfinch, Thomas. *The Age of Fable: Stories of Gods and Heroes*. New York: Review of Reviews, 1913.

Chang Yaoxin. *A Survey of American Literature*. Tianjin: Nankai University Publishing House, 2008.

Graves, Robert. *The Greek Myths*, complete edition. London: Penguin Books, 1992.

Harris, Stephen L. and Gloria Platzner. *Classical Mythology: Images and Insights*. Mountain View, California: Mayfield Publishing Company, 1995.

Hesiod. *Theogony*. Apostolos N. Athanassakis trans. Baltimore: Johns Hopkins University Press, 1984.

Homan, Clarence Hugh. *A Handbook to Literature*. 4th ed. Indianapolis: Bobbs, 1980.

Holy Bible. Nanjing: China Christian Council, 1995.

Jindi Shao and Jinpeng Bai, eds. *An Introduction to Literature*. Harbin: Heilongjiang People's Publishing House, 1998.

Lawall, Sarah, et al., eds. *The Norton Anthology of World Masterpieces*. 7th edition. New York: W. W. Norton & Company, Inc., 1999.

Liu, Bingshan. *A History of English Literature*. Zhengzhou: Henan People's Publishing House, 1993.

Morford, Mark P. O. and Robert J. Lenardon. *Classical Mythology*, 7th edition. New York and Oxford : Oxford University Press, 2003.

Rubinstein, Annette T. *The Great Tradition in English Literature from Shakespeare to Shaw*. Beijing: Foreign Language Teaching and Research Press, 1988.

Scholes, Robert, et al., eds. *Elements of Literature*. 5 Rev. ed. New York: Oxford UP, 1982.

后记

本教材分工如下：

季峥：总编全书，负责厘定篇目，确定体例及统稿工作，并主持课程教学实施。并负责了《圣经》部分的选篇（*Genesis* 1–3，*Genesis* 4，*Genesis* 6–9，*Genesis* 11）以及参考书目的编写。

龙亚：负责小说部分的编写协调工作，以及出版联系部分相关工作。并选编《马丁·伊登》（*Martin Eden*）、《觉醒》（*The Awakening*）、《失窃的信》（*The Purloined Letter*）、《小伙子古德曼·布朗》（*Young Goodman Brown*）。

雷定坤：负责全书的汇总和校订，撰写了前言、目录，并选编《草原日出》（*A Sunrise on the Veld*）、《园会》（*The Garden Party*）、《破碎故事之心》（*The Heart of a Broken Story*）、《伊芙琳》（*Eveline*）。

另外，学院文学课程组的老师们参与完成了教材的不同部分的工作，选编篇目如下：

陈康：负责编写了希腊神话故事部分《宙斯》（*Zeus*）、《赫拉》（*Hera*）、《忒修斯》（*Theseus*）、《伊阿宋》（*Jason*）。

史风晓：负责编写了诗歌部分莎士比亚十四行诗第二十九首（*Sonnet 29*）、《我孤独地漫游，像一朵云》（*I Wandered Lonely as a Cloud*）、《因尼斯弗里岛》（*The Lake Isle of Innisfree*）、《挖掘》（*Digging*）、《啊，船长，我的船长！》（*O Captain! My Captain!*）、《有一道幽光斜照》（*There's a Certain Slant of Light*）、《未选择的路》（*The Road Not Taken*）、《独自进餐》（*Eating Alone*）。

毕丽君：负责编写了散文部分《自然》（*Nature*）、《旅行》（*Of Travel*）、《理想国》（*The Republic: Book X*）、《独立宣言》（*The Declaration of Independence*）、《诗学》（*The Poetics*

I–V）。

庄美兰：《大卫·科波菲尔》（*David Copperfield*）、《弗兰肯斯坦》（*Frankenstein*）、《黑暗的心》（*Heart of Darkness*）、《墙上的斑点》（*The Mark on the Wall*）。

戚晖：《罗密欧与朱丽叶》（*Romeo and Juliet*）、《长夜漫漫路迢迢》（*Long Day's Journey into Night*）、《密室》（*No Exit*）、《送菜升降机》（*The Dumb Waiter*）、《被埋葬的孩子》（*Buried Child*）。

邹莉：《推销员之死》（*Death of a Salesman*）。

图书在版编目（CIP）数据

西方文学选读：英文/季峥主编．—北京：中国人民大学出版社，2018.2
高级实用英语系列教材
ISBN 978-7-300-25455-5

Ⅰ.①西… Ⅱ.①季… Ⅲ.①文学欣赏-西方国家-高等学校-教材-英文 Ⅳ.①I106

中国版本图书馆CIP数据核字（2018）第018567号

高级实用英语系列教材
西方文学选读
主　编　季　峥
副主编　龙　亚　毕丽君　雷定坤
Xifang Wenxue Xuandu

出版发行	中国人民大学出版社		
社　址	北京中关村大街31号	邮政编码	100080
电　话	010-62511242（总编室）		010-62511770（质管部）
	010-82501766（邮购部）		010-62514148（门市部）
	010-62515195（发行公司）		010-62515275（盗版举报）
网　址	http:// www. crup. com. cn		
	http:// www. ttrnet. com（人大教研网）		
经　销	新华书店		
印　刷	北京中印联印务有限公司		
规　格	185 mm×240 mm　16开本	版　次	2018年2月第1版
印　张	18.25	印　次	2018年2月第1次印刷
字　数	380 000	定　价	42.80元